Lady of the Seven Suns

BY

Tinney Sue Heath

LADY OF THE SEVEN SUNS: A Novel of the Woman Saint Francis Called Brother

by Tinney Sue Heath

ISBN (paperback): 978-1-7339933-2-6
ISBN (ebook): 978-1-7339933-1-9

BISAC Subject Headings:
    FIC014020 FICTION/Historical/Medieval
    FIC041000 FICTION/Biographical
    FIC042030 FICTION/Christian/Historical

Cover design by Jennifer Quinlan of Historical Fiction Book Covers

This is a work of fiction. Historical names, characters, places, and events are used fictitiously; all others are products of the author's imagination. Cover includes a portion of Edmond Blair Leighton's 1895 painting, "The Charity of Saint Elizabeth of Hungary."

To Linda W., who has more of Giacoma in her than she knows.

Unless it's the other way around.

CONTENTS

CONTENTS, continued

1

THE first time I saw him, he was flinging handfuls of coins through the grate at San Pietro's tomb like a housewife feeding her chickens. His flamboyant clothes, peacock-bright, made him look like he had just stepped down from the apse mosaic above him. The other pilgrims stared at him wide-eyed, except for a small group huddled together off to one side, pretending not to see.

Probably the unfortunates who traveled here with him.

I had finished my prayers and had already knelt in devotion at the tomb of the Great Apostle, as I did whenever I was in this part of Rome. My next act should have been to make my way outside to the atrium with my maid. There we would distribute alms to the beggars while we waited for my husband to come and collect us once his business was complete.

But I was enjoying the show.

The strange little man must have exhausted the contents of his purse, for he dropped the spent leather bag carelessly onto the ornate pavement and rummaged under his cloak for another. At that, one of his fellow travelers stepped forward and put a hand on his arm, gently but firmly.

"We're not going to pay your expenses all the way home, friend," I imagined that man saying.

These travelers were certainly far from indigent, or they wouldn't have the privilege of looking directly down at the tomb from the grating in front of the altar, as I did. Low-level clerics herded the less affluent pilgrims down the steps to the crypt and into a semicircular corridor lit by flickering lamps, which they then followed to the point in the center where they could catch a brief glimpse of the holy tomb at a distance before being funneled back out on the other side. Those of us up in the church proper were the people expected to make, shall we say, more substantial donations. But the slight man with two purses had flung a great many coins already.

1

I had lingered in this area of the basilica because the endlessly varied parade of humanity fascinated me. A pilgrimage to San Pietro's tomb was a once-in-a-lifetime journey for most, and some traveled for months to get here. Something about the enormity of finally reaching their goal made the saint's awestruck visitors behave in ways that were most completely their own, devoid of any pretense.

Thus the peacock man with the feverish eyes must be all manner of things: excitable, wealthy, agitated, generous, devout, ostentatious. Hungry for something, too. I sensed a neediness about him, a seeking, a searching. He was probably a few years older than me, yet he had a childlike quality about him that reminded me of my two-year-old son.

His plain cloak, incongruous over his colorful tunic, was probably his concession to the dangers of the road. Not very convincing, not with that rich purple tunic trimmed with a green and yellow weave, or, for that matter, the expensive boots and the silver belt clasp, but he'd made it safely here in spite of it all. He must have been well guarded.

I watched as his friend led him away, leaving the coveted spot directly above the apostle's tomb free for someone else. He went reluctantly, looking back over his shoulder at the holy shrine as if he could scarcely bear to leave it. The next man in line moved up and sank to his knees before the saint's relics, but the one behind him reached over and picked up Peacock Man's discarded purse and explored it with his fingers. He smiled and plunged his hand in, drawing out one last silver coin. He was about to slip it into his own purse when Peacock Man stopped and called something out to him, though in the church's vast echoing space I couldn't make out what he said. The pilgrim looked up, and Peacock Man met his eyes and held them. Finally the pilgrim shrugged, reached across the kneeling man, and tossed the coin through the grate, where it clanked against all the others.

My own charitable efforts were aimed at the group of genuinely poor people who gathered outside, hoping for handouts from those whose proximity to the saint's holy relics had made them temporarily generous. Peacock Man and his fellows were leaving and nothing else as entertaining appeared to be coming up, so I nodded to Vanna, who was waiting patiently for me. She joined me, and we walked the length of the nave toward the atrium along with a trickle of pilgrims, stopping to pray at the various altars and papal tombs along the way.

"He's an odd one, monna Giacoma," Vanna said, when we had stepped outside. "Showing off all his money that way." She wrinkled her nose, a sure sign of her disapproval. Vanna had very definite ideas about the proper way to handle money. She frequently despaired of me, and there was no chance at all that she would give Peacock Man the benefit of her doubt.

"Where do you suppose he came from?" she asked.

I shook my head. I had no idea, but wherever it was, it produced entertainingly peculiar people.

"That lot is from Assisi," said the pilgrim woman who had followed us out of the church. "I heard someone say so."

"I hope he can still afford to go back, then."

"So do I. Bless you, madonna," she said, her attention shifting from us to one of the souvenir stands where she stopped to peruse the display of little lead badges with their crudely stamped images of San Pietro.

The atrium was a large space, but Vanna and I had to thread our way through the crowd of merchants, pilgrims, and beggars. The throng almost obscured the great fountain in the center, though its huge stone pinecone towered above people's heads.

Booksellers, merchants selling water and food, cobblers ready to mend worn soles and broken straps for footweary pilgrims, vendors of holy oil collected from the lamps surrounding the saint's tomb, goldsmiths, and moneychangers vied for whatever coin remained in the pilgrims' purses.

One booth, actually a long table covered with a tattered blue cloth, was manned by a pair of brothers who sold brandeas to the pilgrims. These lengths of white fabric were meant to capture some of the saint's holiness when they were lowered through the grating to touch his tomb. One brother enthusiastically hawked the brandeas while the other hunched over a delicate goldsmith's scale, for one of their services-for-hire was to weigh the cloth as they sold it, and then weigh it again on its buyer's return, to prove that it was heavier for having been imbued with the essence of the Great Apostle. I wasn't buying today. I had several of their brandeas at home, near the small altar in my chamber, and I didn't feel the need for another. I had once used one as a hand towel accidentally; I don't think any harm was done, but it did make my next confession rather awkward.

As usual, shabbily clad beggars had scattered themselves through-out the spacious area, hands out, pious expressions fixed on careworn faces. They knew me, for I played my part in this drama often, and they maneuvered their way through the crowd toward me.

I pulled out my alms purse, stocked with a few more coins than I expected to need, just in case. Vanna took out a second purse, and we began to distribute the money with a smile and a kind word.

They thanked us and promised to pray for us, and some of them started to tell us of their misfortunes, because they knew it was my habit to listen carefully. If I learned of a particularly disastrous situation or a gross injustice, I took note and arranged to pursue it later. I knew most of their names and had been to many of their homes. All of them had come to mine for alms in the form of leftover food after meals, and whenever need drove them to seek out a sympathetic friend with a full purse.

But one among them was unknown to me. He surprised me by murmuring his request in French, and clumsy French at that. I placed a coin in his outstretched hand, noting that it was a soft hand, smooth and clean, unlike the others'. I looked at his face and gazed directly into those feverish black eyes.

What was Peacock Man doing in a beggar's grimy rags? I gaped at him, thoroughly confused.

"God's peace upon you, madonna," he said in our Roman language as he accepted my coin. His voice was pleasant and cultured, his soft Umbrian accent unmistakable. He smiled at me, but it was the smile of an equal, not of a supplicant.

"What—" I started. Then I noticed the filthy beggar standing behind him. This one I recognized: Renzo the Tinker, though these days his hands were twisted and useless with age. He was wearing Peacock Man's brilliant clothes. His wide grin displayed a paucity of teeth, and he kept plucking at the fine purplish cloth of the tunic as if he didn't quite believe his luck. Renzo stood a head taller than the man from Assisi, so the effect was rather ridiculous.

Not such a good exchange for Peacock Man, yet he was every bit as delighted as the tinker, and I had to chuckle at the two of them.

"Playing at begging, are you?" I asked the pilgrim.

He shook his head vigorously. "No, not playing at all. I want to learn from these people. I have to know what it's like to be one of the truly poor. What it's like to have to beg for your food." He spoke earnestly, as if willing me to understand.

I took a step back, irritated. "Begging for a day when you eat well all the rest of the time doesn't teach you anything about being poor. Wearing a beggar's clothes for a few hours accomplishes nothing. Would you be a leper for a day, then, to learn how to help the sick?"

It was his turn to be taken aback. He pointed to my own clothing, of fine quality, though nowhere near as colorful as his, and said, "You can't know much about what poverty is like yourself, madonna." As his pointing finger brushed my skirt, I instinctively put a protective hand on my belly, softly rounded with pregnancy.

"No, of course I don't, not from my own experience. But I don't see the point in pretending. And I know these men and women," I indicated the beggars, who were now standing around us and listening, fascinated. "I know their worth, to God and to each other. I know they didn't choose their poverty, and I know they aren't playing at it. I also know that if God had made only slightly different decisions, I could easily have been in their place and they in mine. But he didn't, and I have means, so I use them to do what good I can. I don't dress up and play games."

"I assure you, madonna, this is no game."

"Then why do you take coins these people need so badly?"

He said nothing, only turned to Renzo and handed him the coin I had just proffered. Renzo laughed gleefully as he clutched it.

Vanna came up to me then and showed me her emptied purse, so I handed her mine, still half filled, and then turned back to Peacock Man, but before we could resume our conversation I heard my husband's voice behind me.

"Giacomina, I'm ready to go. Are you?"

I turned to welcome him, and all other thoughts immediately vanished. My Graziano—the handsomest man in Rome, as well as the kindest. I adored him. I could scarcely believe my good fortune that the marriage alliance between our two ancient Roman families was also such a love match. And it didn't hurt that his body made mine sing, every time we lay together. I relished it all. I was singularly, undeservedly blessed.

"Have you given all your alms, my love?" Smiling, he reached over and tucked a stray lock of my hair back under my veil.

I turned to Vanna. "Are we done?"

She nodded and gave the empty purse back to me.

Graziano was holding a muslin sack that bulged with odd shapes. What had my profligate husband bought now? It was never a good idea to let him near the market stalls unsupervised.

"Look, wife, what I found for Giovanni." He drew a bulky wooden object out of the sack and held it up proudly, a broad grin on his face. It was a garishly painted knight on horseback, big enough to come up to Giovanni's chin.

"Watch, Giacoma. See how it moves?"

He demonstrated by pulling on the string attached to the horse's bridle. The wooden animal's stiff legs lurched in the air and the soldier's head turned frantically from side to side, the effect more than a little comical.

He set it down on the paving stones and pulled the string again. This time the soldier and his mount jerked along behind the string for a couple of clumsy steps, then slowly toppled over.

"He'll love it, my dear," I said quickly, as Graziano's face fell. "He always loves it when you choose something for him." *And it's bigger than any of his other fifteen toy knights.*

Graziano reached into the sack again and pulled out a silver rattle.

"This is for our new little one," he said, glancing meaningfully at my belly. I took the toy from him and admired it, turning it round in my hands. The silver was etched with little birds in flight, and through its tiny cut-out windows I could watch the colorful stones as they tumbled around inside, making quite a racket with the slightest movement.

"You don't think babies make enough noise on their own, my love?" I teased.

"Well, if he's anything like Giovanni was, a little more noise won't make much difference, will it?"

"Or she. It could be a girl, you know."

"If it's a girl, she'll need some extra noise at her command to hold her own with Giovanni."

I gave the rattle back to him. He slipped it into the sack, then drew out a cloth-wrapped package.

"I have something for you, too, Giacomina." He handed it to me, smiling again.

I felt it. All fabric, inside and out. Last time he had given me a silver buckle with inlaid garnets, and the time before that, a carved ivory comb. What had he come up with this time?

I unwound the blue linen wrapping while he watched me with that eager, little-boy expression I loved. The diaphanous wisp of silk inside made me catch my breath. I had all manner of costly fabrics in my wardrobe, but this veil was as light as a spider's web and very nearly transparent—it would caress every curl, twist, and turn my mass of turbulent hair chose to take.

"Husband, one would almost think you *want* everyone to see my hair."

His eyes twinkled. "I don't care if everyone does, as long as I do."

"Does that apply to wearing clothes as well?" I asked, all innocence, and he leaned over and kissed me lightly.

"I think they must be content with your hair, sweetling," he murmured in my ear.

Time to go home. I looked around for Vanna, who was waiting alongside a beggar woman. They were a study in contrast: Vanna mildly disapproving, clearly hoping my husband and I would do nothing she considered improper, and the woman beaming at us, just as clearly delighted by our conversation.

I felt a little wave of guilt. I had given that woman a few coins and listened to her story, but I knew—and she must know also—that the silver rattle alone was worth enough to keep her family fed and warm for several months. Yet she was happy for my good fortune. I may have been the almsgiver, but whose was the real generosity?

That reminded me of Peacock Man. I turned back, but he was gone. Then I spotted him near the entrance, humbly begging alms of other visitors, probably in fractured French. I shrugged. Graziano had banished my irritation, as he always did. I could not sustain a bad mood around that man.

He led us back to where his men waited with our horses. We were going only as far as our palazzo and it was a fine day; another time we might have walked, for the city was fairly much at peace in those days, but Graziano was solicitous of my pregnancy and would not have it.

We crossed the Aelian Bridge and rode southeast, parallel to the Tiber's eastern bank. The river was swollen with the spring rains, but nowhere near flood stage. We passed the ruined Bridge of Antoninus and then several floating mills, ramshackle constructions of wooden slats jutting out from both shores. Those obstacles and several permanently-anchored fishing rafts choked the river, but we were moving so sedately that a barge winding its way through the maze outpaced us.

Graziano pointedly looked away as we passed the Tiber Island, where the Pierleoni had recently acquired property near San Bartolomeo. His family and the Pierleoni had a longstanding mutual grudge.

"All went well with your business?" I asked him, mostly to distract him.

"Yes, I got the price I wanted for both mills. And your charities, Giacomina? Any new causes among your poor?" Graziano was less zealous than I about almsgiving, but he was glad enough to have me do it for the sake of both our souls—he simply didn't have the time himself. And he liked it that I did it in such an orderly, well-documented way, keeping careful track of everything.

"Bona is with child and will need some extra help. And Lippo says his sister needs a doctor's care."

"You'll see to it, then."

"Yes."

We had reached a part of Rome more sparsely populated than the

7

area closer to the river. Elaborate homes, like ours, stood proudly on high ground, but only people with little other choice dwelled in the unhealthy malarial lowlands between the hills. Our palazzo, in the ancient Circus where the chariots once raced, was surrounded by orchards, gardens, and a disused well. Graziano's forebears had once kept a leopard which freely roamed the grounds, until one day it attacked and killed a servingwoman. The servingwoman was replaced; the leopard was not.

As we approached our home, now free of wandering wildlife, Graziano spoke again.

"Who was that beggar you were talking to when I arrived? Wasn't he a new one? He seemed different from the rest."

"He's a pilgrim. From Assisi. Wanted to try his hand at begging, apparently."

Graziano laughed and shook his head. "Some rich man's idle son out for experience, bored with the novelty soon enough," he said as we halted.

He dismounted in his usual fluid motion, then came to my side to help his clumsy, pregnant wife down from the world's most docile horse, the only one he would allow me until I brought our child to the light.

"Guess we won't see him again, then. He'll be heading back home, now he's been to the shrine."

"No, we'll not see him again," I said, as we climbed the outside staircase to the piano nobile. And then, as Giovanni came running to meet us, I forgot about Peacock Man altogether.

God must have been laughing.

2

I cracked open the door of my chamber and peeked out. Nobody there.

I stepped into the corridor and checked both directions. Still nobody.

I crossed the corridor in four paces, leaned out over the half wall, and looked down into the courtyard below. Nobody in sight, just a few pots of basil, not yet very far along, drinking in the weak late afternoon sunshine. And the sunken pool, now almost empty.

Having looked, now I listened. I had placed myself in the perfect spot to assess what was going on in all areas of the palazzo. The chambers on this level opened out onto the rectangular covered landing overlooking the courtyard, with the wide stairway to my left, stone from the street level up to where I stood, wood for the stairs leading to the upper floor where the servants slept. All the building's multitudes of noises were captured here, in the open space that defined the heart of the palazzo. Or if not all, all that mattered, for the west wing was closed off and not in use.

The boys' chamber was directly opposite me across the courtyard, and the door stood ajar. My sons chattered away to their nurse as she dressed them after their nap. Had it been only Giovanni, Lucia's job would have been easier, for he was an earnest, serious boy, obedient and eager to please. He was sadder and quieter than a six-year-old should be, but things were as they were and could not be changed. Uccellino, my little bird, was another story. At barely four, he alternated between bursts of feverish activity and querulous discontent, for he was too often ill. Graziano and I had chosen Lucia for her patience, and a wise choice it was. She needed that virtue with our younger son, and yet he had a sweetness about him that melted Lucia's heart, as it did everyone's.

I heard activity coming from the stables off the courtyard, but nothing unusual—probably just the stable boy, saddling up for a trip out to one of our farms. My steward would know. Once I kept careful track of such household details, but now I no longer attended to them.

Less common sounds drifted up from the kitchen. I focused my attention in that direction and realized I was hearing several voices. Mostly men; the only female voice belonged to my cook Amata.

I didn't worry. It was bright daylight and no voices were raised. They were probably poor pilgrims, asking Amata for charitable gifts of food and clothing. She was a kind woman who shared my wishes about almsgiving, so she would be offering the visitors a decent meal even though the dinner hour had passed, and making packets of bread and cheese for them to take with them when they departed. I wondered briefly whether they had already been to San Pietro's tomb, or whether that experience still awaited them. They must have been from out of town, since our local poor arrived right after dinner each day and stayed only long enough to collect alms.

Not so long ago, I would have gone to the kitchen to greet the guests and welcome them to my home. I would have inquired about their needs, asked for their prayers, and made sure they left with more than they expected. I would have made sure they knew their way around Rome well enough not to get into trouble, and if they did not, I would have provided a guide from among the members of my household, or hired a neighbor boy to accompany them. Not long ago I would have offered them overnight lodging, first obtaining my husband's permission—not that he ever refused me.

But not long ago I was a wife, happy in my state, and not a widow. Not a half-crazed, disheveled, sorrowing wreck of a woman who, scarcely a month before, had felt her world tear apart, black despair arriving in the form of the agitated messenger who brought me the news.

How could Graziano have fallen from his horse? He rode brilliantly, as brilliantly as he did everything else. He might have been a centaur, so perfectly did man and animal move together. He loved to ride and hunt on the forested land near our summer villa in Marino, only a few miles outside Rome. He knew every herb, every rock, and every tree on that land. How could a branch reach out and hurl him to the ground? And how could he have been so broken that he failed to get up, failed to remount, failed even to live until I reached him, though I was riding all out on the fastest horse in our stable, hair and clothes flying, while Massimo and the others struggled to keep up with me?

Yet he did fall, and he was broken, and I did not reach him in time to say goodbye.

I ordered our people to chop down the tree and burn it then and there. They were not to dry it for firewood but reduce it to ash immediately. I bound my hair, which Graziano had so loved, in the widow's black benda and swore an oath to him as he lay on his bier that no man would ever see it again while I lived. I gave the necessary orders for his burial, sent the messages that must be sent, did the things that had to be done.

No priest had reached him in time to shrive him, nor to give his soul the comfort of the final anointing. Masses had to be bought, and I did not stint. Graziano's soul would not suffer in Purgatory while I could aid him, so I purchased masses both in Marino and in Rome, a full trentine for the first month and then extra rites for the anniversaries of his death, at one week, one month, one year, and beyond. I expected to add to this schedule as time went on, but it would suffice for a beginning. Some murmured about my extravagance, but I paid them no heed.

Inside I was empty, but the outer Giacoma knew all the rules and procedures, all the proprieties. She—I—was famously efficient and capable, so I let her get on with it. I remember nothing from that time. Many members of my husband's august family and my own came forward to help me. I was not alone, and yet I had never been so alone in my life.

As Graziano's body was broken, so was my heart. And, I think, my soul, for I was contemplating something horrible, a dark sin that would condemn me to hellfire forever—and yet it called to me like a siren.

That was why I listened to my house. With Lucia and the boys in their chamber, Amata busy in the kitchen, and the other servants about their duties, I could go out unnoticed onto the wooden balcony connecting the palazzo to the tower, make my way up those tight, winding stairs, and view the city from the highest point on this part of the Palatine.

The members of my household, fearful of my state of mind since Graziano's death, made sure someone always accompanied me on these climbs. I let them have their way, for I had no will to argue. I had made a daily habit of these visits to the tower for three weeks now, and those who watched me were beginning to relax their vigilance, believing I only intended to gaze sadly out over Rome and remember my noble Roman husband.

That was what I wanted them to believe.

I may do nothing more today, I told myself, as I stepped carefully out onto the balcony and closed the door silently behind me. One day dragged on exactly like the last one, and any time I chose to change that sameness would be arbitrary. I had not made any decisions, plotted any course of action. I only wanted to go up the tower and look out the window, as I had so many times before.

Except this time I was alone.

I trudged steadily up the twisting staircase. Diffuse daylight found its tentative way in through the narrow windows above me, but it didn't do much to illumine the stairs. I knew them by feel, but even so the irregularity of the stone and the uneven heights of the steps demanded my attention. Yet I had no attention to give them, or to give to anything else, for that matter. Not even my poor boys, who were depending on Lucia for the comfort and reassurance a mother should have provided. When you're empty, you can see clearly enough what needs to be done, but that doesn't mean you can do it.

So I didn't care whether I made a misstep and tumbled down, or whether I arrived intact at the large window near the top.

As God or my fortune would have it and through no care on my part, I made no misstep. I reached the great window, and the city sprawled before me. Our tower jutted out of a forest of vines and fruit trees at the southeast end of what had once been the Circus Maximus. The ruins of the Temple of Fortune huddled below me, ignored by the tiny people on the street hurrying past on their various errands. Here and there I spotted columns of smoke from burning marble, where workers were turning crumbling bits of ancient ruins into lime to make mortar to stick other chunks of old marble together into new buildings—Rome's eternal dance of destruction and creation.

Graziano had been at my side the first time I stood here. It was he who pointed out this monument and that palazzo, showed me the churches and the marketplace, traced the winding road through the scattered gardens and orchards and taught me to search for weather patterns in the sky, impossible to see from the crowded street below with its tangle of overhanging balconies, but obvious from up here.

Graziano would never stand beside me again. I kept returning to that thought the way a tongue keeps stroking a painful tooth, unable to leave it alone. Empty I may have been, but there were layers upon layers of pain from which not even emptiness could protect me.

I looked straight down. The wind howled in my ears, and I stood on my tiptoes and leaned over the base of the window.

My aloneness engulfed me. Last night, as usual, I had slept on a pallet on the floor beside the great bed, the bed I could not bear to lie in without Graziano. Even climbing up those tower stairs without him close behind me had hammered me with my loneliness and abraded the raw place where he should have been.

12

Perhaps it was time to pull the tooth.

I tried the idea on, not for the first time. Two things still gave me pause: the thought of my boys, and the priests' insistence that self-slaughter damned one's soul forever.

Graziano's family, the mighty Frangipane clan, would care for the boys. My sons would never want for anything, and Lucia, who adored them, would do her best to shield them from a new loss. I was not much good to them now, I knew. Perhaps they would fare better without their damaged mother. Already they had given up seeking me out when they woke in the morning. They didn't know I watched them sleep at night, yearning to hold them, but I could not bear to see the pain in their eyes—eyes so like Graziano's.

But nothing could save my soul if I did what I yearned to do. I should have clung to the thought of finding my husband in Paradise, or at least in Purgatory, but a voice inside me coldly insisted that a God who cut down a man like Graziano would never show me such grace. And if Graziano's death had not been God's will but merely a cruel trick of fortune, if God cared nothing for our doings here in the world, then perhaps death meant an end to our existence—and thus an end to suffering.

So I wavered. Life without Graziano, or death, bringing me either an eternity in Hell or nothing at all. One chance out of three. The more I tried to conjure visions of hellfire and savage unending punishment, the more I realized I was already there: life without Graziano was infinite pain for me.

That realization drove out any further thought. I am ashamed even now to admit it, but the madness of my grief kept me from hope, from any thought of one day reuniting with Graziano. I saw nothing ahead of me but an infinite extension of the emptiness I was feeling.

I hoisted myself up to the window, one foot on a protruding stone in the wall beneath the ledge. That howling wind pushed at me rudely, violently, making me work for what I wanted. One more movement upwards, and I would be free.

"If you jump, your body will halt when you reach the paving stones, but your soul will keep traveling down."

I didn't release my grip on the window ledge or lower myself to the floor, but I did turn my head to see who had followed me and was speaking to me in such a matter-of-fact way.

A small, dark-haired man in a nondescript patched tunic stood in the doorway. He studied me with bottomless black eyes, his expression mild. I did not know him, yet something about him was familiar.

Why had I not heard him coming up the stairs? Was the wind whistling that loudly? And why was he not trying to stop me?

To my surprise, instead of attempting to seize me or speak to me, he dropped to his knees and began to pray, his arms raised in the ancient way. From his knees he would never reach me in time. One thrust upward would bring me over the ledge and plummeting before the strange little man could react. I was still standing with my left foot on the protruding stone, my hands gripping the ledge, and I started to swing my right leg up.

I couldn't move.

The intruder continued to pray, but it was hard to see him clearly because a fine mist surrounded him. The whole interior of the tower was growing lighter, the light centering on the praying man, the mist taking on a pale apricot color as it eddied gently around him. I felt weak and helpless, and my legs started to quiver uncontrollably.

I made another feeble effort to move my leg. I still could not pull myself upward, but I found I could step down, lowering my foot to the floor as I released my grip on the window ledge. My legs trembled so much they wouldn't support me, and my back slid down the stone wall. I sat on the cold floor abruptly, both legs sticking out in front of me.

The man prayed on. I caught a word here and there, but my mind was in such a state of befuddlement that nothing he was saying made any sense. My head spun. My stomach clenched, and I could not draw a breath.

My body's distress grew until it demanded my full attention, and I lost any awareness of where I was and what I had been trying to do. Was I dying? I thought I must be.

But isn't that what you wanted? The hard little voice inside mocked me. Perhaps, I thought, feeling my gorge rise. But if I wanted it, why was I working so hard to breathe? I didn't understand. I didn't understand anything, except that I was frightened.

And then, as if none of it had ever happened, all of my panic, my sickness, my terror drained out of me and dissolved into nothing. My shivering body relaxed, and I drew a deep, satisfying breath.

The sense of being engulfed by despair had lifted, and with it, something more. The ugly voice urging me to sin was finally silent. I felt a sense of calm, a small tender unfamiliar thing deep inside me, and I knew some kind of healing had begun.

Recalling the sensation of tongue probing painful tooth, I experimented. I called up my grief, my loss, the absence of Graziano. And it still hurt, it hurt enormously, but I was not empty. Not quite. Something of my old self had returned—not much, but something.

What had the praying man done, that the priests and the nuns and even my boys could not do? The mist had dissipated, and now I heard him clearly as he spoke his words of gratitude and praise.

"My Lord God, we thank you, this woman and I, for her release. All praise to you, Lord, for your mercy and your infinite goodness." His expressive tenor resonated in the stone tower. "We two are unworthy, yet in your wisdom you have granted us this gift." He shifted to Latin and began the paternoster.

And then I remembered where I had seen him before.

He had been playing at being poor, begging for alms in the atrium of San Pietro's.

I shook my head to clear it. Yes, it was the same man, but with nothing of the peacock about him this time. He was thin and angular, sunburned, his black beard short and unevenly trimmed. His bare feet, his shabby undyed tunic belted with a rope, his fervent prayer all spoke of a man who had found a religious vocation, and a demanding one at that. His hands, raised to heaven, were no longer soft and smooth. This time he was not playacting.

Why was he in the tower—or, for that matter, in my palazzo? I supposed he must be one of the pilgrims I had heard earlier, but how had he known to find me here?

I wanted to thank him, to explain how I had come to be as I was when he found me, but his praying continued unabated, and I sat and watched him. I should have offered a prayer of my own, but I was still too shaken, too confused.

I was baffled by my own actions. They were so unlike me, so far outside of my true self I scarcely believed I had even thought of such an act, let alone determined to do it. Had I really been willing to sacrifice my soul and separate myself from my husband and my children forever?

How could I be a different person now than I had been just minutes ago?

And if it was madness that had consumed me, how did the little man free me from it? I had spent so many hours on my knees since Graziano's death, a prayer on my lips every waking minute, and still I spiraled down into that dark place where I was nothing but an aching void. Yet in a moment this man, this stranger, spoke to God on my behalf and saved my life.

His conversation with God finally at an end, the stranger stood up

15

and faced me, beaming. He had such an open, joyful smile that to my surprise I smiled back.

"Thank you..." I started to say, my voice faltering, but he shook his head.

"We will speak of it later. Not now. Will you not be wanted downstairs?"

Yes. Yes, I would be. The light outside was fading; it was growing late, so the boys had been up from their rest for some time, and I would be needed. Or at least wanted. Thank God my madness had not gone on so long that my boys no longer wanted their mother. It felt strange to think of resuming my life as if nothing had happened.

But where we're needed, we go, and perhaps we go even more readily where we're wanted. So my rescuer and I wound our way back down the stairs, carefully this time, and took the narrow walkway back to the palazzo. Back to my life, with all its sadness and loss and responsibility, but this time, at least, without the madness. We parted ways, he to rejoin his companions in the kitchen and I to find Lucia and the children, but we agreed to meet in the kitchen later. After a few steps I realized I hadn't learned his name. I turned to ask him, but he was already out of sight.

3

PERHAPS I hugged the boys tighter than usual. Perhaps I confused Lucia when I laughed with them over some bit of their play. Uccellino was feeling well, and he was overjoyed to find me attending to him once more. Giovanni hung back, not quite trusting the change in me, but soon he, too, relaxed, and I joined them in a silly, raucous game of tag, much to Lucia's pleasure. My pretty servant was barely more than a child herself, and she adored my boys and fussed over them constantly. She would be a wonderful mother someday.

"I got you, Mamma," Uccellino squealed, flinging his arms around my knees. "I got you, and Giovanni didn't."

Giovanni swaggered up to us and tagged us both, one with each hand. "And now I've got you, too, Uccel," he said, laughing.

"That's not how you play tag, Vanni," Uccellino protested, but I scrambled away from both of them, dodging and feinting, knowing they would team up to defeat me.

Our game transformed into a footrace, from one end of the hall to the other. Giovanni and I let Uccellino win. People always let Uccellino win, because it delighted him so.

"I'm not very strong, Mamma, but I'm fast, aren't I?" he said as I hugged him and pronounced him the victor. Giovanni rolled his eyes, but he was more amused than annoyed. He was ever his brother's protector and fierce defender, and he worried along with me every time Uccel was ill.

"Yes, you are, my love," I said, stroking his hair. "And you will grow stronger as you get older." *Please, God,* I added silently, *let it be so.*

Somehow we fell into an impromptu tickling match, and then the three of us collapsed in a heap, breathless and giggling, and Lucia seized her opportunity. She bundled the boys off to their chamber for supper while they were still too breathless to argue. I watched them go, overwhelmed with gratitude that I was still capable of being a mother to them.

It was beginning to get dark, for we were still in the first days of spring, with its unpredictable weather and early nightfall. I sat on the floor where the boys had left me—I don't normally sit on floors, but I'd done it twice on this day—and puzzled over my experience in the tower.

Vanna found me there. At first she was alarmed, but I assured her I was well, in fact was better than I had been for quite a while.

"I must go to the pilgrims in the kitchen," I told her. She offered a hand to help me up.

"Must you?" She wrinkled her nose. "They're dirty and shabby, though they do pray a lot. I'm sure Amata can take care of their needs, monna—I mean Giacoma." Vanna found it hard to remember that I wanted my servants to address me by my name, not by a title. Or so she claimed, anyway. It was one more way in which I offended her sense of propriety.

"No, I want to see them and speak with them. They are men of religion."

She gave a slight but eloquent shrug, and then looked at me more closely, her eyes narrowing. "But do you not wish to tidy up a bit first?" She hesitated a moment. "And perhaps you might wish to change your gown?"

For weeks I'd paid little attention to what I wore, but Vanna was right. I was a disaster. The cioppa I wore, in a lugubrious shade of dull brown, was fine enough quality, or had been once. But it had gone too long uncleaned, and I found snags and rips and stains I didn't remember acquiring.

The one thing I had done each day without fail was to bind my hair in the benda. But already I had violated my oath—a strand of my wheat-colored hair, greasy and tangled, had worked its way out of its drab binding and dangled in a forlorn coil next to my face. Did that mean my rescuer had seen it? Or had it come loose during my lively play with the children?

Sorry, Graziano. For an instant I pictured him grinning at me. The thought brought tears to my eyes, and I felt my giddy sense of relief drain out of me like the air from a child's inflated pig bladder. I waited to see what would replace it, but though sorrow and loneliness crowded in like the persistent lodgers they had become, at least madness did not join them.

Vanna's perplexed frown reminded me I hadn't answered her yet.

"You're right. I'll go put myself in order first," I assured her, and she beamed.

"I'll find you something fresh to wear," she said, and we went off to my chamber together to make repairs.

It took a while to turn me back into someone who might convincingly be the lady of the house. I shed that disreputable garment and put on its murky dark red counterpart, every bit as dismal but considerably cleaner. Vanna stuffed my straying hair back into the benda, then dunked a towel into a basin of water and swabbed at my face and hands. When she was satisfied she had done all possible to render me respectable, she surveyed me critically and finally nodded her approval.

Vanna seated herself in front of my writing table with my cioppa across her lap. She adjusted the candlestick, lighted tapers on all three prickets, propped the bronze mirror behind it to double the light, and went to work. She started by plucking off the bits of debris I had picked up from the floor, first in the tower and then while playing with the children. Her lips were pursed in silent disapproval, for Vanna's mission in life was to persuade me to exhibit the dignity she believed so necessary to my station. I wasn't trying to make things difficult for her; I just tended to forget. Vanna was as young as Amata and Lucia, but she never seemed so, especially when she disapproved of me. Yet she was a loyal friend, and dear to me. I would try harder.

I left her there and went downstairs. The kitchen was unusually bright for that hour. The fire crackled, though the day's cooking was long over, and a lamp burned cheerily on the cutting table. Amata sat on the bench in earnest conversation with one of the pilgrims, absentmindedly twisting a dark curl around her finger as she listened intently to whatever he was saying. She had put out food—I saw traces of a cold meal consisting of bread, cheese, fruit, and almonds, and there wasn't much left.

Massimo, my steward and friend, leaned against the wall in the background. He was keeping an eye on everything, but he seemed uncharacteristically relaxed. Something about these men must have put him at ease. Usually he counted the coins and did furious calculations in his head whenever alms were being given out. It didn't matter that I was better at figures than he was, or that I tracked every denaro entering or leaving this house, or had until recently. Massimo kept his own tally, stubborn as an abbot but utterly reliable.

I saw ten or eleven men, clothed much like the man in the tower in undyed tunics with rope belts. They were tall, short, old, young, dark, fair—some of them might have been peasant farmers, but at least two of them had the bearing of knights. All were sun-browned and barefoot. The singular man who had confronted me in the tower was on his knees, this time in a corner of the kitchen. He prayed silently, though his mouth formed words. His companions variously ate, talked quietly, or relaxed, feet toasting near the fire. They stood, leaned on the wall, sat on the bench or on the floor, perfectly at home.

It was an oddly serene domestic sight. Unaccustomed as I was to having my kitchen taken over by a pack of itinerant religious men, it felt quite normal to find them there.

One of them got up to greet me. He was a tall, sturdy man, scruffy, with gingery hair and beard and light, gray green eyes.

"May God give you peace," he said in a surprisingly melodious voice.

An unusual greeting, especially when addressed to a member of a celebrated Roman warrior clan. I liked it, though. Peace, were it possible for me to receive it, would be a great gift, and I told him so and welcomed him and his companions to my home.

"I'm Brother Egidio," he said. "We're from Assisi, and we follow Brother Francesco in his chosen path, trying to live according to the gospels. We espouse poverty as an act of faith in God's providence." He swept his arm in a circle to indicate his companions.

All of them were watching us, except for the man—Brother Francesco?—who had helped me in the tower. He was still praying silently, oblivious to everything around him. Some of the men blinked at me or bobbed their heads uncertainly, others murmured something, and one comical fellow, with tufts of hair sticking out from behind his ears, grinned and raised his hand in a casual salute, waggling his fingers at me. The gesture was so childlike, so like something Uccellino would have done, that without even thinking I waggled mine back. The men broke into smiles at that. They relaxed and returned to whatever they had been doing, leaving me to continue speaking with Brother Egidio.

"I'm monna Giacoma, wife—widow—of Graziano of the Frangipani, of whom you will no doubt have heard. They call me Giacoma dei Settesoli." I raised my chin as I spoke, as proud of my husband as ever. Brother Egidio inclined his head, by which he might have meant either yes, he had heard of Graziano, or he was simply acknowledging my introduction. It didn't matter, really. These men were several days' travel from their home, a city much smaller than Rome, and even I had to admit not everyone in the world knew of my husband. Sometimes I had a bit of a problem with the sin of pride. I was raised to it, after all.

"Giacoma dei Settesoli?" he repeated. "How is it, madonna, that you are named for seven suns? Brother Francesco would say only one Brother Sun shines on our world."

"And he would be right. 'Settesoli' is the name the Romans have given to the noble ruin nearby, which was here and whole in the days of Rome's greatness. They call it the Temple of the Seven Suns, or the Septizonium, in the tongue of the ancients." All that remained of it were the slender columns and partial rooms, now more porches than chambers, west of our palazzo.

"Brother Francesco would say Rome's time of greatness is now, ma-

20

donna. She may have ruled the world once, but she was still heathen in those days."

"And is that Brother Francesco?" I indicated the man kneeling in the corner.

Brother Egidio nodded, his face glowing with pride.

"Why are you in Rome, Brother Egidio?" I asked him.

"Brother Francesco wishes to obtain the Holy Father's approval for our brotherhood. Without it, we risk having the churchmen we meet on our travels believe us heretical, since our way of life is, shall we say, rather unlike their own." His eyes twinkled, but he kept his expression serious.

I couldn't quite imagine these shabby men in audience with His Holiness. I knew Pope Innocente, the third of that name if you didn't count an antipope a while back. I knew him when he was just Cardinal Lotario dei Conti Segni, a family friend. I believed him to be a genuinely religious man, which was not necessarily a given in a Roman pope, but I found it hard to picture him granting his blessing to this ragtag group of penitents. Still, Francesco was an extraordinary man.

I found I wanted very much to talk with this Francesco, but he was still on his knees.

"Will he be finished soon, do you think?"

Egidio's smile was like his leader's but softer and more muted. "He will never truly finish, monna Giacoma. Brother Francesco's entire life is a prayer." He lowered his voice. "He did, however, give me leave to speak with you of your experience in the tower."

I hadn't expected anyone other than my rescuer himself to know about that. But now I was fiercely curious, so I beckoned Egidio to follow me a little distance away from the others.

We moved to the end of the kitchen where Amata kept her washing basins, which reminded me how desperately I needed to wash my hair. Massimo, who never missed anything, approached us with two three-legged stools, carrying them awkwardly because of his damaged left arm. I thanked him and sat on one. Egidio took the other, and Massimo moved back to his post, watching me, though his expression was untroubled. Protecting me was his duty, whether I was in any apparent danger or not, and duty was everything to Massimo, who was himself still reeling from Graziano's death.

I studied Egidio, who was waiting for me to speak. Might as well talk to him, I thought. If he's spoken to Francesco, he already knows all that had occurred. And I'd like to know it, too—know it and understand it.

21

"Can you tell me what happened to me?" I asked.

"You had a demon in you. Brother Francesco cast it out."

"I had a *what*?"

"A demon, madonna. There's no shame in it. In fact, Brother Francesco says demons are attracted to good people, because they see a challenge in them."

"I thought it was madness," I said, shaken by the idea that I had harbored a thing of evil. "And I must not have been much of a challenge for it." In fact, I had been helpless against it.

"Often madness takes hold when a demon is in residence," he told me. "Your grief left you open, and the demon saw it and moved in."

"How did Francesco even know where I was, or... or about my demon?"

"It's not your demon, nor are you its victim. It only tried to take you over. It failed."

"But how did Francesco know?"

He shrugged. "I can only assume God told him."

I must have looked distressed, or maybe he thought my confusion meant I was skeptical.

"You'd be surprised how often he does things like that. We've come to expect it."

My head spun. As a Roman noblewoman, I'd been around the highest churchmen in the world for most of my twenty-four years, and I'd never known anyone in our time who did that sort of thing often enough for people to come to expect it, though I had read of such instances in the saints' lives.

I had heard, though, the wild boasts of some of the traveling religious. Suddenly suspicious, I glanced over at Francesco and then turned back to Egidio.

"You're not heretics, are you?" I asked, immediately regretting my words. *Stupid question.* I could hardly expect him to say, "Yes, we're shameless heretics and we are here to bring down Mother Church." The idea almost made me laugh. What could he possibly say in reply, other than of course they aren't?

"Do you think we'd be seeking an audience with the Holy Father if we were heretics? Brother Francesco is determined that everything we do will work with the Church, not against her."

He did have a point. Certainly the targets of the Holy Father's struggle to wipe out heresy in Languedoc weren't going to come face to face with His Holiness. Not if they could help it, anyway.

"We are grateful for your alms, madonna," Egidio said, changing the subject. "We had not eaten since early yesterday, and the food was most welcome."

I started to reply, and then it washed over me like a sudden downpour. If their Brother Francesco had not somehow known to follow me up to the tower, I would be in hell right now, not chatting with a pleasant man in my warm kitchen. I shivered, despite that warmth, and pulled my mantle closer around myself.

"How can you sit there and talk of almsgiving when you see such a sinner in front of you?" The question burst out of me without my volition.

Egidio's broad face registered concern. He frowned and leaned toward me, reaching out his hand as if to offer comfort.

"You know what I would have done," I said, drawing back from him. "No virtue in me prevented it, only what your Brother Francesco did. You're a religious man, so how can you talk to me as if I deserved your kindness?"

"No one can blame you for what the demon tried to drive you to," he said, looking steadily into my eyes. "Had you damned yourself with your sins, not even Brother Francesco could have saved you. But he was there to help, and it was God's will that brought him to you. You were never alone. How will I condemn you if God does not?"

Never alone. I seized that phrase the way I had once seen a panicky boy clutch at the rope his friends threw him as he struggled against the current in the Tiber. I had felt so alone—and yet when I needed it most, help had come. Francesco had come to me, but God had always been there. I tipped myself off the stool and onto my knees on the cold brick floor. As I uttered my belated prayer of gratitude, Egidio sank down next to me and added his voice to mine.

I don't know how long we knelt, but I became aware of a growing sense of peace as some of my despair and guilt began to lift.

I loved the way praying made me feel. I loved the respite it gave me from living, breathing human beings and their demands, and I loved how it always cleared my thinking, but I never really saw it as a conversation with God. I spoke the words, and he either did or did not listen, as he chose. If God answered me—and in spite of everything I believed he did—it was always an indirect answer, never a resolution in the moment of praying. Yet this time something shifted inside of me. I felt lighter, cleansed, my mind clearer than it had been in weeks. It was nothing dramatic, just enough to remind me I was not alone.

Egidio was still kneeling on my left, but now on my right was Fran-

23

cesco, also on his knees. His face was raised, his arms extended in the *orante* position, and he spoke his rapid words of praise in a soft, clear voice. For an instant I thought I saw something of the apricot mist that had enveloped him in the tower, but when I blinked I could no longer find it. Massimo, Amata, and most of the men in Francesco's party were watching us in respectful silence. Three or four of the men were also on their knees, adding their prayers to ours. Together we gave voice to our gratitude, our praise, and our humble fealty to God.

Never alone.

4

As the fire burned low, we talked together like a reunited family. Our shabby visitors opened my eyes to a way of living I had never known was possible. If the demon who had tempted me to end my life hoped for another chance at me, then the spiritual fire of those men was enough to rout him for good.

If the brothers were bright torches in my darkness, then Francesco was a bonfire. I could not take my eyes off him. He was incandescent as he described to me the brothers' commitment to living what he called "the gospel life"—poverty, service to God and to humanity, reverence, humility, faith.

He would speak for a while, his words passionate, articulate, and shimmering with a keen intelligence, then lapse into the same bad French I had heard from him years ago at San Pietro's tomb. He would suddenly break into improvised song, making up a nonsense ditty and bowing an imaginary fiddle as he proclaimed himself "God's troubadour," and then segue into a prayerful and heartfelt lauda. When Francesco spoke or sang of God, he was a man enamoured. He urged us all to penitence, not for the fear of God but for the love of him.

The brothers, more accustomed to his ways than I was, did not seem to find his abrupt shifts unsettling, so I tried to adapt. It was easier than I would have guessed.

I could have sat up with them all night, but it grew late, and when Egidio stifled a yawn, I knew it was time to let them rest. They were bone weary from travel and had much to accomplish in the next few days.

Amata and I left our guests comfortably bedded down in the kitchen, cheerfully sharing among themselves the pile of blankets Massimo brought them from the upstairs storage chests. I lit a lamp and climbed the stairs, tired, but more at peace than I had been in weeks. Amata walked with me to my chamber door.

"Rest well, Giacoma," she said, placing her plump hand lightly on my arm. "It's a joy to see you more like yourself again."

"I feel different, somehow." I handed her the lamp. "I can't explain it, but something has changed."

"Thank God it has." She touched my hand affectionately. "I've been worried about you." With that she left me, continuing up the stairs to the room she shared with Lucia, and now also with Vanna. I could not bear to have anyone else in my chamber since Graziano's death, not even my

25

personal maid.

In my chamber, two of the tapers had burned down and the third was guttering. Poor Vanna must have worked for hours on that cioppa, for she had fallen asleep on the pallet. I had intended to sleep on the pallet myself, alone in the room as usual, but I decided not to wake her. I slipped out of my dark red gown, tossed it over the rail, dropped my benda on the floor, and after a moment's hesitation, climbed into the big bed. Tired though I was, I was still far from sleep, and I lay there listening to Vanna's rhythmic breathing, not sure whether sleep would find me at all that night.

While I waited for it, I thought about the extraordinary men sleeping downstairs. I was beginning to understand how fluidly these men moved in and out of a state of prayer, some of them never entirely leaving it.

Their way of living was the opposite of mine. They owned nothing, they had no fixed home, and they lived on alms and on what they could earn with manual labor, though they would not touch money and accepted payment only in the form of food, fuel, clothing, and other necessities. I lived in a luxurious and complex world, whereas the brothers' world was simplicity itself.

Their thoughts about the days, weeks, and years ahead were utterly different than anything in my experience. That emerged when I invited them to stay with us during the rest of their time in Rome.

"Monna Giacoma, we are grateful for your kindness and your generosity," Francesco said, "but our way is to leave tomorrow to God. He will provide."

His answer startled me. "Not even to plan for lodgings or food?"

He shook his head. "God provides for the lilies of the field, and for the birds of the air. Will he do any less for us?"

Massimo was still leaning against his wall, standing guard. He scratched thoughtfully at the wiry beard he had grown to mourn Graziano. For such a careful man, making no provision for the morrow must have seemed hopelessly foolish.

I found the idea exhilarating, though I was sure I could never live by it. Yet their attempt to have an audience with the pope was surely a subtle version of planning ahead. I didn't say anything, though. I just listened.

They did not intend to approach the Holy Father on their first full day in Rome. That day, Francesco said firmly, was to be dedicated to a pilgrimage to the tomb of San Pietro. Their business would wait for the following day.

I concealed a smile, remembering how I had last seen Francesco paying his reverence there. Thus far he had shown no sign of recognizing me, and I supposed it had been so long ago he didn't recall our meeting. Perhaps even remarkable religious men couldn't count on God reminding them of everything, and surely our heavenly Father was entitled to keep a few secrets. Which was an idea I wished the Holy Father and his curia would consider, instead of assuming that whatever they wanted was also God's fondest desire.

One could grow old waiting on such wishes, however. And I was far from old, and suffused with new thoughts and hopes I didn't even begin to understand. Instead of being convinced my life had ended, I was awash in new ideas of how I wanted to spend it, devoting myself to God as Francesco and his brothers were doing, helping the poor, making God's world better. Teaching my sons to love God and the church, imperfect as that church was, with the same joy Francesco expressed with his whole life.

How, exactly, a woman was going to accomplish this was another question.

I lay there in the darkness, wide awake, mulling these things over. Even Graziano's empty place beside me was not enough to drain away my exhilaration. Wishing I could somehow share this feeling with him, I rolled over to his side of the bed. By my own command, nothing had changed in this room since his death, and the sheet still carried his scent, though only faintly. I breathed it in and felt the tears start to come, and then found myself praying in earnest, except I couldn't decide whether I was mourning my loss or expressing my gratitude. I think it must have been both.

Some time later I heard the first stirrings in the kitchen, and the first dim sunlight crept in through the gaps around the shutters. I listened to the boys get up, noisy as they had been before they lost their father, not subdued and quiet as of late, and again I was grateful to Francesco. Lucia arrived at their room and started getting them ready for the day, trying to shush their high-pitched voices to allow me to rest longer. She needn't have, for I loved to hear them sounding like themselves.

Vanna slept on. I hated to wake her, but it was time for me to be up if I was going to see the brothers before they left for their pilgrimage to the apostle's shrine. I intended to make sure they would stay with us this night. Lilies of the field were well and good, but the morrow had now arrived, and I wanted it sorted out.

Carefully I climbed out of bed on the side opposite Vanna's pallet and dressed without waking her, though I heard her stirring as I slipped out the door.

In the kitchen, the scene that met my eyes was completely different than the chilly, hushed mornings we had become used to lately. The brothers were up, and two or three of them knelt in prayer, in places where Amata would not stumble over them as she worked. Lucia was there, bemused by this benign invasion. My boys were chattering happily with the tufty-eared brother who had waggled his fingers at me the night before. Amata had built up the fire, and she was sorting through a linen bag of dried fruits, apples and figs and apricots, selecting some and arranging them on the scarred wooden table she used for cutting vegetables. Massimo lounged in the doorway that led to the garden, watching Amata with an inscrutable expression. He didn't notice me when I came in, for she held his full attention.

Hmm. How long had *that* been going on, I wondered? And how had I not seen it before? I stored the information away to think about later, and entered the kitchen.

"Good morning," I called to my boys, and Giovanni and Uccellino came running to hug me. The men who were not praying greeted me cheerfully. Francesco was sitting on the bench, awkwardly trying to mend a rent in his tunic while he still wore it.

He trained those jet black eyes on me and said softly, "May God give you peace."

"Have you been to mass?" I asked him. The bells had sounded while I still lay abed.

"Yes, madonna, and we came back because your cook kindly offered us alms to break our fast. We don't know if we will see any more food today, so we've accepted her offer. Unless you object?"

"No, not at all," I said. "You're welcome to everything we have."

Uccellino interrupted us then. "Mamma!" he said urgently, tugging at my skirt. "This big brother is going to teach us to play the story of Saul on the road to Damascus!"

I looked up. The big brother was Brother Egidio, and Amata was placing a handful of dried fruits in his cupped hands. He thanked her and then turned back to me.

"Your lads wanted a story, monna Giacoma, and I thought this one might be a worthy tale for young ears." He sat down on a stool, smoothed his grubby tunic and began to arrange the wizened fruits in a pattern on his lap.

"I'm sure it will," I said. "May I learn, too?"

"Certainly," he said with a smile, and the boys and I gathered around him.

"Over here we have the Christians in Damascus." He indicated a small pile of dried apricots. "And here we have Saul and his companions, on their way to arrest the Christians." Saul and his companions were the apples.

"Was Saul on a horse?" asked Giovanni.

"I don't know," said Brother Egidio. "Do you think he was?"

"Was it a long way?" said Uccellino.

"Yes, a very long way."

"Then he was on a horse." Such certainty. The barefoot pilgrims, who clearly had not made use of horses to come to Rome from Assisi, watched the boys with evident delight.

"Then we need a horse for Saul. Can you find me a horse? Maybe a piece of wood?" Giovanni and Uccellino both dashed for the kindling basket, squabbling over which twig looked most like a horse.

"Boys, any will do," I said. "You have to imagine it's a horse, the same way you imagine the apple is Saul."

Uccellino chose his stick and dashed back to Brother Egidio, and Giovanni followed goodnaturedly in his wake. Egidio solemnly accepted the twig and arranged the biggest dried apple on top of it. He lined up the other apples in a row behind Saul.

"Do his friends have horses too?" asked Uccellino. "Should we get more sticks?"

"No, we'll just pretend they have horses. My lap isn't big enough for everyone to get a real one."

I grinned at how smoothly the stick had become a *real* horse.

"Do you know what happened to Saul?" Brother Egidio asked them.

"Yes! He fell off his horse!" shouted Uccellino, and Giovanni added, "He got blind because of a bright light from God."

Brother Egidio nodded his satisfaction. "You've been taught well, young lords," he said, glancing at me with a hint of a smile. "We'll want a bright light. I think you might have to ask for your mother's help for this part."

Both boys looked up at me. It lightened my heart to see them like this.

"I'll bring a coal in a little pan, and we'll blow on it to make a bright light," I suggested, and the boys agreed eagerly. Amata had been listening, and she handed me a brass pan, one we often used for eggs. I took the tongs and selected a glowing coal from the edge of the hearth, placing it in the pan, and brought it back to where the small army of apples waited, while the hapless apricots huddled together.

"Now, when I count to three, if you two young men will blow on the coal, we will have our bright light, and Saul can be changed forever," said Brother Egidio, holding the biggest apple lightly on its woody steed.

He got as far as "Two—" but Uccellino couldn't hold back any longer, and he whooshed a lungful of air at the coal, which flickered. But after a moment's hesitation it flared quite satisfactorily, and several of the brothers cheered, though Giovanni protested that he hadn't gotten his chance to help since Uccellino didn't wait for "Three."

I quieted him with a gentle squeeze of his shoulder, the signal I used to remind him that Uccellino was smaller than he was and lacked his patience and understanding. Brother Egidio lifted the apple up in the air dramatically, turning him end over end before dropping him ignominiously onto his lap. He made the twig scurry away, to the boys' laughter.

"Alas, I am blinded," he said in a high, breathy voice. "What must I do?" The boys stared at the apple, fascinated. "I heard a great voice saying, 'Saul, Saul, why do you persecute me?'"

"I want to hear God's voice," said Uccellino. "Say it for us!"

"The voice spoke only to Saul. Even in play, we don't try to speak for God." Uccellino opened his mouth to argue, but something in Brother Egidio's calm gaze made him hold his tongue.

Brother Egidio made another apple walk over to the Saul-apple. "We will guide you to Damascus, signore Saul," he said in a different voice, and then he made the two apples move off together, toward the huddled apricots.

"When poor blind Saul arrived at Damascus, he didn't eat or drink for three days. Then what do you think happened?" he asked the boys gravely, though his eyes danced.

Uccellino frowned, trying to remember, but Giovanni said promptly, "Ananias came and made him see again. And then Saul was a Christian, too!"

"Exactly." Brother Egidio picked up the largest apricot and walked it over to the Saul-apple. In yet another voice—how many of them did he have?—he said, "I am Ananais, and I am here to heal you through God's grace." The apple, which had been lying on its side, disappeared briefly into Brother Egidio's closed fist. When he opened his hand, Saul had been transformed into a fig, drawing gasps of delight from my boys.

"And now he is no longer Saul, but Paul, an apostle of the Lord,"

Brother Egidio finished in his own voice, setting the transformed fig down in the midst of a circle of friendly apricots.

The boys were ecstatic. Uccellino was so excited he was hopping from one foot to the other. "Now Saul isn't a apricot, he's a fig!"

"Saul was an apple, not an apricot. The fig is Paul," Giovanni explained to his brother with exaggerated patience.

Uccellino had more immediate priorities. "Can we eat the Christians?" he wanted to know. He was very fond of apricots.

"Do you think it would be right to eat the Christians, young lord?"

Giovanni solemnly shook his head, but Uccellino was not giving up. "What about the apples?" he demanded.

"You mean because they're Pharisees, Uccel?" Giovanni scoffed.

"We wouldn't eat Pharisees either. But we've finished the play, so now they're just apples," said Brother Egidio.

Uccellino thought for a moment. "Then why can't we eat the Christians?"

Brother Egidio laughed. "You have a point, young lord," he said. "But I think you mean the apricots."

"Oh—yes. The apricots."

Then Francesco spoke, and all of us turned toward him. "I say we may eat the apples and the apricots, now that they are only themselves, no longer Pharisees or Christians. But Paul was a saint and a holy man, so perhaps it would be more respectful not to eat the fig. Can we agree on that?"

Both boys nodded solemnly and turned to me for permission to fall upon the Biblical fruits, permission I gladly gave.

While the boys enjoyed their treat, Francesco and I moved apart from the others to a place against the wall opposite Massimo's doorway, so we could speak more privately.

5

"TODAY, then, you'll be going to San Pietro's tomb?" I asked the man who had saved me.

"Yes. And I assure you, it will be quite different from my last visit." He grinned as he said it, and I smiled at the memory. So he did remember me.

"Then we will find a place to spend the night, and on the morrow we will seek out the Holy Father. We understand our Bishop Guido is in town, and we'll find him too."

That didn't sound like much of a plan to me, but then as a Roman who by birth and marriage was part of the highest social echelon, I knew something about what was required to gain access to the papal presence. And walking into San Giovanni Laterano in a scruffy, patched tunic and asking to see His Holiness was not going to do it, even if he managed to get some sort of recommendation from a small town bishop.

I needed to approach this carefully. "Well, first, I hope you'll consider returning here tonight. The boys are enjoying having your brothers here, and I owe you a great personal debt. Will you please come here after you visit the tomb, and allow us to share a meal with you?"

He hesitated, but then he relented. "We accept your offered alms then, madonna, and you will see us tonight, if you're sure that's what you wish."

I was sure. My boys were talking animatedly with several of the brothers, and I rejoiced to see them acting like children again. Somehow, life had returned to our home. I should never have let my grief cripple me and keep me from my duties to those under my protection, whether my own sons or those who lived with us and worked for us. My household, my responsibility.

"There's one more thing," I said, and Francesco looked at me inquiringly.

"It is not always so easy to have an audience with the Holy Father. He is very busy with all the affairs of Christendom, and often he cannot make time for people who drop in unannounced."

"I know we're asking a lot. Is there any way you can help us?"

I was afraid of that. I didn't want to tell him what I had to say next, but I saw no alternative.

"When my husband died, I learned he had honored me by not only leaving me fully in charge of our children, but also of his property. It means I am extremely wealthy, and that makes me of interest to the church and its leaders, because the church's. . ." what was the word I wanted? "The church's efforts in the Holy Land cost a lot of money."

Francesco nodded. "I understand your position, monna Giacoma, and also the Holy Father's."

"Unfortunately, another thing Graziano left to me was a lawsuit against the papacy. It's nothing too important, just a property dispute, but I'm sure you can imagine how it has strained this house's relationship with His Holiness. I fear my recommendation wouldn't help you much."

Francesco shook his head. "It is not good to contest the will of the Vicar of Christ. Could you not drop the lawsuit, if it is, as you say, not too important?"

"I can't, I'm afraid. I owe it to my husband to see that his wishes are pursued in this matter." Much as I hated to deny this man anything, my first loyalty would always be to Graziano. "Besides, the papacy is wrong about this particular dispute, Vicar of Christ or not. Or are you one of those who insist the church is always right?"

"No. I believe imperfect men make imperfect decisions. But I also believe the men of the church are charged with doing God's will on earth, and we must honor them and obey them, even when men make mistakes, as they sometimes will."

Of course, I thought. To say anything else would make these men vulnerable to charges of heresy. They, of all people, had to be the most loyal of the church's children.

"I understand. But my promise is given, and so it must be, though I would happily be free of the responsibility for that lawsuit, if I could."

My formidable in-laws the Frangipani had no such scruples. They had a knack for using popes and antipopes as pawns in their eternal squabbles with their rivals the Pierleoni. They espoused the not unreasonable belief that you never knew which one was going to turn out to be the pope and which the antipope until all the shouting was over and you could figure out who had won. I found the whole thing faintly ridiculous, but in spite of that I intended to honor my husband's wishes. I wished, though, that I could find a way to help my new friends.

"Nevertheless, we are grateful for your hospitality," Francesco was saying, when I realized there was something I could do, and I interrupted him.

"It wouldn't help you if I sent a message to the pope, but I have a friend on the papal curia, a wise and good man, and if you were to gain his trust, I've no doubt His Holiness would gladly see you." Cardinal

Giovanni di San Paolo was an old family friend. It was he Pope Innocente counted on to sort out what was heretical and what was not, for often the dividing lines were far from clear. The cardinal had no patience with those who enriched themselves in the name of religion, and he would be filled with admiration at the all-out commitment of Francesco and his brothers to living the gospel life.

I told Francesco a little about him, and he listened with interest.

"He sounds like a man much deserving of our respect," he said.

"He is. He's a good man, both learned and wise. Would you like for me to speak to him on your behalf?"

"That would be most kind, madonna," he said with a smile.

We decided that while Francesco and the brothers visited the tomb of San Pietro, I would send a messenger to the cardinal.

Francesco gathered his ragtag band together, and they traipsed off to the apostle's tomb, to the disappointment of Uccellino and Giovanni, who clamored to go with them. Massimo distracted the boys by handing them their wooden swords and offering a bit of combat practice in the courtyard.

While my sons marched happily off to pretend mayhem, I went upstairs to my desk to scribe a letter. I kept it simple, hoping for a chance to talk with the cardinal in person, and when I was satisfied with what I had written, I folded the parchment, added my wax seal, and placed the note in a leather pouch for Ricco to deliver.

With the boys playing under Massimo's supervision, the brothers off on a pilgrimage, Amata busy in the kitchen, Lucia and Vanna folding the brothers' blankets, and my message on its way, I could at last take stock of what I needed to do next.

It was no contest, really. I was going to wash my hair.

*

I had just finished stuffing my blissfully clean, almost dry hair back under the benda when a breathless Vanna appeared at the door of my chamber.

"A prince of the church is here to see you, madonna," she said.

"'Giacoma', not 'madonna'," I muttered. She ignored this.

"It's Cardinal Giovanni di San Paolo." Her eyes were wide. Generally, lay people went to church people, and not the other way around. "He wants to know if you will speak with him."

"Gladly," I said. "Can you find me an overdress, quickly?"

34

She could, and I slipped it on over the dark red cioppa. It was midnight blue, not new, but of a soft, fine wool and well made. It would serve. Deftly, she laced me up, inspected me, and nodded her approval.

Cardinal Giovanni waited below, chatting with Massimo. I heard him inquiring about how the family fared since our bereavement, and the genuine concern in his voice moved me. When he saw me coming, the cardinal smiled.

"Monna Giacoma. A pleasure to see you, my dear. May I say again how sorry I am for your loss?"

The cardinal was almost an uncle to me, and he had been one of the people who helped me arrange for Graziano's funeral and supported me throughout that nightmarish time. He had been a strength to me then, though I had been too distraught to feel gratitude. I felt it now, and I looked at his kind, creased face and rheumy eyes with real affection. I knelt for his blessing and kissed his ring, and he took my hand and squeezed it gently.

"Madonna, his lordship's escort is waiting outside," Massimo said, and I rose. Massimo preferred to avoid using my given name around guests, and I let him have his way.

"Please see them made comfortable in the kitchen and have Amata give them refreshment," I said, but the cardinal shook his head.

"I can't stay long, my dear. Let's just take a few minutes together, and you can explain to me your interest in these men from Assisi."

We went to the courtyard and seated ourselves on a stone bench on the shady side. I told him, as simply as I could, of my encounter with Francesco and his brothers and my impression of them. I did not tell him exactly what had happened in the tower, but I did say that with the help of God, Francesco had kept me from committing a very great sin. The cardinal's face suddenly became serious, and I was sure he knew what I meant, even without any details.

"If this man helped you that much, my dear, then certainly I will see him." He gave me a searching look. "But I cannot promise my support for a papal audience, not yet. First I must speak with him and learn something of his character. It would not be wise for him to come before His Holiness espousing some heretical doctrine, even were it only out of ignorance."

"I think, signore, you will find Francesco and his brothers are neither heretical nor ignorant," I said. "I believe they follow the gospel life, commanded by God himself and obedient to him."

The cardinal stood up, and I followed his example. "Well, we shall see," he said. "I hope you're right, Daughter, for I would like to meet such men. Very few can commit to a life of poverty, simplicity, and pure trust in God, and fewer still can do it without finding themselves at odds with Mother Church."

"You'll help them, then?"

"I will see your friends. I must ask that they stay with me for a few days, to give me time to examine them and learn about what they're proposing. Do you mind losing your guests to me?"

I did mind, and the boys would be disappointed too, but he was right. This was the brothers' best opportunity, and I certainly wasn't going to stand in their way.

"No, signore. By all means make them comfortable, or at least as comfortable as they will let you make them," I said, remembering how we had struggled with trying to persuade the men to eat a full meal and then, in the morning, to take a bit of food with them for later.

"After all," Brother Giannuccio, the tufty-eared man, had mused, "as long as we make sure to eat it sometime today, we're not planning for the morrow." I smiled, remembering that comment. To my ears it had sounded like something a churchman would say.

But not this churchman. I walked to the front door with the cardinal, who turned to me and took both my hands, tenderness on his lined face.

"My dear, may I be sure you are no longer in danger of committing a sin that would damn your eternal soul?" he asked me gently.

"Yes, signore. I am free of that now, I give you my word."

He studied me for a long moment, then gave a nod of satisfaction. He blessed me and left, promising to send a man to the brothers at San Pietro's tomb with his invitation.

Francesco accepted Cardinal Giovanni's offer, though he was kind enough to send Brother Egidio back to us so the boys wouldn't be disappointed. Egidio must have been disappointed himself not to be with his brothers on this new adventure, but he hid it well. He was, we learned, a skillful carver, and he turned part of our woodpile into several charming and ingenious toys, which made the boys squeal with delight. He kept my little lads happily entertained until their bedtime, and then he led them in prayers and told them gentle stories from the gospels until their eyes finally closed.

By then it was too late for him to go join his brothers, though the cardinal's palazzo wasn't far away. Rome's streets are lawless at night. In truth, they are often lawless in the day, as well, but safe passage is likelier in the daylight than after dark. So he bedded down in our kitchen, and by the time we got up in the morning he was already gone, his blanket neatly folded and two perfectly carved wooden horses the size of my palm on top of it, one for each of my sons.

*

The brothers all came back to us a few days later, to share their good news and to bid us farewell before returning to Assisi. Francesco had succeeded well beyond his expectations—or at least beyond the expectations any more worldly person might have had. First, he had won over Cardinal Giovanni. Then, with the cardinal's enthusiastic support, he managed to get his audience with Pope Innocente, and Innocente, to his credit, must have glimpsed something of what was so extraordinary in Francesco. The pope's acceptance of their fledgling order went a long way toward making them safe from charges of heresy, and the fact that not everyone on the papal curia was convinced carried little weight, as long as His Holiness didn't change his mind.

We exclaimed merrily when we saw the fresh tonsures on Francesco and the two other brothers who could read and had a bit of Latin. Later we learned that those men had arrived in Assisi with sunburned scalps, so Vanna and I sewed some hoods in a plain gray cloth and sent them into the Umbrian hills in the care of a hired courier, who, on his return, kept shaking his head in disbelief as he described to us the squalid, ruined building the brothers called home. It was a former hospital for lepers in a place called Rivo Torto; so little of it still had intact walls and a roof that the brothers had to crowd into a space too small even for their modest numbers. But they had papal approval. And hoods.

Giovanni and Uccellino begged for hoods of their own, to play "brothers walking to Assisi." Vanna and I each sewed a little hood, and the game kept them entertained for a few days before the wooden swords began to be more appealing.

Francesco had won the support of the Holy Father, but he had also made the acquaintance of our household, and I was determined to make that, too, work in his favor somehow. I owed him so much.

Spring 1212, Rome

6

WHATEVER Francesco had done two years ago to save our grief-ridden household had not been enough to ward off the problems we were having now. He had left us more at peace than before, but I'm a Roman—I should have known peace would be a fragile and ephemeral thing.

Vanna was sobbing piteously yet again, facedown on the bed in the room she shared only with Lucia, now that Amata and Massimo were married. Lucia was rapidly reaching the end of her patience, and patience was the virtue Graziano and I had hired her for.

I knew Lucia was reaching her limit because she told me so. Loudly, with her left eye twitching frantically. In the presence of my sons. I had never heard Lucia raise her voice until the current crisis, but now she was wielding a formidable soprano with an impressive range of pitch and intensity, quivering with outrage.

"That woman is driving me mad!" Both her hands balled into fists. "She's bolted the door to our room and won't let me in. I know she's suffering, but she's making everyone's life a misery and I can't endure it any longer."

She glared at me. Lucia was always so calm, so gentle, so peaceable. Had it really gotten this bad?

"If you can't get her to stop it, I'm going to leave."

Both of the boys wailed at that, and I was sorely tempted to join them. Vanna had indeed been making everyone's life miserable for weeks, and I couldn't help thinking the wrong servant was threatening to quit.

The boys saved me, at least for the moment. Lucia sank to her knees and hugged them tightly to her, all apologies and caresses and reassurances, wiping their tears with her sleeve and covering them with repentant kisses. I watched her as she comforted my boys, and I tried to think of something, anything, to say or do to help.

Though it was Vanna who moped and snuffled and dripped and cast a cloud of deep gloom over the whole house, I'd been struggling to keep myself from doing exactly the same thing.

Thanks to Francesco, things were much better than they had been. I had not strayed back into madness, and I continued to be a mother for my boys, though some days even that was difficult. But I still ached for Graziano. For the boys' sake I confined my weeping to those rare moments when I was alone, yet despite my best efforts, I sank into a torpor much of the time. And now I had this mess on my hands.

Time to do something, whether I felt up to it or not. "I'll talk to her, Lucia," I said.

"Lucia won't have to go 'way, will she?" Uccellino wiped his nose with the back of his hand.

"No, she won't." *You two have seen enough loss already.*

Uccellino reached for my hand and took it between his own, something he did when he especially wanted me to attend to what he was about to say. "Vanna's sad, Mamma," he said gravely. "She can't help it. You're sad too, sometimes."

All the time, my love. And you are the kindest of us all.

They clattered down the stairs, to play with their toy knights around the pool in the middle of the courtyard. Lucia stood and brushed her skirt with her hands, and her smile faded.

"Talk to her, then, Giacoma. This really cannot go on."

*

I paused outside Vanna's closed door, gathering my thoughts. Her problem was clear enough—Amata and Massimo. Why else would Vanna dart out of the room whenever one of them entered? Why refuse to join us at mealtime, sneaking down to the kitchen late in the evening once Amata had joined Massimo in their chamber? My maidservant was lovesick for my steward. I berated myself for not having seen it earlier, before the wedding, but I had been caught up in my own unhappiness. Not that I could have done much about it, in any case.

Not for the first time, I wished Francesco would come back. He could cast out her demons, if she had any, and if she didn't, somehow he would still make everything come out right.

But in his absence, I was going to have to confront the problem myself. I took a deep breath and knocked.

"Go away," came the muffled voice from within, followed by a loud honk as Vanna blew her nose.

"It's Giacoma, Vanna," I said, and waited.

Several minutes passed, and I was about to knock again when I heard the bolt click. The door opened, and my woebegone servant peered at me with red-rimmed eyes.

"Yes?"

Not even a "monna Giacoma" or "madonna." A simple "Giacoma" would have been too much to hope for.

"May I come in? We need to talk."

She didn't answer, but she retreated into the room and I followed her inside. We sat on the chest at the foot of her bed, which was a chaotic mess of tangled sheets and blankets.

"Vanna, will you tell me what's wrong? I'm worried about you."

"No, you're not. Nobody in this house cares anything about me at all." This was followed by an emphatic sniff.

I reached for her hand, but she snatched it away.

"That isn't true, Vanna. We all love you, and we're worried about you." I was feeling close to the edge myself, and I wasn't sure I could cope with this level of hysteria today. Still, I pressed forward. My household, my responsibility.

"Vanna, I know you're unhappy, and I want to help. Please tell me what I can do to make things easier for you. I think I may have some idea of what's troubling you."

"You don't! Nobody does! Nothing will ever make it any easier!" Her voice rose to a screech, and she jumped up and flung herself dramatically onto the bed, her sides heaving as she sobbed.

This was becoming more than a little ridiculous. Still, the poor girl was genuinely miserable, and it wasn't up to me to decide whether she ought to be or not. She was young, convinced she was in love, and what she wanted most in the world was something she could never have. What could I say that might console her? Yet I absolutely could not lose Lucia. It would destroy my boys.

"Monna Giacoma, you can't possibly understand what it is to want something so much." This was followed by another burst of sobs.

Oh, really? I can't understand that? I felt myself drawing back from her, angered and offended. She must have sensed it too, because she sat up and stared at me, a look of horror on her face.

"Oh, madonna, I'm so sorry! I don't know how I could have said that. Please forgive me. I didn't mean it the way it sounded."

She's young. She's upset. She's not thinking clearly.

I stood. Making an effort to keep the anger from showing in my voice,

I said, "Vanna, we will talk later. This obviously isn't a good time." *For either of us.*

She nodded mutely, and I turned and left. My hand was shaking as I pulled the door closed behind me.

I was still mulling over what to do next when I heard a rapping at the front door. Massimo was downstairs and would respond, so I stayed where I was, listening, curious. It was late in the day for peddlers, the day's beggars had come and gone after dinner, and our gloomy household didn't attract many guests these days.

The heavy door opened, scraping on the stone floor, and Massimo exclaimed. Next I heard a familiar voice, warm and musical.

Egidio! Was Francesco with him? I gathered up my skirt and sprinted down the stairs. Vanna would have been horrified.

"Egidio!" I almost threw my arms around him, but I didn't want to scare him. I don't think he would have known what to do. I had so missed the brothers. I'd received a few visits from some of them over the past two years, whenever they had business in Rome, but never Francesco himself, and none in the winter months. The roads were only now becoming passable for travelers on foot.

"Hello, Giacoma," he said with a grin, and then he turned his attention to the boys, who had come running at the sound of his voice, Lucia hurrying behind them. The man with him was not Francesco, but a brother I hadn't met, an unusually handsome man with a commanding air. His tattered tunic was every bit as disreputable as Egidio's, but he wore it with an effortless elegance that belied his status as one of the humble *frati minori*.

"Monna Giacoma?" he said, his voice deep and resonant. "I am Brother Elias. Brother Francesco has told us much about you, and he has asked us to call on you and tell you he will be in Rome soon."

"You are most welcome, Brother Elias," I said. The boys were chattering excitedly at Egidio, who gave them his full attention. "May I offer you food and drink?"

He inclined his head graciously. "We would be pleased to accept your alms, madonna, and we'll gladly share Brother Francesco's news with you in return."

Egidio broke away from my clamoring boys long enough to greet us. "It's good to see you, Giacoma," he said, and he nodded pleasantly to Lucia. "All the others send their greetings."

"And ours to them, when you return, though I hope you'll stay for a while. Brother Elias, you said Francesco is coming?"

41

It was Egidio who answered. "He is. He has a small matter to discuss with His Holiness, so we're expecting him in a day or two. Giacoma, may we go to the kitchen and greet Amata? We'd like to give her our blessings on her marriage."

Massimo, the proud bridegroom, beamed.

"Yes, of course. Come with me," I said, and we all trooped through the courtyard toward the kitchen, the boys still busily telling Egidio everything that had happened since the last time they saw him.

Amata looked up from kneading her dough and broke into a huge grin. "Welcome back, Brother Egidio!" she said, wiping flour-coated hands on the towel that always hung from her belt. Amata and Egidio beamed at each other, so warmly that I thought Massimo's own smile drooped, but he rallied quickly. Everyone in our house loved Egidio and his brothers, and there was no room for jealousy here.

Soon a contented bustle of activity filled my kitchen. The boys were gathering bits of wood to bring to Egidio for him to carve, and Amata was rummaging around for food to offer our guests. Massimo brought some stools in from the storage area.

I studied Brother Elias while he chatted with Massimo. He was of medium height and well made. His cheekbones could have been carved out of stone, and he had bright amber eyes like a lion's, rimmed with luxuriant lashes. But it was something intangible in his bearing that made him so impressive. I didn't think I was seeing arrogance in this Elias, exactly, but he was certainly sure of himself. I could find no fault in his behavior, which was in all ways courteous, and yet he did not seem to be made of the same stuff as Egidio and the others.

Amata found them some hard cheese and harder bread, apologizing because the best of the day's leftover bread had already gone to the beggars.

"We will be well content with the cheese, if you can spare it," Brother Elias said in his rich voice. "We have no need for anything more."

At that, Egidio's shoulders sagged a little, then he caught himself and sat up straight.

"When did you eat last?" I asked, suddenly suspicious.

Egidio and Elias looked at each other. "Yesterday," Egidio said reluctantly. "But late yesterday."

"Then you're eating now. Amata, heat the soup and bring the brothers some. I'll have Ricco buy us a pie for tonight," I said firmly. Why on earth did these men not eat while they were traveling? It didn't make sense to me, so I asked them.

"Father Francesco says if we are leading the gospel life, we will take no thought for the morrow," Brother Elias reminded me.

"You could have asked for alms," I said.

Egidio grinned. "We did, but none were forthcoming. We planned for the morrow to this extent, though, sin or no—we knew if we came here you would take good care of us."

"And so I shall," I said, giving Massimo a few coins from my purse. "Massimo, will you ask Ricco to find us a couple of pies for tonight? Enough for all ten of us."

He took the money and went off toward the stable to find the boy.

"I see seven of us here," Egidio said, "and there's your stable boy, and Massimo. But where is your gentle maidservant? Will she not come to greet us?"

"Probably not. We're having some problems, Egidio. Vanna is unhappy, and of late she prefers not to spend her time with us."

"But she will join us for supper?" His brow furrowed, and I saw him glance at Lucia, who was glowering. "Is she unwell?"

"I expect she'll choose to stay in her chamber. Egidio, I'd like to talk with you about this, if you will be so kind." I really wanted to talk to Francesco, but I wasn't sure the situation could wait another day.

"Gladly, Giacoma," he said, "but let's also include Brother Elias. You'll find he has a gift for working out problems."

I shrugged. I needed all the help I could get.

While Amata busied herself with the soup, Lucia took the boys out into the courtyard. They protested, but Egidio promised to carve them something new while we talked. He assessed the chunks of wood they dumped in his lap and told them they had chosen well. They wanted to watch him work, but he said he would surprise them with his creations at supper, and that satisfied them.

Now that I had the two brothers' full attention, I sketched out our predicament for them. Amata was stirring the soup, too far away to overhear, so I didn't hold back any of my suspicions about what was amiss with my poor servant. Both of them listened attentively, and Egidio picked up a knife and began to whittle a chunk of wood while I spoke.

"Do you think Massimo misled her?" asked Brother Elias. A fair enough question, so I gave it some thought.

"No," I finally said. "I'm sure he didn't. I think he was so preoccupied with his Amata that he didn't notice what Vanna was going through. I'm not sure he knows even now, actually." Though I did know that Amata had figured it out.

43

"Then I see no fault here, only an unfortunate situation."

"I agree, but what do I do about it?"

Amata came toward us bearing a tray with two steaming bowls of thick soup, a poached egg floating in each. Slices of cheese were heaped on a small trencher next to the bowls. Both men took the food gratefully, and she set the tray down on the hearth bench. She lingered as if she hoped to be invited to join us, but when we were silent, she took the hint and left us.

I let the men eat their soup before pressing them for their advice. They ate quickly and efficiently, as hungry men will. It was comforting just to have Egidio here, and I was willing to believe that Brother Elias also would be able to contribute something of use.

Elias placed his empty bowl back on the tray and sat back. "Francesco may well be able to help your Vanna directly, my lady. I have no such power, but perhaps I can suggest some ways to make your household more peaceful until your servants' problems are resolved." I noticed he didn't precede Francesco's name with "Brother" this time, and I took this to mean he was close to his leader.

"I'll be so grateful if you can, Brother Elias," I said.

"First, then, let's consider Lucia's needs. Do you have any other chamber in the house for her?"

Why hadn't I thought of that? The whole west wing was not in use—I had closed it off after my husband's death, except for the chapel. All we would have to do was open and air one of the chambers nearest to the courtyard for Lucia.

"Yes, I do," I said, already thinking about which room would serve best.

"Then we should call Lucia in and make sure the plan will satisfy her. No point in going any further if she has strong objections."

He was right—that was the logical next step. This man was a good organizer, and while I could imagine his assurance would be annoying to some, I rather liked it. I recognized in him a mind similar to my own, efficient and quick and realistic. The brother I would be, had I been a man.

"Amata," I called to her, "would you please go summon Lucia?"

When Lucia arrived, I took the tray off the bench and motioned for her to sit with us.

"Lucia, Brother Elias is prepared to help us solve the situation with Vanna," I said.

"We're trying to find a solution that will give you a chamber of your own, where Vanna's distress will not be a problem for you," Egidio told her. She looked startled, and I wondered if she had been expecting the brothers to take her to task for her lack of sympathy for Vanna. Perhaps Uccellino's innocent remark had touched her conscience, as it had mine.

"What if we let Vanna keep the room you're sharing now, and we open the near chamber in the west wing for you?" I suggested, and her face brightened.

"You mean a room just for me?"

"Yes. We'd get the room cleaned and furnished for you as soon as possible, but you might need to stay in the boys' room for a week or two."

"Oh, I don't mind staying with the boys," she said, laughing with relief. "They'd like it. And it would be so lovely to have a chamber on this floor. I don't need much, only enough room for my bed and my little chest."

"Then that's what we'll do," I told her, pleased at her response. "I'll have Massimo and Ricco start on it right away."

Lucia thanked me. In fact, she thanked me several times before I persuaded her to go back and stay with the boys. She had tears in her eyes as she got up to leave.

I felt like I had been given a reprieve. This plan was not a complete solution, but it effectively removed the threat of Lucia leaving us.

"You know you must speak to Vanna again," Brother Elias said, watching me. So much for my reprieve, I thought. But he was right.

"Will you come with me?" My last effort had not exactly been a success.

He shook his head. "This is women's business, and she would not be pleased to share her private thoughts with a stranger, or even with her old friend Brother Egidio, I fear."

I sighed. He was right, but that meant I had a difficult conversation ahead of me.

"Very wise, Brother Elias. I suppose I'd best get it over with," I said, and both brothers nodded sympathetically.

I left them with Amata, who had been patiently awaiting her turn, and I marched up the stairs and rapped on Vanna's door.

7

An hour later I emerged, exhausted. We had finally hammered out an agreement: Vanna got the room to herself, and she would continue to work as my personal maid and assistant, but she would not be expected to eat with the others, whether in the kitchen or the hall. Someone—not Amata—would bring meals to her.

Vanna had finally admitted she was hopelessly, helplessly in love with Massimo. And now that he had chosen Amata instead, her life was ruined, and she would probably die of it, no doubt quite soon. I murmured sympathetically, trying not to roll my eyes, and stroked her tangled hair and patted her hand. It wasn't that I didn't take the girl's misery seriously, exactly—remembering my own experience, I kept the door to the tower locked and the key in a pouch on my belt—but something in her plaint sounded so very, very *young*.

Relieved to have that encounter finished, I went back down to the kitchen, which was cheery and warm and full of camaraderie. Our guests were there, and Massimo and Ricco, and Lucia and the boys, and Amata, who was bustling around creating wonderful aromas involving almond paste and spices. The boys were hanging on Egidio, asking questions and chattering. Uccellino kept trying to wheedle him into showing them what he had carved, even though it wasn't yet suppertime.

"You have to learn to wait, little man," Egidio said to Uccellino, but he was smiling. "Else you just might find yourself up—up in the air!" He picked up my boy, tossing him into the air and catching him while Uccel squealed with delight.

"Egidio, that might not—" I began, but it was too late. Uccel's face paled, and just as Egidio caught him after the second toss, he spewed a torrent of vomit all over both Egidio and Brother Elias.

Brother Elias muttered something under his breath and looked down at his tunic as if it were some vile and noxious thing, which I suppose at that moment it was. Egidio ignored the mess and set Uccel down with infinite gentleness as Lucia, practiced in this, dunked a towel in the water barrel and started swabbing at my son's face.

"I'm sorry, little man. I didn't mean to make you sick," Egidio said, crouching in front of Uccel. "Do you feel better now?"

Uccel nodded uncertainly. Unlike the brothers, his clothing had escaped unscathed. Amata brought him a cup of water and a basin, and he rinsed his mouth.

So much for Amata's fragrant spices. The kitchen reeked.

"Uccel, I think you should lie down for a while," I said.

He started to argue, but then he paled and retched, though nothing more came up. After that, he obediently took Lucia's hand and walked away with her, Giovanni following.

Massimo and Ricco absented themselves from the stench, going up to the hall to assemble the trestle table, and Amata wet a few more towels and began to clean up what she could.

"Egidio, Brother Elias, I'm so sorry," I said. "Uccel's stomach is weak sometimes. I should have warned you."

"No matter, Giacoma," said Egidio. He stripped off his stinking tunic and used it to wipe some of the mess from his hair. "I didn't mean to do anything that would harm him. He will be all right, won't he?"

"Oh, yes. He's fine. This just happens sometimes. He'll be back with us at supper, happily eating to make up for what he's lost. But we must do something to give you clean clothing until we can wash your tunics. You can't go around like that."

Elias stripped his tunic off, revealing a muscular chest. He wadded up the garment and dropped it on the floor, wrinkling his nose. "May we perhaps beg a basin of water to clean our hair, madonna?"

"Certainly. Amata?" I turned to her, but she was already filling a washbasin at the barrel. "I'll go find you something to wear temporarily," I told them, and they murmured their thanks.

In my chamber I opened the chest that held Graziano's clothes. The scent of rosemary, his favorite, wafted up to my nose. It brought predictable tears to my eyes, but I ignored them and rummaged through the stored items, dislodging layers of dried lavender and rosemary, searching for something simple enough for the brothers to accept, and for something that might fit them.

Graziano had been a wealthy knight with fine and costly garments, so I didn't find much that seemed right. Finally I settled on a couple of plain linen shirts, some hose with leather soles, and an unadorned but well-made blue tunic for Brother Elias and a reddish brown garment for Egidio. The brown one had been large on Graziano, and I hoped it was big enough for the sturdy brother. These tunics were longer than the men's shabby ones, which would have been too brief, had the brothers not worn breeches underneath. We'd have to make sure we heated enough water to wash the breeches too, if they had also been spattered.

I knew Egidio would wear as little of Graziano's finery as possible, and for as short a time as he could. I had no idea what to expect from

Brother Elias.

I was curious about the man, and this should be interesting. I draped the clothing over my arm and carried it downstairs.

"Here are some things to change into until we can launder your tunics," I told them. "We'll heat some water later."

"Thank you, monna Giacoma," Brother Elias said, taking the garments from me. "I will welcome the chance to wash my clothes. Francesco does not allow us a second tunic, so we are never as clean as I would like." The intensity in his voice told me he was not altogether easy with the brothers' standards of cleanliness.

I had to admit I agreed with him. I could not imagine wearing one garment day after day. I had done so in the thick of my madness, but only during those dark days when I barely knew who I was or what I was doing. I knew I didn't have it in me to live Francesco's version of the gospel life, and yet something in me fervently wanted to try. Whenever I was in the presence of the brothers, especially Francesco or Egidio, I yearned to find a way to change my life completely—more than just redoubling my charity efforts, increasing my donations to the church, attending mass, praying, and teaching my boys to live a life of faith. All of those things cost me little and gave me much, but I honored the price Francesco and his brothers had chosen to pay, and I wanted to emulate them. Yet I couldn't imagine myself, or any woman, walking around barefoot and living on alms.

But we had a meal to serve and no time to think about those things now. While Egidio and Brother Elias went to the pantry to sort out the borrowed clothing, Amata began to carry the food up, starting with bread and a pitcher of wine on a tray. Ricco and Massimo helped her carry the rest, and Lucia and the boys reappeared, Uccello now looking cheerful and pink-cheeked. Before long all of us but Egidio, Brother Elias, and Vanna were seated on benches in the hall, ready to eat. Enough late afternoon light filtered in through the high windows that we had no need yet for candles.

Ricco had brought us two handsome pies, plenty for everyone. We had the rest of the soup, and Amata had finished the batch of almond cakes. The boys were eager to eat, but I wanted to wait for the brothers. It would be discourteous to our guests to start without them.

"I'll go get them, Giacoma," Massimo said, but as he stood, we heard them coming up the stairs.

What a change! In the one case comical; in the other, dramatic. Egidio emerged first, self-conscious in the red-brown tunic. Large as it had been on my husband, it strained across Egidio's shoulders. He had belted it with the grimy piece of rope he always wore around his own tunic, and he had foregone the hose and was still barefoot. He looked mightily uncomfortable, especially when Amata giggled at him.

Brother Elias followed, transformed. He wore Graziano's blue tunic proudly unbelted, and the hose fit his calves snugly. He appeared completely at ease in the fine garment.

"Thank you, madonna," he said to me. "It's a pleasure to be cleaner. We're grateful for your kindness."

Egidio mumbled something polite, too.

"Are you comfortable, Egidio?" I asked.

He squirmed a bit. "My body is comfortable, Giacoma. But it doesn't feel right to be wearing something so fine when we are sworn to poverty."

"Well, you don't own it. You're wearing it out of necessity, and only for a little while," I said, and he gave me a grateful look. I wished I could give them the clothing, but I knew there was no chance of that.

"Brother Elias, would you offer a prayer?" I asked him.

His deep, resonant voice was hypnotic, and our simple supper was well blessed. We fell to.

We had eaten our way through what was left of the soup and at least half of both pies—one mutton and one mostly cheese with raisins—by the time the boys had sated their appetites enough to remember the toys Egidio had promised them. He reached into his sleeve and pulled out two freshly carved wooden animals: a tiny, perfect wooden pig for Giovanni, and a remarkably lifelike miniature cat for Uccellino. The boys seized their new toys, delighted, and even dignified Brother Elias smiled at their pleasure.

I may have been the only one who noticed that Egidio also quietly handed a third carving, an exquisite little horse, to Ricco, who beamed. He slipped it into his sleeve before my sons could see it and demand horses for themselves. I felt a twinge of guilt. Ricco worked so hard and so tirelessly, it was easy to forget he was not yet twelve years old. I resolved to pay more attention to the needs of Massimo's frecklefaced assistant. Perhaps a bit of schooling might be in order. He was a clever lad.

Brother Elias set his wine cup down and turned to me. "Monna Giacoma, how is it that your younger son is called "Little Bird"? It's an unusual nickname, though it does suit him."

"I wanted him named for Graziano, and Graziano wanted him named for me. Eventually we compromised and named him Graziano Giacomo, but it was too much name for such a little thing. He made small chirping noises like a baby bird, and so he came to be called Uccellino."

"Then I've just given the cat to the bird," Egidio observed with mock seriousness. "Was that wise of me, do you think?" Uccellino, delighted, mimed eating the cat, smacking his lips loudly.

At length our meal came to an end. Even the brothers, who had eaten heartily, eventually slowed their pace. I knew the brothers dined frugally on their own, often abstaining from all but bread and water, the better to tame the desires of the flesh. But Francesco believed in taking the gospel literally when it exhorted the faithful to eat whatever was put before them. These men worked hard, for people in need and for their own brotherhood. They covered great distances on foot, sparing themselves no hardship. It was no wonder they had healthy appetites, and it was my great pleasure to put plenty of the best we had in front of them whenever I got the chance.

As we sat talking among ourselves, Amata took a tray from the sideboard. She put a cup of wine on it, along with small slices of each pie, a cup of soup, and a cake.

"Lucia, will you take this up to Vanna?" she asked. Lucia tensed and frowned.

"Never mind, I'll do it," I said, but Egidio stood up.

"Let me take it to her, Giacoma. I haven't had a chance to greet her yet, and perhaps she would like to talk with someone from outside the house," he said, picking up the tray. "If you fear any impropriety, you can certainly come with me, or I can ask her to speak with me in the chapel."

"No, Egidio, Vanna is the only one here who worries over such things, and she'll tell you if it's a problem for her. Thank you, and good luck," I said.

He took the tray and headed for the stairs.

*

Good food, good conversation, a warm hall, and all of us were feeling contented. The light was fading, so Amata brought in candles and lit them at the brazier. Egidio rejoined us, though he said nothing about his errand, and he and Brother Elias sang us a devotional song Francesco had composed. As the rest of us learned the simple tune and words, we joined in, a bit raggedly at first, but enthusiastically. Francesco's words were in the Umbrian dialect, not difficult for us to understand but still odd to a Roman ear, and the boys laughed as they experimented with the new sounds. Ricco's high, pure soprano soared over all the other voices.

The evening wound down, much like the first evening the brothers had spent among us two years ago, with laughter and talk and more song. The boys began to doze where they sat, still clutching their prized wooden toys. We eventually got them up to bed, Giovanni walking sleepily hand in hand with Lucia while I carried Uccellino.

We put water on to heat in the kitchen, and Amata and I prepared two basins. Egidio and Brother Elias brought us their soiled tunics, Brother Elias holding his between thumb and forefinger with evident distaste.

I was about to apologize again for Uccellino's unfortunate aim when a voice behind me said, "Excuse me..."

Surprised, I turned toward the door. Vanna stood in the doorway, her face pale but determined. Egidio gave her an encouraging smile.

"I apologize for my behavior in recent weeks," she recited rapidly, her eyes lowered. "It will not happen again. I ask only that you leave me to myself as much as possible. And when Father Francesco arrives, I beg a few moments of his time, that I may speak with him alone."

Everyone looked at me. "You may certainly hold yourself apart if that is your choice, Vanna," I said, "though you're always welcome to join the rest of us any time you feel you want to. As for speaking to Francesco privately, what do you think, Egidio?"

"I don't see why not," he said. "In fact, perhaps other members of the household would also benefit from a brief interview with Brother Francesco. Can you arrange it, Brother Elias?"

"Easily," Brother Elias said, smiling.

I was beginning to understand a little more about this strange clever brother, sworn to poverty and yet so fond of fine food and clothes. Just give him a problem to solve, and he was as happy as a fish in the river, or a bird in the sky, or Amata in a kitchen.

Vanna vanished, and the rest of us got up to go to bed. Amata, Lucia, and I hauled the wet tunics and breeches out of their baths, wrung them out, and stretched them to dry over the bench in front of the embers, while Massimo fetched blankets for the brothers.

I invited Lucia to sleep on the pallet in my room tonight, rather than risk waking the boys or presuming too much on Vanna's good intentions, and she readily agreed. She fell asleep immediately, and I realized how little rest she had been getting of late.

I had neglected my responsibility.

8

THE next morning, six of us assembled downstairs, ready to go to mass. Egidio had put on his own tunic, though it was still damp. Brother Elias still wore the borrowed blue garment. Lucia would stay with the boys, who still slept. And Vanna was nowhere to be seen.

The strident bells of our parish church summoned us to worship. San Sebastiano was only a few minutes' stroll along our awakening street.

Amata and I entered the church through the women's door. To my delight, Francesco and several of the brothers were already kneeling on the men's side, bathed in the soft light filtering in from two windows high above.

The barefoot brothers looked out of place in the well-appointed church. Their attention was firmly fixed on the striking wooden cru-cifix over the altar, and Our Lord's open eyes gazed serenely back at them. Egidio and Brother Elias joined them, kneeling next to Francesco.

Amata and I knelt among the neighborhood women: noblewomen, their maidservants and their half-grown daughters; sleepy-eyed house-wives; elderly women sitting on stools because they would never be able to get up from their knees unaided; a trio of giggly young women standing in the back, their attention more on the men's side of the church than on the mass. Had I ever been that young? I couldn't remember.

I saw one new face, a small, plain woman of perhaps forty years, wearing an undyed garment that might have been a woman's version of the brothers' tunics. She prayed aloud, her words tumbling out rapidly, eyes scrunched shut and hands raised, on her knees and swaying back and forth. I made a mental note to find out if she belonged among our neighborhood beggars and to make sure she knew she was welcome to come round for alms.

The mass felt like the longest I had ever attended, but at last it ended, and we hurried outside where we could be reunited with the brothers. A flurry of greetings and introductions followed. I welcomed Brothers Bernardo and Giannuccio and my other old friends, and I met Brothers Leone and Rufino, both of whom apparently already knew all there was to know about my household. Leone, a gentle man with a hesitant smile, was an ordained priest, only the second clergyman to join the brotherhood. He served as Francesco's own confessor, but he made it clear he was to be called "Brother," not "Father."

The little woman in gray hovered around the outskirts of our group as we all talked at once, catching up on one another's news. I turned to her to see if she was in need of anything, but before I could speak, Francesco beckoned her over.

"Sister Prassede, come and meet monna Giacoma," he said.

She hurried forward, smiling up at me. I am not a tall woman, yet the top of her head was level with the base of my throat.

"Monna Giacoma, I've heard so much about you," she said breathlessly. "I'm called Sister Prassede and I'm a recluse from Grottaferrata, but now I want to be part of Father Francesco's movement, so when I found out he was coming here to Rome, I walked here myself, so I could meet him, and the very minute I came through the gates, there he was—well, not him exactly, but one of his brothers, so I knew it was a sign, and then the brother took me to Father Francesco, and we talked for a long time, and he said he wanted me to meet with you, because you were his good friend and a virtuous woman and you would make me welcome here in Rome."

She paused for breath. This was a recluse? I hadn't heard such a deluge of words since the last time my sister-in-law visited. Maybe this Sister Prassede saved them up while she was being reclusive, or perhaps she was the kind of recluse who spent her days parceling out spiritual advice to housewives who queued at the window of her cell. What could Francesco want me to do with this woman?

She began again. "And I also learned that Father Francesco is going to start an order for women, back in Assisi, and I would like to go there and be part of it, because I want to embrace holy poverty and help others and live a gospel life and nurse the lepers and beg for alms and—"

Francesco held up his hand. "Sister, enough for now," he said, gently but firmly. "Let us go back to monna Giacoma's house, and we will have a chance to talk more of these things."

A women's order? Could this be the answer to my need? I was so curious I almost wished she would keep prattling, but she closed her mouth, placed two fingers over her lips to indicate silence, and nodded cheerfully to Francesco. He turned to me and said, "Shall we go?" and the two of us started walking toward home. The others fell into place behind us in twos and threes, with the chatty little woman bringing up the rear.

Toward the back of the group poor Brother Elias was taking quite a bit of teasing from his brothers about his blue garment, but he bore it well, and when I glanced back, he was smiling.

The sun was now fully risen and the day set to be mild and cloudless.

Rome is beautiful on such a day, and I was glad Francesco and his brothers were seeing my city at her sparkling best. The interplay of light on the marble of both ancient ruins and new buildings changed with every passing cloud, never the same twice.

Once, I could not have imagined living anywhere else. Where else would my shoemaker ply his trade inside a triumphal arch from centuries ago? Where else could I be living in a palazzo in the ancient Circus Maximus and visiting my in-laws ensconced in their massive fortified house that shared one wall with the Colisseum?

I suppose everyone thinks their own city is the center of the world. The difference is, we Romans are right. But I was no longer sure I wanted to live in the center of the world, and I still had days when I didn't know if I wanted to live in the world at all.

As soon as we arrived, Brother Elias headed for the pantry to collect his tunic and dress himself like his brothers. The rest of us trooped into the kitchen. I thought our presence might be a nuisance for Amata, but she assured me she didn't mind.

Egidio mentioned to Francesco that some members of my household wanted to confer with him, and Francesco readily agreed. First, though, he gave himself over to my sons, much changed in the past two years and waiting with barely contained impatience to gain his attention.

It was as if no time had passed since his last visit. He told them sacred stories, listened to them talk, and admired their new wooden gifts from Egidio. Ricco hovered nearby, his eyes never leaving Francesco, drinking in every word.

Sister Prassede had assigned herself to help Amata with the dinner. She was chopping roots on the cutting table, though she had to stand on a stool to reach the surface. She knew her way around a kitchen. To my surprise Amata accepted her help without argument, perhaps because there was little opportunity to squeeze a word in around her constant chatter.

Egidio distracted my sons long enough for me to snatch a few words with Francesco out in the courtyard. He sat on the edge of the pool, dangling his feet in the water. Had I not been wearing stockings I would have joined him, but I settled for sitting cross-legged next to him.

"How long can you stay, Francesco?"

"This must be a short visit. We have come to speak to His Holiness about the possibility of creating a new women's order. A noblewoman in Assisi passionately wants to devote her life to holy poverty, and I hope to help her achieve her godly wish, but I cannot assist her against the Holy

Father's will. It would endanger our brotherhood, and I would be guilty of the grave sin of disobedience. So I must try to persuade him of the virtue in her desire."

Before I could ask him more about this women's order, Brother Elias came out to fetch us for dinner. I looked at the two of them standing next to each other, Brother Elias in his clean tunic and Francesco in his filthy one, and I had an idea. As Francesco went back inside, I motioned to Elias to wait with me for a moment.

"Francesco and the brothers with him are dirty and their clothes are grimy and torn from their journey," I said. "They don't even smell very good." It was a long walk from Assisi, and even if they had started out presentable, they certainly hadn't ended up that way.

Elias nodded. "This is true, madonna. Were it not for your generosity and your son's weak stomach, I would be no better."

"Do you think you could persuade Francesco to let us launder and mend their tunics before the papal audience? I know it shouldn't make any difference, but I really think the brothers would be more convincing, don't you?"

He stroked his chin, thinking. "I do, but persuading Francesco to have a care for appearances is quite a challenge."

"Could you try? We could do the washing after dinner, and the mending won't take long if several of us work on it. Everything should be dry by tomorrow."

Egidio appeared at the door. "Come on, you two. Everyone is waiting."

I looked inquiringly at Elias, and he smiled back.

"I'll try, monna Giacoma."

"Just Giacoma," I said, on impulse.

"Giacoma, then. No promises, but I'll do the best I can."

*

I continued to wonder about the strange woman in Assisi all during our dinner. My mood darkened, and I felt a surge of something I recognized as jealousy. Who was this noblewoman? Was she to become part of Francesco's brotherhood, while I remained outside the blessed circle? And how could she, when the brothers were sworn to avoid personal relationships with women?

For two years, I believed I was the only exception to that rule. Perhaps I was wrong.

I wondered what sort of noblewoman would want to commit to living in abject poverty the way the brothers did. Perhaps she was widowed, or old, and what she really wanted was to be part of a convent with no luxuries, where she could nurse the sick and help the poor. Perhaps she didn't want the kind of house that serves as little more than a pleasant retreat for wealthy women, and I could admire that in her, whoever she was. But would the Holy Father ever permit women to go out unprotected to beg for alms? I doubted it, in spite of what Sister Prassede had said.

At least one thing had gone right. Elias, proceeding carefully, had managed to convince Francesco that appearing clean before the Holy Father was a way of showing proper respect. While we cleared away the remains of dinner, Massimo went off in search of a few of the neighborhood boys who worked as waterbearers, to restock our water barrel.

The usual local beggars arrived at the usual time. I had completely forgotten about them, but it was entertaining to watch them struggle with finding their benefactress's house full of unkempt men. Old Renzo even sidled up to me and asked out of the corner of his mouth, "Is't well, madonna? Do you want us to get rid of these 'uns for you?"

I assured him the strange visitors were our welcome guests, and he shrugged and wandered off to see what alms might be available. Amata absented herself from the laundry project to make sure the beggars got what they came for, and I wished we could call on Vanna to help out, for it was a big job. Prassede joined Lucia and me, talking the whole while, and the three of us collected the tunics and breeches while Ricco distributed blankets to the men.

Egidio herded brothers and beggars alike out into the courtyard so we women would have room in the kitchen to clean the clothes and lay them out for drying. A laundry of that size is something I would normally send out, but the brothers needed these clothes the next day, so there wasn't time. The three of us formed a line, with Prassede tending the fire under the great pot of hot water, me stirring the garments in the tubs and Lucia hauling them out, wringing out the excess water, and draping them on the bench. It was work I wasn't used to, but I liked seeing the threadbare tunics come out brighter as the water grew murky. Upon reflection, I was relieved that Vanna stayed upstairs, for she would have been shocked to see the lady of the house up to her elbows in dirty water. But it had to get done, and if the brothers could walk barefoot from Assisi to Rome, I could at least make sure they wore clean clothes to meet the pope.

Eventually we had nine clean tunics and nine clean pairs of breeches, draped over every available surface in the kitchen.

We also had a courtyard full of men in various stages of nakedness, some of them wrapped in blankets, others unabashedly walking around with nothing on at all. Good that the day was mild. Egidio and Brother Elias, in their recently washed tunics, were positively elegant by comparison. At least, Brother Elias was elegant. Egidio looked—well, like the big scruffy humble man he was. He tried to take his tunic off and give it to one of our shabbier beggars, but Brother Elias reminded him he could hardly go naked to an audience with the Holy Father, and Egidio reluctantly had to agree. I let him give Graziano's brown tunic to the beggar, which made both of them happy.

When the task was done, I slipped out to the chapel. I wanted to gather my thoughts before I spoke to Francesco, but despite my efforts, I didn't feel any better prepared by the time the bells chimed nones and I had to get back to my guests.

We took a light supper together upstairs in the hall, since every place to sit in the kitchen was covered with drying clothes. By now all the naked brothers were draped in blankets, since the afternoon was growing cooler. After we'd finished, Brother Elias announced he had devised a schedule for the members of my household to meet with Francesco one at a time and ask for his blessing, or his counsel, or whatever each one sought from him.

What did I seek? My thoughts were in an uproar, and I still didn't know what I was going to say to him.

Lucia went first. She and Francesco carried two of the stools into the smaller hall in the west wing, so they could speak in private. Egidio took over for her, settling on the bench with my sons, telling them stories, lulling them toward sleep as they leaned on him, drowsing in the warmth from the brazier.

Two candles burned on the table in front of us with a reflector behind them, for I had fetched my needles and threads and started mending the damp tunics. We brought them up from the kitchen one at a time. They weren't in bad shape, though they all displayed a motley array of patches, but inevitably the walk from Assisi to Rome had resulted in some new rips and snags, best repaired before they became huge rents.

"Who is the woman who wants to follow Francesco?" I asked Brother Leone, who sat next to me. "What sort of person is she?"

"She is young and very fair, madonna, and she comes from one of the wealthiest families in Assisi."

Young and fair. That troubled me. Why should I care? I didn't know, but I was agitated enough that I stuck my finger with the needle and thrust it into my mouth quickly, lest I bleed on the clean tunic in my lap.

Brother Leone smiled sympathetically. "This isn't your usual kind of sewing, is it?"

"No," I said, still sucking on my finger, tasting the metallic blood. "I embroider. But I can do this too, when I need to."

"Do you make altar cloths, then?" he asked respectfully.

"Yes, and vestments, and veils for the chalice." But I had also made veils for my hair, before I put on the benda, and I made cushion covers and other pretty things. I loved the art of it, and the freedom to use as much color as I wanted. I loved creating spring, summer, and autumn flowers together on a single piece of linen, though they could not exist together in the world. I could stitch apples with strawberries, ripe cherries and cherry blossoms together. The beauty I could make with my needle was mine alone to plan and realize, and when I felt sad or troubled I found it was almost as good as praying. Sometimes better.

But I was still thinking of the Assisi noblewoman. "Doesn't that woman's family object?" I asked. Surely they would want her wed, or at least housed in a more usual type of convent, where her comfort and status would be assured.

"They don't know yet," he said. Brother Leone had two little frown lines between his thick brows, and they deepened as he spoke.

"You mean she has spoken to Francesco but not to her family?" That shocked me.

"Yes. There is danger here, but Francesco is willing to take the risk. He is planning carefully. That's what this trip is about—he will not go through with it without the backing of the Holy Father. If he gets it, she will make her escape and come to us honorably and safely, for Brother Rufino is her kinsman and will escort her." He indicated the tall, quiet brother who sat next to Egidio, listening to the stories that absorbed my children. Rufino did have an aura of refinement about him, but he was so self-effacing I hadn't realized he was a nobleman.

Lucia returned, glowing. She waited while Egidio finished his story, then persuaded the boys to climb off his lap and come upstairs. They came to me and hugged me, and I kissed them goodnight.

"All is well, Lucia?" I asked her, softly.

She nodded. "Brother Francesco has blessed me. He says I am in my right place, on my right path, and all will be well with me. Oh, and he says I must be kind to Vanna. I believe I can do it, now."

Ricco was next. He coughed nervously as he left the hall, but when he came back he was grinning ear to ear, even more cheerful and energetic than usual.

Amata and Massimo followed together, hand in hand, and Egidio went to fetch Vanna so she would be ready for her turn with Francesco.

The newlyweds returned, unsmiling. Massimo's shoulders slumped, and Amata seemed uncharacteristically subdued. I maneuvered her over to one side so I could ask her privately what troubled her.

"He blessed our marriage and told us we had chosen well," she told me. "But he also said we will have sorrows ahead, though with God's help and each other's we will bear them patiently."

"I think surely all of us will face sorrows in our lives. I know of no one who has avoided them entirely. Did he say anything else?"

She blushed. "He said we must be careful not to indulge excessively in the pleasures of the flesh and we must always put God first. I know he's right, but I fear we do indulge. I don't want to sin, but I love my husband, and we take such joy in each other..."

Tears filled my eyes, and I blinked hard. How well I remembered that feeling. And nothing in the world, not even Francesco, would cause me to want it and miss it any less.

I was at a loss to come up with something encouraging to say, but fortunately Brother Leone had come up behind us and overheard.

"Daughter Amata," he said gently, "Brother Francesco sometimes asks of us what we are not yet ready to give. Yet he is never disappointed in us; he knows we each do what we can, and we grow in grace, and that's all he asks. What matters is that we not turn our backs on God. Even Saint Augustine prayed to God to give him chastity and continence—but not yet."

That delighted Amata, who was unlearned and had never heard it before. I remembered reading it in the *Confessions*. I hadn't understood then, but I did now. Chastity and continence were granted to me far too early, and against my will.

"Go and take joy in your love, Daughter," Brother Leone told her. "Love is never a sin. You'll have your time to be older and calmer. There's no need to rush it."

She thanked him prettily, then rejoined Massimo. She took her husband's hand and I saw her whisper something, standing on tiptoe to be nearer his ear. His lips brushed the top of her head, he put his arm around her shoulders, and the two of them then bade us goodnight.

By this time Egidio had reappeared, alone.

"Would Vanna not come?" I asked. She was the one who had set this project in motion, after all, and she needed what Francesco could give her as much as any of us did.

"She's already with Francesco. I'm afraid you'll have to be last, Giacoma," he said, sitting between Brother Leone and me.

Of course I would go last. It was my duty to see to my household first, and only then to my own needs. Whatever those were, and I still wasn't sure.

Sister Prassede approached me then. She hesitated, but I could tell she had something she wanted to ask.

"Sister, thank you for your capable help with dinner," I said, to help her along. "You made Amata's work easier."

"Oh, I don't like to be idle," she said. "I believe in working with my hands, and earning my dinner. I can sew, too, if you'd like me to help you with the mending."

"Your help would be most welcome," I said. "We could work on it together."

"I'd be honored, monna Giacoma, but I was wondering if you'd mind if I also took a turn to talk with Father Francesco."

"Oh, I didn't realize you wanted to speak to him." *I didn't realize you were part of my household, more like.* "I thought you had seen him earlier, when you first arrived."

She shook her head. "No, not privately, and I do have something I want to ask him. I promise I won't take much time, but could I please see him?" She looked flustered, as if she was embarrassed to be asking.

"Yes, certainly. Please go to him as soon as Vanna comes out, and I'll take my turn when you're finished. I wouldn't mind a little more time to consider what I want to say, anyway."

"Oh, thank you! I'll go get another tunic first." She bobbed her head at me and left the hall. I sighed. Longer to wait, longer to think. And Vanna had already been with Francesco for quite a while. It was growing late, and I was tired—laundry is exhausting work.

Vanna poked her head in just long enough to say, "Whoever's next, Brother Francesco is ready for you," and disappeared again before I could assess her state of mind. Prassede was right behind her; she placed her wet tunic on the table next to where I was working and hurried out to talk to Francesco.

Given Prassede's tendency to talk at length, it surprised me that she was back so soon. She smiled as she entered, but like Amata and Massimo earlier, her smile did not reach her eyes. Her shoulders slumped. She sat next to me and picked up a needle, but her hands trembled as she tried to thread it, so I handed her mine.

"Use this one, Sister. I'm going to Francesco now."

She nodded uncertainly at me and took the needle but did not speak.

60

I was concerned for her, but I couldn't think about her problems now. It was finally my turn.

9

I joined Francesco in the room, smaller than the great hall where the others were gathered, yet spacious compared to the other chambers in the house. A lamp flickered on the floor by his feet, but the room was in deep shadow all around us. I sat on the stool opposite him.

"Giacoma, it's good to see you again," he said. He looked at me, waiting.

So many things I needed to say. I was drowning in my loneliness, I could no longer keep my household running as it should, and what I most wanted, I realized all at once, was to take myself far away from everything here in Rome. My wealth and my life of privilege had become a burden, not a comfort, and I wanted to begin again.

"Francesco..." I began, and then, to both our surprise, I fell to my knees in front of him, my hands clasped in front of me like a beggar. He reached down and moved the lamp a little to the side, away from my skirt.

"Let me come to Assisi and join your women's order," I pleaded. "Please, Francesco, I need to make a new beginning. I'll gladly take a vow of poverty and obedience, and I can divide my money between my sons and the poor. I can work. I can nurse the sick, and I can sew and spin, and I can—well, I can probably figure out cooking. I've never really had to do it, but it can't be too hard."

At that, he burst out laughing. Stung, I sat back on my heels and glared at him. I was baring my innermost thoughts, thoughts that frightened me, offering him my obedience and my loyalty and my life, and he laughed. I should have been crushed, but the first thing I felt was exasperation. Was no one, even Francesco, ever to understand what I was going through?

"Giacoma, Giacomina," he said, shaking his head but still chuckling. "What have those boys of yours done, that every time I see you you're trying to get away from them?"

Now that was just not fair. "I love my boys! They would be well cared for. The Frangipani would raise them, and they'd have wealth, and comfort, and every opportunity, and Lucia..."

"But not you."

No. Not me. Francesco was right. I sat back onto the floor and tucked my legs underneath me as the tears came. He let me weep for a few minutes until the torrent started to slow, and then he spoke, his voice gentle.

"Giacomina, my dear, your right place is with your children. You know that as well as I do."

I sniffed and wiped my eyes with the end of my benda. "You tell your brothers to give away all of their possessions and leave their families behind, to be worthy to join you."

"My brothers are men, not young women with children to care for."

"What if a man wants to join you and is willing to leave his wife and children behind? Do you allow him to do it?"

"It depends. We make sure no family is left without what it needs, but sometimes, yes, it is right for a man to join us, even so."

The unfairness of that made me argumentative. "So you're leaving me stuck with all this wealth, even though the gospels say it's easier for a camel to pass through the eye of a needle than for a rich man to enter the kingdom of Heaven?"

Francesco grinned. "Yes, I'm leaving you 'stuck with all this wealth,' as you put it, my Giacomina. Remember, the text also says with God all things are possible. You can do more good where you are than you could tucked away in a convent somewhere."

"Well, what about your young, fair Assisi noblewoman? Won't she be giving up her wealth?"

He leaned over and placed a hand on each side of my face and tilted my head so I had no choice but to look into his liquid eyes. He had never touched me before, and I was startled into silence.

"Chiara is different. Her path is not yours, Giacoma. It remains to be seen whether we can do anything for her, and even if we can, she will not get everything she wants. She would like nothing better than to share our poverty and beg on the streets with us, but the Holy Father will forbid it. Nor can I permit it. It is not for my brotherhood to be spending our time in the company of women. Chiara's best solution may be to found her own convent, based on poverty and service, but even that will be a challenge, because His Holiness will not wish to see a house of women without any source of revenue. Yet nothing less than total poverty will satisfy her." Gently he withdrew his hands from my face.

Curious in spite of myself, I asked, "How will this resolve for her, then?"

Francesco shook his head. "I don't know yet. I've prayed, and I believe it will be well, but I don't know yet exactly what that will mean. What I do know is that it is Chiara's path to tread, and yours is your own. Have you prayed about this?"

"I asked God the same way you did."

He raised one dark eyebrow. "What do you mean?"

"Last year when Brother Bernardo was here, he told me about how you consulted the missal three times, letting the book fall open to the messages God intended for you. So I did the same thing."

"When?"

"This afternoon. Remember when I absented myself after we finished the laundry?"

"Did Bernardo tell you what answers we received?"

"Yes. 'If you wish to be perfect, go, sell your possessions, and give the money to the poor, and you will have treasure in heaven.' And then you got 'Take nothing for your journey, no staff, nor bag, nor bread, nor money, nor even an extra tunic.'"

"Right. And what was the last one?"

"'If any want to become my followers, let them deny themselves and take up the cross and follow me.'"

"Very good. And what did the missal say to you?"

I was afraid he was going to ask that. Still, I wouldn't hold anything back from him. "The first time the book opened and I put my finger on the page, it said 'And Zoroba begat Abiud; and Abiud begat Eliakim; and Eliakim begat Azor.' It's from Saint Matthew's gospel."

"I see. And the second time?" I thought I saw a twinkle in his eye.

"'Which was the son of Joanna, which was the son of Rhesa, which was the son of Zoroabel, which was the son of Salathiel, which was the son of Neri.' That one is from Saint Luke."

The corner of his mouth twitched. "Ah. And the third?"

"'And there accompanied him into Asia Sopater of Berea; and of the Thessolanians, Aristarchus and Secundus; and—' and somebody else, and then two other people, but I forgot their names. That's from the Acts of the Apostles."

Francesco threw his head back and guffawed. He had an infectious laugh, and overwrought as I was, I found myself tempted to join him. I knew my results were ridiculous, though I had earnestly hoped for some real guidance. I settled for waiting for him to finish, maintaining as much dignity as possible.

Finally he wiped the tears of laughter from his eyes, though he was still grinning.

"And what do you believe your divination means?" he asked.

"I have no idea," I said testily. "I hoped you could explain it to me."

"Oh, I can. It's very clear."

"Well?"

"It means you shouldn't be trying to figure out your life based on playing a game with holy scripture."

"Even though you did?"

"Even though I did."

"It didn't mean anything, did it?" I had memorized all those names—or at least most of them—for nothing.

"Well, with that many sons and begettings, it probably means you shouldn't even think about leaving your boys behind."

An irresistible wave of mirth welled up inside me, and then we were laughing together. As I dried more tears, tears of laughter this time, he lowered himself off his stool and joined me on the floor, and we sat together in a companionable silence for a time.

Eventually he spoke. "If all goes well, I'll be able to set Chiara on her path, and I think she'll probably start a community of women, though I don't know what form it will take. In fact, I'd be surprised if she did not. That woman is determined, and she's extremely resourceful. If the Holy Father pits his will against hers... well, if betting wasn't a sin, my money—if I had any money, which I don't—would be on Chiara."

"I wish her well, then," I said, and realized I meant it. "I can accept that her path is not mine, yet I wish I understood what my path should be. I want to live a gospel life, and I don't see how I can do it in this palazzo, with all my money."

"It will be hard," he agreed. "Maybe harder than anything Chiara or I will try to do. But God has given you these tools, Giacoma—your wealth, your intelligence, your goodness—and those are the things you have to work with. Graziano would have told you to stay with your boys." Doubtless that was exactly what Graziano would say. I knew I couldn't fight both of them, so I reluctantly relinquished the idea of withdrawing from the world, letting it depart like a butterfly released from my cupped hands, a little gossamer thought too beautiful to be real.

"Giacoma, you are not meant to be a sister," he said. "Not like Sister Prassede, and not like the leader of women Chiara will become, and certainly not like one of her followers. You are powerful, forthright, a doer as well as a thinker. You have courage and intelligence. The tools God has given you could as easily be a man's, but it is with the additional burdens of a woman that you must wield them. I cannot call you 'Sister,' my Giacomina."

I knew this. I knew it, and yet hearing him say it made me feel desolate. Other women could be accepted as Francesco's sisters, yet I could not. It hurt. But I said nothing.

"No, you are not Sister Giacoma. But I will give you this instead: to me and to my brothers, you will henceforth be Brother Giacoma. I will expect from you the same high standard of virtuous behavior I expect from my other brothers, and I will trust you as a brother and offer you a brother's love. Will you accept that title?"

Brother Giacoma. "With all my heart, Francesco," I said, overwhelmed.

"And do I have your vow of obedience and chastity?"

"You have it. You would have my vow of poverty too, if you'd accept it."

"Which I can't. No, Brother Giacoma, use your wealth to help people. I don't even have to tell you this—your own generous nature guides you better than ever I could."

"I will. And I can live a simple life, if not a poor one, even here in Rome, in the midst of all this wealth."

"I know you can, and I trust you to do it. Shall we pray together?"

On our knees, we prayed. Francesco offered thanks and praise to God, and I could only echo his words. Somehow I had emerged from defeat with more than I could ever have hoped for.

*

We sent the brothers off in the morning in clean and mended tunics, with many expressions of friendship and good wishes, and then we settled in to wait for their news.

It wasn't long in coming. They returned in high spirits, to report to us and to join us for supper and for a night's rest before they began the long walk back to Assisi. All of us, even Vanna, crowded around to hear them tell of their audience.

The pope had directed them to include their bishop, Guido, in their plans, and Francesco was happy to be able to tell him Bishop Guido already knew of Chiara's vocation. I knew Francesco trusted Bishop Guido, and I was glad the brothers would have powerful support at home, for I still thought the business might become contentious, perhaps even dangerous.

They glossed over the detail of how to spirit her away from her family. God would work it out, and besides, Brother Rufino was Chiara's kinsman, and so everything would be respectable. Vanna, our arbiter of all things respectable, raised a skeptical eyebrow, but she didn't say anything. I

66

wondered if Rufino might share her misgivings, but as usual he kept silent.

I hoped God was planning to keep a tight rein on a certain noble family in Assisi and not let Francesco and his brothers be blamed for Chiara's actions. Francesco may have known God's will, but I knew a little something about noble families. For example, they would be perfectly capable of making a spectacular mess out of everything if they decided their honor was endangered.

But all we could do was wish the brothers well and watch from the street outside the palazzo while they walked away the next morning, threadbare but clean, singing and waving to us.

As they moved out of our sight, I turned to Sister Prassede. Tears were running down her lined cheeks. I recalled her obvious distress two nights before, after her private talk with Francesco. She had been subdued and taciturn since then, and I had almost forgotten she was among us. In fact, I wasn't sure why she was still here.

I put a hand on her shoulder, trying to offer some comfort, though I didn't know the cause of her sorrow. "What is it, Sister Prassede?" I asked. Amata, Massimo, Ricco, Lucia and the boys had gone back inside, for a light rain was beginning, but the two of us and Vanna had stayed outside to see the brothers depart.

Prassede sniffed loudly. "It's nothing, Giacoma. Only... I asked Brother Francesco for something he couldn't give me, and I'm still trying to accept God's will. I will accept it, but it's hard."

"What did you ask him?" I had a feeling I knew.

"I asked him if I could join the new women's community in Assisi," she said, almost reluctantly. "He told me it didn't even exist yet, and anyway my path lay elsewhere. I tried to explain to him that I wanted to work, to nurse the sick, to—"

"I know. To help the poor and nurse the lepers and beg for alms. The Holy Father will never let women go a-begging, Sister Prassede, you know that."

"Women go a-begging all the time," she said almost tartly, wiping her tears on her sleeve.

"Not if they're part of the church," I said. She had a point, though. No one was ever concerned about how ordinary women gained their living. Only holy virgins merited that kind of consideration.

"So Brother Francesco reminded me. He told me I would find my way as part of the larger community, not in a small group of women kept separate and protected. And he said my place was with you."

67

With me. So that's why she was still among us. I wasn't sure what to think. Sister Prassede was certainly a good woman and a willing worker, free of the sin of pride and full of kindness, and yet if she recovered from her disappointment and started chattering again, I wasn't sure I could bear it.

But right now she was suffering, and I wanted to console her. I hadn't meant to say anything to anyone about my own interview with Francesco, yet now I felt compelled to share the experience with Prassede.

"I asked him the same thing, Sister. And he gave me a similar answer. I understand how you feel."

Prassede looked up at me, surprised. "*You* wanted to join too? I didn't know that. Why didn't he let you? He admires you so, I can't understand why he wouldn't want you to join. He must have other plans for you, or else he knows that God does. He always knows what God wants. Did he talk to you about that? Were you going to take your sons with you, or let somebody else raise them? What would happen to this house? It's a big house, and I'll bet you could even turn it into a convent if you wanted to, except you wanted to go to Assisi, just as I did, and the house is here in Rome, so it wouldn't be the same at all, because you'd be much farther away from the brothers. . ."

She was back. I sighed, put an arm around her shoulders, and let her prattle. It was better than her tears, anyway.

We started to go in out of the drizzle, for we were already getting damp, and I realized silent Vanna was still there with us, and had been listening to everything.

I didn't understand why at the time, but I thought I saw the ghost of a smile on her face.

Assisi, summer 1213

10

I pulled the sheet up over my head and scrunched down further in bed. Here in my host's elegant third-floor guest chamber there was no escaping Assisi's cathedral bells. They were emphatically announcing early mass, and they were relentless.

Yesterday had been a long, hot day of travel, the last of many. The fierce July sun had beaten down on us as if to demand that we surrender and return home, but we persisted. I was going to see Francesco, and a summer heat wave was not going to stop me.

My hosts, the gracious monna Mengarda and her husband Arnolfo, had welcomed us and provided us with every luxury—everything except quiet. As usual following a miserable day on the road, sleep had not come quickly, so I would have enjoyed the luxury of waking slowly, but it was not to be. Not even Ulisse's crewmen, their ears stuffed full of wax, could have slept through those bells.

This wasn't even my first waking of the day. Vanna and Prassede had already tried to rouse me so I could go to mass with them and with our hosts. Mengarda and Arnolfo were among Francesco's most ardent and influential followers in Assisi. They had been eager to do him a service by hosting me, and now they wanted to show off their distinguished guest to their friends and neighbors, so already I had disappointed them.

I had pleaded exhaustion, but in truth, after so many miles on the road with my traveling companions I was more in need of solitude than either sleep or worship. My soul was likely to survive a morning without mass, since this whole journey was a kind of pilgrimage.

I got out of bed. Sleep would have been welcome, but another treat awaited me.

I leaned out the window and feasted on the magnificent church, as the night retreated and the sky gradually brightened. Only one other palazzo—the one where Francesco's fair and devout young noblewoman had grown up—separated us from San Rufino, at the end of the piazza. Its facade was a glorious explosion of intricately carved decorations, animals and birds, vines and flowers, saints and evangelists, Christ's holy mother with her infant at her breast, the saintly bishop himself, a she-wolf, griffins and lions, a king on his throne, all in the warm rosy stone of the Umbrian hills that surrounded us, with enough added color to make it rich and real.

Nothing in Rome had ever captured my imagination the way this church did. I had seen it for the first time the day before, at sunset, and it glowed with a fierce ruddy fire that made me gasp. I fell in love with the three figures standing on the backs of strange animals, their arms extended to support the huge rose window. Something about those little men, straining to hold up that window for eternity, touched me deeply. They made me think of Francesco.

The cathedral and its piazza were proudly positioned to gaze down on the rest of Assisi, except for the ruins of the fortress, which loomed above all else. In our imperfect world Mars ranks higher than the saints. From here we could almost see across the valley to the humble huts and makeshift chapel of the brothers, Francesco's Porziuncola, or little portion, as he called it. Had it been winter and the trees bare, I would have seen the smoke from the brothers' fire, though they were perhaps an hour's walk away.

The sky over Assisi was just beginning to display the colors of early morning. I wished Graziano could see it with me. He had taught me how to read the sky over Rome and over Marino, and he would have loved this. He would have been gleefully predicting the weather like a native within days.

Pink and blue chased each other across that vast brightening sky like playful children. Blue was gaining, and as the day grew brighter, pink abandoned the contest altogether and took refuge in Assisi's stone buildings.

Everywhere Rome is hard, Assisi is soft. Rome's summer sun emerges harsh and aggressive even before it fights its way up beyond the seven hills, but Assisi's is mellow burnished gold, warm and gentle. Sunlight flashes on Rome's brilliant white marble, sometimes sudden and sharp enough to blind you, but in Assisi it caresses pink and white stone and seduces the eye.

Even the sounds are different. Rome's streets with their hard surfaces clatter and rattle, and the voices of people and animals and bells ring out clear and sharp, edgy, piercing. In Assisi, sounds wind their way down curving streets, merging with their own echoes, caught by the buildings and tossed whimsically in new directions until they fade away altogether.

When the bells were still at last, the people inside the church, and a blessed quiet reigned, I leaned my elbows on the windowsill and enjoyed my silent contemplation of Francesco's city, now fully blessed by his Brother Sun.

Silent, that is, until the child burst out of the house across the street, singing nonsense words tunelessly but at the top of his voice, and started bowling his wooden ball against the wall of Arnolfo's palazzo. It hit with a crash each time, and the child cheered for himself as he ran to retrieve it. He bellowed his incomprehensible song as he flung the ball repeatedly at the palazzo.

The racket was singularly annoying. I watched the houses across the piazza, thinking his mother or his nurse would emerge at any moment and get him under control, but no one did. He had the piazza and the street all to himself.

A holy mass was being conducted in the church, and the doors stood open to let the air in, for the day was already getting hot. Surely this child's rudeness was disrupting Bishop Guido's efforts.

I grabbed my dusty travel dress and pulled it on over my shift, then marched down the stairs and headed for the front door.

A servant intercepted me. "Can I help you, monna Giacoma?" she asked, an anxious frown on her face.

"I'm going to go shush that child, since nobody else will."

She had planted herself directly in front of me, so I moved to my left to go around her.

"But madonna, you can't," she said, now visibly alarmed, moving to her right to stop me. "He's the miracle child."

The wooden ball crashed into the wall.

This was a miracle? "Explain," I said shortly, then thought better of it. "If you will."

She gamely tried. "Last summer when they found San Rufino's relics, there were some wonderful miracles happened here. First the German pilgrim whose hands and feet were all withered, and he got healed because he prayed inside the church. And the next one, out in the piazza, was this boy."

The high point of Assisi's last summer had been the rediscovery of their patron saint's relics, and Bishop Guido had paid for an elaborate celebration when they were reinterred in a spot where with a bit of luck they would not get lost again. The usual spate of miracles had followed, some of them indisputable, some questionable. But I hadn't heard of this one.

"What's so miraculous about him?"

"He got knocked down by an oxcart, and he lived," she said, crossing herself fervently. "They thought he'd die for certain, but San Rufino saved him, and he lived."

Another crash and bellow from outside. I found myself wondering how the ox had fared.

Much as I itched to dash out and snatch the ball away from Miracle Boy, that would clearly be an unpopular move in the eyes of the Assisians. Reluctantly I resigned myself to putting up with the noise. I thanked the girl and trudged grumpily back upstairs, where I realized my hair still hung loose, a mass of tangled curls in a furious chaos down my back, so perhaps it was lucky I hadn't charged out into the piazza to confront the young miracle. I wrapped my hair in my benda, all the while listening to regular crashes punctuated by incoherent cheers and chanting.

The black benda, now faded to a dull charcoal, had become my main concession to mourning. I had left off the dismal dark-hued gowns. My goal now was to keep my clothing simple, without ornamentation, as close to the spirit of Francesco's and the brothers' habits as possible, though I did allow myself a bit of color to keep my spirits up. And I liked my clothes to be clean. I still mourned Graziano; I would mourn him for the rest of my life. But I didn't need to prove that to anyone, so I wore what I pleased. If my noble friends and kinsmen were taken aback at my utilitarian clothing, and Graziano's family thought I should still be in full mourning, and Francesco's brothers in their turn disapproved of my bright colors, well, they would all simply have to make of it what they would.

I was like a duck these days, a creature of both air and water but not entirely of either: not a grand lady and not a humble friar, and yet something of each. If I ever figured out what exactly I was supposed to be, I would dress accordingly, and until then I would waddle around like the duck I was.

I took off the dusty travel gown and donned a robe of lightweight wool, cloth the merchant had described as "colore di leone." It shouldn't leave me sweltering, even once the day's heat was fully upon us. The color flattered me, though not as much as red, and it almost matched my hidden hair. No one was going to get me into an overdress, though. Not if today was to be hotter than yesterday, as seemed likely. I shrugged my way into the garment, fiddled inexpertly with the laces, and snagged the benda on a hook on the bedpost and had to rewrap the end.

Throughout this process, the appalling child continued crashing and bellowing. I did my best to ignore him, but it was difficult.

In fact, when Mengarda, Vanna, and Prassede appeared at my door I was sitting on the window seat with my washbasin half on my lap and half balanced on the windowsill, contemplating how much uproar would ensue if the visitor from Rome happened to clumsily tip the contents out onto the little miracle's head the next time he came to retrieve his ball.

Vanna, who knew me entirely too well, gave me a look of pure horror. I relented and set the basin on its small table.

Prassede, naturally, entered talking.

"Oh, Giacoma, you should have come with us! The church is so beautiful, and Bishop Guido is such a wonderful man, and the whole experience was just so uplifting, and we prayed for peace and harmony, and he mentioned that Brother Francesco will be preaching later, and I'm sure the image of Our Lady was smiling down on all of us—"

"That's lovely, Prassede," I said automatically, though it was exactly the way she always reacted to mass. I held my arms out, and Vanna adjusted my gaping laces. If I was going to live the gospel life, I should learn how to get my clothes on without help. The brothers seemed to manage it. But poor Vanna would be so disappointed if she didn't feel needed.

Mengarda eyed my dress, smiled, and stood straighter. No competition for her here, I thought, amused. Her own gown was an elegant figured surcoat in a rich dark blue. *She's going to be hot in that today.*

Francesco had commended Mengarda and Arnolfo to me, and me to them. They were among his most ardent and influential followers in Assisi, and they had been eager to do him a service by hosting me. I wanted to make sure I didn't disappoint them, for his sake but also for theirs. They had welcomed us warmly, providing us with every luxury at their disposal, and I found I liked them very much.

"Monna Giacoma, Brother Francesco has sent us a message," Mengarda said. "He wants you to meet with Sister Chiara at San Damiano, and he has asked me to take you there, if you will."

I felt let down. Curious as I still was about that remarkable woman, I had hoped Francesco would be the one to take us, for I could hardly wait to see him.

"Very kind, and I thank you," I said. "But will we see Brother Francesco later?"

"Oh, yes, only he needs to meet with someone from the hospital,

73

so he wanted you to go and dine with Sister Chiara and the others, and then he'll meet you later, after he preaches." She walked over to the window and beckoned to me. "See the second palazzo down, right next to the church? That's where Sister Chiara's family lives. The men are still unhappy with her decision, but with everybody so excited over Brother Francesco, there isn't anything they can do about it. Chiara's sister Caterina—she's Sister Agnese now—has already joined her, and I wouldn't be surprised if more of the women in her family do too. I'm bringing her a message from her lady mother."

I leaned out and peered in the direction she was pointing. The palazzo was indeed right next to the church. I supposed that meant Chiara's family got jolted out of their beds every time the bells pealed and had to listen to the noisy little miracle just as we did.

"We should go now, monna Giacoma," Mengarda reminded me. Obediently I trooped down the stairs with her, Vanna, and Prassede following us. At least this would get us away from Miracle Child, who was still chanting and crashing his ball into the wall.

We went out the door and I turned to glare at the boy, but then I saw the jagged scar along his forehead and temple and his blank eyes. I was suddenly ashamed of my annoyance. God chose to let this child live, despite his injuries, and here I had resented his pleasure, never stopping to ask myself what it would have been like if one of my own boys had suffered such an accident and been so damaged.

Obviously I wasn't as good at assessing a situation as I thought I was, nor was I as kind and charitable as I wanted to believe, and wanted Francesco to believe, too. I resolved to make sure the child received a gift of something that would please him. Something quiet—though I supposed that something noisy would be more appropriate, as a penance on my part.

11

MENGARDA proudly linked arms with me, nodding to the people we passed, Vanna and Prassede behind us, two of Mengarda's servants bringing up the rear. We walked, a gentle downhill stroll, out of one of the city's gates and along a lane with an olive grove on either side. The silvery green of the leaves shimmered in the morning sunlight. Behind us Prassede chattered to Vanna, who was even more silent than usual.

Vanna had rejoined our household in recent weeks, but she was not the same. She seldom spoke unless someone asked her something, and then she answered as briefly as possible. I knew she still suffered, but she refused to speak of it, so I left her alone. Once or twice I even caught her smiling when she thought no one was watching. I pretended not to notice, but I was glad.

"There it is," said Mengarda, pointing ahead. "And I must confess I'm relieved—these are not the best shoes for walking." She reached down and tugged at her delicate shoe. "Ouch!"

I clucked sympathetically. We still needed to get all the way back later, and that way the path was uphill. Not good if she already had a blister. I was wearing my usual sturdy shoes, but she must have forgotten to change after mass.

San Damiano was a modest place, smaller than I had expected. It had a tidy little chapel and a ramshackle building that I assumed housed the sisters, and a well and a few wooden outbuildings that might have been a kitchen, a bakehouse, perhaps a place for laundry. An orderly kitchen garden peeked out around one side of the building, and I guessed it probably extended a good distance back behind the premises. Mengarda had said if we walked a bit farther along the path we would come to an infirmary staffed by the sisters, but I couldn't see it for the olive grove.

Three women were waiting for us in the diminutive cobbled courtyard. One was older, slightly stooped; another was plump and cheerful; and the third, the youngest of them, was tall, willowy, and striking. They wore starkly simple gray tunics, narrow to the body and with no excess cloth. I felt fussily overdressed in my simple gown.

The tall one had to be the redoubtable Chiara. I had heard the tale of how she escaped from her house in the dead of night, making her way in the dark with only a single companion, to the gate where her kinsman Rufino waited and then all the way down to the Porziuncola, to Francesco and the rest of the brothers. I admired the courage and resourcefulness such an act must have required; I couldn't imagine myself doing the same thing successfully when I was a maiden still living with my family. I'd probably have stumbled and awakened everyone or gotten lost on the way to the Porziuncola.

All three women watched us as we approached, their expressions mild and pleasant. I stopped a few paces away from them, to let Mengarda greet them first and make the introductions.

She strode forward, a warm smile on her face. She took both of Chiara's hands in hers and started to kneel, but Chiara murmured something and she straightened. Mengarda was taller than me, but not as tall as Chiara.

Mengarda beckoned and I approached, ready to meet this remarkable woman. I couldn't see any of her hair, hidden as thoroughly as was my own, but her brows were lighter than mine, so I guessed her hair must be paler than my tawny curls. I knew it was cropped short under her veil. Francesco himself had cut it for her, the night she made her daring, breathless escape and joined him at the Porziuncola. Her eyes were a clear gray, large and round, rimmed by dark lashes. Her mouth was wide, her skin delicate, her nose long and narrow, and her chin was softly pointed. She carried herself with a perfect balance of humility and dignity, and immediately I felt a stab of envy. I had never mastered that combination.

I recognized in Chiara another noblewoman, not only by her appearance but by her speech, which was measured and cultivated, though it employed the same peculiar Umbrian accent I heard from Francesco and his brothers.

"I am grateful to have the chance to meet you at last, monna Giacoma," she said, so quietly I leaned forward to make sure I didn't miss anything. "Will you and your friends honor us by joining us for a simple meal after we sing the office of Terce?"

"The honor is mine, madonna..." I stopped, confused. What was I to call her? Monna Chiara? Mother Chiara? Sister Chiara? Could this woman be mother or sister to me?

"Call me 'Sister,'" she said, seeing my hesitation. "It is the name that applies to all of us here."

"Sister, then." Something about the woman both awed me and intimidated me, though nothing in her appeared to seek such a response.

"May I make the acquaintance of your fellow travelers?" she asked, indicating Prassede and Vanna. "I know Sobilia and Dialta, for we were neighbors for years." She smiled at Mengarda's servants, who gazed at her reverently.

"This is Sister Prassede, from Grottaferrata," I said, indicating my suddenly silent companion. "And this is Vanna, who lives in my home." I did not feel comfortable calling her my servant, not here where women renounced their lives of privilege and embraced what Francesco would call "monna Poverty." Was it perhaps "messer Poverty" to these women?

Chiara inclined her head in gentle acknowledgement, then turned to the two women in gray who waited nearby.

"Sister Balvina, Sister Cristiana, please take Vanna with you," she said, and to my amazement Vanna stepped forward, her face radiant.

What was going on here? I glanced at Prassede, but she was as surprised as I was. Her mouth fell open and she stared at Vanna as if she'd never seen her before.

Vanna walked away between the two gray-clad sisters, and she didn't look back. Chiara led the remaining five of us into the chapel. I kept turning my head, trying to see where they were taking Vanna, but the three women disappeared around a corner. In the chapel other sisters waited, heads bowed in prayer. One young girl raised her head as we entered, but she caught herself and lowered it quickly. The chapel was austere, with a wooden painted crucifix hanging high on the back wall and a rather primitive painting of the holy Mother and Child on a wooden panel just above the altar. The only hint of luxury anywhere was a beautifully embroidered altar cloth, which I hoped to study someday.

There followed a lengthy melange of singing and praying and listening to readings of psalms, but all I remember was my sense of bewilderment about what was happening to my maidservant. I stood and knelt when the other women did, and sang with them, but uncertainly. I loved singing lauds with the brothers, where my voice floated above theirs in a pleasing effect, but in this place, my voice was low to the point of sounding harsh in my own ears, as the sisters' ethereal sopranos soared above my hesitant alto.

We sang the hymn *Nunc nobis Spiritus*, and Chiara moved noiselessly to the front of the chapel and faced the rest of us.

"Sisters, let us welcome among us the great friend of Brother Francesco, monna Giacoma of Rome," she said, and everyone looked at me. I felt my cheeks reddening, and I wondered whether Chiara was aware that I was now Brother Giacoma.

"And let us also welcome Sister Prassede, a holy woman, and three virtuous women many of us knew while we were still in the world, Mengarda, Sobilia and Dialta." To my relief, at least some of the attention shifted to the others. These somberly clad women must have been friends, neighbors, even relatives of the women of Mengarda's household.

"And most especially I want you to welcome our new sister, Sister Vanna."

The door to the chapel opened behind us. I whirled and saw Vanna, now barefoot and clothed in a coarse narrow gray habit, walking solemnly through the door flanked by Sisters Balvina and Cristiana. Her head was uncovered, and her straw-colored hair hung loose down her back. Sister Balvina held a wad of white linen in one hand.

The three of them approached Chiara, and the two sisters veered off and moved to the sides of the chapel. Vanna sank to her knees before Chiara, and Chiara lifted her hands to the ceiling and began to sing in an otherworldly voice that made my breath catch. She sang in the Umbrian dialect, where every time I expected to hear an "O" I heard a "U" instead. It was a song of praise and thanks, much like some of the songs Francesco sang. Then other voices joined in, alternating in a joyful call-and-response, and Vanna prostrated herself on the floor, her arms outstretched.

Prassede's eyes met mine, and she gave a helpless little shrug. At least I wasn't alone in my lack of comprehension. Mengarda and her servants beamed, their attention fixed on Chiara, seemingly unaware that I was not a party to whatever was happening to Vanna.

Chiara signaled with her hand, and the youngest of the sisters, the one who had noticed us when we came in, stooped and picked something up from the floor, then brought it to Chiara, taking care to step around Vanna's outstretched arms.

It was a pair of shears, the kind one might use to cut fabric—like the shears used by cloth merchants, but smaller. We watched silently as Chiara knelt and lifted Vanna's hair, then began to cut it off at the nape of her neck.

How comfortable that will be in this summer heat, I thought irrelevantly. Then, as handfuls of Vanna's hair accumulated on the floor, I wondered how I would have felt had Francesco allowed me to join Chiara's sisterhood, and it had been me instead of Vanna splayed out on the chapel floor. I had sworn never to display my hair again, my thick, curling, easily tangled lion's mane of hair Graziano had loved so much, but I still wasn't sure I could have parted with it.

So. Vanna must have planned this, probably from the time of Francesco's last visit to us. She had wanted an interview with Francesco alone, and she'd gotten it. I supposed they made their plans then. I was hurt that she hadn't said anything to me. As my servant, she should have asked my permission; as my friend, she should have trusted me. But perhaps since Francesco had rejected my plea to join this sisterhood, and Prassede's too, she thought we would have been distressed when he accepted her.

She may have been right.

My thoughts roiled. I could tell from the way Vanna had entered the church—eager, excited, proud—that she was doing this of her own volition, so I did not fear for her on that score. I did fear she might be driven to this irrevocable act by her pain and disappointment, which might have faded in time, rather than by a true vocation. Had she committed herself to an established Benedictine order, she would have spent a year as a novice, to learn whether it was the right path for her, but instead she had chosen to cast her lot with this band of religious radicals, who never did anything in the normal way.

The same radicals who had my own oath. No substantive difference existed between Chiara and Francesco when it came to the religious life.

Chiara must have been in on this deception, and that did not incline me to trust her, but my more immediate problem was Francesco's secrecy. Was I so unreasonable that he didn't feel he could tell me? What did he think I would have done? Naturally I didn't want to lose Vanna, but Francesco knew I would have put her wishes first. I felt betrayed by three people, two of whom had been dear to me for a long time.

The shearing complete, Chiara stood and said, "Rise, Sister Vanna, and accept your veil." Vanna hauled herself up to a crouch and then stood, awkwardly. She brushed some invisible matter from the front of her narrow gray garment, which at least appeared to be new, if coarse and stark.

Sister Balvina moved forward, holding out the length of white linen, and Chiara took it from her and covered Vanna's raggedly shorn hair with it, adjusting it until it fit like the other sisters' veils, showing none of her remaining hair and shrouding her neck as well as her head.

So much for being comfortable in the heat, I thought vindictively, and I immediately regretted my waspishness. Vanna's veil wasn't any more restrictive than the benda I wore by choice. And I would be accepting my own veil now, had Francesco only acquiesced.

Given the consternation I was feeling, however, I began to suspect he had been right, at least about me. I hoped he had been equally right about Vanna.

Once my former servant was introduced to her new sisters in a flurry of hugs and warm and welcoming words, Chiara announced that we would have time to talk with each other and to enjoy the garden in the courtyard until dinner was ready. Two of the women left, to finish dinner preparations, I assumed, but Vanna—I should say Sister Vanna—was still surrounded by gray people, so Prassede and I slipped out the door unnoticed. It gave us a few moments to talk before the others emerged.

"You didn't know either, did you?" I asked her.

"No. I had no idea."

I shot her a quick look. That was terse, for Prassede. I waited, but she had nothing more to add.

"Why didn't Francesco tell us?" I wondered aloud.

"Why didn't Francesco *want* us?" she countered.

Yes, that was at the heart of it. Why my foolish lovesick servant, and not Sister Prassede, penitent and recluse? Or, for that matter, why not me? Surely if I renounced my earthly goods and embraced poverty it would accomplish more for Francesco's beloved poor than Vanna renouncing hers.

Sister Vanna and the others tumbled out the chapel door into the courtyard, laughing together like old friends. Mengarda, Sobilia, and Dialta followed, each arm-in-arm with one of the sisters, talking as if they had months of news to catch up on. I supposed they did.

One of the sisters who had gone out earlier appeared in the door to the refectory and rang a small bell to announce the meal. Obediently we filed in. There were perhaps twenty gray-clad women present, plus us, their guests. Two rough-hewn trestle tables at right angles gave us plenty of room for dining, but I hung back to see where Chiara wanted us to sit.

Mengarda, Sobilia, and Dialta followed their companions over to a bench and stood with them. The older woman who had been waiting for us in the courtyard approached Prassede and led her to a place in the center of one of the tables. No one sat.

I hesitated, feeling awkward and isolated. Others arranged themselves in what I supposed were their accustomed places. I thought of asking someone, but as soon as the women entered the refectory all chatter had ceased, and a decorous silence prevailed.

Finally, after an interminable few moments beyond the point where everyone else had found her way to a spot behind a bench, Chiara came to me and touched my arm lightly. She indicated I was to follow her. I did, and she placed me near the end of the table closest to the door, while she took the end place to my left. On my right side was Vanna, her eyes lowered. No word was spoken.

The women stood motionless, many of them in silent prayer. In front of each pair of women was a wooden cup to share. In the center of each table was a platter of brown bread in slices and chunks, an earthenware oil jar, a wooden dish filled with salt, and a cracked maiolica bowl full of eggs. At the point where the ends of both tables met were a basket containing salad herbs and a smaller basket of plums.

Chiara began to pray aloud, her hands raised in the orante position Francesco favored. Some of the sisters imitated her, but others bowed their heads and kept their arms down at their sides. All of them closed their eyes, including Prassede and the other members of our party. God forgive me, but rather than do likewise, I took advantage of the opportunity to look around me.

There wasn't much to see. The refectory's walls were bare, and no white linens covered the tables. The platters were of wood, chipped and darkened with age. I glimpsed a patch of garden out the window in the back wall; that and the open door let sunlight in, though the middle of the room remained in shadow. I saw no washbasin waiting to be passed to us, neither spoon nor knife, and no napkins to clean our fingers. Probably someone would bring those things in when the prayer ended, I thought, and when they brought the rest of the food. No point in letting good food sit on the table and get cold while the sisters prayed at length. Very sensible.

Except there wasn't any more food. Chiara finally finished praying and gestured for the sisters to sit, and they passed the platters of coarse grainy bread and each one took a piece, so I did too. Trencher bread, I assumed, probably with better bread to come to accompany the meal. But when the eggs were passed, still warm from the pot, and then the greens and plums, and the sisters began to eat their bread, I realized with a start that the entire meal was already before us. No hot dishes would follow, no delicate sweets, no cheeses, no pie, no little dishes of candied almonds. I hadn't expected meat, but a bit of fish would not have been unwelcome, or at least something with pulses in it, and some flavor. Was it a lean day? No, eggs would not be on the table had it been a day of fasting. My stomach rumbled. We had eaten nothing before walking here, and I was more than ready for a satisfying dinner.

Even our wooden cups stood empty, I noted morosely, but then two sisters came in bearing pitchers, and I brightened a bit.

But it was water, not wine, the sister sloshed into our cup. Cool, clear water, but water nonetheless. Surreptitiously I peeked at my Assisi hostess and her servants, but they wore beatific smiles as they munched that unappetizing bread and sipped their water. I thought glumly of the

81

box of Amata's almond cakes we had brought for the brothers, which were back in Mengarda's palazzo in town.

All this time, Vanna and I avoided acknowledging one another. No one spoke, so we didn't have to try to converse, but our proximity was still awkward. She nibbled a chunk of bread. I cracked my egg on the table and peeled it, letting the bits of shell fall on the age-darkened wood, for I had no plate and there was nowhere else for them to go, since the empty egg bowl was out of my reach and apparently I wasn't permitted to speak to ask someone to pass it.

Chiara must have been watching me, for she chose that moment to stand up and rap on the table. All eyes turned to her.

"Sisters, we have served you eggs today in honor of our esteemed visitors. But I would like to ask anyone who does not feel the need of this extra nourishment to give up her egg, so we may take them to the patients in our infirmary as a special treat. If anyone wishes to keep her egg, she may do so, but I encourage you to make this act of generosity with a glad heart." Obediently, the sister closest to each egg bowl passed the bowl down the table, and each sister placed her egg back inside it. So did Prassede, Mengarda, Sobilia, and Dialta, and Chiara gave them an approving nod.

I was the only one who had started on my egg. My face reddened with the knowledge that I had been singled out for humiliation. How did they expect me to obey the rules if no one told me what they were? How did Prassede know? Or Mengarda?

Francesco was right. I would have failed as a sister. The egg bowl reached me, Vanna holding it out to me without meeting my eyes. My egg was the only peeled egg in the room. I felt my annoyance growing. Nobody told me, so what did they expect? The patients in the infirmary were just going to have to survive without my egg. I passed the bowl on to Chiara and took a defiant bite of egg. Chiara glanced at me, and I was almost sure I saw a flicker of amusement cross her flawless face.

I don't care, I said to myself sourly. I had been deceived, I was losing my servant, I had been humiliated, and to top it off, I was hungry. Also the day was growing unpleasantly warm, and my body was slick with sweat under the gown that no longer looked so simple, compared to the gray habits all around me. And this was the life Francesco had denied me. A wise man, Brother Francesco.

12

CHIARA stood. "Sisters, I thank you for your generosity, and our patients will thank you too. Now, as a special privilege to celebrate our distinguished guests, you may speak with one another."

That elicited an excited buzz of murmurs. Mengarda and her servants picked up the threads of their previous conversations with their companions, other sisters turned to one another and began to converse, and Vanna finally faced me.

She took a deep breath. "Mon—Giacoma, I must apologize for withholding this from you. I didn't know how to ask you, because I knew you wanted to come here yourself." She was perspiring, and not entirely from the heat.

"Did you not trust me, Vanna? Did you fear I'd fail to support you in this?"

She shook her head emphatically. "No. I was sure you would help me in any way you could. I can't explain why I couldn't ask you, but I just couldn't." She paused, swallowed hard, then went on. "I had nothing of my very own, only this secret. Brother Francesco agreed to let me come, as soon as Sister Chiara had a place for me and I had a way to get here, and I was so miserable about... about the situation at home..."

"About Massimo." I wasn't ready to let it be quite that easy.

"Yes. About Massimo. It's clear to me now that God had other plans for me. Marrying Massimo would have been a huge mistake."

Not that you ever had that choice, my girl. On the other hand, if Vanna had wed Massimo and Amata had come here instead, we might at least have had a decent meal.

Vanna's lower lip quivered. I felt a rush of sympathy for the poor girl, so unhappy for so long. Maybe here she would at last find what she needed. Then all of this would be worthwhile, although it still chafed me that Francesco accepted her while rejecting me.

"And please, Giacoma, don't blame Brother Francesco or Sister Chiara. They honored my request not to tell you. They didn't like it, but they agreed it was my decision. So you mustn't be angry with them. If you're angry, let it only be with me." Somehow, my very youthful servant had found the strength to prevail over those two extraordinary people. Or possibly they hadn't tried very hard to resist. Either way, I had to respect that—it couldn't have been easy for her.

"Vanna, I'm not angry," I told her, and it was almost true. "I'll miss you, but the important thing is that you've found what you want. I suppose this means you won't be coming back with us, back home to Rome—or even back to town today?"

"No. I will never leave here. Sometimes I might go to the infirmary to do some nursing, but otherwise, this is my home now, I've given my oath, and I am not free to go."

Her words hit me like a blow to my stomach. I hadn't grasped the enormity of the commitment she was making, and I had foolishly hoped to make myself, until that moment.

"I'll have your things sent from Assisi as soon as we get back," I said, but she shook her head.

"No, please take my things to San Rufino and leave them for the poor. I won't be wanting them anymore. I have this." She indicated her coarse undyed garment. "It's all I need."

My mind went blank. There must be something I could give her, or do for her, or at least say, to wish her well and help her in her new life, but nothing came to me.

She turned to Chiara. "Sister, may I go get the dress I wore today, so monna Giacoma can give it to the poor?" At Chiara's nod, Vanna slipped out the door.

All through the refectory women were talking quietly, enjoying the rare chance to speak. Chiara turned to me. "Monna Giacoma, I must add my apologies to Sister Vanna's if our secrecy has caused you pain." She spoke softly, but her face was serene.

"I understand," I said, though I didn't yet, quite. I had no wish to make things more difficult for my friend, or even for Chiara. Their apologies had taken the edge off my resentment. Ruefully, I realized I need not have worried over Vanna's distress if I dressed myself without her help. Nothing I did would be of any importance to her any more.

The thought left me feeling saddened and lonely, for Vanna had been with me since we were both young girls. But one thing I was learning about loss, whether small or great, was that the only thing to do is to pick yourself up and move forward.

"And don't feel bad about the egg," Chiara added. "We served them because of your visit, as I said."

I still thought I had been embarrassed, possibly even ridiculed, in a way I didn't deserve, but Chiara's calm demeanor shook my confidence. Perhaps I was merely being selfish and greedy.

"Prassede and Mengarda and the others did without their eggs," I said.

Chiara gave her thin little smile, a private, secret smile I was to come to know well. "Yes, but they'll go back home and eat whatever they want," she said, and I knew it was true. "They are not sisters, and they have not taken an oath to live in holy poverty, as we have. All are good women, generous women, but their paths are not ours. They fast when the church requires them to, but they do not share our privations. Our ways are not for everyone."

Fair enough. She sounded as if she meant it, and so I would take her at her word.

"I hope your ways are right for Vanna. She has lived in some measure of luxury in my household, and this will be a great change for her."

"Yes. But she has chosen this of her own will, and we will do all we can to help her adjust to her new life. If you can give me any advice on how to make it easier for her, I would be pleased to consider it."

Consider it. Not necessarily take it. There wasn't much doubt about who was in charge here.

What could I tell her that would be of help to Vanna? I puzzled for a moment, and then I had it.

"She's very good at prodding people to do things properly. If you tell her how you expect the sisters to behave, she will make absolutely sure they do. She's like a prized sheepdog. Not a single lamb will get away from her."

That smile again, and this time it triggered a dimple. Suddenly I saw Chiara as a lovely and marriageable young woman, and I could imagine how much her kinsmen believed they had lost, though they probably had never really had it.

"Wise advice," she said. "It will be a way she and I can serve each other, and I thank you for your suggestion."

Vanna came back then, carrying her folded blue gown and chemise with her shoes on top. Chiara turned away from me to a sister who had been waiting for a chance to speak with her, and I accepted the package from Vanna, who handed it to me silently. Her eyes were moist, and I felt tears sting my own. It was strange to see her in her gray habit.

"Oh, Vanna, who will keep me respectable now?" I asked her, almost choking.

"Giacoma—madonna—you are worthy of all respect, always. Even when your laces aren't done up properly."

Reflexively my hand went to my side, and she laughed. "I knew you'd check. They're fine, Giacoma. You'll be fine. You have Sister Prassede now, remember."

I did, I supposed. Prassede had been living in my palazzo about half the time since we first met her during the brothers' visit, and the rest of the time she stayed in a house of penitents near the hospital where the women helped with the nursing. With us she was invariably cheerful and loquacious, practical, well organized, indefatigable. The boys liked her, Lucia was fond of her, Massimo trusted her judgment, Amata welcomed her competent help in the kitchen, and I had come to regard her with a certain respect and affection, though it was often tempered with exasperation at her constant talking.

Chiara offered to show us Vanna's new home. We saw the dormitory upstairs, the kitchen shed, the garden, the tiny outbuildings the brothers had been constructing for the sisters, and the shack a short distance away where at least two of the brothers lived at all times. The brothers served as questors, begging for food and fuel for Chiara's growing sisterhood.

At my request, she took me down the road to see the infirmary. In it were only four elderly women in narrow white-sheeted beds, but I also saw another four empty beds. Chiara explained: when the brothers came across impoverished women in need of help, they could not accept them in their own hospital, for they were not to have to do with women. Instead, they brought the sick women to Chiara. I met the two patients who were alert enough to exchange a few words with us, and Chiara introduced me to Sister Agnese, her sister by blood as well as by vow, who was on duty as the nurse and therefore had not joined us at dinner. We prayed with the women and tended to them, helping one to sip water and propping another up on cushions to ease her back.

One woman's bed was soaked; I took one side of her sheet and Chiara the other, and we lifted her while Agnese pulled off the wet bedding and put a clean pad and a fresh sheet on the mattress. Then we had to roll the patient gently onto the new bedding. The procedure required some skill, but both Chiara and I had done it before, so we accomplished it with little discomfort for the disoriented woman.

It seemed to me Chiara viewed me with more respect after that, which pleased me in spite of myself. On our way back to San Damiano, I told her about Prassede's hospital. Like Francesco's brotherhood, the Benedictines who ran the hospital would not consider housing men and women on the same premises, so the female patients were scattered around in private houses, often including my own. Chiara offered some solidly practical ideas, and I listened to her carefully.

When we arrived at the courtyard, Prassede was deep in conversation with an older sister, and Mengarda and her servants were chatting with their friends. I followed Chiara into the chapel and took the opportunity to ask her about the beautiful embroidery on the altar cloth.

"That is my work," she said, and I heard no pride in her voice, though the artistry of the embroidery was extraordinary. "I prefer doing simple sewing, or spinning thread, but I was inspired to make this for our chapel for the glory of God."

I looked more closely. It was exquisite work, a well-proportioned design in the Assisi style, where the figure—in this case a cross bordered by vines and flowers—is left void and the surrounding area is defined by color. I praised it, but Chiara shook her head.

"I may not take pride in my skill when it is God who lends it to me for his purposes." Was she pleased at my words anyway? I thought perhaps she was.

Our visit with the sisters soon came to an end. Egidio came to get us, and all of us, sisters and guests alike, greeted him warmly. He told us Francesco was preaching in the piazza in front of San Rufino and would not be able to come to meet us here. Chiara's face did not change as she thanked him for bringing the message, but I knew she was disappointed. This was becoming something of a game—the less she showed of what she was feeling, the harder I tried to figure it out. Was I succeeding, or was I only imagining she felt as I would feel in a similar situation?

I was becoming more comfortable with Chiara than I had been at first, but I sensed a certain mutual wariness between us. Much as I hated to say goodbye to Vanna, it would be something of a relief to be on our way back to Assisi, and Francesco.

Vanna and I hugged each other, and this time our tears flowed freely. As our party started back toward Assisi amid farewells and promises to pray for one another, Prassede took my hand and squeezed it. We were walking two by two, and she and I followed Egidio and Mengarda.

"She'll be happy," she said. "It was what you and I wanted for ourselves, wasn't it?"

It had been, but now I was less certain. Could I have lived with Chiara making my decisions for me? With anyone except Francesco having authority over me, for that matter? I felt a failure, but I was not sure I could have donned one of those awful gray dresses and lived on bread and the occasional glimpse of an egg.

"Are you still disappointed?" I asked her.

Uncharacteristically, she hesitated.

"I don't know," she finally said. "I trust Brother Francesco to know what's best. Yet I did so want to be part of this. Yes, I guess I am disappointed, but I accept it—this is not to be my path."

"Will you talk to Francesco, then?"

"If I get the chance. He's told me what I can't do, so maybe now he'll help me come to know what I can do instead."

Prassede was not yet back to her usual talkative self, so we walked along through the olive grove in near silence, sweating in the heat. It gave me a chance to think about our meeting with Francesco, and what to expect.

The previous fall, Francesco had tried to go to the Middle East to preach to the Saracens, and only a disastrous shipwreck had prevented him. Francesco was determined to do everything in his power to convert the Moslems, so no more blood would be shed. Yet I had feared for my impractical, otherworldly, barefoot friend, setting sail for such a hostile land. It would have been wrong to rejoice in his shipwreck, and indeed it must have been terrifying, but I was glad he had not reached his destination. Now I wondered what his next project might entail, and whether it would be as dangerous.

13

By the time the six of us arrived at Assisi's gate, we were exhausted from the heat. We were also still hungry. Fortunately, Prassede had insisted on Mengarda wearing Vanna's shoes. Otherwise, I'm not sure our poor hostess would have made it. Even after we were back inside the city, we still had plenty of walking to reach the piazza of San Rufino, where Francesco was holding the crowd spellbound.

My beloved friend was in front of the central church door, preaching animatedly, practically dancing, words and sweat pouring from him. The crowd filled the piazza. Since I couldn't get close enough to hear, I stationed myself in front of Mengarda's palazzo. Elias was standing opposite me, doing exactly what I was doing—surveying everyone, observing their reactions, watching, always watching. His arms were crossed in front of his chest. His eyes met mine and he gave me a nod, which I returned.

Francesco must have been approaching the end of his sermon, because he slid into his troubadour persona, miming playing a fiddle while he sang a lauda, to the crowd's delight. I looked about me for other outliers. Francesco was not universally accepted, not even here in his own city, and his sermons sometimes drew troublemakers, though this crowd seemed benign and enthusiastic. I couldn't help smiling as I watched him.

I heard a soft noise to my right, at about the level of my waist, and turned to see what it was. Miracle Boy was sitting next to me, his back against the building and his wooden ball resting at his side. He peered up at me from under that terrible scar. I didn't know what to say or to do, but then he said to me, clearly, "Good man."

Tears stung my eyes. "Yes," I said. "He's a good man." And then, for some reason I can't explain, I sat next to him on the paving stones and put my arm around his sturdy shoulders. He did not resist; he watched me, silent and still, and I could hardly believe it was the same child who had been so obsessively agitated before.

"Lady cry," he observed, and I nodded, unable to speak. I didn't know why I was weeping, but I was. Then the child picked up his wooden ball, which despite its lengthy assault on the palazzo wall still had a few flecks of red paint, and placed it in my lap.

I was hugging the child and sobbing when I noticed a pair of bare feet in front of us, and a gray tunic that stopped short of its wearer's knees. I looked up. Elias was watching me, a worried frown on his handsome face.

"You sorrow, Giacoma?"

"No, Brother. I was moved by Francesco's words, that's all." I hadn't been able to hear most of those words, but it would do for now.

"Francesco has been wanting to see you." He extended a hand to me. I set the ball down next to the child and let Elias help me to my feet. "He'll be free of the crowd soon, and he'll come here to Arnolfo and Mengarda's palazzo and meet with you inside. Shall we go in and wait for him?"

I wiped my face on my sleeve and took a gulp of air to try to calm myself, with partial success, though it left me with hiccups. "Yes," I said to Elias, "let's go in." The child was no longer paying any attention to me. One of his hands rested lightly on the ball, and he looked absently straight ahead.

We went in, and Mengarda and Arnolfo soon joined us. Mengarda sent for a cup of well-watered wine to help my hiccups. From the window we could see Francesco and the brothers working their way through the crowd toward the palazzo, but everyone wanted a word with him, so we would have to wait. I spotted Egidio and Rufino and Leone and Bernardo, talking with townspeople who had attended Francesco's sermon. Elias offered to go outside and speed things along, but I didn't think it necessary, and besides, I felt better for having him near. I was surprisingly at ease with this man, so like me in so many ways.

Mengarda fussed around the room, torn between bringing out her embroidered cushions and hangings because company was coming, and keeping everything simple because that company was Francesco. We let her buzz about like a nervous honeybee, and Elias and I took a few moments to share each other's recent news. I told him of Vanna's decision, and he told me more of Francesco's ill-fated journey by sea.

The first ones to join us were Egidio and Prassede. Prassede must have recovered from whatever disappointment she felt about not joining Chiara's sisterhood, because she was talking even faster than usual. Elias drew her off to give me a chance to greet Egidio. More brothers arrived, but not yet Francesco.

"Giacoma, I'm so glad you're here," Egidio said, and I felt warm all over, knowing this dearest of Francesco's brothers never said anything he didn't absolutely mean.

"And I you," I said, then hiccuped. I took another mouthful of my wined water, held my breath, and swallowed it in a series of tiny gulps.

He glanced at prattling Prassede. "How did you ever manage, all the way here?" he said, raising his eyebrows comically.

I grinned back at him. I hadn't been planning to admit this to anyone, but I couldn't resist. "I talked her into taking a vow of silence before we left, as a penance."

He whooped with laughter. Several of the others turned toward us then, but I kept my attention on Egidio and tried to control my face. It was not easy, especially since I hadn't yet rid myself of the hiccups, but I didn't want to have to explain the joke to anyone else, lest Prassede be hurt.

"And how was your trip?" he finally said, still chuckling.

"Lovely. Very quiet," I said, and we both giggled. "I vowed silence too, and it worked out well. But I'm afraid you and the others will bear the brunt of all those stored-up words."

Before we could jest any more at Prassede's expense, Francesco entered the room, with Leone and Bernardo behind him. He came right to me, and the affection in his smile lifted my heart. I promptly forgot—for the moment, at least—my annoyance that he had not told me of Vanna's plans.

"Welcome, Giacoma, to Assisi," he said. "Does my city please you?"

"I love it here," I said, and I was not exaggerating, or speaking out of mere courtesy. Assisi was a revelation to my Roman eyes—to all my senses, really. "The facade of San Rufino alone would be enough to make Assisi one of the most beautiful places in the world."

"Yes. Did you notice the lions flanking the door? I was preaching about them, but I don't think you arrived in time to hear me."

I had seen them, two statues that came up to my waist when I was on the step, to my chest when I stood on the paving stones. One lion feasted on some hapless prey animal—I wasn't sure what it was intended to be—but the other feasted on the head of a seated man, huge paws resting on his victim's thighs. The man's back was upright, his hands bound behind him as he faced the beast. It was a disturbing picture of martyrdom, troubling and yet beautifully carved. Francesco had rested his hand lightly on the man's head as he spoke to the crowd.

I was going to ask Francesco what he had said about the lions, but Prassede bounded up to us, already talking.

"Father Francesco, it was so inspiring to hear you preach! And it's wonderful to see you! And we met Sister Chiara, and Vanna is Sister Vanna now, and Bishop Guido said mass this morning, and Arnolfo and Mengarda have been such perfect hosts, and we brought you some of Amata's almond cakes—"

"Almond cakes! How kind, Giacoma. You make it hard to renounce the world," he said.

I laughed. "Perhaps you can permit yourself a taste of the world now and again, to remember what you're renouncing."

"It is our policy to accept alms when they are generously offered to us," he said, mock-seriously. "Perhaps we might sample your gifts soon, for preaching is hungry work."

"I'll bring them," Prassede said, already moving toward the door. She took Sobilia to help her, and they went up to our chamber where the gift waited, carefully packed.

Elias joined us, and he, Egidio, Francesco and I enjoyed a few moments together before the women came back with the almond cakes. Mengarda had her own delicacies to offer, but she graciously allowed the cakes to take pride of place. It was pleasant and convivial, but after the day's activities—the loss of my servant, meeting Chiara, and the strange exchange with the miracle child—my own hunger was for a chance to talk with Francesco. He was aware of my yearning, and he assured me we would find time.

"Mengarda has invited all of us for dinner tomorrow," he said. "It is too much for her to tend to us all, so only Elias and I will accept, and then we can take the afternoon to talk and pray together."

For the time being, I would have to be satisfied with that.

The brothers stayed at Mengarda's palazzo for perhaps another hour or two, leading us in prayer and in song, and Francesco told a couple of stories, tales with a moral lesson but also imbued with humor and playfulness. He was adept at finding that artful balance; it was one of the great strengths of his preaching.

Later, as Francesco and the brothers prepared to leave, I remembered Vanna's belongings. I asked Francesco what to do with them, and he told me people who had items to donate to the poor took them into the church and left them in a designated area. The churchmen then gathered everything and stored it in the sacristy until the next Saturday, when it was distributed to the beggars after mass in the morning. Elias and Egidio offered to take Vanna's things to the church for me, so Mengarda left to fetch Vanna's shoes, and Prassede and I went to our chamber to collect the clothing.

I watched out the window as Elias and Egidio took the donations into the church. Egidio had whispered to me not to let Francesco do it, because he could never enter a church without sinking to his knees and praying for a long time, and they wanted to get back to the Porziuncola before nightfall. Prassede was unwittingly doing her part to keep Francesco out of San Rufino by chattering with him, though he and the other brothers were on their feet and ready to leave.

Egidio went into the church. Elias was right behind him, but he stopped and looked up at the carvings over his head—I suspected he admired them as much as I did—and I saw him rest his hand unconsciously on the statue by the door, as Francesco had done.

Except I was almost certain Elias rested his hand on the lion, not on the man.

*

The next day, midmorning, Elias was the first to arrive. He told us Francesco would be along as soon as he could, but always there were townspeople eager to talk to him and ask for his counsel and his blessing.

We settled down on two facing window seats to wait for him. The delay suited me, because I had wanted to ask Elias's advice on some financial matters. I knew plenty of financially astute people in Rome—I was, in fact, such a person myself—but they seldom addressed the moral issues I was wrestling with, being very much in and of the world. I thought Elias might supply the needed balance between pragmatism and the gospel life.

"Elias, I would very much like to drop the lawsuit against the Holy Father—"

"That would please Francesco."

"Hear me out. I'd like to, but I don't feel that I can, because my husband would never want me to. But there are other changes I could make to aid the poor and set aside some money for our hospital project, only I want to be sure those measures don't harm my boys or their future in any way. Do you see my problem?"

"Yes, clearly. What are you considering?"

"I'm considering liquidating half of my possessions."

Elias whistled. He had a rough idea of what that would amount to. "Did your husband not intend for his estate to go to his sons?"

"Nobody needs as much money as they will inherit when they come of age. Francesco always says wealth creates only temptations and danger."

"It does a bit more than that, I think." Elias was smiling. "Especially in your hands."

"What about a third? Plus the income from my dowry properties?"

"What if the third included *all* of your almsgiving? And how about half of your dowry income?"

I did a quick calculation. Given my current level of almsgiving, this would be a losing proposition for the hospital.

"A third, to include any donations I make to the church but not alms given directly to the poor. And half my dowry income." The church would survive without my aid better than my beggars would. And my dowry was mine by law to use any way I chose, so I was already making something of a concession.

Elias laughed aloud. "Done. I feel like I'm arguing on behalf of your husband, Giacoma, and I didn't even know him. If that's what you want to do, then by all means do it. It's a generous impulse, and as you say, it should still leave plenty for your heirs."

My thoughts exactly. I probably would have done it in any case, but it was comforting to have the approval of the one brother I knew who I could count on to be sensible about money.

Our conversation wandered onto other topics, and soon Francesco joined us. We enjoyed a lavish dinner, and Mengarda basked in our praise. Elias excused himself to go pray in San Rufino, and Mengarda hovered for a short while, but she was gracious enough to give Francesco and me our privacy when she realized we needed some time together.

We sat on the bench in the hall where we had eaten, though the table had been put away. I was sewing a set of brightly colored cloth balls for the miracle child, balls which I stuffed with rags. Lovely, *quiet* balls. From that same bag I produced a pouch with the last four almond cakes. Francesco took one and bit into it with gusto.

"You really do like those, don't you?" I said, wadding up scraps of linen and pushing them into a yellow ball.

"I do indeed, Giacomina. But I would like them even better if they were made by your own hands."

I hooted at that. "No, you wouldn't. You've never eaten anything I tried to cook."

"And yet you told me you'd learn to cook, and it couldn't be too hard."

"I may have misspoken. But why not just eat Amata's cakes? You know they'll be good."

"Do this for me, Giacomina? Learn to make the almond cakes?"

I could never tell Francesco no, though we hadn't yet cleared the air about Vanna's little surprise. "If you wish it, Francesco, I'll ask Amata to teach me. But I warrant the difference between hers and mine will be obvious, and it will be hers you want to eat."

"And I warrant you'll test me," he countered, and I flushed. That had indeed been in the back of my mind. He saw it on my face and chuckled.

"And you're hurt that I kept Vanna's plans from you, aren't you?"

I nodded. I was getting used to having no secrets from Frances-co—probably the reason it rankled so much when he kept something important from me.

"You know the reason. Also, the final decision was Chiara's."

"You mean Chiara might have said no to Vanna?"

"Yes. I expected her to interview the girl and then decide, but it sounds like she took one look and gave her approval. I trust Chiara when it comes to things like that. God makes his will known to her."

I didn't answer. Instead I finished stitching up the opening in the yellow ball and moved on to stuffing the blue one.

He watched me for a while. "Are you at peace yet with the way things happened for Vanna?" he finally asked.

"No. Not in my heart. I still think you could have trusted me, and I don't see what any of you accomplished by keeping it secret."

"Giacomina, I know you don't understand, and it doesn't matter. You are bound by a vow of obedience to me, remember? And that means you accept my decisions, even when they're wrong."

Yes, I supposed it did, and I lowered my eyes to my work. But there was something about "even when they're wrong" that carried a hint of apology, and I found that comforting. I decided to let the whole thing go, and I felt better immediately.

I started stitching the blue ball. Francesco finished his almond cake and refused a second. Never greedy, he was abstemious enough to concern me, for he was alarmingly thin. He had summoned abundant energy and passion while preaching to the crowd, but in private he was more subdued than I recalled.

"I've had a dream," he said, and something in his voice made me look up.

"I dreamed of a small black hen with the feathers of a dove. She had many, many chicks—so many she could not even begin to protect them all under her wings. They darted about, going in all directions at once. It was a sorrow to her, and a worry, for she loved them all."

I had seen how rapidly Francesco's order was growing. Branches of the brotherhood had sprung up in other cities, both near and far away. Every day more men chose to follow Francesco, so it didn't take any special gifts to figure out what such a dream meant.

"As many as that, then?"

"Not yet. But there will be."

"You don't have to take care of all of them by yourself, Francesco."

"They are nonetheless my responsibility. But you're right, I do have help. I have Pietro Cattani, and I will leave the order in his care when I go to Spain. And God has given me Elias, who has wonderful skills in dealing with people and who is devoted to the order. So as you say, I am not alone. Still, it feels like a burden sometimes, and perhaps that's why the hermitage on La Verna tempted me so."

He lapsed into a moody silence, and I finished my stitching on the blue ball, feeling ashamed of myself for letting my own responsibilities overwhelm me at times. I had only a household to manage, albeit a large one; Francesco had what may have been the fastest growing religious order in the history of the world.

At least Spain didn't sound as dangerous as the Holy Land, and Pietro Cattani was a good man, if not decisive.

But I didn't share those musings with him, and soon Elias rejoined us and our conversation turned to other topics.

*

The rest of our time in Assisi passed quietly. We saw a little more of the brothers, and we made another trip to San Damiano, where we reported to Vanna that her donated clothing had been well received by poor women who were delighted to have it. Chiara and I discussed the hospital idea further, and while I can't say we became friends, we did establish a civil and efficient way of working together, based on mutual respect. She agreed to allow me to make a donation for the infirmary and for certain needs at San Damiano, though she wouldn't accept money, so I had to hire a cart and go and make the purchases myself.

I didn't mind. Shopping was a way to get to know Assisi and its environs better, and the city did please me, though I overpaid drastically for linen to make sheets and chemises. I couldn't very well hide my wealth, and I was well acquainted with that gleam in the merchant's eye.

He probably didn't realize that prices were even higher in Rome.

Our day of departure arrived. We assembled our men-at-arms in the piazza outside Mengarda and Arnolfo's palazzo, along with all our mounts and beasts of burden, and packed everything for the journey. We distributed gifts: for our hosts, fine ceramics; gray cloth for the brothers; coins to be given to the poor; and the set of red, blue, green, yellow, and white balls for the Miracle Child, who had been serene and silent ever since Francesco's sermon. I handed him the balls and he smiled, though he did not speak.

We said our farewells. Francesco and most of the brothers were at the Porziuncola that morning, having said goodbye the previous day, but Elias and Egidio had come to see us off.

I was eager to see my boys, but the trip would take us at least two weeks and probably longer. When I sent a messenger to Francesco, we counted it as a five-day trip each way in fair weather, but that was one man plus a guard, moving fast, with a planned change of horse and no carts or laden pack animals to slow him down. It took much longer to transport this many people, all these clothes and furnishings and new purchases, and a chatty recluse with a weak bladder.

Also, I had arranged for one final gift—a crate of eggs, carefully packed in straw, to be delivered to San Damiano two days after our departure.

November 1215, Rome

14

THE lopsided almond cake sagged and puddled, a pathetic mess on the worktable. I wrinkled my nose in frustration.

Amata clucked sympathetically. "It's better than the last ones, at least."

"Not by much," I muttered. The last batch had been floury and dry, practically inedible. If I could have merged the two batches, I might have produced something more like the tidy cakes, all perfectly square and identical, lined up in front of Amata in four neat rows.

"Do you want to try baking them?" she asked. She was smiling, but I heard the weariness in her voice. We'd been at this a long time, and Amata's pregnancy tired her.

"No." I frowned at the sticky blobs melting in front of me. "Let's just bake yours, and then at least there will be something to feed Francesco and the brothers."

"We still have another two days," she reminded me. "They aren't coming until Tuesday."

Francesco and a large portion of his burgeoning crowd of followers were in Rome to attend the Holy Father's long-awaited church council. Actually, the brothers weren't attending it so much as taking advantage of the presence of so many influential churchmen, which was why they were staying in the hospice of Santo Spirito in Sasso instead of with us. Cardinal Giovanni, God rest him, had died two months before, and Francesco and the brethren wanted to find a new protector. Some in the pope's inner circle wanted to crack down on new orders, lumping them together with the most outlandish of the heretical sects, and the order needed someone to speak for it.

I knew the churchman Francesco had in mind, and I'd been doing what I could to smooth the way, but it remained to be seen whether

Bishop Ugolino, Cardinal of Ostia, would agree. The crucial meeting between Francesco and the Cardinal was set for Monday.

We'd had only one brief visit from the brothers since they first arrived in Rome, and we were eager to see them. I had been alarmed at how thin Francesco had become. He seemed tired and ill, and all of my instincts were to feed him. I was determined to serve him almond cakes made with my own hands, albeit with a lot of coaching from Amata.

This was my third attempt, and my arms ached from having crushed a vast quantity of almonds in the mortar. Amata had offered to do it—her pregnancy didn't affect her muscular arms—but I insisted. Every bit of these cakes was to be my own work, starting with grinding the nuts. I had pulverized enough of the little devils to provide for an army, but after three batches the supply was finally running low.

"My hands lack the skill and delicacy of yours, Amata," I told her.

She snorted, and held up her calloused, reddened hands and made a face at them.

"I don't mean they *look* delicate, my literal friend. I mean you can do such intricate things with them, and shape things just right, and read temperatures, and textures—"

"Giacoma, your hands are much more skilled than mine." She pointed at my doughy fingers. "I've seen you spend five days embroidering a single butterfly's wing, and it was gorgeous."

"Oh, embroidery," I said, waving my hand and dismissing my favorite form of relaxation as if it were nothing, though in truth I enjoyed her praise. "Embroidery is easy. It's all colors and lines, and the different stitches." And it let me make beautiful things that didn't dissolve into sticky disasters in front of my eyes.

"It's not so easy for everyone, you know. I can't do it. Even Lucia can't do it as well as you can. Remember how quickly you learned the Assisi style. One visit there and you had it."

I did have some gift for the art of decorating cloth, and I took a lot of pleasure in doing it. It was generous of her to remind me, but it didn't solve the immediate problem, which was my determination to have almond cakes of my own ready to put before Francesco. I hoped to fool him into thinking they were Amata's work, just to prove I could.

"Well, if Francesco doesn't like my almond cakes, then he should have to wear a tunic that you've embroidered," I said, and she laughed.

"That would show him," she said. "If you're not going to try again tonight, let's get mine baked, and then we can take a rest." She studied the fire, looking for the place where the embers were exactly right, and used the poker to smooth an area for the lidded pan. We did own an oven, out in the courtyard, but it wasn't worth firing for a small batch of cakes, and the ovens in the bakehouse down the street would be cold by now, so the covered pan would have to do.

Fortunately, Amata had the knack. She and Brother Fire, as Francesco called it, spoke the same language, and I knew the technique would work for her. My relationship with cakes was more contentious. In a long-ago moment of culinary overconfidence I had tried frying some ricotta cakes, since I couldn't figure out how long to bake them or where in the fire to put them. The experiment was not a success. The boys still liked to tease me about those cakes, though Amata had been diplomatically sympathetic. We'd saved the fry pan, but barely.

Amata prodded the pan into place and used the shovel to heap its flat lid with glowing coals. Satisfied, she sat back, put her hands on the small of her back, and arched to stretch herself.

"My belly's getting so big it makes my back hurt," she said, grimacing.

A cough from the doorway caused us to turn. Renzo the Tinker, formerly our most faithful beggar and now one of our permanent guests, hobbled into the kitchen, one hand clutching the door frame for support.

"What do you need, Renzo?" Amata asked him.

"Have either of you seen Salvestra?"

We both shook our heads. Our elderly former midwife, another permanent guest, spent most of her days meandering through the corridors and rooms of the palazzo, in slow but constant motion. We had given up trying to keep track of her.

"She's probably wandering, Renzo," I said.

"Sister Prassede says she hasn't seen her since Sister Bartola started to bathe the other two ladies. That's why I left, you know. Wouldn't have been proper to stay," he said primly.

Amata and I held back smiles. Renzo was incorrigible. He was ancient, but his eye for the ladies had not faded, and if he wasn't pursuing Salvestra, he'd be turning his attentions to poor bedridden Isotta, who was terrified of him. One of the nurses had to stay in the women's chamber at all times, thanks to our lovable but amorous Renzo, whose abject need for shelter had made us scuttle our plans for a women-only hospital. After his hovel burned down and the religious at Santo Spirito claimed they were full and couldn't take him, we could hardly have left him out on the streets.

He was probably the reason Salvestra spent hours walking around the palazzo. Though aged, she could outmaneuver Renzo, whose joints pained him more every day. She lived in a world of her own, but once in a while she emerged from her fog and startled us by becoming sharp and incisive, though it never lasted long.

Renzo, Salvestra, and Isotta were our first patients, along with wizened Meliorata who did nothing but lie in her bed and hum or sing softly to herself. Also, at the request of our parish priest, we had taken in a pair of foundling twins, a boy and a girl, and with them Nuta, the wetnurse the church had hired to care for them. Prassede and her fellow penitent, the redoubtable and dour Sister Bartola, had their hands full taking care of everyone.

I had ambitions to purchase an appropriate property and set up a real hospital soon, but meanwhile we practiced on the four old people and the infants. Circumstances had left each of them without a home, so we had reopened the closed wing of the palazzo and welcomed them into our household. Most of the time neither they nor we regretted it, though there were occasional exceptions, usually involving Renzo.

As for the infants, the old ladies doted on them, and so did the rest of us. Nuta, a quiet, self-effacing young widow, went about with sad eyes, for her own child had not lived to taste her milk, but she was gentle and loving with the babes.

Renzo shuffled closer to us and peered conspiratorially in both directions, then, satisfied we were alone, he whispered hoarsely, "I think Salvestra wanders because she's feeling jealous of the time I spend with the lovely Isotta."

I heard Amata sputter, and somehow I managed not to look at her. Fighting to stay serious, I said, "Renzo, Salvestra wanders all the time, whether you're with Isotta or not. You know that."

His expression was one of wounded dignity. "Aye, Giacoma, I know she does, but did you ever think perhaps she wouldn't, if she'd just settle down with me? We could wed, and she could move into my chamber, and I'd see that she was content. And I'd be faithful to her, I would—Isotta is pretty, but it's Salvestra I love."

"Renzo, Salvestra doesn't want to marry again. For one thing, she's noticed that she's seventy years of age or more. As are you, if you recall."

"Well, you never know. Maybe she'll come around. The sisters asked me to find out where she's gone, so I'm back to searching for her. If you see her, send her up to Sister Prassede." And he shuffled back out.

As soon as he was out of earshot, Amata and I allowed ourselves a chuckle at his expense. We adored Renzo, but he did keep us slightly off balance much of the time. He had got it into his head that his job was to protect us, and the fact that he could barely walk did not deter him. When the beggars arrived each day, if any new men were among them it was all we could do to keep Renzo from charging at them as fast as he could hobble, brandishing the poker. The first time Egidio and Brother Bernardo visited after our gallant tinker moved in, Renzo almost succeeded in driving them off, until we persuaded him they were welcome guests.

We were trading jests about the many loves of Renzo the Bold when the elusive Salvestra appeared at the kitchen door.

"Ah, you've been found," I said. "Everyone's looking for you, Salvestra."

She turned her mild, filmy gaze on me. "Everybody's looking, nobody's finding. Not looking very well, then, are they?" She sniffed the air. "Burned soon."

Amata hastily prodded the pan out of the embers, tipped the lid off with the poker, and used the spatula to remove the fragrant cakes and set them on a tray. They were on the verge of being overdone, but still edible, so we would at least have those to put before our guests at Tuesday dinner.

"Sit down, Salvestra, and when the cakes are cool enough you may have one," I said, and she sat obediently on the end of the bench. Prassede could wait a few more minutes. I enjoyed Salvestra's unpredictable remarks and her gentle detachment from reality; sometimes she made more sense than most of the other people in my life.

"Isotta and Meliorata like cakes too," she observed, her eyes on the steaming sweets. "And Sister Prassede and Sister Bartola. Or maybe not Sister Bartola. She likes vinegar, I think. But Renzo likes cakes. Renzo will take all the cakes, if you let him. You won't let him, will you?"

"No. We won't let him," I assured her. I began to worry that we wouldn't have enough cakes for our guests. As if to reinforce my fears, both of my sons dashed into the kitchen, the ever-vigilant Lucia right behind them. The boys' tutor Tommasso, who was besotted with Lucia, brought up the rear. I fully expected to see Renzo and Prassede next, and even Nuta and the babies. It must have been that scent of sweet almond cakes wafting through the palazzo.

"Cakes!" Uccellino exclaimed, grinning. He grabbed one.

"Hot!" I warned him. Too late—he yelped and dropped the cake and stuck his fingers into his mouth.

I sighed. I would need to make a new batch of cakes on Monday, if I hoped to have any of my own for Francesco, and now Amata would have to make more as well, if we wanted to keep everybody happy.

When, exactly, had I taken on the task of keeping everybody happy? I could almost hear Graziano's voice saying, "Giacomina, you were born trying to keep everybody happy." It had amused him, and he told me it was one of the things he loved about me, even though it got expensive sometimes.

We were dividing the rapidly cooling sweets to distribute among all interested parties when Massimo stuck his head in.

"Guests, Giacoma," he said.

I remembered hearing some activity at the front door while we were talking with Salvestra, but I had left it to my steward, thinking it was probably a delivery of some sort.

"Who's here?"

"Your brother-in-law and your nephew. I've sent them up to the hall. It sounded a little crowded in here."

And my late husband's family were not people you could entertain in a kitchen, but Massimo was diplomatic enough not to say so.

"Thank you, Massimo. I'll be right there. Here, have a cake." He didn't have to be asked twice; Amata was already handing her husband one, with a smile sweeter than any cake.

I wasn't in the mood to be a gracious hostess to the Frangipani. But there they were, and I would have to play lady of the house. I knew what Cencio wanted, and we might as well get it over with.

15

I left them to it, first asking for someone to bring up some wine and a few cakes from our rapidly dwindling supply, and went upstairs to the hall.

I thought it unfair of him to bring his son Pierino along. Cencio wanted me to let him foster my boys for military training, which involved learning a lot of new ways to skewer and bash people and make life difficult for horses. Both Giovanni and Uccellino were in awe of their cousin Pierino, a cocky, strutting lad whose voice had finally finished changing, and his presence would be enough to make them add their pleas to Cencio's relentless attempts to make me feel guilty.

My brother-in-law hadn't paid us a visit since we opened our modest hospital. Maybe Renzo would hobble in and threaten them with a poker, or Salvestra might float through the hall and say something strange to them. Maybe Amata would send up my almond cakes instead of hers. One could always hope.

Cencio sat on the bench, and Pierino stood next to the window. Cencio got to his feet as I entered the hall, and we greeted each other with artificial smiles.

"You and the boys are in good health, Giacoma?" he asked. Pierino deigned to glance over his shoulder and nod to me, then resumed looking out the window.

"We are, Cencio. And I trust all is well in your household?"

"Well enough. This gathering of the Holy Father's has filled our city with all manner of people, not just the men of the church—and some of those are churlish enough—but the rabble they insist on bringing with them. The noise never ceases. You can't ride in the street without scattering peasants and country boys gawking at our ruins and monuments and holy places while their mouths hang open."

Pierino sniggered. Cencio loved that boy, but for my life, I couldn't see how he did it. Still, a parent is a parent. Always.

Cencio's view of the world had never fit well with my own. The money flowing from the purses of those pilgrims keeps our diminished city alive, and as far as I was concerned, all were welcome.

A long pause ensued, while I tried to think of something light and casual to say. The awkwardness was broken by Lucia, who had been elected to bring us the wine and cakes, and my boys, who rushed in and greeted their cousin noisily.

Lucia asked if we would like anything more, I said no, and she withdrew. I couldn't put this discussion off any longer.

"Boys, why don't you take Pierino down to the stable and show him the new pony?" I suggested, and off they went in a boisterous knot of half-grown masculinity, leaving me alone to grapple yet again with Cencio's inexhaustible ambitions.

"That wasn't the kitchen girl, was it?" he said, taking a cup of wine and a cake.

"No, she's the boys' nurse." I suppose he thought it unusual to see the nurse carrying a tray of cakes, but since Vanna's departure we had become a bit lax about separating everyone's traditional duties.

Cencio frowned but said nothing. I didn't want to join him on the bench, so I sat on the window seat, which meant he would have to turn around if he intended to talk to me.

He swung his legs over the bench and faced me, brushing cake crumbs from his lap. "Giacoma, we must talk," he said, staring at me as accusingly as if I had suggested a vow of silence instead.

"Very well, then, Brother-in-law. What do you wish to say to me?"

"Two things. First, as the head of the Frangipane family, I must again ask: are you considering remarriage? If that is your wish, the Frangipani will not hold it against you, and we will gladly care for your sons. We care about your happiness, Giacoma, and we are prepared to be generous."

That was different. Not that he hadn't brought it up before, but then the emphasis had certainly not been on my happiness. His wife must have been coaching him. Also, Graziano had two other brothers and not a few cousins who might have disputed Cencio's claim that he was head of the family.

Bringing up the possibility of my remarrying was only his blatant attempt to stake a claim on Graziano's fortune. That property was mine alone to control, as long as I remained a chaste widow. Those were the terms, and I liked them just fine. Graziano knew his brothers; he had written his will with care.

"How odd you should ask, Cencio," I said sweetly. "My brother and his lady wife were here recently asking me the same thing. I assured them, as I'm now assuring you, I have no wish to marry again. I will live out my life as Graziano's widow, fulfilling his wishes for his sons and his estate. You need not fear on that score." I was sure his persistent efforts to get my boys into his house had more to do with the estate than it did with any concern for his nephews. If he took on the care of my sons, he gained a toehold in claiming some share of Graziano's wealth—or at least that's how Cencio would see it.

"I am delighted to hear it, Giacoma," he said.

No, you aren't. You look like you just swallowed vinegar, or possibly one of my almond cakes. It was a challenge for him. He could not appear to encourage any disloyalty on my part to his late brother, nor to urge me to abandon my sons, yet he would have liked nothing better. Too bad. We don't always get what we want. For one thing, Cencio had no idea that I was now Brother Giacoma, which involved a vow of chastity. That was not general knowledge in Rome.

"When I married your brother, I promised him my love forever, not only until one of us met our death. I will be with him in Paradise one day, and until then I neither want nor will take any other husband."

"Very commendable." He refilled his wine cup from the jar Lucia had left. "Let's talk about the second thing, then."

Here it came.

"Giacoma, your boys are more than old enough to begin learning the skills they'll need so they can take their proper place in Roman society. Had my beloved brother lived, he would have taught them well. He excelled in all the knightly arts—in weaponry, strategy, leadership, courtly behavior, godly acts of charity and mercy—he was even a fine rider, despite the accident."

My hand gripped my wine cup so tightly my knuckles went white. Cencio had a lot to learn about persuasion.

"Understand, Sister-in-law, I'm not blaming you. Your grief is laudable and appropriate, but it has had some unfortunate results."

I waited, saying nothing.

"When my brother lived, this house was run the way a nobleman's house should be run. There were no filthy, lice-ridden old beggars wandering around, getting in everyone's way and eating their fill of your food."

Ah. He's met Renzo.

"The hospital patients are our guests, and we can well afford their food," I said shortly.

"And you permit your servants to call you by your given name. You work alongside them like a serving maid, living like threadbare penitents sharing some hovel in the name of God."

Guilty as accused, except it was a palazzo we were sharing, and we weren't exactly threadbare.

"You have a problem with doing things in the name of God, Brother-in-law?" I asked him, working to keep my voice calm. How was it that this ridiculous man could be so closely related to my Graziano? I was beginning to understand why Francesco told the brothers to leave their families behind if they aspired to live a gospel life. It would give me the greatest pleasure to leave this one behind. Far, far behind.

He scowled. "Giacoma, I revere the church and her teachings as much as you do. But it remains true that this house has gone downhill since my brother's death. I share your grief, but you've no right to throw away your sons' heritage. You've been too influenced by that malodorous heretic from the hinterlands and his grimy followers."

All right, Cencio, you obnoxious lackwit. Now you've done it. Out comes the heavy weaponry.

I looked him up and down, coolly, taking my time. "I fear you may be alone in your worries, Brother-in-law. When Cardinal Ugolino, the Bishop of Ostia, dined with us last week, he had nothing but praise for the way I teach my sons, and for our charitable efforts and our generosity to the church. I think it may have been in part because the cardinal is soon to become the protector of Francesco's order"—I hoped, at least—"and because he approves of those who try to follow in the footsteps of Our Lord."

Cencio had started when I mentioned the cardinal's name. Ugolino was one of the three men closest to the Holy Father, and though Cencio was not a clever man, he was shrewd enough to avoid placing himself deliberately in opposition to such a one. A point for my side.

But my brother-in-law was a man of little imagination and a firmly fixed agenda, and so he plunged onward.

"Giacoma, my dear kinswoman," he said, a false smile plastered on his face, his open hands turned upward in a placating gesture. "I meant no criticism of you. I have the utmost reverence for your virtuous life and for your charities."

Of course you do. I ate an almond cake, all the while watching his face as he tried to figure out what to say next.

He stalled, setting his wine cup on the floor and adjusting his robe. Finally he remembered his script. "My meaning is only this, Giacoma: my brother's sons, my dear nephews, have certainly benefited from your careful teaching, and they will continue to do so. But it is essential for their futures that they also begin to learn knightly ways so they can grow into their heritage. It's what Graziano wanted for them."

I was in a vulnerable position, and we both knew it. That was indeed what Graziano had planned for them. I would fight like a she-bear protecting her cubs for Francesco and the brothers, for my patients, and for all the beloved friends in my household, but when it came to my own sons, I was too much a creature of my world. They were Graziano's heirs, and Cencio was Graziano's brother and their uncle and, to hear him tell it, the head of the family they belonged to and I never truly could. My boys were not mine to raise as I would, or at least not mine alone. They had other allegiances I was obliged to respect for my late husband's sake, and therefore I was not free to make this decision for them, young though they were.

My hesitation must have showed on my face, for Cencio pressed his advantage.

"My brother would have begun their training by now."

"They have a tutor. Their Latin is coming along, they're both adept at figures, and Massimo is teaching them about horses and riding."

"The tutor is fine enough, Giacoma, but they will have to know how to use a sword, how to ride into battle, how to joust, how to conduct themselves in war. Would Graziano have left *that* up to a mere steward, especially one with a useless arm?"

A small part of that was true. Graziano would have worked with the boys himself, and he no doubt would have begun before this. I felt uneasy, and unsure what Graziano would want me to do next. He had loved his brothers, even though he knew better than to trust them about money. And he had certainly intended for his sons to be part of the knightly caste.

I suppose I had been lax, thanks to my total lack of enthusiasm for knightly culture. There's nothing like being born into a social niche to help you see its limitations. Unless you're as simple as Cencio. Then you believe all the foolish talk without question.

Massimo's damaged arm doesn't keep him from riding like a prince compared to you, with your fat backside.

But before I could compose a more acceptable rebuttal to speak aloud, we were interrupted by Pierino and the boys, who thundered up the stairs and burst in, talking excitedly. Did boys of that age never just *walk* anywhere?

"Mother! Pierino says we're to come and live with him! We'll learn to fight with swords, and we'll joust! We'll be knights, like Father!" Giovanni couldn't contain his delight, though Uccellino was subdued.

"That hasn't been decided yet, Giovanni," I said, and his face fell.

"But, Mother—"

"Your uncle and I were just discussing it. If you want to be part of the discussion, sit down, and talk with us calmly."

Cencio smirked. He thought he was winning, but I wasn't through yet. Both boys obediently sat on the bench, and Pierino stood behind them, leaving me to face all four Frangipane males.

Very well. I'd give it my best.

"First, you have your lessons with Tommasso. Second, if you leave this house, what will Lucia do for work? Third, Massimo is perfectly capable of teaching you everything you need to know at this age, and the finer points can be learned in a year or two, when you're older. And fourth, Uccellino, your health is not robust enough to be training with weapons, and you're only nine. You, at least, must stay here and become stronger first." *Listen to me. I sound like I've already given up on keeping Giovanni.*

"Tommasso is their tutor?" Cencio asked. The boys and I nodded. "I've no problem with letting him teach them at my house. Pierino could use some practice with his Latin, too." Pierino stuck his lower lip out in a childish pout. "I'll pay the man whatever you're paying him, and enough extra to teach Pierino as well. No problem there."

I faced my boys. "Remember, Tommasso teaches Ricco too," I said, and Uccellino squirmed, though Giovanni was untroubled. "Do you want Ricco to do without lessons, then?"

"You can hire someone else to teach him," Giovanni said, but at the same time Uccellino murmured something about Lucia.

Cencio turned his attention to my younger son. "You've no need of a nurse at your age, have you, lad?" he asked, not unkindly, but clearly not brooking any arguments.

Uccellino shook his head and stared at the floor.

"Also, my boy, you're too old for a nursery name," Cencio added. "You bear your father's name, and from now on you'll use it. You're Graziano, and you should be proud of that." Uccellino did not look up, but he nodded his head once, which was enough to satisfy his uncle.

He bears my name too, for whatever that's worth. Probably not much, to Cencio.

"What about Uccellino's health?" I demanded, deliberately ignoring my brother-in-law's comment. "It's no small consideration, Cencio."

"He's under maestro Marco's care, is he not?"

"Yes."

"So is our entire household. The man comes at a run whenever we call for him—he knows how to earn his coin. Your boy'll be fine. If at some point he requires your motherly care, we'll bring him back to you until he's healthy. You can see our houses from here, so it's not as if they'll be going far away."

"Uccellino? Do you want to go?"

He glanced at his brother. "I want to be with Giovanni," he said in a small voice.

I knew that would be his answer. He adored his older brother, and the boys had always been inseparable. I was losing this battle, and I didn't even entirely understand how it was happening.

"You wouldn't be here when Francesco and the others come to visit," I said, a little desperately. Both boys looked forward to seeing the brothers as much as I did.

Cencio snorted. "The boys are Frangipani, Giacoma. They don't need the company of a bunch of ragged, smelly bumpkins from Perugia, or wherever it is they come from."

"Assisi," I said automatically, watching my boys. Uccellino had stiffened at Cencio's words and his worried frown deepened, but his brother hadn't even been listening, so busy was he formulating his own plan.

"We could come back here on Sundays, Mother, and attend church with you," Giovanni said earnestly, "and then we'd see them whenever they're in town. They always stay over a Sunday. And we could spend time with Lucia then, and we could eat Amata's cakes and chicken and sausage pie and fruit tarts, and we could tell Ricco and Massimo all the things we've been doing. And we'd be learning all the things Father would teach us, if he were here." And then, because he was only eleven, he couldn't help adding, "And we'll have *swords*! And *lances*! And our own horses, big ones!"

"Would you not miss home?" I asked, my shaky voice betraying me. "And our patients?"

Pierino spoke, finally. "You mean those old beggars you harbor? I saw the old man, walking like this." He started to lurch around the room in an ugly, exaggerated caricature of Renzo's painful gait. His father laughed, but Uccellino frowned. Even Giovanni was taken aback, though he rallied quickly.

"Mother, it's time for us to do this. Everything will be fine, you'll see. Please allow us to go." We held each other's eyes for a long time. I was the first to turn away.

It all moved very quickly, then. I agreed reluctantly that Cencio would come for the boys on Tuesday after dinner. At least they'd enjoy one meal with Francesco and the brothers. And I'd have their things packed and ready to send with them. They would return on Sundays. I would try to persuade Tommasso to transfer his services to Cencio's household, and I would further try to persuade Lucia to stay on as part of mine. That last shouldn't be too difficult, in light of the two babes already living with us and Amata's child coming soon. She'd have plenty to do, and she'd see Giovanni and Uccellino on Sundays.

I would do what I could to make the best of it. Sometimes I wearied of trying to keep everything running smoothly, and I just wanted to retire to my chamber and let the pieces fall where they would. But I was never able to do it, somehow. Certainly not this time.

On one level, I feared losing the boys to Cencio. On another, deeper level, I did not believe it would happen. They might live in his house, but they would never truly be his. I knew my boys. I knew their hearts, and I trusted their true natures to keep them from turning into power-crazed, arrogant men like their uncles. Somehow their father had escaped that fate; the boys could, too. With luck, they might even avoid an obnoxious adolescence like Pierino's.

I held one additional advantage: Cencio could push me only so far, because in his bid for the Frangipane consortium to become the primary bankers to the pope, he needed Graziano's money. And I controlled that money. If I pulled out of the consortium, Cencio and the others would lose out to the Pierleoni, and they knew it.

No, Cencio alone could never have made me agree to this plan for the boys. The plea in Giovanni's eyes, so like his father's, had done that.

16

Cencio and Pierino, their objective achieved, wasted no time in leaving. Giovanni and Uccellino raced off to decide what to pack, and I summoned Lucia, Tommasso, and Ricco so I could explain the situation to them, though I dreaded the conversation.

It was a sobering discussion, though I already felt glum enough. Tommasso couldn't stop staring at Lucia, obviously terrified of losing his connection with her. She, in her turn, dissolved into tears because she wouldn't be taking care of "her boys" any more. And Ricco, who had blossomed under Tommasso's tutelage, understood immediately: he was going to lose his privilege. He sat stony-faced, looking at the floor.

"We'll still have Sundays," I reminded Lucia. "You could help with the babies, and with Amata's child when it comes. She'll need you, if she's to continue to cook wonderful things for us all."

She brightened. "Yes. I could do that. I don't want to leave, Giacoma."

"I don't want anyone to leave. But things are changing, and we'll have to adapt. Tommasso? Are you willing to work for Cencio?"

"If I teach the boys at messer Cencio's house, I could escort them back here on Sundays," he offered, a hint of desperation in his voice. I sympathized with what he was trying to accomplish: it would mean spending at least one day every week around Lucia.

And Ricco. Sundays did Ricco no good, for no lessons could take place on the Lord's day. I was determined to do something for him, as well.

"Ricco, we won't have Tommasso coming here anymore, but I'll arrange for you to attend one of the schools in the neighborhood, so you won't have to stop your learning. Will that suit you?"

To my surprise, he slowly shook his head. "I've been thinking, madonna."

"Giacoma." Sometimes even now they forgot.

"Giacoma. For a long time, I've hoped to join Father Francesco in Assisi and to be one of his brothers—"

"I thought we had agreed, Ricco. Not until you're sixteen." Everything was moving so fast. It was worse than when Vanna went from servant to nun in an instant, and I wasn't sure I had quite recovered from that yet.

"But I will be sixteen in less than half a year." So soon. "Couldn't I leave Rome with the brothers, after the council is over? Then we wouldn't have to worry about the schooling, though it's been kind of you to include me, and I'm grateful. But I want to be a brother. I want it more than anything, Giacoma, and Father Francesco said I can come to him as soon as you give me leave."

Ricco was right. We all knew he would join Francesco—it was only a matter of when. Also, I had just given permission for my nine-year-old and my eleven-year-old to move out of my house; how could I hold back this fine young man who was already almost sixteen?

"If that's what you want, Ricco, then of course you may go. We will miss you, very much, but I understand your wish, and you have my blessing."

He broke into a huge smile, and his whole body relaxed. I hadn't realized how stiffly he had been standing.

"Thank you! Thank you, Giacoma! I'll pray for you every day, I swear it!"

"And I for you, my friend. You'll take my greetings to the other brothers, won't you?"

"Oh, yes! And whenever Brother Francesco lets me, I'll come with him to Rome to visit all of you."

Lucia and Tommasso hugged him and congratulated him, and he beamed. At least Ricco and Giovanni were unreservedly happy with today's decisions, even if the rest of us had our doubts.

"Prassede and I will make you a habit, Ricco," I said, and his face fell. Now what? "Do you not want your own habit?"

"Yes, but..." He hesitated.

"Go on, Ricco. Whatever it is, you can tell me."

"It's just... if you and Prassede make my habit, it will look too nice. Too clean, and new, and well made. I want to have an old, patched habit like the rest of them. Otherwise I won't really be poor, will I?"

Not really poor. I thought that an extraordinary statement, coming from a stable boy, but I did see his point. He only wanted to be like all the other brothers, and I had no right to interfere.

"I understand. They'll provide you with whatever you need, and you will be content. But perhaps I might be allowed to give you and the brothers—the other brothers—some almond cakes and sheep cheese and white bread as alms for your journey."

"I don't think Brother Francesco will refuse cakes, Giacoma." His grin was back. I was going to miss that grin. "I didn't mean to offend you. I didn't, did I?"

"How could I be offended? You've told me you can't wear anything I've sewn because it will be too good. I'm flattered, not offended." Somehow

I produced a smile, and all of them laughed.

We dispersed then, to tell the sisters and Amata and Massimo of the upcoming changes. I was heavy-hearted, but at least we had managed to keep Lucia, and to keep our ties with Tommasso. It could have been worse. Still, I found myself wishing my boys shared Ricco's desire to follow Francesco, rather than to take up swords and lances and become knights.

*

I woke in the middle of the night and couldn't get back to sleep, so I prayed instead. I knelt before the image of the Virgin that hung in my chamber and asked for her care for Giovanni and especially for my fragile Uccellino. I asked for help in accepting this change, for guidance in making it as easy as possible for everyone involved, and for wisdom in making decisions for those who depended on me. And it may not have been entirely appropriate, but I also asked for a little help with those almond cakes, for I hadn't given up.

The Virgin's eyes were kind—it was for those gentle, fathomless eyes I had chosen this image from among those the artist offered—and I felt reassured. I still dreaded the departure of my sons, but I had faith that all would be well with them. With that comfort, I crawled back into bed and fell into a deep sleep, unbroken until the bells pealed to herald a Sunday morning.

*

Sunday was to be the day of the great procession. We were well positioned; it would snake right past us, on the way from San Giovanni Laterano to the bridge and then over the Tiber to its goal, the ancient church of Santa Maria in Trastevere.

Rome was flooded with churchmen in town for the pope's council. The streets teemed with bishops. At any moment we could look out a window and see cardinals, abbots, canons, Cistercians, Premonstratensians, Hospitallers, Templars. Not only clergy and established orders, but representatives of kings and princes filled our streets, along with their entourages. And on a much humbler note, there were Francesco and his brothers, a ragtag group of unofficial religious in Rome to swell the crowds and watch history being made.

It was good custom for the innkeepers, shopkeepers, stablers, sellers of food and wine, scribes, and for the cozeners who hired themselves out as guides and porters. For the rest of us, it amounted to a huge traffic problem that snarled the markets, bought up commodities the locals needed, and increased the noise in the city tenfold, not to mention the danger from the sheer size of the crowds. We had already heard lurid tales of tramplings.

Those crowds did, however, provide unending entertainment. Every day Prassede and I watched men flock past our windows on the way from their lodgings to San Giovanni Laterano. The banners, the well-dressed noblemen representing their kings, and even the hordes of servants, assistants, guards, and followers provided enough color to satisfy the greediest eye, which feasted on emerald greens, egg yolk yellows, every kind of vivid blue from lapis to cornflower to ocean, and reds—always my favorites—of strawberries, of cherries, of darker, secret things. Only the soft colors were missing, the gentle pinks, the uncertain, shifting blues and grays, the hesitant peaches and creams. For those, I had to close my eyes and remember the Assisi sky.

And then there were Francesco and the brothers, wearing no particular color. Gray, if anything, or dirty brown. Whatever color the sheep were, so were the brothers' frugal habits. With so many new people in town, we had been giving more alms than ever, and in that spirit, I had quietly funneled some funds to the hospice where the brothers were staying, to defray their expenses. I was always searching for ways to help Francesco, preferably ones he would not notice.

Our balconies were already hung with our most sumptuous drapes. The Frangipane colors flew, with their two fierce golden lions juggling four roundels of bread against a blood-red background. They did not fly for me, but for Graziano's sons, still in residence for a few more days.

Prassede and I had decided to take Isotta out onto the balcony so she could watch the spectacle, though we would wait until the procession approached us, so she wouldn't grow tired of waiting. Salvestra and Renzo would join us, and the rest of the household would watch from outside in the street, along with most of Rome.

"Will Lapo be here?" Isotta asked, her voice still raspy from her recent illness. A flicker of annoyance crossed Bartola's face, but she didn't let it show in her voice when she answered.

"Not today, my dear. Today is only for the men of the church, and for some of our city's grandest noblemen." Isotta's missing son was neither of those. Rather, he was a condemned thief who had fled the city to avoid punishment—not that I blamed him for that—and deserted his poor mother, which was why we took her in. She never ceased asking for him, and we were often taxed to think of anything to say which would not distress her.

"Pope Adriano will come?" Isotta said drowsily. Prassede gave a startled little laugh, and Bartola shot her a warning glance.

"The pope will come, sweetling. You'll see him soon. Won't that be lovely?" Bartola stroked Isotta's thin hair. One had to be quite sick and weak to merit that gentle voice from our cantankerous nurse.

"Lovely," Isotta agreed.

Prassede made a wry face. "Adriano was five popes ago," she whispered.

"Six, actually. And four antipopes," I whispered back.

Prassede pursed her lips. "We don't talk about *those.*"

"Some of us do." My own family had been responsible for several of them. They're every bit as interesting as the real ones, and besides, if a different faction had won, they'd *be* the real ones. But Prassede had that stubborn look on her face, so I changed the subject. "Let's get Isotta ready to go outside now, shall we?"

We had already lifted our fragile patient into a chair with a back. Renzo hovered behind her, which clearly made her nervous, but we could hardly send him away on such a festive occasion. Once he even put a wizened hand on her shoulder, but Bartola slapped it away and glowered at him, and he raised his hands in a placating gesture and took a step back. No one was eager to incur Bartola's righteous wrath.

Now Prassede and I maneuvered Isotta and her chair out onto the balcony, and Bartola draped a shawl over her patient's thin shoulders despite the mildness of the day. Renzo and Salvestra joined us, Salvestra carefully placing herself on the side between Isotta's chair and the railing to avoid our amorous tinker. Meliorata no longer left her bed, nor did she show any awareness of anything around her, so there was no point in trying to prop her up at the window or take her out onto the balcony.

And here they came. From our right, from San Giovanni Laterano, came the musicians, followed by the rest of the glittering parade. Two ranks of trumpeters raised the bells of their instruments high and blared their fanfares. Two wagons bearing shawm players trundled along behind them, the musicians clad in the livery of their various employers—nobles, cardinals, the pope—in a cacophony of colors. The cacophony was not limited to colors, as the shawms from different households did not agree on tuning. Draped from the strident instruments were gaudy banners. I saw the Frangipane lions among them, and the colors of my own family, the Normanni.

Isotta covered her ears with her bony hands as the trumpets passed below us. I leaned over the edge and peered down at the rest of our people gathered in front of the palazzo, watching the procession. Uccellino was bouncing gleefully to the music, which made me smile.

Below us the Frangipane contingent passed, banners flying. Cencio rode in the fore, with Pierino beaming with arrogant pride and riding barely a pace behind his father. I spotted Graziano's other brothers with their sons and assorted cousins and nephews. They ostentatiously maintained their distance from the Pierleoni, who had been given equal precedence by some genius who wanted to avoid problems but might well have created some. The Frangipani rode two or three abreast on the left, and the Pierleoni on the right in a similar configuration.

If one knew what to look for, the procession was a microcosm of Rome's competing factions. In the perennial struggle for power that defined our city, the nobles could have been a lot stronger if they hadn't been so zealous about fighting each other. They did work together often enough to keep both pope and emperor off balance, but there were plenty of times when the people on the street had even the nobles running for safety.

Who wields supreme power in Rome? The emperor, the pope, or the nobility? If you ask that question of the Roman people, there's only one answer you will get: none of them. So the contenders do their best to avoid asking it, but every now and then the Roman people insist on answering it anyway. The populace was seldom wholly benign, and it could turn dangerous in a heartbeat. That's when the supreme prince of the church decides it would be pleasant to conduct his business from a villa several miles away, the emperor finds himself terribly busy elsewhere, and the nobles suddenly—and loudly—remember the needs of the populace. Bread and circuses.

After the nobles came the churchmen. Whoever had to work out their order of precedence would have made enemies for life, no matter what or how he decided, for the churchmen were fully as competitive and contentious as the noblemen. They marched along in front of us, pious expressions on their faces, singing the appropriate antiphons.

Isotta got to see her pope at last, and she clapped her hands with delight. Pope Innocente the Third—not counting the eponymous antipope—passed directly in front of us, his head high, his expression solemn and saintly, his vestments gorgeous. My older brother told me I called him "Zio Lotario" when I was a child. Perhaps he reminded me of one of my real uncles, or perhaps he had told me to call him so. I had no memory of it.

Ugolino, the distinguished Bishop of Ostia and cardinal of San Giovanni, passed beneath our window, and he smiled up at me and inclined
his head graciously. Pleased, I returned the gesture, more certain than
ever that he would take on the duty of protecting Francesco and the
brothers.

One could have randomly selected any five of those dignified and
wealthy churchmen, and the value of the magnificent cloth they wore
would have kept all our beggars well fed for a month.

Ah, but not so with the monks. They were more dignified in their
simplicity than the men of the church hierarchy. They sang better, too.
In fact, when a rank of Cistercians passed beneath the balcony singing,
I heard Meliorata's soft, true voice behind me, singing along from her
bed. She knew every word, every note. I don't know if she was aware of
anything else, but Meliorata opened herself to music as a flower opens
to the sun. The beauty of the men's voices below and her voice floating
lightly above them moved me, the first thing today that had, and I felt
the pricking of tears.

Inside, we heard Nuta arrive with the babies, and Salvestra immediately lost interest in the pageantry below us and went inside to coo over
the twins. She and Isotta doted on both infants, and even Renzo watched
the little ones with a lopsided grin on his face. Meliorata gave no sign of
knowing they existed, and yet I had heard her sing something very like a
lullaby when one of them was in the room and in need of soothing.

Most of the panoply had already passed us, and the nobles at the front
of the procession must have already reached the bridge and headed across
the Tiber. At the end came our own—Francesco and the other brothers.
Elias and Egidio walked on either side of Francesco with Brothers Rufino,
Leone, and Bernardo following, and then the others, ragged and barefoot
and disheveled but singing enthusiastically, straggling out behind. It
always amazed me how much pure joy the brothers could manifest in
any situation. And in the midst of them, grinning from ear to ear and
wearing a tunic meant for someone twice his girth, was Ricco, the most
joyful of them all. I was going to miss that lad.

Egidio waved at those of our household who watched from the street,
and then looked up and saluted the rest of us by raising his clasped
hands to us, smiling broadly. We called our greetings to them, and a few
brothers broke off from singing long enough to call back, but Francesco
was lost in an ecstasy of praise. He walked along singing, his eyes closed,
Elias guiding him by the elbow.

Seeing him like that made my heart swell with affection. Something had spattered on his tunic. I supposed some watcher along the way was unimpressed with the scruffy brothers and had flung some missile at him, mud or dung or some rotting thing. I doubted Francesco would have noticed, so transported was he by his faith, though I could imagine Elias would find it hard to control himself if someone insulted Francesco. I know I would.

When the last of the procession had passed, Prassede and I hauled Isotta's chair back inside. Nuta had gone, probably to the nursery to put the little ones down for a nap. Prassede and Bartola settled Isotta, who was tired from all the excitement. Even Salvestra, who was rarely off her feet until just before she succumbed to sleep at night, stretched out on her bed, and Renzo eventually came in from the balcony and went directly to his own chamber, not saying a word to anyone. We promised our ladies we would watch again later, when the parade returned in the evening by torchlight. It would be late by then, but with the music and the voices and the noise of tromping feet, there'd be no sleep until it was done, anyway.

I left them there, heading down to the kitchen for one more try at the almond cakes.

17

A couple of hours later, I beamed at my perfect row of cakes. I had finally done it. It had taken two more batches, and I'd sent Massimo out for more almonds which I then blanched and ground, but at last I had learned the knack. I would be able to put a plate of almond cakes, cakes made entirely by me, in front of Francesco, thanks to Amata's patient teaching. Massimo went to the cookshop to pick up dinner so Amata and I could concentrate on our task, and it had paid off. Now we were two hours past dinner, with perhaps another three or four hours left before the procession came back past us, and we could sit back on the bench, lean against the wall, and relax.

I was about to thank Amata and urge her to take the rest of the day off, but when I looked at her, I checked my words. She was pale, a chalky white verging on green, and her face was uncharacteristically puffy. She had been rather quiet, but I had been busy working on my cakes and hadn't thought anything of it.

"What is it, Amata?"

"Nothing. I'm fine, just a bit tired," she said, but she sounded uncertain, and I noticed a sheen of sweat on her cheeks.

Her time was not yet close. If the babe were to come now, there was little chance it would live.

"Could it be something you ate?" I asked anxiously. Yet she had eaten scarcely anything at dinner.

She shook her head.

"Perhaps the babe dances a saltarello inside you," I said as lightly as I could, though the more I looked at her the more worried I felt.

"Oh, the babe's not dancing today. She's been sleeping so well," she said, attempting a smile. Prassede had convinced Amata the babe was a girl. "We'll wish her so calm once she's been brought to the light."

I wasn't sure I liked the sound of that.

"But it's been moving some, hasn't it?"

She considered this. "Not really, not today. She was quiet yesterday, though she did move a little, around vespers. But there's this." She hiked up her skirt to show me her alarmingly swollen feet. Yesterday they had been normal.

I jumped up and grabbed a stool. "Amata, you should have told me," I scolded her, as I lifted her legs and arranged her distended feet on the wooden seat, tucking a folded towel under them for cushioning. "We'd best send for the midwife. She'll know what to do to make you more comfortable." I refused to consider the possibility that the babe could be coming already, but I said a quick silent prayer anyway.

We had contracted with an experienced midwife, one of the penitents from the house Prassede and Bartola used to live in, but we hadn't expected to require her services for several more weeks.

I poured a cup of good red wine and brought it to Amata. She sipped it, and I thought her color began to return, but that may have been my wish rather than my accurate observation.

"How are you feeling?" I asked her. We were alone in the kitchen, but I could call for Massimo if we needed him. He'd be in the tack room next to the stable, on the other side of the courtyard.

"I'm well enough. It's just that I've a bad headache, and my back is aching, and I feel a little tired."

"But you're not going into labor, are you?"

"No, of course not. It's much too soon." But she rested a hand lightly on her swollen belly.

"May I?" I asked. She nodded and moved her hand away, and I knelt next to her and placed my own where hers had been. I hoped to find some reassuring movement, but I found nothing.

They don't always move, I reminded myself. They do sleep, and sometimes they're still for a while.

But for all those hours? I couldn't remember a period that long in my own pregnancies when Giovanni or Uccellino had not been moving. I felt a rising panic.

"Where's its—where's her head?"

Amata indicated a bulge down low and on her left side. I explored gently with my hand, found it, and pressed gently, then moved the roundness back and forth a thumb's breadth. *Time to wake, little one.*

Nothing. I left my hand there a moment longer, hoping, but found no flutter, no motion, however small, to reassure me. We were going to have to send for help. I got up and took another look at my friend.

No better. If anything, she was even more wan, and her face was much rounder than it should have been.

"Amata—" I began, but suddenly she clutched at her belly and bent double, moaning.

"Massimo!" I put an arm around Amata to steady her. "To us! Quickly!"

She rocked back and forth, whimpering. I called Massimo's name again, my hand still on Amata's shoulder, but he was already in the doorway, wild-eyed. He hurried to her, sinking to his knees in front of her, and took her hands in his.

"Amata, my love, what is it? What do you need?"

She clutched his hands and gasped, as if trying to draw a breath.

Who could I send? Ricco was with Francesco and both of our nurses were upstairs. Where was Lucia?

Right behind me, standing in the doorway, as it happened. She made a strangled little noise in her throat when she saw Amata, and then she hurried past me and crouched next to Massimo.

"What can I do?" she asked him. Massimo just shook his head, never taking his eyes off his wife, who punctuated her rapid breaths with whimpers.

"Lucia, will you go get Prassede? And find one of Massimo's men? We must send for the midwife," I said, and she stood up.

"She needs a doctor, not the midwife," Massimo said harshly. "It's not yet time for the birth."

I needed to approach this carefully. "But her illness comes from her condition, Massimo. The midwife will know best how to help her." I was guessing, but that terrifying stillness in Amata's belly had convinced me we needed someone knowledgeable about childbirth.

"Who should I get, then, Giacoma?" Lucia asked, looking from Massimo to me and back.

"Nobody. I'll fetch the midwife, if you're sure she's the best one to help," Massimo said, getting to his feet. His voice was rough, but in control. He still held Amata's hands. "I'll go because I'm the one who knows how to find the woman. We'll take Amata to our chamber, and Giacoma, you'll stay with her, won't you?"

"Yes, of course. And Prassede will, too. But take a couple of your men with you, in case the woman isn't home. Then you can split up and search in three different places at once." My mind was beginning to work again, like a mill wheel that has been stilled and is slowly returning to life.

Everything that happened from that moment onward moved either very quickly, or very slowly. It didn't take us long to get Amata to their ground floor chamber; it was next to the kitchen, and Massimo and I each supported her by an arm. She groaned softly, but she was able to walk, and in a faint voice she thanked us for our help. I felt her wrist, and her pulse was racing. Lucia had fetched Prassede, and both of them watched us wide-eyed as we helped Amata into the chamber and onto the bed.

Massimo hugged his sweating wife carefully, as if she were a fragile thing, and then left at a run, with the three men who had come in answer to his bellowed summons. That was when time began to slow for those of us who stayed. I prayed the midwife was not already out on a call, for I didn't see how we could justify asking her to leave one woman in her need only to attend to another. And yet Amata had to have help.

Prassede made a quick examination, at my suggestion checking Amata's swollen feet. Lucia hovered, her fist at her mouth, her eyes enormous. Prassede had solid basic nursing skills, but she was no midwife, and her helpless shrug underscored that. My sons peeped in, but I shooed them away and prodded Lucia to go after them, for there was nothing she could do here, and the boys would be upset by what they had seen.

Amata was white as flour and shaking. I spoke to her as calmly as I could, telling her the midwife was on the way, help would arrive soon, she looked better. That last was a lie, and for all I knew, so was the rest of it, but I wanted to soothe her. Prassede murmured reassurances too, but Amata would have none of it.

"It's too soon," she gasped, clutching at her belly. "I'll lose her. She can't come now—she's not ready. Giacoma, make her wait."

"We'll pray," I told her. "Prassede, will you please go get her more wine?" Prassede took the cup and hurried out.

I sat on the bed next to Amata, took her hand, and we prayed together, to Holy Mary ever virgin and to her Son, but also to a few other saints Amata especially revered. I spoke for us both, a hodgepodge of bits of various prayers, and she murmured an occasional word or two with me. Every time a pain took her, her hand gripped mine so hard I clenched my teeth.

And then we waited. That was the slowest part. In my mind I sorted through our stock of healing herbs, wondering if I had whatever the midwife would ask us for. I had borne Giovanni and Uccellino easily, almost alarmingly fast, both of them out and crying lustily before I had need of any concoctions.

If only the midwife would come! I felt so helpless, and even Prassede could do little more than offer Amata a sip of unwatered wine after every pain.

Prassede remembered something about anointing a woman's belly and sides with oil of violets, so I sprinted upstairs to rummage among my scents to see if I had any. I hadn't used such things since Graziano died, and I had no idea what might still be on my table. Lucia and the boys appeared at my chamber door while I was searching, wanting to know how Amata was doing. I couldn't tell them much, but I asked them to pray for her, and they obediently went to the chapel, their faces solemn.

I didn't have oil of violets, but I did find some oil of roses, so I brought the little bottle downstairs, and Prassede pulled Amata's gown up and arranged the blanket over her legs and private parts, then set to work doing gentle massage on and around her distended belly. A strong and unseasonal scent of roses filled the room, but in combination with Amata's fear and pain it was more overwhelming than pleasant.

At one point, while Amata tried to relax between pains, Prassede whispered to me, "I can't feel it moving."

"I know," I said, my voice low. "I couldn't either. Do you think . . . "

"I'm afraid so, but I can't be sure." Then Amata tensed, and Prassede went back to the bed and helped her sit up, tucking cushions behind her back.

A priest, I thought. If the babe was going to die, we should have a priest. The child must be baptized. But if it was already dead, how could it be baptized? Yet if it lived even briefly, the midwife could perform the baptism. If she had not yet reached us, any of us could do it in an emergency. All it took was a few words, in any language if the speaker did not know her Latin.

But if the babe had died. . . I couldn't bear the thought of Amata's child never drawing breath in this life and also being denied Paradise in the next. I prayed, desperately and ferociously. This could not be happening to one of mine. I wouldn't let it.

Then the front door banged open, and we heard Massimo's voice. "This way!" And the waiting was over.

Massimo rushed to Amata's bedside, stifling a sob when he saw her. She gave him a weak smile, but then her face clenched as another pain struck.

A short woman followed more sedately, carrying a canvas satchel. She was perhaps Prassede's age, broad and sturdy, simply dressed in undyed wool. She had a self-important air about her, but none of us questioned it, because at that moment she was indeed the most important person in our world. She nodded briskly to us, greeted her fellow penitent, and marched up to her patient.

She said nothing to Amata. She placed her squarish hands on that swollen belly and squinched her eyes shut. All of us held our breath, waiting to hear what she would say, but it was a long time in coming.

Her eyes flew open, and she looked Amata in the face. "Tell me," she commanded, and Amata tried, weak and tearful, to describe what she was experiencing.

"Headache, swollen feet, pallor, rapid pulse," echoed the midwife. "How long has it been since you felt the babe move?"

"Not this morning." Amata's answer was so faint I barely heard her. The midwife frowned.

"Last night, then?"

"Yes. Last night. A little."

"During the night, or before you slept?"

"Before. I was wakeful last night; I didn't sleep much. But I didn't feel her in the night."

"Sister Prassede, continue your massage," she said, and Prassede took up her position.

"You, madonna, and you, the woman's husband, come with me," she said, and strode out of the chamber, waiting for us in the courtyard. Massimo and I followed. Salvestra and Renzo were in the courtyard, but they did not approach us.

"I believe the child is dead," the midwife said without preamble. "I cannot be sure, but even if it is so, still she must bear the babe, and as soon as possible. Not until the child is out of her body will we have a chance to save her."

Massimo gave a despairing sob and grabbed my shoulder. I put my hand over his.

"We don't know yet about the child, Massimo. And Amata will be safe, now that—I'm sorry, should I call you Sister Donata, as Prassede does?"

Somehow she gave the impression of looking down at me contemptuously, though I was the taller. "To Sister Prassede I am Sister Donata," she said, "but to you I am monna Donata."

"Well, then, welcome, monna Donata. We are grateful you're here. What can we do to help you?" I didn't like this woman, and if I let myself, I would give way to rage at her blunt way of speaking to Massimo, who trembled at my side. But we needed her.

"Get me wormwood and mint, boiled in wine. As much as you would give a sick child, and half again."

We had done this for Uccellino on several occasions, so I was familiar with the mixture. There should be some fresh mint left in the garden.

"Anything else?"

"Yes. I don't suppose you have any oxizaccara?"

"We do." The medicament was costly, specially prepared by an apothecary I trusted, and even my wealthy household kept only a small supply on hand.

"Good. Add an ounce and a half of that to the wine, and bring it to me. If the child is dead, I will want rue and mugwort, ground together with some pepper, but you need not boil it. It can be stirred into the wine. Make it ready. And make a poultice of ground savory with a little of that wormwood added to it."

"I thought perhaps you would have supplies with you," I said.

"If you have these things, there's no need for me to use mine, is there? And I can save mine for someone who can't afford her own." She had a way of talking that suggested a sneer, even when her face didn't change.

"We have them," I said curtly. I beckoned to Renzo, who had crept closer and was shamelessly eavesdropping.

"Renzo, would you please find Lucia and ask her to come to me? She may have gone to the chapel."

"Aye, Giacoma," he said, and began to make his painful way up the stairs, both hands gripping the railing to help him pull himself up, step by step. *Well, that wasn't a good idea.*

My thought had been to return to Amata's chamber with Massimo and the midwife, leaving Lucia to prepare the herbal mixture, but considering the rate Renzo was moving, I decided to go to the kitchen and begin the process myself.

I turned to the midwife and Massimo to tell them where I'd be, but they had squared off, glaring at each other.

"When a woman's in childbed, there'll be no man around," Donata was saying emphatically. "You'd be in the way. A birthing chamber is no place for a man."

Massimo's eyes went wide. "She's sick, she's not giving birth. It's too soon," he insisted. "She needs me!" His voice was strangled, and he kept glancing toward the chamber he and Amata shared. "She's not in labor, I tell you."

Donata shook her head. "I will be the one to determine that, not you. She doesn't need you. She needs me, and I'm not going back in if you're there."

Now I really didn't like this woman. I knew the customs as well as anyone, but she had just told Massimo the wife he adored might die, and now she refused to let him go to her. Some sort of compromise had to be possible. But the woman's hard face and her small, mean eyes told me she meant it. She would leave if she didn't get her way.

Better do something, then. My household, my responsibility.

"Massimo, go find Lucia and tell her what needs to be done in the kitchen. You heard it all, didn't you?" He nodded wordlessly. I calculated

Renzo would have reached the chapel by now, so Massimo should meet Lucia on her way down.

"Go, then, and once Lucia has her instructions, you go to the chapel and pray. It's the best thing you can do for Amata right now."

"I will," he said, obviously relieved to have a mission, and he headed up the stairs, taking them two at a time.

Donata smiled smugly. I ignored her and returned to Amata's chamber. Amata's breathing was fast and shallow, and Prassede continued to massage that swollen belly.

Donata followed me in. She studied Amata critically.

"Any motion, Sister?" she asked Prassede, but Prassy shook her head.

"Hmm." Donata went to her satchel and rummaged in it, then pulled out a chunk of coral about the size of a child's fist, hanging from a tattered cord. I wondered how many laboring women had worn it, and whether it had helped them. She draped it around Amata's neck, not ungently. Amata clutched at it with both hands.

And now time slowed. Donata prayed loudly and ostentatiously, and Prassede and I joined her, more quietly. Amata whimpered from time to time. Lucia came in briefly to make sure she understood the midwife's instructions correctly, and I took her arm and steered her out into the courtyard where we could talk. Prassede and Donata continued to pray.

I reviewed Donata's instructions with Lucia and sent her to the kitchen to begin pulverizing the dried herbs. The youngest of Massimo's men, one of the three who had gone with him to get Donata, was still in the courtyard. I called him over and asked him to remind me of his name.

"It's Gualtiero, madonna," he said. "Will it be well with Massimo's wife?"

"We don't know yet, but we pray it will. Will you be ready to help if we need to send for anything?"

"Aye, madonna, I will," he said, his young voice earnest. "I'll stay where I can hear you."

"Thank you, Gualtiero. Will you go pick some mint from the kitchen garden? You'll be able to hear me from there if I call."

I braced myself to hear him complain that picking herbs was women's work, but he only said "Aye, madonna," and then hurried off, just as Massimo came heavily down the stairs. He gave me an inquiring look, but I had nothing to tell him.

"I'll go check on her and bring you any news," I told him, and he sat on the stone bench, his elbows on his knees and his face in his hands. Behind those powerful hands he murmured another prayer.

127

18

INSIDE the room, the midwife had taken a strip of fabric from her satchel and was attempting to tie it around Amata's belly. Prassede supported Amata from behind as she half sat, half lay in the bed. Donata struggled with the fabric, which appeared to be quite fragile, but she finally succeeded in tying it in front. I came closer to see it and realized it was not fabric at all, but the empty skin of a huge snake.

"She'd best not tear it," Donata warned. "It's very, very expensive, and if I have to replace it, it's going to cost you. Snakes that big, there's not many of them, and they seldom leave their shed skins in one piece."

"What's it for?" I asked.

"Makes the babe slide out as easy as the snake wiggled out of its skin."

I wondered if anyone had thought to ask the snake whether freeing itself had been easy or not. But at this point I supposed out was out, whether hard or easy, and out was what we needed, the sooner the better.

Amata started to lie back, but Donata grabbed her arms.

"That'll tear the skin," she said sharply.

"So she has to sit up until she gives birth?" I said, just as sharply. Prassede looked first at Donata, then at me. She shook her head slightly.

Fine. For Amata, I'd play by Donata's rules.

"Let's lay her back gently," I said. "If we're careful, the skin won't tear. And if it does, I assure you I can afford to buy you a new one."

The hard-eyed midwife scowled at me. I stared back at her until she turned away. She and Prassede maneuvered Amata back against the cushions, with no apparent damage to the papery snakeskin.

I went out to tell Massimo that Amata was calm and nothing alarming was happening, then returned to find I had inadvertently lied. Amata whimpered, tossing this way and that, and Prassede tried to soothe her. Donata was wholly engaged in rescuing her snakeskin, which she held up triumphantly, oblivious to the fact that no one else cared.

Amata was now indisputably in labor, though whether with a living child or a dead one I did not know. I tried to think how long it had been since she first doubled over in the kitchen, and I concluded that some hours had passed.

Time continued to be unpredictable. Amata's pangs came closer together and lasted longer. Periods of intense activity alternated with periods of nothing happening, and I reported to Massimo whenever anything changed. Young Gualtiero waited with him, and I blessed the boy for that kindness. It was growing late; we brought in candles and lamps, a lot of them, to give the midwife the light she would need. The courtyard was enveloped in gloom, except for a lantern flickering at Massimo's feet.

The procession must already have come back this way, but we were so busy with Amata that we had missed it altogether. I didn't even recall hearing anything, but Amata's chamber faced the kitchen garden, away from the street.

Lucia brought in her herbal concoction, and it was duly pronounced adequate. Prassede offered her patient small sips of the mix in between contractions. It must have tasted foul, judging by Amata's sour expression. Lucia stayed, deliberately huddling in a corner where Donata was not likely to notice her.

Donata pulled a grimy bit of parchment out of her satchel and handed it to me. "Here's a prayer of great power," she told me. "Go write it on a piece of cheese, and she will eat it, and it will help." I did as I was told, though the "prayer" looked like gibberish to me and the difficulties of scratching even a few characters into a chunk of cheese should not be underestimated, but Amata couldn't get any of it down.

Nuta appeared at the door briefly, having put the little ones to bed for the night, and her face showed her fear plainly. Amata was pale and sweating, but we saw no progress. And we all knew it was too soon, much too soon.

In my mind, the question had shifted. It was no longer "Will Amata's babe live?" but "Is there enough life left in the babe that she can be baptized?"

At one point I noticed Salvestra standing in the doorway. I went to her and put my hand on her shoulder. "Should you not be resting?"

She turned her pale blue eyes to me. "The snake didn't need its skin anymore. Amata didn't need it either." She must have peeked in before, and none of us had noticed her. I was tempted to agree with her, but I didn't want to if there was a chance Donata could hear me. And indeed, the midwife turned her attention from her sweating patient to peer out at us and glare.

"Get that old woman away from here," she said harshly. "It's her, not the snakeskin, we don't need."

Salvestra regarded her calmly and walked into the chamber. I reached out to stop her, but then some impulse made me check myself.

In her day Salvestra had been renowned as one of the best midwives in Rome. Was it possible she could offer Amata something Donata could not?

"You don't need me," Salvestra said dreamily to Donata. "But Amata needs me."

Donata snorted. "What for, old woman? Go away before you upset her."

Salvestra ignored her and went over to the side of the bed, looking down at Amata, who moaned and writhed in the throes of another useless contraction. The old woman placed one slender hand lightly on Amata's belly, now covered with a damp sweaty sheet. She held it there for a moment, then shook her head. "Little one will never sin," she said softly.

Donata started toward Salvestra, but I held up my hand to signal her to stop where she was.

Salvestra dipped her hands in the midwife's basin of water, then dried them on her skirt. She lifted the sheet from Amata's belly and let it fall to the floor. She began to explore, her fingers moving delicately, then inserting one slender finger into the birth canal, her movements deft and sure.

Donata turned to me with an outraged glare. "Monna Giacoma! What is this? Why do you let her interfere? Do you not care if harm comes to your servant?"

"No harm will come to her, Donata. Salvestra is a midwife too—she has the skill."

"It's *monna* Donata!" she snarled. "And she's a doddering old woman, not a midwife."

"Monna Donata, then." Should I persuade Salvestra to leave Amata alone? I supposed I ought to, but something in me persisted in saying otherwise. I wished I could talk to Francesco, but I was on my own with this decision, for it was far too late at night to fetch him.

God will speak to you in whatever way will make you listen, Francesco had once told me. *Be sure you heed him when he does, and all will be well.*

My household, my responsibility. I took a deep breath.

"Monna Donata, you will let Salvestra examine Amata. You will not interfere. Mayhap she can find some way to help," I said, silently adding a prayer that I hadn't alienated Donata just at the point where we most needed her.

Donata recoiled as if I had slapped her. "If she stays, I go."

Go, then, I wanted to say. What I actually said was, "What will your fellow penitents say if you abandon a woman in childbed, monna Donata?"

Salvestra didn't look up from her exploration, but she murmured,

"Two midwives. One to watch, one to touch. Twice the help."

Two midwives. "Monna Donata, is it not possible for two midwives to work together?" I asked her.

Sullen silence.

I persisted. "Does it not happen, sometimes?"

"It does, sometimes," she muttered.

"Then it will happen this time, if you still wish to bring my donation back to your Mother Superior."

Donata's face was distorted with rage, but she said nothing.

Salvestra finished her examination and reached down for the sheet and covered Amata with it. To Donata she said, "You have the wisdom to help the babe come. Tell me how we will do it."

I was startled at her lucidity, not to mention her inspired tact. This was not the vague, dreamy Salvestra I knew.

Donata must have seen Salvestra's question as a way to regain control. She straightened and squared her shoulders. "I have tried the herbs," she said, her voice beginning to regain its former confidence. "I have tried the snakeskin. I have tried a powerful prayer written on cheese, but the woman would not eat it. The only thing I have left to try is to make her drink another woman's milk mixed with oil, but we have no woman with milk here, and it is night, so it will be too dangerous to send for someone."

Lucia, Prassede, and I spoke at the same time, our words coming out in an incomprehensible jumble. I held up a hand to silence the others. "We do have a wetnurse, monna Donata."

"Then by all means bring her."

I looked at Salvestra, my eyes asking the question.

"It is a good plan," she said. "Bring her."

Donata nodded her head in fierce satisfaction.

Lucia fetched Nuta. Confused and uncertain, our wetnurse entered the chamber, not sure what was wanted from her, and Donata explained. Nuta fumbled with her clothing and exposed a breast, while I held the emptied wine cup to catch the milk, but nothing came.

"I fed the babes before I put them down," she said, agitated. "There should be something left, even if it's not much, but I cannot make it come."

Now what? Could we milk her, like a goat? It was Salvestra who suggested the obvious.

"Bring a babe," she said peacefully, stroking Amata's curly hair, soaked black with sweat.

131

Of course. If one of the babes woke and cried, Nuta's milk would let down. I started to go fetch one of them from the nursery, but Lucia was already on her way to the door.

From the bed came Amata's faint voice. "Bring the girl. Bring Cilia."

"I will," Nuta said, and then she was gone.

Amata began another contraction, her face contorting with the effort. Salvestra let Amata squeeze her hand, though I worried that the sweating woman would crush those fragile old bones.

Nuta kept trying to coax her milk to come, but the whole situation was so strange and so fraught with worry that her body fought stubbornly against her efforts.

It wasn't long before we heard an outraged squall, getting progressively louder as Lucia carried the child swiftly down the stairs and toward us. As we had hoped, Nuta's body responded. I had to hurry to put the cup to her breast in time, but now the milk started to come, only a trickle, but steadily. Prassede had gone for the oil in the meantime, and we mixed oil and milk in the cup and offered it to Amata, who struggled to a sitting position and drank, though she made a face at the texture. Cilia continued to wail in sleepy indignation at this interruption of her rest.

"Was that enough?" asked Nuta, raising her voice to be heard above Cilia's complaints.

"It should be," Donata said, and Nuta put the infant to her breast. The sudden quiet was welcome, and Cilia fell back to sleep after suckling for a few seconds.

"It tastes better than the herbs," Amata said, wiping her mouth. That was the first thing she had said other than incoherent moans in some time, and I was heartened by it.

I remembered Massimo, waiting in the courtyard. "Did anyone tell Massimo what's going on?" I asked.

"I did," Lucia said.

"Massimo," Amata said weakly. "I want Massimo."

Donata opened her mouth to object, but then it didn't matter, because Amata gave a loud grunt and Salvestra said, "The babe is coming."

Amata's cry had reawakened Cilia, and Nuta left to take her back to the nursery, crooning a lullaby into the child's ear. Both midwives hovered close to Amata's bed, Prassede wiped Amata's forehead with a wet towel, and Lucia and I held back, watching and praying. We couldn't see much with the two midwives between us and Amata, but I did notice that Salvestra had her fingers in the birth canal, while Donata massaged

Amata's belly, trying to help the babe along.

"I feel the child," Salvestra said.

"Push, now," said Donata, and Amata grimaced as she bore down.

Donata moved to one side, and I saw Salvestra's wrist make a peculiar little motion.

"The babe moved," she said, and I gasped.

"You're imagining it, old woman," Donata snapped, but she continued to stroke Amata's distended belly with a gentle, practiced hand.

Did the babe live? Was it possible? I closed my eyes and prayed, my quick, all-purpose, emergency prayer. If only we could get the child safely baptized, the worst danger would be averted.

Salvestra withdrew her hand from Amata's body. "Water," she said, and it was a command. Prassede hurried to place the basin of water within reach, and the old woman dunked her hand in it, then inserted her fingers into the birth canal again. Every movement was economical and sure.

"*Ego baptize te in nomine patris et filii et spiritus sancti*," Salvestra murmured. Her pronunciation was perfect. How often had she done this? The last time must have been years ago, but she hadn't forgotten anything. I felt an enormous sense of relief.

But Donata drew back, indignant. "That babe is dead! You can't baptize a babe that's died." Amata groaned at her words, even through the hard work of pushing.

"The babe moved," Salvestra repeated, her hand working inside Amata.

"You moved it!" Donata was shrieking now.

I didn't know what to do next, but Amata interrupted their argument with a loud yell.

"It comes," said Salvestra, and then they were both between us and Amata, and we could not see what was going on. Massimo, unable to bear it any more, stood in the doorway, terror written all over his face.

And it came. Not easily, not quickly, but it came, guided by our remarkable Salvestra's sure hand, Donata pressing on various parts of Amata's abdomen, the two of them exchanging murmured words, two skilled practitioners working together at last. I didn't have the heart to shoo Massimo away, but I stayed with him in the doorway to keep him from rushing to his wife's side and getting in the midwives' way. Lucia and Prassede watched each move the two midwives made, their breathing stopping and starting in sympathy with Amata's grunts and breathless cries.

When at last the babe was out and Amata sank back on the cushions, all was silent. No indignant howls from the infant, newly released from the womb; no admiring coos from the midwives. Only silence. Salvestra did something quick and deft with the cord and then placed the inert babe on the towel that awaited it, and Prassede, who was standing behind the bed, took one look at it and blanched. She hurried around and scooped up the infant, adroitly wrapping it in the towel as she did so. She held the little bundle protectively, resting on her bosom.

Amata did not ask for it. No one spoke, and there was no sound other than Amata's tortured breathing.

Then Salvestra stood, turned to face the rest of us, and said, "A girl. She is baptized and sinless and has gone to her home in heaven."

19

I willed Donata to be silent. Her face was an angry red, but she said nothing as she dipped a cloth in the basin of water and began to clean Amata's thighs. Then she began kneading Amata's belly gently, to encourage the afterbirth to come.

Still no one else spoke, until Amata opened her eyes and said weakly, "Massimo?" That was all the invitation he needed, and he ran to her, sinking to his knees beside the bed and grasping her hands. Both of them were weeping. Donata scowled at Massimo, then stepped back into a shadow, just outside the pool of light from the lantern on the floor, and I could no longer see her expression.

Prassede brought the babe to me. She opened the towel, and I flinched at the sight of the child's discolored abdomen and purplish lips. Her face was distorted, her mouth and eyes were open, and the brownish-red stain to her skin made her appear as if she had been scalded. I started to close her eyelids, but Prassede stopped me.

"If you touch her, more of her skin will rub off," she whispered. Bits of the infant's skin already adhered to the open towel. Prassede wrapped it back around the tiny girl.

"How will we show her to her parents?" I whispered. But before we could discuss it, Massimo rose and came over to us. He looked at the little face and winced. At least we had covered the child's body, I thought helplessly.

Finally he faced me. "I'll tell her what to expect, Giacoma, but then she'll have to see her."

Numbly, I nodded my agreement. He returned to Amata, they exchanged a few words, and then he came back, holding his arms out for the baby.

Reluctantly Prassede handed her to him. "Don't unwrap the towel," she said quietly, and I saw him think about that, look at the babe again, and understand. Slowly he carried his daughter back to Amata. He said something we couldn't hear, and then he set the tiny bundle down on the bed some distance away from his wife. Tears ran down Amata's pale cheeks. She propped herself on one elbow and reached out to touch her daughter, but Massimo caught her hand and said something to her. She wept, but she lay back on the cushions and let her hands fall to her sides. She and Massimo spoke to each other, and he gathered the bundle in his arms. Amata reached up and gently touched the part of the towel covering her daughter's shoulder, and then Massimo brought the babe to us.

"Giacoma, will you take care of the rest?" His voice was almost pleading.

"Of course, Massimo," I said. "We'll arrange everything with Father Paolo tomorrow." Prassede held her arms out for the child and Massimo handed her over, both of them handling her with infinite gentleness. Prassede slipped out the door with her burden.

Massimo and I walked back to Amata together, and both of us knelt, one on either side of her bed. I took one of her hands and Massimo took the other.

"She would have been beautiful, Amata," I said.

Her tears were still flowing, but she squeezed my hand. "Did you see her, Giacoma?" she said, her voice hoarse.

"Yes."

"She was not beautiful." The pain in Amata's voice tore at my heart.

"She was only damaged, poor little thing. Had she lived to be born, she would have been as lovely as you are, my friend."

Amata wept, Massimo helpless beside her. Lucia stood in the corner, tired and dejected. Nuta had come back downstairs, but she was waiting just outside, in the courtyard. Salvestra paced in circles around the edges of the room. And Donata moved into the light, felt Amata's belly, and peremptorily shooed Massimo away, for the afterbirth was coming.

It came swiftly, and Donata caught it in another towel and took it out of the chamber. Massimo resumed his place at Amata's side, and Salvestra came forward to assume the task of bathing Amata's thighs from the new slick of blood and glistening liquid that coated them. I found it hard to believe our elderly patient had taken charge of the situation so efficiently. I was going to have to completely reconsider my opinion of Salvestra.

I was still standing in the doorway when Donata came up to me, having done whatever midwives do with afterbirths, and touched my arm.

"Madonna, we must talk," she said, and her face was hard and determined. I did not want her to broach the topic she intended while Amata and Massimo could hear her, so I tried to steer her out to the courtyard, but she would not go. Instead, she entered the room and took a position midway between Amata's bed and the door, speaking to all of us.

"This is important, madonna. The mother and father of that poor dead child need to hear it too. God knows I wish it were otherwise—my heart aches for them—but I cannot, in good conscience, pretend the babe was baptized. That babe had died in the womb, and no baptism was possible. As a witness, I must affirm God's will in this. The child died without the sacrament. I don't understand why God willed it so, but he did. Perhaps some sin committed by the parents led to this. A man so eager to intrude on a lying-in chamber might be capable of many another sin."

Amata sobbed, and Massimo's free hand curled into a fist. Salvestra put the wet towel back in the basin and faced us.

"The child was baptized," she said simply.

"She was not." Donata's voice was strident.

"She was."

"You perjure yourself, old woman. Will you lie before God?"

"God knows us both, and he knows the truth," said Salvestra calmly.

I didn't believe her, yet I admired her. She was unshakable.

Massimo faced Donata and rasped, "What kind of a monster are you, you vicious hag, that you say these things in front of my wife?" He released Amata's hand and took a threatening step toward the midwife.

"A penitent and an honest and God-fearing woman is what I am," Donata replied defiantly. "I serve my God and I cannot lie."

This was not going to solve anything. I desperately wanted to believe Salvestra, yet I knew what Donata said was likely true. But unlike Donata, I did not feel capable of speaking for God. I so wished Francesco were here to help us, with his wisdom and compassion and understanding.

"Monna Donata, let us discuss it elsewhere," I said. "Amata needs to rest." I grasped her firmly by the elbow and started to propel her out of the chamber when I heard a tapping on the front portal.

All of us stopped and listened. It was now the middle of the night— who could be abroad at this hour, and what did they want of us?

I called to Gualtiero, who was still sitting on a bench in the courtyard. "Would you go see who's there? Call and ask, first, before you unbolt the door. We'll all be right here."

Gualtiero approached the door cautiously. I followed him into the entryway and the others trailed behind us, except for Prassede, who stayed behind with Amata. I thought Massimo might have stayed too, but he strode past us, pushing between Donata and me on his way to the portal, ready to back his man if necessary and to protect us from whatever waited without.

Through a crack in the wooden door, Gualtiero spoke. "Who goes there? What do you want?"

I heard a muffled voice reply and recognized it instantly.

"It's Francesco," I said. "Unbolt the door!"

Gualtiero threw the bolt open.

Francesco, Elias, Egidio, and Leone stood outside. They had no torch or lantern with them, and I didn't know how they had come to us or why, but relief surged in me.

"Brothers, be welcome," I said. "How come you here now, so late at night?"

Francesco and the others entered in single file, stepping from darkness into the pool of flickering light cast by Massimo's lantern. Francesco made a swift gesture of blessing the house, and all of them threw back their hoods while Gualtiero bolted the door behind them.

"I'm here so late at night, Giacoma, for the same reason you are up so late at night," he told me. "God has told me you have need of us here, so we've come. May God give you peace."

Peace was not what had been given us, this night. In a few words I sketched for the brothers what had happened, including the argument their arrival had interrupted. Donata's face was flushed.

"Will you comfort Amata, Francesco, and help us understand what has happened?" I concluded.

"I'll do what I can. She is in there?" He indicated the chamber. We moved out of the way to let him come in. The other brothers and Massimo followed him, and the midwife and I followed Massimo, though we stopped just inside, as did Elias, Egidio, and Brother Leone. Salvestra paced at the far side of the chamber.

The light from the two remaining lanterns on the floor illuminated Francesco's face—Massimo still held the third—and I could see an expression of profound sorrow and compassion as those liquid eyes studied Amata. He made the blessing gesture again, and she watched him solemnly. Massimo moved to the other side of the bed and took her hand.

Francesco murmured to her, so quietly I think only Amata and possibly Massimo could have heard. Amata said something back to him. I couldn't hear what.

Curious, I glanced at Donata. She gazed at Francesco with the same worshipful expression Prassede wore at the elevation of the host. The penitents revered Francesco and thought him a holy man; apparently even our abrasive midwife was no exception.

Finally Francesco patted Amata's hand, received a weak smile from her, and walked over to the rest of us. He beckoned to Salvestra, and she altered the course of her pacing to approach us.

"Now," said Francesco, "what is the source of the disagreement about baptism?"

"Here, Francesco?" I asked, indicating Amata and Massimo with a tilt of my head.

"Here. No one is more involved than they are. All of us must understand this, together."

Donata stepped forward. "Father Francesco, I have no wish to bring sorrow to these good people, but I am a midwife, and I have to tell you we have every reason to believe the babe had been dead for some time before I was even summoned. There had been no movement, and the girl's skin was fragile and discolored."

Be silent, you horrible woman. She was making things worse, though I knew she spoke the truth.

Francesco listened courteously. "Amata has told me when she last felt the babe move, and I understand how you have drawn your conclusion. But now I must hear from the other woman who served as midwife for this birth."

He turned to Salvestra, who stopped her pacing and faced him serenely.

"I am Brother Francesco, my good woman, and I believe you are called Salvestra?"

"I am *monna* Salvestra," she said, emphasizing the title. "A midwife." Well, why not? She had earned it.

"And you live in this palazzo?"

"I do, thanks to the charity and kindness of monna Giacoma."

"Just Giacoma," I said, the correction coming automatically to my tongue. The irony was lost on me then, though I realized it later: one woman asserting her right to a title, another perennially trying to get rid of one.

"You were a midwife, then?"

"Was a midwife, helped birth a child this night, am a midwife still," she said firmly.

Francesco inclined his head. "You have done well, monna Salvestra," he said. "And you say you baptized the babe?"

"Inside her mother. I felt her head and I spoke the words."

"And did she move?"

"She did."

Donata couldn't stand it any longer. "You moved her yourself! She was dead! She couldn't have moved by herself. There was no living babe to baptize."

Francesco silenced her with a raised hand. "Sister Prassede? Do you know if the babe moved?"

Prassede shook her head agitatedly. She wrung her hands, then looked at Donata and then at me, but found no help there. "I don't know, Brother Francesco."

I dreaded what was to come next.

"One says the babe was dead, the other says she moved. What say you, Giacoma? What do you believe?"

I couldn't lie to Francesco. I could not. I never had, and I had sworn to follow him in all things. I couldn't lie. And yet—the forlorn pleading in Amata's eyes was more than I could bear, and I had to turn away from her.

My household, my responsibility. I would sooner take that sin upon myself than hurt Amata any more than she had already been hurt.

"The babe moved," I mumbled. I could not meet Francesco's probing gaze. God help my soul. I heard Donata draw a quick, indignant intake of breath.

Francesco looked long at me, then at Salvestra, then at Donata. "I will pray," he said, and he left the room.

"Where will he go, Egidio?" I whispered.

"The babe is in the chapel?" he whispered back.

"I think so." That would have been the logical place for Prassede to take her.

"Then I think he'll be there."

And we waited. Brother Leone sank to his knees in prayer, and Egidio and Elias quickly followed his example. Lucia followed suit. Donata glared at me before kneeling and praying in a loud voice. Salvestra began to pace. I leaned against the wall, too agitated to pray, too tired to think. Amata and Massimo were in their own world, she with furrowed brow and anxious expression, and he doing all he could to soothe her, though his own agitation was plain enough.

We waited a long time. Donata lapsed into silence, finally. The murmurs of the brothers were oddly restful, but it was Francesco's conclusion we were waiting for. Had the babe been baptized? Had she lived long enough? Was she with God?

And for me: Would Francesco know I lied? Would he reject me for it?

When he finally returned and we saw him silhouetted in the door, the moonlight spilling down in the courtyard behind him, I heard a chorus of hasty "Amens" as those who had prayed scrambled to their feet. Salvestra stopped pacing and waited, untroubled.

Before he spoke I knew he brought good news. I could see in his jubilant face that he would say something to ease Amata's heart, and I was glad, and yet—I wondered. If he had been led astray by my untruth, would what he said be true?

But this was Francesco, and God spoke to him. How could it not be true? How could he not know who had spoken truth and who had not?

Francesco raised his arms to heaven, beaming. "The babe is with God," he announced triumphantly. "She dwells in heaven and she is joyful. You need have no fears for her."

Amata wept, overwhelmed with relief, and Massimo hugged her shoulders tightly.

Donata lowered her eyes in defeat. Yet even now she couldn't let it go. "Brother Francesco, I told you true." Her voice was low but determined.

"Sister Donata, you have performed your task well, and you told me the truth as you saw it. But our human truth is not always God's truth."

She hesitated, then nodded, accepting. "I am glad of it, then." Perhaps she actually was.

"Go now, and get some sleep," he told her, his voice gentle. As she passed me, I pressed a purse full of coins into her hand.

"For your Mother Superior, and for your house," I said, "and with our thanks for your work here today. We will prepare a chamber for you for the rest of the night."

"I would prefer to go back to my house, madonna," she said coldly. "Can you send a man with me?"

It would have to be Gualtiero. If he took some men with him, all should be well.

I found him in the courtyard, and he was overjoyed to be able to do something to help. I told him to wake two more men, make sure they were armed, and then wait by the door. Then I returned for Donata.

I heartily disliked the woman, but she had done what we contracted with her to do, and I think in her own unimaginative way she meant well. Also, I was uncomfortably aware that she had been more honest than I had.

She picked up her cloak from the rod along the far wall of the chamber, collected her satchel, then turned without another word or even a glance at Amata and left the chamber to join Gualtiero and his companions. The four of them left by the front portal, and I pulled it closed and latched it behind them. I heard their footsteps clicking on the paving stones, receding. I hoped Gualtiero had the sense to keep to the streets where lighted candles flickered in front of the tabernacles and offered some illumination beyond the lantern he carried. I didn't know the lad well, but his accent told me he was born a Roman, so he probably knew what he was doing. I spoke a quick prayer for their safety on the streets.

I lingered out in the courtyard, standing in the moonlight, my thoughts roiling. I was trying to pluck up enough courage to go back in and face Francesco when he came out, alone.

"Giacoma," he said. "May God give you, especially, peace. You've taken on a great many heavy burdens today." His voice was warm and affectionate, which made me feel even worse.

I knelt before him, my eyes on the ground.

"Francesco, I have to tell you something," I said.

"I know it, Giacoma."

"No, I have to tell you—I lied before. I don't believe the babe lived to be baptized."

"I know that, too." He reached his hand out to me, and I took it, though I stayed on my knees.

"But have we told Amata and Massimo what they want to hear, even though the truth is something much worse?"

"No. No, they have taken a great loss today, but whatever comfort I've been able to give them is real. We've not misled them."

"But..."

"I know what you did, and I know why you did it. The literal truth is not the only truth."

I tried to absorb this. "I lied, and yet you say we were right to bring comfort to Amata."

He smiled that beautiful wise smile of his, and then it widened, into something like a holy grin.

"Giacomina, I know you lied," he said. "But I also know I didn't."

20

I woke the next morning to Bartola's hand on my shoulder, briskly shaking me.

"Wake, Giacoma," she said. "I've something to show you."

Bleary-eyed, I looked at the window. Shutters open, full daylight. How had I slept through the bells? Not as close or as loud as the ones in Assisi, but enough, usually. More than enough. But last night had been very short, probably no more than two hours of sleep for me, and if the others were up already, even less for them.

And then I came fully awake. Bartola. Had anyone thought to tell her what had happened last night?

She must have heard my thought, for she said, "There are no secrets in this house, Giacoma. Salvestra and Nuta both talked to me, and I came down to greet Brother Francesco after you had gone to bed and Prassede came upstairs to stay with the ladies. I knew what was going on all the time, but someone had to take care of our patients, or I'd have been there to help."

"Did the ladies hear the commotion?"

"Oh, yes. Isotta was anxious, but I managed to calm her, and when Nuta came in to tell me what was happening, I had her go fetch some herbed wine to help the ladies sleep. Meliorata wouldn't stop singing, though. She sang the Miserere in such a sweet, sad voice that I think she must have known everything, somehow."

"Isotta's anxiety was well founded, this time. We had a thoroughly horrible night, and it would have been even worse, had Francesco not arrived when he did. Your fellow penitent, monna Donata, has a few things to learn about kindness and tact."

Bartola snorted. "Pity I couldn't have been in the chamber with you. Sister Donata listens to me. In fact, I think she's half frightened of me. And I take care of my own."

So do I. I noticed with both surprise and pleasure that Bartola considered the people of my household to be her people as well. Perhaps she was not so different from the rest of us. She seemed uncharacteristically cheerful, but then, she hadn't been there to see Amata and Massimo and that poor little girl who never drew a breath.

She pulled my gown down from the rod and spread it on the bed. "Here. Get dressed—I have something to show you."

I would have sworn her eyes were sparkling. What could possibly cause so much pleasure after the night we had just been through? But I got up and pulled the gown on over the shift I had slept in. I'd been so tired I hadn't even bothered to finish undressing.

A splash of water on my face and I was ready to go with Bartola. And once I had seen whatever was so important, I'd go to Amata and check on how she was doing. If she didn't need me, then I'd seek out Francesco. He and the brothers had finished the night here, rather than go back to the hospice and risk waking everyone as they came in.

In the spot outside my chamber where I listen to my house, I heard a muddle of voices coming from somewhere downstairs. Not the kitchen, I thought—too far away. Amata and Massimo's chamber? What could have happened? Alarmed, I turned to ask Bartola, but she was already moving quickly down the stairs, so I followed her, afraid something else might have gone wrong.

Renzo and Salvestra sat together on the bench in the courtyard. I murmured a greeting as we brushed past them, then we came to the door of the chamber. Bartola stood aside to let me see.

The room was bright, with the shutters open and the morning streaming in. I took it all in: Amata in bed, Massimo sitting next to her, Nuta on a stool on her other side, both of my boys grinning at me, Lucia pouring water into Amata's cup from a pitcher, and Francesco and Egidio just getting up from their knees. Leone was probably in the chapel with Amata's child, standing vigil. Ricco had returned, still wearing his patched and oversized habit, and he stood next to Gualtiero. Nuta held Benino to her breast, where he nursed greedily.

And Amata was feeding his sister. She looked up at me and an extraordinary sequence of emotions blossomed on her face, one after another. Sorrow. Pain. Regret. Gratitude. The beginning of acceptance. And then she caressed the cheek of Cilia, who was sucking industriously at her breast, and smiled, a sad, tired smile. I had no illusions that Amata had finished with her grieving—I of all people know that grieving is never really finished—but I had just seen the path her healing would take, traced on her fair face.

Before I could say anything, Massimo strode forward. "Giacoma, we've decided to adopt," he told me, and in his voice I heard a mixture of pain and newfound calm. "Father Francesco has helped us and prayed with us, and we want to do this, with your permission."

"Oh, Massimo," I said, overwhelmed. "You don't need my permission, but you have it, and my blessing, and my promise of all the help I can give you. Will you adopt one or both?" I would hate to have to separate the twins and send one back to the church when weaning was complete, but it was not my decision to make.

"Both," he said promptly, and Amata nodded. "Nuta is here to help, and she says she wants to stay on as part of the household, so we'll care for them together."

Everyone beamed, even Bartola. I felt almost giddy at this outcome, so soon after such a tragedy, but on some level I knew it would be a mistake to act as if the tragedy had never happened. I approached the bed, admired Cilia and stroked her shock of soft brown hair, and put my hand on Amata's shoulder.

"Amata," I said softly, "what was your daughter's name?"

Her eyes filled with tears. "Thank you, Giacoma." She swallowed, then lifted her chin proudly. "Her name was Bella." And with that naming she gave her child back the beauty lost in the womb, the beauty she had not lived to enjoy.

"Bella," I echoed. There was a general murmur as the others spoke the name.

One thing more. I turned to Nuta, who had finished feeding Benino and was wiping his lips as he drowsed.

"Nuta, what was your child's name?" I asked her. She looked up, surprised. How had I never thought to ask her that before? How had I not realized it was important?

"His name was Arturo, Giacoma."

I echoed the name. And this time, so did another voice. Amata quietly said "Arturo." She and Nuta looked at each other, sharing a private world of grief and loss, each of them gently cradling an infant not born of her body.

Another murmur in the room, everyone repeating the name. The face of each person in the chamber told a different story. Uccellino was weeping silently, unashamed. If any of us had given a thought to Nuta's loss before this, it would have been my younger son. Francesco's warm gaze bathed me in a welcome combination of affection and approval.

Amata's milk was not yet fully in, so she handed Cilia over to Nuta to finish nursing, and Bartola clapped her hands twice and told us all to get out and leave Amata in peace. Massimo ignored her and Nuta stayed to finish feeding Cilia, but the rest of us duly filed out into the courtyard.

I tried to gather my thoughts. First, we had to figure out food for the day. I asked Lucia and Gualtiero to go to the cookshop and get us something for dinner. I didn't think anyone was eager to prepare a meal after such an exhausting night, even if it did mean cookshop food two days in a row. Fortunately, we still had a day to produce a good meal for Francesco and the larger group of brothers.

We dispersed, Lucia and Gualtiero to their errand, Bartola up to the women's chamber to relieve Prassede, the boys to play, and the brothers, with Ricco among them, back to the bustling world of His Holiness's great council, for they must not fail to monitor developments that might affect the order's future.

Salvestra was pacing slowly around the courtyard, and I fell in step next to her. Renzo watched us from his spot on the bench opposite, but he didn't approach.

"Good morrow, monna Salvestra," I said, and she rewarded me with a smile of ineffable sweetness. "May I ask you something?"

She nodded and waited for me to speak.

"You may answer me truly. Nothing will change because of it."

Another nod.

"Did the babe move?

"The babe moved."

"Did she move on her own?"

"That, I did not say."

Ah. It was true, she had not said what caused the motion. And if Salvestra had moved it, then it had moved. Or at least that was one way to see it.

Lawyers, all of us, I thought wryly. Or churchmen. But if Francesco said all was well with the babe, then it was so.

And with that consolation, I thanked Salvestra again for her work the previous night and went to the storeroom to begin hunting up the necessary candles and burial cloth to lay Amata's little girl to rest.

21

THE next day, Tuesday, we began to prepare for our midday visit from Francesco and the brothers. Amata was still abed, and in her absence we all thought Prassede had the best chance of producing an edible meal, so we gave her command of the kitchen, and Lucia and I would help as best we could.

Meanwhile, Gualtiero took the most recent batch of almond cakes to Coppo's bakeshop for us. He would return to collect our finished cakes before dinner.

Prassede and Lucia worked well together. They didn't need me, so I went to the hall and started digging table linens out of a chest, and Massimo came in to help me set up the trestle tables. As I supported my end of the heavy board and waddled awkwardly along backwards, with Massimo supporting the other end and giving me directions, I couldn't help chuckling when I thought of what Cencio and Pierino would say if they saw me thus.

And that thought jarred me back to the thing I had almost forgotten in the flurry of events we'd been through: today Cencio was coming for my boys. I did not imagine my loss was to be as hard to bear as Amata's or Nuta's, and yet I felt downcast at the prospect. Even now I expected sometimes to turn a corner in my palazzo and bump into Graziano; what would life be like without Uccellino and Giovanni? I imagined my household without their youthful energy, the rest of us growing somber and dull without them. I'd be living for Sundays and just filling the time in between.

The weather had turned colder overnight, and a chilly drizzle was falling. The brothers had reached us around midmorning, after slogging through the rain from the hospice, and they entered shaking water from their hoods and wringing out the hems of their tunics. They left wet footprints on the herringbone brick floor as they filed through the kitchen, heading for the warmth of the hearth.

Francesco greeted me affectionately, but then he went to the chapel to pray, as was his wont. Egidio unselfconsciously stripped off his tunic and draped it over the bench near the fire to dry, though he kept his damp breeches on. He sat down with the boys, who wanted to tell him all about moving to Cencio's palazzo to become knights, and he nodded solemnly from time to time as Giovanni described their chivalrous future in colorful detail.

I led the others up to the hall to give Prassede a chance to finish cooking, though she would have chattered happily away at all of them while she worked, had I let them stay. But Massimo had kindled a fire in the hall, so they could warm themselves there instead.

When we got to the hall, I noticed the barefoot brothers were making their way across the floor rather gingerly. The tiles must be cold, I thought, though surely no colder than the streets outside had been.

"Giacoma, there's one thing you need to learn about playing hostess to friars—we don't do well with your herbs," Elias said, grinning as he reached down to pluck a sprig of rosemary from between his toes. Oh. I hadn't thought of that; I had scattered the rosemary, marjoram, and lavender around as usual for honored guests. Not very practical, under the circumstances.

"I'll get a broom," I said, starting for the door, but he put his hand on my arm to stop me.

"No, don't bother. We've probably picked up most of them by now anyway."

"Well, if you could walk here from Assisi in November, I expect you can cope with a few bits of lavender," I said, sitting back down.

Elias chuckled. "It's never an easy journey, Giacoma, but you make it worthwhile."

I relished the compliment, coming from him. Elias was the one of the lot of them who actually saw all the little things I did to make Francesco's path easier. Egidio and the others assumed I was like them, a joyful follower who never questioned Francesco's policies, but Elias and I, and Francesco himself, were made of more complex, more convoluted stuff. From time to time I longed for Egidio's simplicity and kindness and for Leone's gentle wisdom, but apparently those weren't part of my nature, and they weren't part of Elias's, either. We would have to make do with cleverness and good intentions, and the deep love for Francesco that we shared.

"How do you make sure there's food, Elias?" I asked. "And how do you find safe places to sleep?"

"You know Francesco's thoughts about planning ahead. We simply eat what people offer us and sleep when we are tired. It's my role to do what you would do, were you to travel with us—I make sure we arrive in towns where we know people whenever it's time to eat, and similarly, before it gets dark I try to get us to someplace where we can count on an offer of shelter. If Francesco realizes what I'm doing, he fights me on it. He stops to preach, or pray, or arbitrarily calls a halt to the day's travel in the middle of nowhere. But if I'm careful—and I'm getting subtler all the time—he doesn't notice."

"Do you not feel a need to let God provide? Don't you feel out of step with the others, when you plan ahead?"

He shook his head. "Giacoma, I'm the reason Francesco can be so trustful and innocent. Because I do what I do, Francesco can walk lightly through life, with things working out more often than not. You're no different from me, you know. He has friends in high places in the Church because you do what you do."

"Oh, Francesco himself is the cause of that, Elias. Cardinal Giovanni believed Francesco is a living saint, and Cardinal Ugolino says he's never met another man like him."

"Francesco is a saint, and the cardinal's right—he'll never meet another man like him. There is no one else like Francesco. But those men gave him a hearing in the beginning because of you."

"Do you believe you sin by steering him in certain directions and making sure certain things happen?" I had long been curious about this. It was plain enough what Elias was doing, but I didn't understand how it fit with Francesco's teachings.

"It may be that I do. I would love nothing more than to emulate Francesco in all things, but my nature will not permit it, and I've come to believe God led me to Francesco because we need each other. I need his goodness to keep me from sinking too far into pride, ambition, and the temptations of the world, and he needs my skills to free him to be the saint he is. My role is to make his role possible. I've reached peace with that."

"Do you mean Francesco can't be a saint by himself?"

"By himself, he certainly can. The problem comes as he gathers more and more followers. They are the reason he needs our help—and I assure you, Francesco does need our help. He is no administrator. He is a leader of men, but he will never be an organizer of them."

Before we could discuss it any further, Egidio, now wearing his tunic again, arrived in the doorway, bearing a pitcher of wine. Lucia and Prassede followed with trays of food, and the rest of my household and Francesco were right behind them.

We gathered around the table and stood with our heads bowed while Francesco prayed. The meal he blessed was convivial, tasty, and hearty enough for us to give out plenty of leftovers as alms later, both to our regular beggars and to the brothers, should they want to take something along for an evening meal. Francesco ate sparingly despite my urging him to try the delicacies we had prepared for him. He didn't touch the capon, only taking a little bread and a cup of soup. Leone whispered to me, as we nibbled at candied fruits, that Francesco had been fasting to prepare himself spiritually for whatever might come of the council.

"What will come of it, Brother Leone?" I asked.

"Many things, Brother Giacoma, from a new military venture in the Holy Land to renewed struggles with heresy here at home. But for us, we were lucky. Lucky and helped along by Cardinal Ugolino. The council decreed there are to be no new orders for people to join, but His Holiness acknowledged recognizing ours when Francesco first came to him."

That was a relief. I could imagine Ugolino diplomatically reminding the Holy Father of his casual long-ago remark. If he had not, it might well have meant trouble, for many in the curia insisted every order must have some source of revenue so it would not become a burden to its parish church or host city. But Francesco had espoused madonna Poverty, and he would never forsake her.

"Our main concern now is for the ladies of San Damiano," he went on. "They received no such acknowledgement, and the churchmen are even more anxious about communities of women than about the likes of us."

I understood. Chiara was, if possible, even more determined than Francesco to own nothing at all in this world, and that probably meant trouble ahead.

I asked Leone what else had been decided, but before he could answer, Elias stood and clapped his hands for attention. Everyone fell silent and turned toward him.

"Brothers, friends," he said, in his I'm-making-an-announcement voice, "our brother Francesco has something he wants to say to us."

Francesco stood and faced us, smiling his beatific smile. "Giacoma, and all our other beloved friends, we give you thanks for this wonderful meal and for your good company. You've made us welcome, as you have done so often, and we are grateful for your kindness. We have no gifts of our own to bring you in return, for we own nothing. But we do come with gifts, nonetheless, for Sister Chiara and her sisters have given their labor and their skill to make these tokens for your household."

Elias clapped a second time, and Ricco appeared in the doorway, staggering under the weight of a large basket filled with cloth. Massimo hurried to help the boy with his burden. It was still strange to me to see our Ricco in his habit, and yet the simple undyed garment suited him. He and Massimo were poised to dump the contents of the basket out onto the floor, since the tables were not yet cleared, but I bade them wait and fetched another tablecloth, the better to protect the Poor Ladies' handwork from dirt and shredded herbs. Lucia and I stretched it out on the floor as everyone watched, and then Massimo upended the basket, and wondrous gifts tumbled out onto the cloth.

The brothers had brought us embroidered veils, fringed towels, cushions for our elderly patients, an altar cloth for the chapel, baby clothes and cloth poppets, sturdy hose and shirts for the men and boys, and a few extra items in case my ever-shifting household had expanded yet again. Elias, his eyes sparkling, oversaw the distribution. To no one's surprise, he effortlessly remembered who was to receive each item.

I think the others were as moved as I was to be so remembered by the women of San Damiano. A crimson swaddling cloth had been intended for Amata's baby, but I surreptitiously added it to the small pile of baby linens sent for our foundlings. Chiara was well informed about us. No one was left out, and each gift was perfectly suited to its recipient.

My gift, a red linen purse with a border of lozenges in brilliant blue, was worked in Vanna's unmistakable tiny, perfect stitches. It never fails to amaze me how a woman's needlework is as unique to her as a scribe's handwriting is to him. Vanna did beautifully precise work, but she always needed someone else to come up with the design. She was helpless to produce one of her own.

This pattern, I suspected, was from Chiara herself. Certainly the altar cloth was Chiara's own work; it closely resembled the one I had seen at San Damiano. Tears stung my eyes. I didn't know if Chiara and I would ever be entirely easy with one another, but this was a lovely gesture, and I felt humbled.

Lucia, smiling as she displayed a pretty veil, came up to me and admired the purse. "Exquisite work," she said, and I nodded.

"We still have the almond cakes," she reminded me, and Egidio perked up.

So we did. It was time to produce them and put Francesco's perception to the test, but most of the delight of that idea had vanished, after all that had happened in the past two days.

Lucia and I went down to the kitchen to fetch the cakes. We carried them back to the hall on two large platters, for we had enough to feed a crowd. We set them on the table and let the diners help themselves; I chose to say nothing about having made some of them, since the whole game seemed so childish now.

Francesco took one, examined it, and nibbled a corner.

"Brother Giacoma made this cake for us," he announced. The rest of the cake he was holding looked normal, not obviously misshapen or under- or over-cooked. How did he know?

"Amata is a fine cook, and I don't doubt some of these fine treats are of her making. But this cake. . ." He held it aloft. "This cake is made by the hand of Brother Giacoma."

The brothers, their mouths full of almond cake, mumbled their compliments, and I found myself blushing in spite of myself. How could Francesco be so sure? Did God really reveal even unimportant things to him?

And then Elias stood up and clapped a third time. What now? More surprises? Everyone grew quiet and waited.

"We bring you one more gift," he announced, looking straight at me. The corner of his mouth twitched. He faced the door. "Brother Michelino," he called. "You may come in now."

Brother Michelino obediently appeared in the doorway. He was the youngest and newest of Francesco's flock, saving only Ricco. "God give you peace," he said in a muffled voice.

"Ba-a-a-a!" said the thing that muffled him. Brother Michelino was struggling to hold onto a lively, wriggling lamb, clutching it to his chest. The lamb, however, had a different idea and was doing its not inconsiderable best to escape the young brother's grasp.

Uccellino exclaimed in glee, and suddenly everyone was murmuring and commenting. The brothers all watched me as I sat there dumbstruck.

"Giacoma," said Francesco, "we were in the marketplace yesterday and we saw an opportunity to save this innocent creature from a cruel fate. We were going to try to buy it somehow, but when we preached the word of God to the farmer who was selling it, he was moved to offer it to us. We rejoiced to save this symbol of God's pure Son himself. But we've talked it over, and we don't believe we can take the beautiful creature back to Assisi with us, nor are the brothers at the hospice eager to host it for another night, so we give this gentle lamb to you, Giacoma. May it live with you long and happily, and remind you always of our Lord."

I was at a loss for words. I turned to Massimo, hoping he would have some idea what to do, but to my surprise it was Renzo who got up and hobbled over to Brother Michelino and his woolly charge. He lifted the animal's tail unceremoniously.

"It's a wether, Giacoma," he said. "That should help."

The lamb, alarmed at this indignity, redoubled his efforts to get loose, and at last he wiggled out of Brother Michelino's grip and landed with an undignified thump on the floor.

"Ma-a-a-a-a!" he announced to the room in general. And then he noticed the herbs. He put his wet pink nose down and snuffled among the sprigs and scattered leaves and flowers, rejecting some, tasting others.

Everyone in the room watched him in fascination. Uccellino couldn't contain himself any longer, and he crept toward the lamb, speaking to him in a gentle voice.

"Hello, little lambie, do you like the herbs?" he crooned. "You don't care for the rosemary, do you? But I think maybe you do like the marjoram." Uccellino crouched an arm's length away from the lamb and scooped up some herbs, sorting through them, throwing the rosemary aside. Cautiously he extended his hand, offering the selected herbs to our new resident. The lamb looked at him appraisingly and must have decided he posed no threat, because he snaked his tongue into Uccellino's palm, eating the proffered herbs.

Francesco beamed. "You see, Giacoma, already he is part of your family," he said.

I wasn't so sure, though Uccellino appeared to be convinced. Massimo, Lucia, Ricco, Gualtiero, and Salvestra were gaping at the lamb, but Prassede had that ecstatically transported expression I knew well, and that was when I began to realize what had happened: we had just acquired a sheep. In my palazzo. On the Palatine.

Uccellino was not the only one thrilled by the newcomer. Giovanni had been trying to hide his delight, but he couldn't stay silent. "Is he eating the lavender too, Uccel?" he asked.

Uccellino studied the lamb and its flicking tongue, then shook his head. "No, the only thing he wants is the marjoram."

"He'll need more than that soon," observed Renzo, who stood watching the lamb, arms folded across his chest and head tilted to one side.

"Is he weaned?" I asked, finally finding my voice.

Renzo made a show of looking around in all directions. "I don't see his dam anywhere about, so I'd say he's weaned, whether he wants to be or no," he said. "Young brother, if you'll pick the creature up, quick before he runs off, I'll check his mouth."

The lamb started to scramble his way upright, but Brother Michelino obediently scooped him up, holding the struggling animal awkwardly but with an almost comical determination. Renzo expertly pried the startled lamb's mouth open and peered inside.

"He's easy six, seven weeks old, maybe a bit more. A late one—a fall lamb. It happens, sometimes." He released the lamb's mouth, and the

153

creature bleated its delayed protest. "I'd have thought they'd intend him for the Christmas market. Don't know why they'd sell him now. Probably couldn't afford more feed this late in the year."

And that poor farmer was moved by Francesco's preaching to give away his valuable wether, a prize purchase for some wealthy man's table at this time of year. I'd have Massimo track down the farmer and see him compensated. How did Renzo know so much about sheep? Had he been a farmer before he was a tinker? I knew so little about him.

"And that makes him all the more special, don't you see, Giacoma?" Francesco said. "God meant him for you."

"Brother Francesco, may I put him down now?" said the muffled and strained voice of Brother Michelino. At least that's what I think he said. It was hard to tell with a wiggling sheep between him and us.

"By all means, give him his freedom," Francesco said. "Let him explore his new home."

So Brother Michelino did.

This act of kindness may have been a little premature, for the lamb was understandably terrified by everything that had happened to him. He'd been distracted once by tasty herbs and had let my son approach him, but now he realized he was in a new and unprotected place, surrounded by human beings who hauled him around unceremoniously, with not another sheep anywhere in sight, and he began to tremble.

He also dribbled some noxious-smelling yellow stuff onto the floor as he made a dash for the door of the hall. Brother Michelino froze. Renzo hobbled after the lamb as fast as he could go, which wasn't very fast. He had no hope of catching up, and he surrendered the chase before he even got out of the room.

So twenty or more people sat or stood helplessly watching, fully expecting the creature to career down the stairs and wind up in the atrium, or the kitchen, or perhaps in Amata's chamber, which would probably give her a start. But we hadn't figured on the lamb's unfamiliarity with stairs. Frustrated by the alarming steps, the poor thing ran in frantic circles, following the corridor past the chambers. Fortunately he was going at such a breakneck pace that he completely missed the side corridor leading to the west wing, so Bartola and our old women wouldn't find themselves confronted by a hysterical sheep. Not yet, anyway.

"Sheep can climb," Renzo mused, "but I don't think their hooves are very good for going down stairs."

By some unspoken agreement, Massimo, Uccellino, and Francesco all rose and went out to try to corral the sheep. Uccellino grabbed a handful of herbs, and Brother Michelino trailed reluctantly along.

Prassede had shaken off her state of bliss and was swabbing up the yellow stuff. I hoped she had found a towel and not one of Chiara's gifts, but I didn't want to look too closely.

Then I remembered Elias. Elias always knew what to do. I could ask him how to deal with this situation. I turned to where he had been sitting, but his place was empty.

The ever-resourceful Brother Elias was leaning on the wall, his chest heaving with helpless, silent laughter, tears racing down his handsome face.

A distraught sheep was coursing around the piano nobile with a probable saint, a child, and my steward in hot pursuit and an elderly shepherd-turned-tinker offering advice, and Elias was laughing. Actually, I felt a bit tempted myself, but that might have been a touch of hysteria welling up inside me. Graziano would have loved this. He had always taken delight in the ridiculous.

We heard voices and a lot of commotion in the corridor, and occasionally the sheep raced past the door with Francesco, Uccellino, Massimo, and Brother Michelino close behind. Everyone but Brother Michelino appeared ready to last for quite a while. Especially the lamb.

Then came the pounding on the door downstairs.

22

OH, *sweet Mary, mother of our Lord, please don't let it be Cencio and Pierino.* Though I knew full well it was. Massimo left the chase and clattered down the stairs.

Massimo said something, then Cencio spoke, curt and dismissive, and I heard footsteps on the stairs. Meanwhile the lamb and his remaining three pursuers continued to sprint along the corridor, repeatedly passing the door to the hall—and, of course, the head of the stairs. *Maybe it wouldn't be so bad if our little wether happened to find that side corridor just about now, but I'm not optimistic.*

"Giacoma! What's going on here?" Cencio bellowed from somewhere on the stairs.

I thought it was fairly obvious, but I went over to stand in the doorway to talk to him, since he wasn't going to risk crossing the corridor to reach the hall. To do so would have been like stepping into a racecourse in the middle of a palio. Cencio and Pierino were halfway up, glowering as lamb, Uccellino, Francesco, and Brother Michelino dashed past. Cencio had that outraged, how-dare-the-world-do-this-to-me expression, the one that always made me want to prick him with a needle and see if he'd deflate.

"Hello, Cencio," I said as calmly as I could, and Elias gasped for breath and then snorted. Apparently he'd gone beyond the silent mirth stage.

"Giacoma, what's the meaning of this?" Cencio demanded again, and he and Pierino both glared up at me. They looked so much alike I hardly knew which one to pity more.

"Well, our lamb is a little upset at the moment—" I began, but just then the lamb raced past me, close enough to brush my skirt. I jumped back, and my son, my spiritual father, and my steward—who had rejoined the chase—pounded past right behind him. Brother Michelino was panting in a corner and had given up, at least for the moment.

Fortunately the lamb finally noticed the side corridor, which was directly across from where I stood. He galloped down it and his pursuers followed, all headed straight for the women's ward of our hospital wing. I heard a loud squawk from Bartola, but I felt I needed to turn my attention to our guests for the moment. Probably Bartola could cope with it.

Now that the stampede had moved elsewhere, Cencio and Pierino climbed the rest of the stairs, while I watched them from the doorway.

"Would you like to join us for almond cakes?" I asked them politely.

For some reason that set Elias off again, and I heard him behind me wheezing for breath. It must have been contagious, because Egidio, Leone, Bernardo, and even Ricco were in various stages of laughter-fueled helplessness. Lucia tried to shush them, but Salvestra sat at the table giggling happily, dabbing at her streaming eyes with the tablecloth. Only Prassede, loyal little Prassy, came up to me and stood at my side. She was holding a foul-smelling wadded cloth, which wasn't going to help me placate my in-laws, but I was glad she was there anyway.

"I've come for the boys, Giacoma, and not any too soon, I see," Cencio said, glowering at me. He and Pierino shoved roughly past Prassede and me to enter the hall.

"I'm taking these boys out of this shambles you call a palazzo while there's still some hope for them," Cencio said. The brothers were making heroic attempts to control their hilarity, but it did take a few moments before they succeeded, and I think Cencio may have taken their mirth personally, for he practically quivered with indignation.

He was wearing an appalling concoction of plush emerald green with a fur-lined black mantle and an ostentatious belt with an absurd silver clasp studded with stones. Pierino's outfit was even more ridiculous, purplish-blue with too much gold thread in the trim. I must have become accustomed to gray habits and simple clothes, because I couldn't figure out why anyone would even want to wear such things. Elias, finally serious, was looking Cencio up and down with an expression of utter contempt.

"Giovanni's here," I said, "but Uccellino is, um, busy elsewhere at the moment. Can you wait a moment, and I'll fetch him?"

Cencio gave me a withering glance. "No, I cannot wait. We're going. Now. With only one of them, if necessary. Come!" This last was aimed past me and to my son. Giovanni scrambled to his feet and started to say something, but he was interrupted by the sound of weary footsteps approaching from the corridor.

This time Francesco was in the lead, carrying a docile, serene lamb and followed by Uccellino and Massimo.

Francesco nodded pleasantly at my glowering brother-in-law. "The fault is entirely mine, messere," he said. "Allow me to settle this precious creature, and then we will speak of how I may make amends to you."

Francesco carried the uncomplaining sheep to the far side of the hall, away from the tables but within the hemisphere of warmth around the hearth, and set the creature down, asking the creature courteously to wait a few moments. The lamb half sat, half lay, and watched Francesco deftly assemble a sort of nest, using Chiara's unclaimed gifts. Massimo and Gualtiero both contributed their new hose. I thought it might be best to avoid telling Chiara and her sisters what had become of their needlework. Not to lie to them, exactly, but to tactfully omit mentioning this detail.

Meanwhile Cencio and Pierino, ignored, were looking ever more furious, but they said nothing—probably waiting for me. I kept my attention on Francesco.

When the nest was complete, Uccellino tried to lead the lamb over to it, but he met with firm, if passive, resistance. Frustrated, he turned to Renzo.

"Why won't he come with me, Renzo?"

"You can never lead a sheep anywhere, young lord, unless you're another sheep yourself. If you're a person, or a sheepdog, and you want to make a sheep move, you have to stand behind it. Back of its shoulders, like this." Renzo demonstrated, and the lamb awkwardly started to get up. "Then you just sort of nudge it along, and it trots away ahead of you," he said, gently prodding the animal, which did indeed trot right to the nest and plop down in the middle of it.

Uccellino was puzzled by this. "But people always say sheep are easy to lead," he argued. "And when people stop thinking for themselves and follow other people, they say those people are acting like sheep."

Renzo grinned at him. "Folks aren't always right, are they, young lord? You want to make a sheep go somewhere, you don't expect it to follow you. No, you convince it that it wanted to go there anyway, more'n anything else in the world, and then it goes. And it thinks it decided for itself."

"Does that work for people too?" Uccellino asked.

Francesco, who was crouched next to the lamb and stroking it, smiled. "I think it may be true for more than just sheep, Uccel," he said, and his voice sounded tired. He hid his fatigue well, but his face was pale, and his thin chest heaved faster than I liked to see. The chase had been hard on him; he was not as strong as he used to be.

Soon the lamb was nestled peacefully among the bits of cloth while Uccellino fed him sprigs of marjoram. He was relaxed with both Uccellino and Francesco, but when Cencio, plainly tired of waiting, took a step toward him, he stiffened. Uccellino quickly placed himself between Cencio and the lamb.

"Hello, Uncle," he began, but Cencio had had enough.

"I want to know exactly why a sheep was running around the piano nobile of your palazzo," he said. "And I want you to explain it to me right now."

He scowled at Uccellino, who looked up at him with an expression of perfect innocence. I glared at Cencio for him. Somebody needed to.

"The brothers brought him to us, but he got scared," my son said, as if he were patiently explaining a lesson to a younger child.

"Well, tell your man to take him downstairs and slaughter him out in the back. Animals don't belong in your hall, even if your mother doesn't know any better, and these filthy friars you're feeding are nothing but animals themselves."

I think of myself as slow to anger, but something about Cencio invariably hurried the process. I drew in a breath to tell Cencio exactly who was the animal in this hall, but Prassede took my hand and squeezed it and Leone came up to me and put his arm around my shoulder, and to my surprise I found myself holding my tongue. Perhaps Francesco's gentle teachings were finally getting through to me.

"Oh, we're not going to *slaughter* him—" Uccellino said, but Cencio roared at him.

"You and your brother will go down those stairs right now, and your servants are going to fetch your things, and we are leaving this house. And don't think you'll be coming back here, on Sundays or any other days. This palazzo is not fit for my brother's children."

Out of the corner of my eye I saw Elias stiffen, and I'd almost swear he reached for a blade—a blade which naturally was not there.

Uccellino's upper lip trembled, and with that I forgot Francesco's teachings. I started to shake off Prassede and Leone so I could confront my idiot brother-in-law with the full fury of an irate mother, but Renzo chose that moment to tug at my sleeve.

"Giacoma, the little fellow needs something more than herbs," he said, pointing at the lamb. "We should take him to the stable and see him properly fed."

That did it. Whatever control Cencio had left vanished.

"Keep out of this, you flea-ridden old fool! And never call my brother's widow by her given name! Who do you think you are?"

He shoved Renzo hard, and I gasped. Renzo went down in a tangled heap on the floor. Prassede dropped the malodorous cloth and crouched next to him, and Elias hurried toward us from one side and Francesco from the other, but somehow Giovanni got there before either of them. While Prassede and I helped Renzo sit up, checking him for injuries, and Elias loomed in front of Cencio with a face like a thundercloud and his

159

hands clenched into fists, Francesco took the measure of the situation. I knew him well; I noted the precise moment in which he decided not to speak.

Giovanni stood with his hands on his hips, staring coldly at his uncle. He, too, was slow to anger, but I recognized that flash in his eyes. He was his father's son.

"Uncle, we are not going home with you," he announced, and his voice was clear and firm. "We thank you for your offer of hospitality, but what we've seen from you today is not knightly behavior, and we have no wish to learn it." He swallowed hard and continued. "You have insulted our guests and attacked a good man who dwells with us. This is unworthy of a Frangipane. My brother and I will learn what we need to learn elsewhere."

Cencio gaped at him. Pierino let out a string of vulgarities, which I thought nicely underscored Giovanni's point. I had never been prouder of my son.

"I'll *make* you come with me, you arrogant little fool," Cencio barked, taking a menacing step toward my boys.

He didn't get far. Francesco, Elias, and I moved quickly, putting ourselves solidly in front of my sons. I didn't take my eyes off Cencio, but I sensed several of the others moving closer to us as well.

Giovanni came forward, wriggling between Elias and me to stand at my side. I tried to pull him back behind me, but he resisted and stood his ground.

"I am my father's heir and master of this house, Uncle, and I have made my decision." It was strange to hear such adult words in a boy's voice, not yet changed to its adult pitch.

"Brother-in-law, you will go now," I said, my voice dangerously quiet. Cencio and I locked eyes. I watched the play of emotions across his face; I have no idea what he saw in mine, but he made an abrupt gesture to Pierino.

"Let's get out of this pigsty, son," he growled. "It belongs to a mad-woman." Pierino ostentatiously held his nose as they made their way down the stairs and out the front door.

I hugged my boys, who suddenly seemed like children again now it was over, and then the three of us turned to Renzo to see how he fared.

Prassede looked up at us. "I think he was lucky, Giacoma. He's bruised, but nothing's broken."

Renzo groaned, still sitting on the floor. The more I thought about that act of casual brutality, the more I wanted to run to the window and start dropping our dinner dishes on Cencio as he went out the door below, or even better, that cloth Prassede had used to mop up the mess. But I suspected Francesco would not permit it.

Everyone crowded around Renzo, who let Massimo help him to his feet, where he wobbled uncertainly for a moment until Uccellino fetched him his stick. He insisted he was fine, but he leaned heavily on the stick and on Massimo and Prassede as they helped him back to his chamber. Salvestra walked alongside, her hand on Renzo's arm, a worried frown turning her aged face into a pattern of lines and wrinkles.

"I'll have Bartola examine him too, Giacoma," Prassede said over her shoulder as they left the hall.

Uccellino put his hand on his brother's shoulder. "Thank you, Vanni," he said. "You spoke for both of us, and I'm proud of you," and Giovanni, who was trembling after his confrontation with his uncle, smiled weakly.

"I'm proud of you too, son," I told Giovanni. "I'm proud of you both, and your father would have been, too. Giovanni, I know you wanted to go, and to get your horse and your sword and to learn to be a knight. I'll speak to my brothers and see what we can work out." Were my brothers any better? Maybe a bit, but the more I thought about it, the more I was sure it would be best for now to keep the boys here at the palazzo and arrange for occasional lessons. I could afford the best, and I resolved that they would have it, here, safe at home.

Giovanni shook his head slowly. "I did want to go, Mother, but I didn't realize what kind of man Uncle was. I know I shouldn't say that about Father's brother, and I probably shouldn't have said the things I did. But he hurt Renzo, and he insulted Brother Francesco and the other brothers, and I just couldn't—I don't know, I understood all of a sudden that I couldn't go with him. And Uccel shouldn't either."

"I agree. Massimo can work with you on horsemanship, and I'll get a swordmaster to come in, and then you won't have to live somewhere else. Will that suit you?"

"Yes, very much," he said, and Uccellino nodded vigorously.

Francesco came up to us holding the lamb, now perfectly contented and munching on a sprig of marjoram. "Uccellino, Giovanni, this little one needs his dinner. Can you take us to the stable, as Renzo suggested?"

The boys led Francesco downstairs, with the lamb bleating in mild alarm, and I sank down on a bench, exhausted. Lucia sat next to me and patted my hand, and Elias pulled up a stool across from me.

"Your boys did well, Giacoma," he said.

"They did, didn't they? There's a lot of their father in them." I beamed with maternal pride as I remembered Giovanni's extraordinary speech to his uncle.

"I would have said there's a lot of their mother in them," Elias said. "That took a rare courage." His words, and the way he was looking at me, made me blush.

"Oh, I've no particular courage, Elias."

"I think you have. But, in any case, I hope you'll forgive us for creating such a debacle, and for foisting a sheep on you."

Ah, yes. The sheep. "Well, I'm not quite sure what I'm going to do with it, but I suppose it's better than a leopard, anyway."

"A what?" Elias looked puzzled.

"Never mind. If Francesco wants the lamb to live here, then I guess it lives here."

"Francesco has that effect on people, doesn't he? It may be rather like convincing a sheep that it really wants to go where you want it to go. So, are we forgiven?"

"Elias, my brother, the sheep is indeed a sign from God. It's the reason I still have my sons. The only thing I can't forgive is you dissolving into laughter at the precise moment when I needed your organizational skills." I was only half joking.

"Oh, come now, Giacoma. Don't tell me you weren't tempted to do the same. There stood your red-faced kinsman in that ridiculous costume with his sneering, pimply son, and the lamb was pelting along as fast as it could, and the others were madly running after him..."

Elias grinned at the memory, and I couldn't help it—I felt mirth rise up inside me, and then we were all laughing, Elias and Lucia and Massimo and I, and also Leone and Egidio and the other brothers. It was a welcome release. Every time I tried to pull myself together, some other memory came into my mind, and I was off again. The same thing was happening to everyone.

"The look on Cencio's face—"

"That squawk from Bartola!"

"Giacoma, the way you calmly asked them if they wanted almond cakes—"

"Did you see poor Brother Michelino? He's not used to moving so fast!"

"That situation was completely beyond anybody's organizational skills!"

Francesco appeared in the doorway, his breathing now back to normal, to my relief. "But what happened to Renzo was not funny," he said, and it felt like a mild reproach.

We sobered. "No, it was not," I agreed. "Will you visit him before you leave?"

"Yes. I'll go to him soon."

"Where's the sheep?" said Egidio, trying to stifle a last chortle.

"He's made friends with a donkey, and he's eating a nice dinner. Gualtiero is watching him."

A donkey? Did we even *have* a donkey here? I thought they were all stabled in Marino. Oh, yes, now I remembered. A sweet, scruffy little thing, brought to town to carry light burdens. Uccellino was fond of her, as he was of all animals.

I wanted to talk to Francesco about everything that had happened, and to Elias too, but it was time for the brothers to get back to the hospice, and to the business of the church council. The various tragedies and comedies of my household could not occupy them any longer, I understood, yet I hated to see them go.

As they were leaving, Elias asked me quietly, "Will this rift with your kinsman be a problem for you, Giacoma?"

"No, it shouldn't be. He needs me in the consortium. I think he'll send round a conciliatory message in a day or two, along with a gift of some sort. He won't come himself, but he can't afford to lose our alliance." It would be awkward, but Cencio was a practical man. The only effect this would have was the desirable one of making him keep his distance.

And thus it happened—a gift of wine from his villa's vineyards, a brief, stiff note saying we could work together despite our disagreements, and nothing more. So much drama for nothing. But I still had my boys, and that was everything.

My household was back to normal, or at least to our new version of normal, which encompassed our grief at the loss of Amata's child, Ricco's departure, the now-permanent residence of the two foundlings, a distinct chill between my household and my brother-in-law's, and my new facility in cooking.

And a sheep.

Rome and Assisi (and points in between), early spring 1217

23

I drifted toward wakefulness, aware of a powerful odor of rancid wool. Either Prassede had taken another step in her quest for ever more humble attire, or Lotario needed a bath.

Cautiously I opened one eye. A large, wet, glistening-yet-soulful sheep eye stared back at me, a handspan away from my face. That sort of thing could startle a person who wasn't used to it.

I closed my eye and tried to breathe through my mouth. Lotario nudged my cheek with his warm nose, insistently.

I groaned and turned onto my stomach, pulling the cover over my head. "Lotario, you could have been a roast shoulder of lamb. Studded with garlic," I muttered. He shoved his muzzle into my side, emphatically.

"And parsley. Lots of parsley." I curled up defensively and pulled away from him. He put his front legs on the edge of the bed and butted me, none too gently. Time to rise. It was a lot harder to argue with Lotario at this age than it had been when we first got him. Or he first got us, depending on your point of view.

"With a nice sharp vinegar-based sauce. It's not too late." I sat up and glared at him. Unperturbed, he wandered off to see if I might for once have left something edible on my washbasin stand.

Ah, well. My malodorous woolly conscience was right, it was time. Today was my day to travel, and I welcomed a little extra time to finish my preparations. Everything was packed and ready, and I probably had at least an hour before Cardinal Ugolino appeared to collect me, but it wouldn't hurt to review pending household business with Massimo one more time, and to take a few extra minutes with my boys, for I would not see them for several months.

164

I was curious about what to expect of traveling with an eminent churchman and his retinue. It had seemed the most prudent way to get to Assisi, which was why I was leaving from Rome in late February rather than from Marino after the household moved there for the summer. This way I could get away with bringing only Gualtiero and a couple of his men, plus Prassede as my companion, for the cardinal would be traveling with all the protection anyone could ask for.

Part of the cardinal's protection was uniquely his own. As if allowing me a rare privilege, he had shown me the exquisite jeweled reliquary he always wore on a finely wrought chain around his neck, removing it and placing it reverently in my hands.

"It contains a potent relic, monna Giacoma. Herein is the blessed finger of the holy woman Marie d'Oignies."

I knew of this remarkable Flemish woman, not a cloistered sister, but a laywoman dedicated to living a holy life while remaining in the world.

"What protection does it give you, signore?" I traced the reliquary's delicate pattern with my fingertip.

"I don't know if you are aware of it, madonna, but I struggle with a most un-Christian temper. When the black rage is upon me, I have been known to commit the terrible sin of blasphemy."

Yes, I was aware of it. Everyone in Rome knew of the cardinal's irascible nature and his tendency to swear like a dockworker if anyone crossed him.

"And this holy finger prevents you from blaspheming?"

He nodded proudly. "It does, at least when I remember to call upon it. This relic may well save my soul, monna Giacoma. Thus I count it my most valuable safeguard." He clasped it in his hand and squeezed it before putting it back on and tucking it away inside his robe.

So it was under the protection of numerous armed guards and a holy finger that I would travel to Assisi. The guards assured my bodily safety, and the finger should save me from any unpleasantness should I run afoul of the good cardinal, which I intended to avoid doing if possible.

I took Elias's letter from the coffer in the wall niche above my bed, unfolded it, and read it again.

"Watch over Francesco, Giacoma," he had exhorted me in his elegant, lucid hand. "He harms himself with constant penance, and he has never been strong. I fear for him. The other brothers will obey him in all things without question, even though they should be standing up to him for his own good. Only you and I are strong enough to do that, and since I am where I cannot help him, I beg you to go to him, as soon as you can, and persuade him to—no, *make* him take proper care of himself. Ask Sister Chiara to help you, if you need her. He will lose everything if he weakens himself so much that he cannot lead this movement. Though God has caused the brotherhood to grow wonderfully fast, it will not yet survive without his guidance."

Elias had written to me from the Holy Land, where Francesco had sent him with a few brothers. He was to spearhead a missionary movement ahead of the main thrust of the papal forces, now under the command of Innocente's successor Pope Honorius. Francesco still hoped, against all reason, to spread the word of God to the Sultan's people and avoid bloodshed. How Elias managed to get his letters to me I didn't know, but I had learned not to question his resourcefulness. By the time they reached the couriers who at last delivered them to me, weeks or months after Elias wrote them, they had gone through so many hands in so many places I couldn't even begin to trace their journey to Rome.

I refolded the parchment and placed it back in the coffer with Graziano's coif and the diaphanous veil he had given me that day when I first saw Francesco. There was more, much more, but what I had just reread was at the heart of why I was making this trip.

I dressed in my travel clothes, sturdy and practical and with a wide skirt. The road from Rome to Assisi is long and mountainous, and I wanted to be as comfortable as possible. Prassede hadn't even blinked at the idea of riding. She did ask for a donkey or mule, saying it would be more appropriate for her humble penitential status than a horse. We had plenty of both in the party, for his lordship the cardinal intended to stay in Assisi long enough to sort out whatever problems that city's truculent bishop had caused recently, and then he was off to Florence, where he would take up residence as the pope's legate for a period of at least a year or two. Thus the cardinal's entire household, including furniture, was on the move.

I traveled more modestly. I must admit, however, that when I looked at the pile of chests and baskets I was taking, and saw Massimo leading my palfrey out of the stable, followed by the mounts for my guards and my companion, our pack animals, and the cart, I didn't think we had exactly achieved Francesco's ideal of poverty.

It was an enormous undertaking. Still, I was well organized—Elias would have been proud of me—and when the cardinal's train arrived, we were able to merge our parties smoothly and efficiently. I said my final goodbyes to my household, leaving Massimo in charge, and kissed my boys before I mounted. I even gave Lotario a hug, since Giovanni had carried him downstairs to see me off. It meant I carried a strong whiff of sheep on my clothing, but on the bright side, running my hands through Lotario's greasy wool always left them remarkably soft and smooth, and this would be my last chance for a while. The poor sheep was going to miss me almost as much as he would miss his donkey friend, who was to be Prassede's mount.

The boys could hardly wait for us to leave. They were bouncing with barely suppressed glee. They even volunteered to help load the pack animals. I hid a smile at this, for I knew—my household, my responsibility; nothing escapes me in my own palazzo—I knew they had persuaded Massimo to help them build a ramp on the stairs for Lotario, and work on it was set to commence once I was safely out of sight.

It actually wasn't too bad an idea. Lotario had no problems climbing the stairs, but he couldn't get back down on his own. It took my strapping Giovanni, now thirteen, to pick up the Frangipane sheep and lug him down the stairs, for our woolly resident had grown too heavy for Massimo to carry with his damaged arm. Lotario came from compact stock; he was not large for an adult wether, but he squirmed and wriggled enough to present a challenge to anyone trying to carry him. It did mean our hooved friend would have full access to the palazzo, going wherever he liked whenever he liked. And the whole project would perforce take place in the presence of Amata's adopted, raucous two-year-old twins. This promised to be interesting.

Soon after I arrived in Assisi, my household would relocate to our lakeside villa some miles outside Rome, near the rustic village of Marino. There our spacious grounds would provide Lotario with all the best of country life. He would love it. I loved it there too, and I was almost sorry to miss those three months of rural bliss, but Assisi called to me, and it was time to get moving.

With luck, they might have everything at the palazzo back under control by the time I returned, sometime in the fall.

*

Cardinal Ugolino rode up beside me. "We're making good time, don't you think, monna Giacoma?" he asked, smiling.

I looked at him, incredulous. It was day twenty-one of the journey. The rider I sent from Rome to Francesco in Assisi the previous fall had made the trip in four days. True, we had arranged for a change of horse for him each day, and he and his hired man-at-arms were traveling light, unencumbered by carts and wagons and companions on foot. We, on the other hand, traveled with everything from men walking barefoot to palfreys who chafed at our sedate pace and felt the need to move as much as I did. We had been slowed by a broken cart wheel and then a lame horse, and the man who walked alongside our pack animals insisted on lengthy pauses to let them rest. He was a brother, wearing the scruffy gray habit, so fond of the animals that I suspected we'd be carrying them, if he had his way. Still, the single biggest difference was that my messenger didn't stop in every town to hold services, bless the people, conduct papal business, and preach.

The March weather had been fine for the most part, yet we were only now getting into mountainous country. We hadn't even reached Trevi yet, though we would by nightfall. I was eager to see Francesco and the brothers, eager to revisit Assisi, eager to make an end to this plodding, tedious journey and arrive where I could take a bath, wash my hair, and eat something besides road food, which during Lent was even more uninspiring than usual.

Some of this must have shown on my face, for the cardinal reached over and patted my hand. "We will arrive soon, madonna," he assured me. "I know you're eager to see Brother Francesco, as am I. We've no more than an hour to go before we arrive in Trevi, and then it's a matter of perhaps another six days, if all goes well."

He couldn't mean that. "Six days?" I said. "How can it be six days? I could do it in one!"

The cardinal studied me as we rode along side by side. He was not a young man, but he was as vigorous as a man half his age, and the eyes gazing out of that seamed, weatherbeaten face were sharp and alert.

"I do believe you could," he concluded, smiling again. "You're a fine rider, monna Giacoma, and you're young. But you must take pity on the rest of the party." He gestured vaguely at his elite armed guard out in front, and the long string of riders, vehicles, and men on foot trailing along behind us.

"But six?" I persisted. "We can almost see Assisi from here."

He laughed. "We're not *that* close. Six it will be, because I have business to transact for His Holiness in Trevi. We will bide there a while, and I have a case I must hear in Foligno, so that too will take us an extra day. But then we'll pause in Spello only overnight, and from there it is but a short ride to Assisi."

Nothing to be done, then. Six days. I rode in grumpy silence, but he kept glancing at me, and I wondered what he was thinking. I was too annoyed to ask.

At length, he nodded to himself as if he had just made a decision. "Monna Giacoma, will you ride ahead with me? I would speak with you privately about a certain matter."

I agreed, immediately curious, and we prodded our mounts to a trot, pulling out to either side of the party and moving forward until we were well ahead of the caravan.

The cardinal's bodyguards, half a dozen of them under the dour command of one Dino di Pietro, moved to follow us, but the cardinal waved them back.

"Leave us," he called. "We will ride a little ahead."

"But, signore," Dino called back, "we are charged with protecting you, and here the road is wooded—dangers may be hiding."

"It's the middle of the afternoon, Dino, and the trees aren't even leafed out yet," the cardinal said irritably. He touched his reliquary. "We'll be fine. Leave us, I say, and go back to your places."

Dino obeyed, but his scowl told me he wasn't happy. I didn't particularly feel endangered. The trip had been uneventful so far, and we were a formidable party, not an easy target for wolves or for bandits. I was curious, though, about what the cardinal wanted of me. I assumed it had to do with money, that being what most people think of when they think of me, but what might require this unusual secrecy?

We rode along at a quick pace for long enough that I could no longer see our party behind us. It felt good to move briskly after three weeks of plodding.

"Madonna, there is something I must ask of you," he said, slowing his horse to a walk. I reluctantly followed suit. "It concerns the lawsuit you inherited from your late husband, the lawsuit against papal property." He looked at me sidelong.

Ah. That. I almost opened my mouth to assure him it was no longer a problem: when I read Francesco's letter to the faithful, that wise document aimed at his lay followers, I was persuaded that both Graziano's soul and mine would benefit from dropping the suit, and I had determined to do so.

But then, God forgive me, it occurred to me that the lawsuit could be valuable as something to barter with.

As a major property holder representing two of the most important families in Rome, I learned certain negotiating techniques, and it had become second nature to apply them, even to situations involving the Holy Father. Francesco would not have approved, but I suspected Elias would understand completely.

169

So I looked at him, all wide-eyed innocence, and said, "What of it, signore?"

"Do you not believe it would be wise to relinquish your claim? It would set a shining example, for everyone knows of your deep devotion to the church."

Did I have a deep devotion to the church? I was devoted to Francesco, but I had a Roman's informed skepticism about the church as an institution.

"And it would please Brother Francesco, who always urges us to put spiritual things ahead of material things." He sounded rehearsed.

"And yet, I act under my husband's instructions," I said slowly, as if I was thinking about it for the first time. "And on my sons' behalf. How can I make such a decision for my boys? Is that fair to them?" Not that this particular decision would make much difference to their future, but for Graziano, it had been a matter of principle. And however wealthy you may be to begin with, you don't continue being wealthy by flinging away possessions at every turn. It was a matter of prudence as well as principle. Also, for what it was worth, I did believe we were legally in the right.

"I understand your position, monna Giacoma," he said—still sounding rehearsed—"but kindly consider what it could mean to your spiritual father, if you were to take his words so much to heart."

I replied with a noncommittal murmur, and he fixed his steady gaze on me.

"I know Brother Francesco has spoken to you of this," he said.

Ah. An efficient man, the cardinal, his preparations all in place. We ambled on while I considered how to reply, and he didn't rush me.

At length I had it. "Signore, may I be frank?"

"Of course," he said promptly. "We speak in private."

"Is there not possibly an advantage for you also, should I agree to what you ask?"

This time he hesitated. "What do you mean?"

"I mean, signore, the day may come when you yourself wear the tiara, and so this action may well serve you in the future." Frank indeed. I waited to see what he would make of that. Cardinal Ugolino was old, but not as old as our current pope. He still had a chance.

To his credit, he appeared to be considering my words. I do enjoy it when eminent men take me seriously.

"It is possible, I suppose," he said finally. "But I beg you to remember that I am not a young man, and our beloved Holy Father may outlive me, should God grant him the long life we all pray he will have." He turned those shrewd eyes toward me. "I wonder if we might identify some kindness I could do for you, madonna, as a token of my gratitude should you agree to my suggestions."

There it was. I had no immediate use for this verbal promissory note, but I would file it away until I needed it, which meant I must not give him my full agreement yet.

"This is a serious matter, signore. You must allow me time to consider, and to consult with my advisors," I said, hoping he didn't know I wasn't much in the habit of taking advice from anyone but Francesco.

"But you will consider it?"

"Yes. And I will give my answer directly to you, as soon as I have it."

He nodded, apparently satisfied, and we rode on in an easy silence. I thought perhaps I would like to play chess with this man one day. I'd not seen more than a hint of the subtle maneuverings he was said to practice, and yet I had a feeling he would be a worthy opponent.

We had long since lost sight of the rest of our caravan, and I was about to suggest we halt and let the others catch up to us when we heard a violent rustling in the trees alongside the road.

We reined in our horses as five men burst out of the woods just ahead of us, yelling and brandishing weapons.

24

PART of me wanted to scream, but most of me was fully occupied trying to control my mount. I twisted around, hoping to see our party coming up behind us, but we must have ridden farther ahead than we intended.

The men had been well hidden. The branches were still bare, but they had crouched in a shallow pit behind a fallen tree. Two of the bandits moved quickly to the middle of the road in front of us. One of them grabbed the reins of both our alarmed horses, speaking gibberish to calm them.

"What is the meaning of this?" the cardinal roared. He too was working to keep his horse under control. Either we were succeeding or the bandit horse talker was good at what he did, for our mounts, though skittish and wild-eyed, did not panic.

The leader faced us defiantly, standing with his legs wide apart and his weapon raised—a long knife, or a short sword, if you weren't too particular. "Hold right there! We'll have your money, both of you, and your jewels too, lady!" The bandit's accent was pure Umbrian.

I spread my arms and displayed my plain travel gown. I never wore jewels when embarking on an overland journey. In fact, I hadn't worn jewels at all since Graziano died.

He looked me up and down and harrumphed.

"Then we'll take *your* jewels, churchman," he said to the cardinal. He'd have richer pickings there, no doubt, including a certain ornate reliquary. "But first, your purses."

I had no idea how far behind us our party was or how long it might take them to catch up. The wind was at our backs, so I didn't think the shouting would have carried to our companions' ears.

Cardinal Ugolino made a great show of slowly untying his pursestrings. I knew he was stalling. For my part, I did nothing. It would take longer if they had to order me a second time to give them my purse.

"We've got to hurry," one of the bandits muttered, looking anxiously back along the road. "They won't be alone."

"We certainly are not," huffed the cardinal.

From among the bearded buffoons who were trying to scare us by waving their weapons and grunting at us, one man came around behind us and approached me on my right. I stifled an urge to spit on him.

"You too, little lady," he said, leering at me. "Mebbe you got no jewels, but you're a pretty thing, and you got something else I might want to take instead."

I decided to ignore the implications of that and concentrate on what to do about my purse. Surely the cardinal's guards would come within sight of us soon and see our predicament. They wouldn't have forgotten about him just because he had demanded privacy.

I wasn't carrying a lot of money, just a few coins, for Gualtiero had most of our travel money. My purse was tucked inside my garment. I'd have to reach through the hidden slit at my waist, under my simple cord belt, to retrieve it.

And if I did, I could also retrieve my dagger. The honor of a noble-woman is a valuable commodity; we are taught from an early age to defend it. I wouldn't need to hold this oaf off for long, and I'd have the advantage of surprise. Slowly, as if I was too frightened to move more quickly, I reached inside my clothes.

And that was when I heard a voice booming inside my mind: *"You don't want to do that, Giacoma,"* it said.

"Yes, I do," I said, and the bandits and the cardinal looked at me in surprise.

"No, you don't," said the voice, which sounded suspiciously like Francesco. I glanced at the bandits and then at the cardinal, who raised an eyebrow quizzically. As far as I could tell, no one else could hear it.

"This is a poor man, Giacoma. Give him the money. Think of it as giving alms. You have no wish to harm this man."

I might. This time my reply was silent. *After all, he is pointing a grubby short sword at me and trying to take my purse.*

"If you harm him, you will regret it. Do you really want to risk taking this man's life and leaving his poor wife and starving children alone and helpless?"

Well, no. When he put it that way, I didn't. And besides, there were four more of them, the cardinal was unarmed, and their leader's ridiculous excuse for a sword was still longer than my dagger. I pulled my hand back out, holding only the purse, and tossed it at the bandit's feet.

"Buy something for your children with this, you irritating little man," I said, perhaps a bit ungraciously.

He snorted and stuffed the purse—my gift from Vanna—up his sleeve. "Don't got children, lady," he said with a smirk. "You want to give me some?" He put his filthy hand on my thigh. I stiffened, more with indignation than with fear, and the cardinal roared in outrage. I swatted at the bandit's hand, and he laughed, displaying a shortage of teeth.

Hmph. *We have to talk, Francesco.*

"Later. Right now, you've got company."

So we did. I heard galloping hooves behind me, and I knew what I'd see.

And I was partly right, because Dino, two of his guards, and Gualtiero thundered toward us, blades drawn, hunched forward and riding all out. What I hadn't expected was to see Prassede astride her donkey, short little legs sticking straight out, determinedly trailing along behind them. It made me think of Renzo and his poker, and I had an incongruous moment of homesickness. Gallantry turns up in unexpected places sometimes.

The bandits had heard them coming, too, and the two on the cardinal's left plunged back into the woods without a backward glance at their companions. The one who had my purse dashed headlong into the woods on our right, and that was the last I saw of Vanna's gift.

Leader and Horse Talker were either slower to react or bolder. My money would have been on the former, had I not just given my money away. Leader did finally catch on, and he turned tail and ran into the woods, with four of the fastest horses in Rome barreling along the road toward him. This was not a palio he was going to win. Had it been only Prassede and the donkey, it might have been a contest.

Horse Talker stood there hanging on to the reins as if his life depended on it.

"Don't move," I hissed at him, and he stared at me in amazement. "You're safer there than if you run."

Maybe I could figure out a way to save this one. I was pretty sure it was too late for the leader.

And it was. Moments later, Dino and one of his men pulled up next to us, one on either side, and Gualtiero halted directly behind us. But the third guard passed us and crashed into the woods after the terrified bandit, his sword drawn, and cut the fleeing man down before I could even cry out. The bandit crumpled with a scream and a spray of blood, and the guard slowed his horse abruptly and turned to face us. Horse Talker whimpered.

"Are you and the lady unharmed, signore?" Dino panted. First things first. While the cardinal reassured him, I leaned over my horse's neck and whispered to the one remaining bandit.

"Don't talk. Don't run or try to fight. I'll do what I can to help you," I told him, and he nodded, stark terror in his eyes.

Then he looked past me and let out a strangled yelp. The other guard had dismounted and with sword drawn was walking slowly and inexorably toward the trembling miscreant.

"Get between our horses. He won't use his sword if you're close to us."

The bandit dropped the reins and scurried between our mounts. His would-be assailant stopped in front of us, snarling in frustration.

I turned to Gualtiero, waiting close behind me, and saw him swiftly comprehend my wishes, though I hadn't said a word. I liked that young man. Simply by staying where he was, he blocked access to the trapped bandit from the rear.

I put on my rich noblewoman face and spoke to the guard we had foiled.

"Good man, I thank you for your care for us, but I would see this man brought to justice, and not just dispatched here on the road," I said firmly, and the guard gave me a curt bow and backed away.

"Dino, I thank you and your men," the cardinal was saying, "and I acknowledge that you were right to warn me of danger on the road. Henceforth I shall be guided by your wisdom in such matters. Accept from me this modest reward for your courage and your diligence." He presented Dino with the purse, which somehow had never been handed over to the bandits. I admired his forthrightness and his willingness to admit his error, not to mention his shrewdness in hanging on to his purse while I let mine get away.

Speaking of courage, Prassede and her donkey finally caught up to us. She looked first at me, worry written across her face, and then shifted her gaze toward the woods, to where the bandit lay broken in his own pooling blood. Then she slid off the donkey, sat down hard on the road, and threw up.

I wanted to go to her, but first I had a bandit to protect. "Signore Cardinal Ugolino, I beg of your mercy and your generosity that this man not be harmed, at least until we can discuss what should be done with him. I ask in Brother Francesco's name for a trial, not a summary decision."

The cardinal looked a little taken aback, but when I invoked Francesco's name he gave a nod of agreement. I dismounted, patting the poor bandit on the shoulder as I went to Prassede.

Ugolino himself offered a leather flask of water, and I held Prassede's veil out of her way while she rinsed her mouth.

"You were brave to come after me," I whispered to her, "but how did you think you could help? What could you have done?"

She was beginning to regain a little color, but she avoided looking in the direction of the slain bandit. "I was going to pray," she said.

"But did you have to be here to do that? Couldn't you have prayed from back there, where it was safer?" I brushed a stray lock of hair out of her face and dampened the end of my sleeve with the water to clean her face.

She flushed. "I guess so, but I was afraid for you, so I thought I should come to you and try to help. And after that I was mostly praying just to stay on the donkey."

I managed to disguise my laugh as a cough. But what of Horse Talker? Dino, Gualtiero, and the other guard had taken his knife from him and tied his hands behind his back. Though they were not gentle with him, I didn't think he was in immediate danger.

Rescuing the unfortunate bandit was going to require ingenuity. The cardinal's bodyguards were furious; not only might they have lost their master while they were on duty, but they genuinely loved the old man, and they were outraged that anyone would threaten him. The rest of our caravan had finally caught up to us, and the cardinal indulged me by convening an impromptu court involving all the other churchmen in the party and the witnesses, namely Dino and his guards, Gualtiero, a wide-eyed Prassede, and me. At my suggestion, he also requested the presence of the brother who travelled with us, Brother Alessio, the keeper of the pack animals. I wanted him there so his shabby gray habit would remind us of Francesco and his wisdom and mercy, because I certainly had no intention of telling anyone about the voice.

We sat in a circle, most of us on stools hastily fetched from one of the wagons, but Brother Alessio and Gualtiero sat crosslegged on the ground. The cardinal presided, with me at his side, and the Horse Talker knelt in the midst of the circle, his wrists still bound, facing us.

Ugolino, his reliquary grasped firmly in his right hand, succinctly described the attack to the group, then invited me to speak. I gave my version, emphasizing that the bandit, who gave his name as Feo, had calmed our mounts and thus protected us from the dangers posed by panicking horses, for they could have reared and dumped us off, or run away with us. The cardinal was an even better rider than me, and he raised a skeptical eyebrow at this, but he didn't contradict me. I also mentioned that unlike his fellows, this bandit had in no way threatened us nor demanded anything from us.

Dino and the other guards argued for a summary hanging. It was certainly one possible outcome. While a man of the church would not pronounce a death sentence, he could choose to leave the matter in the hands of his guards, who would have found it easy to justify their actions to the secular authorities.

I watched the cardinal while his guards spoke. Both of us knew well that this frightened man was not like the brutish lout who seized my purse, or the blustering leader. Ugolino was a fair man, a man perceptive enough to appreciate Francesco, but he was also a commanding leader, impatient to continue our journey, so I wasn't sure what he would do.

The cardinal called on Prassede to speak, but for once she was at a loss for words. She stammered that she had not arrived in time to see anything but the dead bandit in the road and our prisoner cowering between our horses. When she spoke of the dead bandit, Feo made a peculiar noise, something like a sob.

That set me to wondering. I turned to Ugolino and asked his permission to speak to the prisoner, and he gave it.

"Feo," I said, and the eyes that looked back at me were swimming with tears, "the man who died on the road was your friend, was he not?"

Feo gulped. "He were my brother, Mistress. Will he be buried proper?"

Dino glared at him. "A miserable thief who attacked the Holy Father's legate doesn't deserve a proper burial."

But Ugolino raised his hand, commanding silence. "Was your brother a Christian man?"

Feo held his head up. "He were. He done some bad things, but he were a believer. And he might've repented, while he was running away."

All things are possible.

"When was he last shriven?" the cardinal demanded.

Feo's face was blank. Then, to my surprise, Brother Alessio spoke.

"May I ask the prisoner a question, signore?" he said.

Ugolino hesitated a moment, then nodded.

"Feo di Lottiero, you had another brother, did you not?" he said.

How did he know that name? "Feo" was all the prisoner had offered. I glanced at the cardinal; he had noticed, too.

"Aye." Feo looked sullen, but not surprised. "Me older brother Eusebio. He joined up with that Brother Francesco and the men who live with him, in Assisi. You're wearing the same kind of tunic they wear, so likely you know him."

Brother Alessio did. He explained to the group that Francesco and his brothers had befriended a group of outlaws who had been harassing them. The friars brought them bread, offered them clothing, carried firewood to their rough camp. It was a perfect opportunity to turn the

177

other cheek, and exactly the sort of thing Francesco loved to do. So persuasive was Francesco's example that three members of the group left their thieving ways and joined the brothers. Alessio named them, and I realized two of them were men I had actually met, though I had known nothing of their background. I did not know Feo's brother, however.

"Were you one of the group then, Feo?" the cardinal asked him.

"I were one of them, and so were my brother Sergio, who your man run down," he said.

"And you two elected not to join the friars, even though your elder brother and two others did?"

Feo said nothing.

Brother Alessio got up and stepped into the circle. He put his hand gently on Feo's shoulder.

"Your brother Eusebio is also my brother, and he would be overjoyed to have you join us at the Porziuncola as one of Brother Francesco's followers," he told the prisoner. "And since you know animals, I would welcome your help with the pack animals for the rest of the trip. If his lordship agrees, will you come with us to Brother Francesco, where you can ask him if he is willing to accept you?"

Feo's mouth had fallen open, and he seemed unable to speak.

The cardinal saw a chance to wrap this up so we could be on our way, and he said briskly, "Well, then, Feo, you will follow one of your two brothers. Which will it be? Eusebio, who does good works and lives a holy life with Brother Francesco? Or Sergio, who lies there on the road? We can see if you do any better than your brother at outrunning my guards, if you like."

Feo swallowed. "Eusebio, signore. But now can I bury my brother?"

It was agreed. Ugolino delegated a handful of churchmen and servants to go with Feo to see his brother properly buried and prayed over, but he instructed them to be quick about it, as time was passing and we needed to arrive in Trevi before night. Brother Alessio went along with Feo. I offered a silent prayer for the soul of the dead outlaw.

The rest of us made ourselves ready to leave. Dino and the guards grumbled, but they accepted the cardinal's decision like the loyal men they were. By the time Feo and his escort returned from their solemn task, we were already starting to move, and they scrambled to catch up with us and take their places in the caravan.

Again I found myself riding next to the cardinal.

"You are a woman of great courage and wisdom, monna Giacoma," he said, his good humor restored now the unpleasant interruption was past and the matter resolved.

"I thank you, but it's your wisdom that has made this day less of a tragedy than it might otherwise have been."

The forest around us had given way to olive groves, and we were climbing. We were approaching Trevi, a town of stone towers and strong city walls clinging to the slope of Mount Serano, silhouetted against the pale March sky.

"I must confess to you, monna Giacoma, that when those ruffians demanded our money, I considered drawing the dagger I wear hidden under my robe. It may not be a churchman's place, but a man is a man, and I believe God would have forgiven me had I acted to protect you, a devout Christian woman. And perhaps even to protect myself, as God's servant."

So he was armed, too. Interesting. "I knew I was safe with you, signore," I said, trying to sound impressed. I gazed up at him admiringly and then modestly lowered my eyes, a trick all women learn early in their lives, right along with the part about defending their honor. I had tried it—the gazing, not the defending—with Graziano when I first met him, but he only laughed at me. I think it was then I fell in love with him.

Still, it pleased the cardinal, who sat straighter in the saddle, and we wound our way up the hill and through the olive groves to Trevi, where we could at last take our rest after that extraordinary day.

25

I loved being back in Assisi. Before Graziano's death, I had considered bucolic Marino our out-of-town haven, yet now no other place delighted both my soul and my senses as Assisi did.

I loved being back in my airy chamber in Arnolfo and Mengarda's home, looking out on the magnificent facade of San Rufino and on that extraordinary Assisi sky. I found Assisi's mountains lovelier by far than Rome's famous hills. I loved reuniting with the brothers—though I missed Elias and the brothers who had gone with him to the Holy Land—and I loved seeing our own Brother Ricco happy to be part of Francesco's community.

I loved celebrating Holy Week and Easter in this small, intimate setting, so different from the papal ceremony and pageantry in Rome, all worship and celebration centered in the cathedral of San Rufino. I looked up at those three carved men standing on the backs of their mythical beasts, straining to bear the weight of the rose window—the world, perhaps?—for all eternity, and they made me think of Francesco holding up his brothers, and Chiara and her sisters, and those of us who were beginning to follow him even as we continued to live in the world, we who some called Francesco's Third Order. It was said that the late Pope Innocente had a dream in which Francesco was holding up the Church itself, and I could believe it was so.

I did not love learning that Miracle Boy had succumbed to a fever the previous summer. Because he was a miracle, he was buried in the crypt of San Rufino instead of in the parish churchyard, and I visited his tomb and lit candles for him. Men said more miracles had occurred at his tomb. I prayed for him, though the words that came to me were no formal prayer, but only "God give you peace."

I did not love that Bishop Guido had created such agitation and animosity among the clerics of San Rufino, squabbling with them over tithes and the right to conduct ordinations. Guido, a good man but contentious and territorial, was the second of the name, not the Guido who had helped ease Francesco through his conversion and his break with his family. This Guido also supported Francesco and the brothers, but he was always involved in some battle or another. The cardinal was going to have his hands full sorting it out. Francesco and Bishop Guido shared a close friendship, but even so the bishop's aggressive behavior was not something the cardinal could afford to tolerate, speaking as he did for His Holiness. The holy finger was soon to be invoked, I suspected.

I did not love that I had yet to find a time to speak with Francesco alone, though he had welcomed me warmly and enthusiastically. Always Francesco was surrounded by others—brothers, hangers-on, supplicants, admirers. I needed to talk with him about hearing his voice in my mind during our encounter with the bandits on the road. Had it really been him, or God speaking to me in his voice to get my attention? I did not think it would please Francesco to know I paid more attention to his voice than to God's, but after my experience with Amata's child I had resolved to hold nothing back from him.

Most of all I did not love the alarming deterioration I saw in Francesco's health. While he still burst into song often and laughed easily, it took him longer to make his way on foot to Assisi from the Porziuncola, and he rested often, where before he would have walked tirelessly to his destination, no matter how long the journey. Egidio confided to me that Francesco was weakened by fasting, and his long hours of prayer late into the night left him hollow-eyed and exhausted the next day.

"And do you do these things also, Egidio?" I asked him. We were walking along the path atop the ridge just inside the city walls, stopping at the high points to look out across the valley or up at the ruins of the castle.

Egidio wouldn't meet my eyes. "Brother Francesco tells us we must not mortify our bodies to the extent that we cannot do God's work," he said slowly. "And yet we see how he disciplines himself, and we are often moved to follow his example, in this as in so many other things."

It was not an answer, not really. I studied him. He was thinner, and his tunic betrayed an odd stiffness about the chest. A hair shirt? I couldn't make myself ask him.

It is a fine and noble thing to emulate Christ's suffering, we are told, yet I found it hard to grasp why even while we give alms to ease suffering in others, we must impose it on ourselves. I fasted when the church said I must, and I prayed as I was instructed as well as when I felt the need, but these things were not the building blocks of my faith. What I wanted in my heart was to take away the world's suffering, not to add to it. I wanted the joy, the exhilaration, the vast alleluia of praise Francesco had shown me, not this gratuitously imposed pain. Did we not already have pain enough, by virtue of being human?

Egidio and I were on our way to my second-favorite Assisi church, sturdy little Santo Stefano, and I preferred this route atop the ridge to the lower one through the more peopled part of town. Santo Stefano was small and plain, built by stonemasons for their own use. No frescoes or ornaments graced its simple interior, but it was serene and peaceful, and angled windows cut in the thick walls admitted shafts of soft light that pooled on the rough stone floor. Sometimes in this part of Umbria the earth trembles, but Santo Stefano always stands firm, even while stones and bricks and wooden balconies rain down from grander buildings nearby.

Often I was the only person praying there. On this day, though, as Egidio and I made our way down the steep and uneven steps and through the open portal, an old woman knelt beneath the crucifix, her lips moving in prayer. She was covered by a dark brown mantle, and something about her was familiar to me.

She heard us come in and turned her head sharply toward us. Her deep-set eyes passed over me quickly, but she fixed on Egidio and her pale face formed itself into a fierce glare. The color drained from his face. He looked away from her, then sank to his knees, arms and hands extended, and fixed his attention on the crucifix as he began to pray.

The woman was not as old as I had first thought, though she was not young. She was older than Prassede, but hardly Salvestra's age, as I had first assumed.

And finally I realized who she was. I saw pain in those flashing eyes, and rage, and a hint of madness. But they were Elias's eyes nonetheless.

She stood up and brushed herself off, an unconscious action so like Elias that I knew I was right. She made straight for the door, but as she passed Egidio she reached for his triple-knotted cord belt and gave it a vicious jerk. He lost his balance and toppled back onto his rear with a surprised "Oof!"

She laughed mirthlessly. Then she brushed past me with a rustle of cloth, and she was out the door and gone.

"What was that all about?" I asked Egidio, as I helped him up.

He dusted himself off and shook his head.

"But why does she hate you?" I persisted.

"She doesn't. It's Francesco she hates. She only despises me."

"She's Elias's mother, isn't she?"

He hesitated. "Yes," he finally said, "but don't ask me any more. Francesco doesn't want us to talk about our families, or each other's."

Fine. I'd ask Mengarda. Egidio and I, after making an unsuccessful attempt to continue praying, gave up and walked back to the palazzo. We didn't talk. Silence was never awkward with Egidio; it was one of the many things I loved about him. I was glad he hadn't gone to Syria with

Elias. I would have been twice as disappointed to miss them both.

Mengarda, a clever and efficient collector and purveyor of all sorts of information, did not disappoint me. We sat together on the long chest that flanked my bed, both of us working on our embroidery, and she promised to do her best to answer my questions.

"That does sound like Elias's mother," she said when I described the woman. "I never really knew her. She's widowed now, lives outside the walls. The family's poor but not indigent. She couldn't accept the loss of her firstborn to the brotherhood, and she's never forgiven Brother Francesco. Or her son, for that matter."

"Does she have other children, then?"

"Oh, yes, but Elias was always the clever one, the one who got an education. And he was ambitious—he didn't want to spend his life helping his father stuff mattresses. So he taught children to read their psalms, and people thought he would eventually become a notary..."

"And then he met Francesco."

"No, he had always known Francesco. But one day he just abandoned all his plans, and suddenly he was a brother."

I said a silent prayer of thanks that he was, because Francesco needed him. We all did. I hoped he would return from Syria soon.

"It can be hard on the brothers' families, can't it?" I tied off my thread and studied my work. The border was done; I would tackle the central part later.

"Francesco says they have to leave their families behind, leave everything, mother, father, sisters, brothers, children, and serve only God."

"Did Francesco talk to her, at least?"

"He tried. He really wanted her to understand, and to give Elias her support."

"What did she say?"

"Words I would be ashamed to repeat. The gist of it was that she didn't want his explanations—she wanted her son."

We sat quietly for a while, thinking about that woman and her situation. I also thought of my own sons, and I imagine Mengarda was thinking of hers. How would we have felt in similar circumstances? I might well have uttered some unrepeatable words myself. It was not only the brothers who paid a steep price for following Francesco.

"Did Francesco visit his own mother?" I asked. He had never said anything about his family to me, though I knew monna Pica had died not long after he and his earliest brothers had come to my palazzo in Rome.

Mengarda shook her head. "As far as I know, no. I always thought he should have, though. She took his part against his father, and that can't have been easy. My father was there, you know, the day Brother Francesco stripped himself naked in front of the bishop's palazzo and announced that he wouldn't call Pietro di Bernardone his father any more, but only his father in heaven."

"Your father saw it?" I was curious about that oft-mentioned scene.

"Oh, yes. It was ten years ago, or even a little more."

That must have been soon after I had first seen him at San Pietro, dressed like a peacock and flinging his coins at the saint's tomb.

"He'd been arguing with his parents, then?" I prodded her.

"With his father, yes. You know how Brother Francesco is about giving things to the poor. It's almost more than the brothers can do to make sure he isn't naked even now, because he keeps giving his tunics away. They all do. I tell you, half the people you see in Assisi wearing those scruffy tunics aren't even brothers, but just poor men who got a brother's old tunic as alms."

That was true. One had to look for the thrice-knotted rope belts to recognize a true brother.

"Brother Francesco took some cloth from the workshop and sold it while his father was away, and then he tried to give the money to the priest at San Damiano, which was pretty much a ruin in those days, only the old priest living there as caretaker. But the priest had seen Pietro di Bernardone's famous temper unleashed before, so he was afraid to take the purse. And Brother Francesco wouldn't take it back. Poor Pica was caught right in the middle. She knew her husband was going to be furious when he came back from his trip and found all that cloth gone."

"What did she do?"

"Brother Francesco went into hiding. Nobody knows to this day where he was living—some say in a cave, others say in the crumbling old crypt at San Damiano. But Pica knew, and she took food to him, and clothes, and she tried to talk him into coming back home. He wouldn't, though. Everyone felt bad for her. She was well liked, a lighthearted, pretty, generous woman who loved music and dancing, but nobody had any sympathy for Brother Francesco."

She gave me an apologetic little smile. "My own father was a friend of Pietro di Bernardone, and he and many others thought Pietro should surrender his son to the authorities. You can't go stealing the very thing your father sells for his livelihood, my father said. Though some of us thought a man as rich as Pietro could have been a little more generous. And if it had only been the money for the cloth, maybe he would have been. What he really wanted was for Brother Francesco to renounce his share in the inheritance of his mother's dowry so his brother Angelo would get it all, because Angelo would invest it back into the business instead of giving it all away."

"What happened when Pietro came back?"

"He flew into a rage, as everybody expected. And once Brother Francesco finally came back home several weeks later, he was so dirty and shabby and had such a straggly beard and hair that children jeered at him in the street, and then their older brothers threw things at him, rotten food and dung and stones." Mengarda had tears in her eyes as she described it. "I'm ashamed of my city, Giacoma. What must you think of us?"

"You wouldn't be ashamed if you could see what the people in my city do. They've chased popes out of the city and taken over fortresses and torn down towers and mocked pilgrims and insulted churchmen, and nobody thinks a thing of it. It's how Rome has always been. Assisi couldn't have been that bad."

"You are kind, kinder than we deserve. Well, Brother Francesco came home, as I said, and his father was even angrier when he saw his neighbors' reaction, because he felt his son had brought shame upon the house. He beat Brother Francesco and berated him and then locked him in a tiny closet in their palazzo, to make him 'see reason,' as his father said, and promise to come back to work in the family business and give up his talk of God and restoring churches. But Brother Francesco had heard the crucifix at San Damiano speak to him, and he knew he couldn't go back to the way things had been."

No. Francesco had had a true conversion, and there would be no going back.

"What did Pica do during all of this?"

"She was miserable. My mother knew her well in those days, and she says Pica was too frightened of her husband to defy him, but then he left on another business trip, and she somehow found the courage to disobey his orders and unlock the closet and let Francesco out. He went to San Damiano straightaway to work on restoring it, because that's what God told him to do."

"And when Pietro came back from his second trip, Francesco renounced him?"

"Yes. Pietro was furious, and we can only guess what passed between him and Pica, because I don't know of anybody who talked to her after that. He tried to get the consuls to throw his son into prison, but Brother

Francesco refused to return to the city, because he said he was God's servant and only the church had jurisdiction over him. That was why the first Bishop Guido got involved."

"A good thing he had, or it might well have been the end of Francesco's vocation and his order might never have come into being."

"True. So it came to trial, and Brother Francesco readily agreed to give back his father's money—the bag of coins had been sitting on a windowsill in San Damiano all that time—and then he said he'd give back the clothes that belonged to his father too. He stripped off everything he was wearing, folded it all up neatly, put the bag of money on top, and handed the stack back to his father. And then he said he would no longer call Pietro di Bernardone his father, for God alone was his true father. The bishop stepped forward and covered Brother Francesco with his own cloak, just as if he was welcoming him into a confraternity, and Pietro took his money and the pile of clothes and skulked back home."

"Did people continue to think Francesco's father was in the right?"

"Nobody knew what to think. Having the bishop support Brother Francesco made a big difference. People started to wonder, and they weren't quite so sure anymore that Pietro was in the right."

Assisi was divided even now. Francesco had devoted followers like Mengarda and her husband, but there were those in town who scoffed at the brothers' chosen way of life, and even at their message. The second Bishop Guido, like the first, was firmly on Francesco's side, and we didn't see much outright hostility these days. But the earlier days had been harder.

I still didn't entirely understand. "Francesco split with his father, but how could he not acknowledge his mother? She tried to help him and protect him as best she could."

"She did," said Mengarda softly. "We're both mothers, Giacoma, and so I know you'll understand when I say that as much as I revere Brother Francesco and follow him in every way a laywoman can, I have a hard time grasping this. I cannot explain it for you."

I had asked him, but he would only quote from the book of Luke: "If any man comes to me and does not hate his father, and his mother, and wife, and children, and brothers and sisters, yes, and his own life too, he cannot be my disciple." It had never satisfied me; I could not help wondering if a good woman had been sacrificed to make a point.

26

THE next day Mengarda and I set out on foot with her two servants to visit Chiara and Vanna. With us were Chiara's youngest sister Beatrice, a lively twelve-year-old with a deep dimple in her left cheek and eyes of a startling light blue, and their mother, monna Ortolana. The child fairly bounced up and down with excitement to be visiting her sisters, but her mother moved with quiet dignity.

We left the city through the Porta San Rufino and took the winding downhill path, the olive grove still ahead of us. The day was bright and fair and mild, and birdsong accompanied us as we followed the path toward San Damiano. In response to my questions, monna Ortolana regaled us with stories of her various pilgrimages, for she was far more travelled than any of the rest of us. She told us of Jerusalem, of the tombs of saints, and of the great shrine called Santiago de Compostela in Spain. Egidio had also spoken of his pilgrimage to Spain, and I found it fascinating to compare the impressions of a barefoot brother with those of a wealthy noblewoman, both for the predictable differences and for the marked similarities of their experiences. Ortolana had lodged in luxury at every stop, and Egidio had slept rough, under the stars. Yet both of them found themselves moved to tears as they knelt in front of the holy sepulchre, and both of them came away filled with eagerness to make a new beginning. Perhaps devout people had more in common than their stations in life would suggest.

As Chiara's mother talked, I found myself thinking of the differences between mother and daughter. Monna Ortolana possessed great wealth, or at least great wealth by Assisi standards, and she followed her faith all over the world, travelling when and how she chose. Yet her daughter, for the sake of her own faith, stalwartly refused to own anything, and thanks to the church's policies about women, she was immured in a small complex of buildings, perhaps never to leave, as Vanna had said.

Mengarda asked her neighbor a question about the Holy Land, and I took advantage of the interruption to move back to Beatrice's side and fall into step with her. The servants, Sobilia and Dialta, walked ahead of us and the girl's mother and Mengarda were in front of them, so we had a bit of privacy.

"Do you see your sisters often, Beatrice?"

Her face lit up with a quick bright smile that made her look even younger than her years.

"I don't often get the chance, madonna," she said. "I'm grateful to you for asking me to come along today." The invitation had been Mengarda's idea, though I had readily agreed.

I decided to take a bit of a risk. "Does your father object to your visits, then?"

Her smile faded. "My father is away on business, madonna." Not quite an answer, but I wasn't going to push her.

But I couldn't resist asking one more thing. "And your mother? Does she go to San Damiano often?"

The smile tentatively reestablished itself. "My mother does much as she pleases, madonna, and it pleases her to see her daughters often. But my father usually says it's not appropriate for me to go with her to San Damiano, because he says I'm to be married."

"Are you already betrothed, then?" She was so young.

She shook her head hard enough to make her pale blonde plaits swing. "No. Not yet. Not ever," she muttered. I recognized that stubborn set of the jaw; both Chiara and their mother had it, and fresh young Beatrice was clearly their kinswoman. I suspected the men of Chiara's family were going to have another battle on their hands soon. They had certainly made a big enough fuss over Chiara's choice, and her poor sister Caterina, now Sister Agnese, had fared even worse, only saved by Chiara's prayers. I hoped this pale child would have an easier time than her older sisters had.

And now we were through the olive groves, and San Damiano was within our sight. Once more Chiara was standing in the yard waiting, a slender column of gray with another woman—Vanna?—at her side.

Chiara greeted all of us warmly, but her chiseled, perfect face broke into a grin of pure delight when she saw her sister Beatrice in our party. Mother and daughter embraced, then older sister and younger. Chiara and Beatrice both glowed with happiness to be in each other's company, and Ortolana radiated pride in both her girls.

The other woman, a column a little less tall and a little less narrow than Chiara, was indeed Vanna—Sister Vanna, I reminded myself—and she welcomed me shyly, almost hesitantly. She accepted my embrace passively.

"Vanna, thank you for the beautiful purse," I said, choosing not to mention that it was probably hanging on the belt of a bandit's wife or mistress. "The workmanship is exquisite."

"Thank you, monna Gia—thank you. I'm glad you liked it. I haven't been doing much embroidery lately, just some basic sewing, mostly for the hospital patients," she said.

I wanted to hear more about what Vanna had been doing since I saw her last, and to tell her all the news from home, but before I could say anything more, Chiara pulled us all into the chapel for prayers. The other sisters were already there, waiting for us. I knelt with the other visiting women, and noticed Beatrice between Agnese and Chiara. I felt a sudden rush of envy. *She belongs here. Beatrice belongs, Vanna belongs, and I do not.*

I prayed, or at least I tried to. My thoughts were scattered, and I had a hard time clearing them away to allow myself to concentrate on the divine. Finally I gave up and watched Chiara instead.

Chiara at prayer, even in an open chapel at midday, somehow gave an impression of kneeling in a shaft of moonlight. There was a silvery and otherworldly quality about her, more sensed than seen—a coolness, a smoothness that made the rest of us look coarse and awkward.

When Francesco prayed, he vanished into a sphere of light. Well, he didn't exactly vanish—I could still see him on his knees, his face raised to heaven—but at the same time he was surrounded by a soft golden glow, the color of ripe apricots. It was diffuse but brilliant, like the sun rising behind the fog of an Assisi dawn.

I never entered that light when I prayed. Often I saw it before me, and what I saw was closer to Francesco's gold than to Chiara's silver. Sometimes I was able to approach it. Once or twice I touched it, and the feeling was indescribable. But I never stepped into its welcoming glow as Francesco did, nor did I bathe in soothing moonlight like Chiara. I just said what I had to say and hoped God heard me.

It was some time before Chiara drew our worship gently to a close and invited us to stand. She announced free time and freedom to speak, as she had done on our previous visit, and then she came over to me.

"Will you come into the refectory, Sister Giacoma?" she murmured, touching my arm lightly. "I will call you 'Sister' now, since you worship with us." She steered me into the modest dining area, and we sat on a rough wooden bench in front of the scarred and ancient table. We were alone in the room. I knew the rules here: no private space, no separation. But when Chiara wanted to speak privately with someone, somehow everyone else simply vanished.

"Sister Vanna mourned most sincerely when she learned of the death of your steward's child," she told me. "It touched her deeply. The love she used to bear him has been transformed by God into something holier and more compassionate."

How interesting that Vanna should think of Bella as Massimo's. I always thought of her as Amata's, though I had seen Massimo's devastation with my own eyes. "It was a difficult time for Amata and Massimo, but their faith and some timely help from Francesco helped them get through it. And now they have the twins. As I'm sure you can imagine, two-year-old twins keep us off balance most of the time."

Chiara smiled. "I can indeed. And I hear your home is now also home to a sheep?"

Ah, yes. I wondered how Lotario was doing, and whether he had yet learned to climb his ramp. "Yes. Francesco made us a gift of a beautiful little lamb, and he is a part of our household."

Chiara raised one perfect eyebrow. "I should think it would be difficult, sharing your home with a sheep."

"It does have its moments. But we've all become quite fond of Lotario."

"Lotario!" Her breathless laugh startled me. I had never heard Chiara laugh before. "You named him for the Holy Father?"

Automatically I recited the rationale I had come up with to soothe Prassede, who had not been happy with my choice of a name. "The Holy Father at that time was Pope Innocente, Sister Chiara. I chose a name for our sheep that happens to be the same as the name the pontiff bore before he was pope. It is not the same as naming him after a reigning pope."

"Why did you call him so?" Chiara had a look of pure delight on her lovely face, nothing like Prassede's pursed-lips disapproval, and it immediately disarmed all my caution.

"I watched him snuffling around among the herbs on the floor, munching on the marjoram and pushing the rosemary aside, and it reminded me of the way Lotario Conti used to go through a legal document, picking at every detail." It had been an interesting process to observe. The canon lawyer in him would not be gainsaid.

"You knew Pope Innocente well, didn't you? May God give his soul peace."

Well enough to miss him. A good man, a good friend to Francesco, and for the most part a good pope, maybe even a great pope, though the Albigensian heretics certainly would not have agreed with me. "He was a family friend, Sister Chiara," I said.

"How strange it must be, to live so near the papacy, and to have known the Holy Father before his elevation."

I shrugged. "Rome isn't that large a city, I suppose. We all know each other." All of us from the ruling families, at least. Best to keep your friends close and your enemies closer, my father often said. Especially since families tended to move from one category to the other with little warning.

She paused, collecting her thoughts. "Then you also know Pope Honorius?"

"Yes, I do," I said, then waited to see what would come next.

"There is a service I need from you, if you will help me."

"If I can," I said, opening my hands in a gesture of readiness. I respected Chiara, and I recognized her steely courage. I honored her close ties with Francesco. I was in awe of the pure austerity of her life. But despite her disarming laughter, I still wasn't absolutely sure I *liked* her. Still, for Francesco's sake, I would do whatever I could for her.

"His Holiness fears that by owning nothing, my sisters and I will become a burden on the brothers, or on the church itself."

A position Cardinal Ugolino shared and had expressed most eloquently. I waited for more.

"And he wants us enclosed, trapped in these walls, as if we were followers of Saint Benedict and not of Father Francesco." I had not heard such vehemence from her before. And "Father" Francesco? That was new.

"And if you are enclosed and can't work, you can't earn your bread, and since he doesn't want women going a-begging..."

"Precisely. And there is the small matter of trusting to Our Lord to provide for us. 'And seek not what you shall eat, or what you shall drink, nor be of a doubtful mind.'"

"'But seek the kingdom of God, and all these things shall be given you.'" I finished the line for her, at the same time thinking how easy it was for a woman of my wealth and easy life to say it and how different the meaning was for her and her sisters. What if one day no one brought them food? What if they had no wood in winter? What then? Would someone else not then have to rescue them, bringing them what they required no matter the cost to their rescuer? Or would they starve or freeze? Clearly I lacked Chiara's strong faith, or perhaps I had just fed too many beggars at my hearth.

"I need time, monna Giacoma. Time to strengthen San Damiano, to prove we can trust in God. We are still too new, too weak, and too disorganized to stand up to the Holy Father in this. I wish you could persuade him to leave us alone for now. I know this struggle is far from over, but if I could have a respite before anything is decided, I could be ready for him."

"You will want to persuade the cardinal, too," I said. "His Holiness expects Ugolino to be his connection with Francesco and with the brothers and the sisters."

"So they are as one in this?" She frowned.

"They are."

She paced the length of the table and back, her hands at her sides, fingers drumming along the outsides of her thighs. Even thus she did not appear agitated; she merely seemed to be thinking hard.

Finally she halted and faced me. "You have the cardinal's ear?"

I thought of my recent adventures with Ugolino. I thought of the mounting costs of His Holiness's upcoming Crusade. I thought about Graziano's lawsuit.

"I can rent his ear," I said, and she allowed herself a small smile.

And so we settled it. Chiara turned out to be even more practical than I had realized. She recited a list of things to ask for and a much longer list of things to resist, and I memorized them. Between us we agreed on which points were not negotiable and which allowed for some haggling—not that we were going to let the cardinal know which were which. We were not so foolish as to believe I could protect her indefinitely, but both of us hoped this approach might gain her the time she needed. I thought it a good use of my bargaining currency.

She would accept the title of abbess if she must, though she didn't want it. She was willing, albeit reluctantly, to haggle on the issue of enclosure, as long as enough loopholes could be built in to protect the little hospital and allow the sisters' other charity work to continue. But she would not bend on the issue of owning property, individually or collectively. She was totally committed to poverty for herself and the other sisters.

"If you speak to His Holiness, will you witness to him how God cares for our humble community? We lack for nothing that is needful, and we have no wish to acquire possessions."

"I may find the chance to tell him," I said. "Soon I'll be taking a legal action that will clear away most impediments, and I'll almost certainly see more of His Holiness and the curia than I have in recent years. I'm not sure whether I'm looking forward to that or not, actually." They were a formidable group of men, many of them deeply traditional and immediately opposed to anything that smelled like change. Francesco and Chiara both smelled a lot like change, and in some ways, so did I.

Once our business was complete, I asked how Vanna was doing. Chiara told me it had taken Vanna some time to settle in, the main problem apparently being the equal status of all the women in the community.

As a serving sister, Vanna had expected to be more subservient and less responsible than she turned out to be. She was always more comfortable with hierarchy; she would have been miserable with the way my household ran these days. At least here the egalitarian structure was intentional, whereas at home it had just gradually happened. I suspect it had been going in that direction for years, in truth, and Vanna's dogged insistence on propriety may have been all that held it off.

But Chiara said Vanna had become more comfortable. In accordance with my suggestion, Chiara had asked her to mentor new young sisters, and she loved that task.

"Does she perform it with kindness?" I asked.

"Oh, yes. That's one area where I think she has made real progress. She empathizes with these young women, newly separated from their families and contemplating a future so little like what they grew up expecting. She is extraordinarily patient with them."

"I thought she seemed anxious when she greeted me."

"She's been worrying for weeks over how to address you," Chiara said wryly. "I've even spoken with her about it—as you know, we usually keep silence, but when I see a need I arrange to talk with the sisters, individually or together—and I've tried to help her, but she remains concerned. I told her she could call you anything she wanted and you wouldn't mind. Was I correct?"

"Yes. I tried for years to get her to drop the 'monna,' but she found it so difficult that I finally gave up."

"She only means to show respect, but I still hope she will reach an understanding that all the sisters are equal to one another, and we are all of us the smallest and meekest of women."

I couldn't think of this great-souled woman as either small or meek, but Francesco often spoke of himself and of the brothers in the same way. Was I small? I thought not, but neither was I any bigger than anyone else. Meek could be a problem. I'd been raised to give orders and see them carried out, so I might have to work on that. With me it had never been a matter of social position, which is probably why my parents were relieved to see me safely wed to Graziano instead of falling in love with some apprentice and disgracing them. But I had far too little patience with people whose minds worked more slowly than my own, whatever their station in life. It was why someone as quick as Elias won my trust so easily.

As if she had heard me thinking, Chiara asked me if I had news of Elias. I told her briefly what he had written about Francesco's health and his instructions to ask for her help if I needed it, but she shook her head, slowly.

"I fear for him too, Sister Giacoma, but I cannot interfere with Father Francesco's penance. He is a holy man, and I would not presume to dictate to him. Like you, I am under obedience to him."

"What penance does he engage in?" I wasn't sure I really wanted to know.

She paused, and I suspected she was judging how much to tell me. "He often wears a shirt with horsehair knots on the inside. Sometimes he replaces it with a pigskin garment, wearing the bristles next to his skin."

I shuddered. My habit, as I liked to call it, was plain cloth, not as soft or luxurious as the clothes I used to wear, but it was smooth and tightly woven, and I couldn't imagine deliberately wearing a garment that caused not only discomfort, but pain.

"And he fasts," she went on. "He severely limits what he eats, and should he find his food too tasty, he mixes it with ashes." That surprised me. At my table Francesco was abstemious, but not exaggeratedly so. And he relished his food, though he never allowed himself large portions of anything. I could imagine Amata's face if he started smearing ashes on the meals she prepared for him.

"Does he sleep, at least?" I asked.

"Little. He prays for most of the night. And the penitential garments can make sleep hard to find."

I looked at her sharply, for she spoke as if she knew this from experience. She looked calmly back at me.

"He wears them even at night?"

"That is when they cost us the most, and therefore accomplish the most." Her matter-of-fact voice suggested this was perfectly reasonable; I did not find it so. I didn't see how Francesco could lead a growing religious brotherhood while in constant pain and hunger and exhaustion. Nor could he hold sickness at bay, for he was not strong by nature. But I didn't feel these were things to discuss with Chiara. Our approaches to such things were worlds apart.

With that realization the moment of closeness between us faded, and we were back to being guarded with each other. By tacit agreement, we left the refectory to join the other women, who milled around in the courtyard speaking quietly in clusters of two or three. All fell silent when Chiara emerged, and she gestured for them to continue. She went over to her sisters and her mother and joined them, the pleasure they took in one another's company a joy to behold.

The rest of our stay with the sisters passed quickly. I persuaded Vanna to call me "Sister Giacoma," since Chiara did, and she seemed relieved to have it decided for her. Knowing that Francesco had specifically disallowed that title for me, I was uncomfortable, but it was the easiest solution. She showed me the kitchen garden, proudly pointing out the plants she tended, and she told me about welcoming the new sisters.

I had brought her three almond cakes and tried to slip them to her, but she put her hands behind her back. "I cannot, Sister Giacoma," she said earnestly. "Not unless all of the sisters were to have them."

We had arrived after dinner this time, so I didn't have my chance to ignore an egg, but I thought of pouring ashes on good food, and going hungry, and never eating almond cakes again, and I was glad our evening supper would be back at Mengarda's well-supplied palazzo. I was probably hopeless, I decided. Mengarda, Ortolana, and Beatrice ate the three almond cakes on the walk back to Assisi.

27

Two weeks had passed since our visit to San Damiano, bringing warmer weather and longer days to Assisi. I was walking back from Santo Stefano, enjoying the afternoon's gentle warmth on a light breeze, when I saw the horses tied outside Mengarda's palazzo.

I quickened my step, for it was likely this would be a delegation to me. Arnolfo's business brought an occasional guest, but not a half dozen at once. Something must be wrong at home.

The portal stood open, and I hurried in. Arnolfo, Mengarda, and Prassede stared at me in alarm, and I recognized one of Massimo's men standing in the entryway with them. Our household would have arrived at the Marino villa by this time, so he must have come from there.

"Is it Uccel?" I asked breathlessly. That was always my first fear.

Prassede came up to me and put her hand on my arm, murmuring soothing words as if I were a child.

"Is it? What's happened?" I heard the hysteria in my voice, but I didn't care.

"Madonna, your son is ill, but it may be nothing serious," the man from Marino said, offering me a rolled parchment. "Here's a letter from Massimo."

I snatched it from his hand, but I wanted answers immediately. "Tell me. Now."

"Massimo sent me because he thought you should be told, but he cautioned me not to alarm you."

"How can I not be alarmed? What are his symptoms? How long has he been ill? Who's taking care of him? Is he eating? Does he have a fever? Did anyone send for maestro Marco? We have to pack right away. I'm going back to Marino." *Listen to me. I sound like Prassede.*

The poor messenger looked flustered. "Madonna, I don't know the details. They will be in Massimo's letter, I am certain."

I broke the seal with my thumbnail and unfurled it—two pages in Massimo's utilitarian miniscule hand, which always made me squint—and scanned it.

Uccel had fever, chills, weakness, all familiar symptoms, but I didn't see anything more alarming than any of his previous illnesses. The second page was only a detailed household report, expenses and minor news items, and I ignored it for the time being.

I reread the first page slowly, trying to read between Massimo's tidy lines to discern whether there was something he wasn't telling me. He assured me the doctor had visited twice, and Lucia was with Uccel every minute. Bartola was the more experienced nurse, but she was in Rome with our elderly patients.

I had a flurry of questions for the messenger, whose name I didn't recall, but the unfortunate man didn't have the answers. He said he had been on the road for six days and nights. The pace suggested a certain amount of urgency on Massimo's part, but not an all-out race against time. So, serious but not an imminent disaster, or perhaps only Massimo being cautious. Or that's what I told myself, not that it helped much.

"Is there anything we can do, Giacoma?" Mengarda asked. She squeezed her clasped hands tightly. Mengarda understood my fears. She had two grown sons and a daughter whose every mishap, however inconsequential, sent her into a frenzy of worry and urgent prayer.

"I must go home," I told her. "If you and Prassede could gather our things, and perhaps make arrangements..." I looked at the messenger. The man was mudspattered and disheveled, clearly tired, and I did not think he would be eager to turn around and escort me back immediately. His companions, who were probably taking refreshment in the kitchen, wouldn't be in any better condition. "And arrange for an escort, just a few armed men who can move fast. We'll leave as soon as they get here. This afternoon."

Arnolfo was horrified. "But, Giacoma, it's too late in the day. You'd not reach a place to lodge by nightfall. You mustn't try to leave until morning."

I started to overrule him, but then I paused to think. He might be right. I had no wish to find myself somewhere in the wilds of these Umbrian hills come dark. Between the wolves and their human equivalents, we would not improve our chances of reaching Uccellino soon, if at all. We would have to wait, and there was little I could do for now except pack. Unless—yes.

"And please send a messenger to Francesco and the brothers. Ask for Feo as a guide, and tell him to bring his brother Eusebio," I instructed Mengarda. "If anyone can get us there quickly and safe, it will be those two." What better protection from bandits than to hire some?

Mengarda hurried to find a servant to bear the message. I pestered the man from Marino with more questions until I was satisfied he had told me everything he knew, and then I finally let him join his fellows in the kitchen.

Arnolfo promised me an armed contingent to guard us and his fastest

197

horses for our use, and he swore everything would be ready by dawn. Prassede hurried off to pack, and I went to the chapel to pray.

I prayed first for my son's health. I prayed for relief from my own agitation, to enable me to think and plan clearly. I prayed for Francesco, for I had hoped to stay here long enough to try to help him as Elias had asked, at least long enough to be here for the brotherhood's upcoming chapter meeting, and to turn my renunciation of my lawsuit to his advantage as well as to Chiara's, if I could. God listened to all of this without comment.

But when I started to rise to go help Prassede with the packing, it was Francesco's voice, not God's, that I heard in my mind. I stayed on my knees.

"Giacoma, there is no need for you to leave tomorrow. Wait three days, and then if nothing has happened to change your mind, you may go."

My child needs me. I must go.

"Brother Giacoma, I'm putting you under an obedience. I say you will wait. Wait through tomorrow and the next day and one more, and then if you still want to go, you are free to leave."

Francesco had never before ordered me to do something I didn't want to do, unless I counted not pulling a dagger on the bandit, and I had to admit he was probably right about that one. Still, this time everything in me resisted his command.

Once before, I learned from a messenger that someone I loved was in trouble. I didn't get there soon enough. I can't let it happen again.

"It won't. You have my word. And I have your oath, and I say you will wait. Three days."

I struggled with that. My trust in Francesco was strong, but this was my son, my youngest. With so much at stake, could I trust anyone absolutely? And besides, Francesco hadn't been exactly forthright about that bandit, as I recalled. Yet I could not believe he would lie to me about my son's safety.

Nothing in Massimo's letter told me I needed to come immediately. He had not asked me to come home, yet he must have known I would. My instincts as a mother drove me to do so. But Francesco was my spiritual father, and I meant it when I promised him obedience. I felt wrenched apart inside and completely at a loss.

Why, Francesco? Why must I wait?

"Does your obedience depend on being given a reason you can accept?"

No. It didn't. Obedience was absolute, or it was not truly obedience.

Francesco, if you're wrong, I will never forgive you. Not in this life or beyond.

"I know."

It hung there in the air between us, between the woman on her knees in front of an altar and the man who wasn't even physically present. I closed my eyes tightly and directed one last prayer to Our Lady, beseeching her to help me find my way through this thicket of conflicting desires and help me fulfill my obligations—to my sons I owed my care and protection; to my spiritual father, my obedience and loyalty. All of them possessed my unconditional love, so how could I choose?

Our Lady must have been busy elsewhere. She offered me no help; I was on my own.

I tried to think clearly. Uccellino was with people who loved him deeply, and he had the best care they and the doctor could provide. The messenger said Massimo had sent for Bartola. Everything I would have done had I been there was already being done.

Also, Francesco had my word. Was I to prove myself foresworn on the first occasion where my wishes differed from his? Was I, then, unfit to be a brother? Was my word worth nothing?

No choice. Not for Brother Giacoma.

I will wait. Three days, and three days only.

"God give you peace." And his presence was gone. Had it really been there?

Did I still have to ask?

I went downstairs and found Mengarda and Arnolfo in a whirlwind of activity trying to arrange my journey. I told them gently that I had changed my mind, and I would not be leaving until first light on Friday. They looked at me as if they were unsure whether I had been mad before and returned to my senses, or the other way around. I mumbled something about having prayed and received an answer, which would be hard for them to argue with, and went off to the kitchen to thank the messenger and his escort.

The messenger was courteous to a fault, but he was clearly relieved not to have to escort a hysterical mother back to Marino immediately. I gave him ample coin to cover lodgings for the six of them in town, and he readily agreed to meet me on Friday morning for the journey home. That would simplify things. We would take the precaution of hiring two or three more armed men, and of course we would take Feo and Eusebio, though this time they would have to ride instead of walk. It should be enough. I wished Gualtiero was in Assisi to lead our party, but he had gone back to his duties in Marino after the Easter celebrations were over.

And so the waiting began. I barely slept, I paced and growled like a caged bear, and I snapped indiscriminately at anyone who had the temerity to speak to me. I trudged down to Santo Stefano and back, twice the first day, thrice the second. Considering the state of mind I was in, it was probably a good thing I didn't encounter Elias's mother.

I gave generous alms to anyone brave enough to approach me, asking them—no, ordering them—to pray for Uccel.

I was prepared to argue with my spiritual father and insist on knowing why I must wait, but he evaded me. I marched up to every brother I saw on the street and demanded to speak to Francesco, but each one said he was busy, or elsewhere, or they didn't know how to find him, and soon they learned to avoid me altogether.

On the third day I walked all the way to the Porziuncola, the first time I had ever done so, and there on the path just outside the complex it fell to an anxious Ricco to turn me away. Because he was my dear freckle-faced boy, I somehow managed not to be unforgivably rude to him, though my disappointment must have been obvious. But I had not so far forgotten myself that I was blind to the difficult spot he found himself in. If Francesco would not see me, Ricco could do little to help me.

Loyal Prassede had come with me, ignoring my prickliness, and she and I had already started back to Assisi when Ricco called to me to wait. I stopped, my heart hammering. Had he changed his mind? Would he help me get to Francesco?

"Giacoma, if you'll give me a minute I'll fetch Feo and Eusebio for you, and they'll go with you and stay at the palazzo tonight. Then you'll not have to wait for them on the morrow. They can't make this walk in the dark, and if they're already with you, you won't have to wait for them—you can leave at sunup. And Francesco has given leave for them to ride."

That was something, at least. I thanked him, and he loped back to the Porziuncola to find the former bandits.

The two brothers hurried to join us. Feo introduced his brother. Eusebio was taller, leaner, and shabbier than Feo, whose face still had a youthful softness, but their identically cleft chins marked them as brothers. We wound our way single file along the narrow uphill path.

I wanted to learn about the bandit business. I wasn't planning to waylay anyone, but if I understood the dangers ahead I would be better prepared—and besides, I was curious. Eusebio was a humble friar now, courteous and eager to serve me, but once I got him started sharing his professional wisdom he proved a treasure trove of information. I learned not only how to spot an ambush, but how and where to set one up. I learned how to make a small group appear larger than it was, and how to be undetectable to a mounted party passing so close you could smell their horses. He told me how to persuade a stolen horse or dog to accept its new master's commands, but that only worked if you had Feo available. We had apparently robbed the bandit gang of a valuable tool.

When we reached Mengarda's palazzo, I asked Sobilia to find a place for the brothers to sleep that night and to give them some dinner, for I suspected they had missed their meal in order to come with me, and then I went to the chapel to pray.

The late afternoon light slanted through the narrow window in the chapel wall, falling on the altar with its tidy embroidered altar cloth and its workmanlike crucifix. I had just sunk to my knees when I heard a commotion outside, in front of the palazzo.

Now what? Instantly alert in case it was another messenger, I scrambled back to my feet and rushed to the window. I wasn't tall enough to see out, but I could hear the voices below.

And one of those voices I knew very well. It was changing registers erratically, like the voice of any thirteen-year-old boy, and it belonged to my elder son.

As I sprinted down the stairs, my skirts hiked up in a way that would have made Vanna swoon, I felt my gorge rise. He must be bringing me news of Uccellino—and what news would cause my older son to follow the messenger to Assisi at such a close interval?

What had Francesco cost me?

28

GIOVANNI had not come in yet, so I burst out the door and came to an abrupt halt when I saw him astride his horse, chatting with one of Arnolfo's men. His companions, Gualtiero and seven or eight other men, were also still mounted.

"Giovanni! Why are you here? It's Uccel, isn't it? What's happened?" I clutched at his arm. Even if I dreaded hearing his news, I had to.

"Mother, calm yourself," he said hastily, placing a reassuring hand on mine. "All is well. I bring you good news—Uccel is much improved."

Much improved. I had been so certain of disaster that it took me a moment to grasp the meaning of his words.

"He's not ill now?" My voice was scratchy.

"He was still ill the morning I left. Or at least he was resting from being ill. But the fever has broken, and he was eating, and Sister Bartola and Massimo urged me to bring you the good news. In fact, we were sure you'd be on your way home, and I've stopped in every town to ask if anyone had word of you, or if they had seen a party that could be yours, to make sure we didn't miss you."

No fever. He was eating. A wave of relief washed over me, like a sudden welcome downpour on a sweltering day.

"Come, dismount, my son. Come inside, and refresh yourself. I'm overjoyed to hear your news, and grateful to you for bringing it." I stroked his mount's neck. She was the mare I often rode at the villa in Marino.

Mengarda and Arnolfo welcomed Gualtiero and the other men into their home while I held tightly to my son's arm and walked with him up to my chamber. We would rejoin the others soon, but first I needed news from home.

I sat on the long chest that flanked my bed, and Giovanni went directly to the window, gazing out appreciatively.

"They've given you a wonderful view, Mother," he said, turning to smile at me. Indeed they had—the cathedral with its gorgeous carvings, the ruddy rooftops of Assisi, the winding streets and closely packed pink and white stone buildings, the hazy blue mountains far away, the peaceful wooded valley, that vast sky freely giving away the weather's secrets. And unlike me, my tall son could see it all without standing on the window seat. But this time I was not interested in the view.

"Tell me of your brother," I begged him. And then, as his face fell, I caught myself. "But first tell me of your journey. You met with no dangers, I hope?"

He brightened. I was going to have to be more careful to balance my worries about Uccel, lest I wound Giovanni.

"No, Mother. I had good men with me, trained by Massimo, and Gualtiero to guide us here. We rode through rain on the second day, but we said our prayers to San Giuliano l'Ospitaliere, and thus each night we found adequate lodgings and no one interfered with our travels."

That probably had as much to do with Massimo's solid planning and Gualtiero's good sense as it did with San Giuliano, but I did not comment.

I still wasn't sure whether I wanted to return with Giovanni or do as I had originally planned and stay in Assisi for the chapter meeting. If he went back without me, Feo and Eusebio could go with him for an added layer of safety. Now that I knew how easy it was to set up an ambush, I felt more anxious for my son.

I urged him to tell me all the news, starting with Uccellino. Most of what he told me of his brother was reassuring, though I worried about a lingering weakness. But Uccel had been very ill for more than two weeks, so it was not surprising that he tired easily.

After Giovanni had patiently answered my questions, some of them more than once, he brought me up to date on the household news. Tommasso and Lucia hoped to wed, waiting only for my blessing, which I assured him they had. Lotario was in excellent health and had developed a taste for turnip greens. Our elderly patients did as well as could be expected. Renzo struggled with his painful joints and Salvestra drifted in and out of a state of dreamy vagueness, but they had formed a singular friendship, spending their days in each other's company. Ancient Meliorata was no longer with us. She had given up her soul to God peacefully, singing quietly till the end. I would pray for her soul and have masses said for her.

Isotta, however, presented a problem, or at least her ne'er-do-well son did. Lapo had turned up on the doorstep of our Roman palazzo at dawn one day, and a new hired girl, knowing nothing of his history, took him in. By the time Massimo and Giovanni got wind of it in Marino, Lapo had been in residence for more than a week, eating and drinking everything in sight.

It was Bartola who sent for Massimo. She held Lapo in little regard, yet she didn't want to upset Isotta, who had wept over her prodigal son and hugged him and thanked God for his return. So Bartola presented the problem to my steward and my son, who straightaway rode back to

Rome to deal with the interloper.

They knew Lapo was wanted for thieving, but they couldn't make themselves turn him in, for turning him in would have cost him his right hand at the very least, and possibly worse. They couldn't do that to Isotta, even if her son might deserve it.

They had intended to make him leave, at least, but Isotta was so grateful and so happy that they lacked the will to send him off. Lapo took over a guest chamber and made himself at home. At least he wasn't getting the benefit of Amata's cooking, for she was with our family in Marino. Only the household guard, the old people, and Sister Bartola had remained in Rome, though two neighborhood girls came in during the day to cook and clean.

"But, Giovanni, our household is defying the law. If anyone sees Lapo—"

"No, it's all right, Mother. I took care of it."

Had I been in Rome, I would have had a discreet word here, passed a generous purseful of coin there, called in some favors, and expertly righted Lapo's situation for him in those ways. He didn't deserve it, but I would have done it for Isotta. What could my son have done? At thirteen, he didn't yet know any of these subtleties of being a Roman noble, though it was time for him to learn.

"How did you do that?"

He blushed. "I consulted with Massimo, and he told me it would take a bribe to fix things for Lapo. He said I'd have to do it, since I'm the master of the house, but he came with me, and it went well. You'll see he put it down in the books as a charitable donation, which it is, in a way."

My boy's first bribe. I felt a surge of pride, even as I realized how ridiculous it was. I could just imagine Graziano grinning at both of us. Francesco never approved of flouting the authorities, and of course I wanted my sons to follow my spiritual father's example wherever possible, but I didn't think Francesco would choose to see Lapo handed over to such brutal treatment, even if it was in the name of justice. And given my sons' position in Roman society, they needed to learn practical skills as well as spiritual virtues.

I scanned Massimo's report for the relevant entry, found it, and whistled. I could have done it for half that. Still, it was Giovanni's first, so I felt he had done well.

"You did as your father would have done, Giovanni, and I'm proud of you." That was actually quite true—Graziano never balked over amounts of money less than the price of a palazzo, so he would have overpaid too.

He always had more important matters on his mind. "You've given Isotta the one thing in the world she wanted, and that's worth a lot. Thank you for taking the responsibility."

He beamed.

Once I returned home, we'd have to figure out a way to get Lapo out of the house. Perhaps I could install him and his mother in one of the rental properties I owned in the neighborhood. I reminded myself to make sure Giovanni took a letter from me to our parish priest when he went back, as a precaution.

When he went back. I guess that meant I was going to stay, though I hadn't been aware of making the decision. But if all was as right as it could be back in Rome and Marino, then I might as well stick with my original plans. I had things to accomplish in Assisi, and apparently I had passed Francesco's test in spite of myself.

*

Giovanni stayed for a week. It gave his men and horses time to rest, and it gave him time to make the acquaintance of this city I had told him so much about. He even got to visit Francesco at the Porziuncola, a privilege which left me wrestling with envy of my own son. I may have been Brother Giacoma, but that didn't mean a woman could be traipsing around the humble shacks and prayer cells of the brothers.

He made the trip in the company of Brother Giannuccio of Cappella, the amusing tufty-eared brother who had waggled his fingers at me endearingly that first night in my kitchen in Rome, years ago. I hadn't seen him often since then, because he seldom left his duties at the leprosarium.

His was not a job many men wanted, even among the brothers, but Brother Giannuccio was devoted to his patients. The more presentable lepers, and the ones from wealthier families or with property to give, were attended to by the Cruciger knights, but responsibility for the patients who were shambling wrecks, near to death and terrifying to behold, inevitably fell to Brother Giannuccio and the brothers who volunteered to help him.

My almost grown son and the childlike brother quickly rediscovered their rapport, and I watched them affectionately as they wandered off together, chatting in the way of old friends. Giovanni bore with him a gift to Francesco from me, a fine cushion filled with down, its red cover painstakingly embroidered with the wildflowers and herbs Francesco most loved. I hoped it would please him and he would see in it a reminder of my love and my devotion.

So when Giovanni returned hours later with the cushion still in its cloth sack, I was disappointed. Had Francesco rejected my gift? If he thought the cover too ornate, surely he could at least have kept the plain cushion inside it.

Giovanni eagerly described his visit for me. "Mother, they live so simply! Their homes aren't the least bit like houses—more like sheds. Only the chapel is really finished, and even it is small and plain. They do have a little garden, but that's about all. They showed me around, not that there was very much to see, and I got to talk with Francesco and pray with him!"

I looked at him sharply. Was I going to lose my son, Graziano's heir, to Francesco's brotherhood, as I had lost Ricco? If it were so, I wouldn't know whether to be joyful or sad, creature of two worlds that I was.

"He gave me a message for you," Giovanni went on. "I don't know what he meant, but he said to tell you he was grateful for your obedience and proud of your courage. And he hopes you'll trust him sooner next time."

Well, he had been right about the three days. But he could have told me. "And how is Francesco?" I asked.

Giovanni hesitated. "I'm not sure," he finally said. "I think he might be ill, or else at least very tired. He doesn't seem as strong as I remembered."

I'd had the same impression, and I shared Giovanni's concern.

It was my turn to hesitate, but I needed to know. "I see you've come back with the cushion. Did he refuse it?"

"He never said so. But when the brothers showed me where Francesco sleeps, I saw what he was using to rest his head, and I realized he would not have used your gift, so I said nothing about it. I'm sorry if that was wrong. I know you wanted him to have it." Diffidently he handed me the sack.

"Why wouldn't he? What pillow does he use, then?"

"No pillow at all, but a stone."

"A stone? He rests his head on a stone?" This was a penance I hadn't yet heard of.

"It was a rounded stone," he said hastily.

Well, I suppose that's something. "So do you aspire to join our Francesco and sleep on stones, my son?"

He laughed. "Is that what you fear, Mother? No. I admire the way the brothers live, but I'm my father's son, and I will be a knight. A virtuous knight, I hope—a knight Francesco would approve of—but I have no wish to turn my back on my legacy. I'll serve God and follow Francesco in the world, just as you do. Francesco assures me we can do much good that way."

I found his words comforting, for their reassurance and for the implied compliment. Reluctantly I stored the cushion in one of my travel trunks. It belonged to Francesco, I told myself stubbornly, and one day he would have it from my own hands. Until then I intended to keep it for him.

*

More than three weeks had passed since the day Giovanni departed for Marino, guarded by Gualtiero, Feo, and Eusebio and accompanied by an armed escort strong enough to protect him, yet not large enough to embarrass him. A messenger had already reached me with word of their safe arrival.

We were now in the second full day of the brotherhood's Pentecost chapter meeting. It drew hundreds more of Francesco's followers than he had expected, some from far-flung parts of the Italian peninsula, both north and south of Assisi. The weather had been fine, which was fortunate because most of the gathered brothers slept in the open, though the sick and the elderly had makeshift tents. The people who brought them carts of food marveled to see so many barefoot men scattered around the Porziuncola, praying, singing, talking with one another, stretched out on the ground to get a little sleep, or taking turns at cooking or tending the fires. All of them wore the same simple, undyed garments we knew so well. The mood was joyful, with a strong sense of camaraderie.

Chapter meetings were for brothers only, but the townspeople who counted themselves friends to the brotherhood, or who were merely curious, crowded along the outskirts to watch. They brought food and blankets and firewood, and the brothers cheerfully made them welcome and thanked them for their gifts.

My own position was ambiguous. I was—I am, always—Brother Giacoma, but I am still a woman, and therefore could not take my place with my brothers, though I had paid for several of those carts filled with supplies. But I did have a vantage point, a shady spot under an ancient oak tree where I would be close enough to hear everything. And with me was the cardinal.

Cardinal Ugolino's entrance had been consummate theatre—or so I thought, until I saw his radiant face and understood at last how thoroughly he, too, had come under Francesco's spell. He had approached the

Porziuncola on horseback, dressed in his clerical finery, accompanied by three mounted attendants. But when Francesco emerged from the chapel to welcome him, the cardinal impulsively dismounted and came to him on foot, humbly, like a brother, while his attendants waited dumbstruck. When they were face to face, Francesco tried to kneel and kiss his ring, but the cardinal sank to his knees first. Francesco gently helped him up and they exchanged a few words before Egidio escorted the churchman to where I sat inelegantly on a blanket.

I had never seen the cardinal so transported. He murmured a prayer over and over, and his eyes were shining. He acknowledged me with a nod, but said nothing to me, for the meeting was about to begin.

Francesco and a few other brothers, those who intended to speak, were on a makeshift dais cobbled together out of bits of scrap wood. Francesco had at first rejected the idea of being placed higher than the gathered brothers, but Egidio and Leone persuaded him that it was the only way for him to be heard all the way to the back of the crowd.

The meeting began with prayer and continued with song, Francesco's sermon, and more prayer. I knew the brothers' ways well, and none of this surprised me.

What I hadn't expected was the direction the meeting took once the brothers settled down to business. Egidio had told me Francesco intended to bring up some new ideas, but he wasn't willing to say more than that.

Francesco stepped forward to speak, and a hush settled on the huge gathering. The cardinal leaned forward intently, eager to catch every word.

"My brothers," Francesco said, spreading his arms wide to encompass us all, "you have my heartfelt thanks for your presence here today. May God give all of you peace."

The brothers murmured the words back to him.

"I have a new venture to put before you this day. God has told me it is now time to spread our message into more distant places—to bring the joys of brotherhood to any and all who may be ready to embrace them."

Another murmur, this one pulsing with curiosity and anticipation.

"I want us to assemble groups of brothers to serve as missionaries. Some will go forth to France, some to Spain. I want some to travel to the Germanic lands, where few yet know of our movement. And I want to send additional brothers to Syria, where Brother Elias has made such a promising beginning."

He went on, going into more detail about what he hoped to accomplish. I studied him carefully. He was animated, excited, smiling, his

208

inimitable zeal there for all to see, and the brothers, to a man, were fired with enthusiasm. Yet I thought I detected in him a darker mood lurking beneath the surface, a mood of foreboding, of resignation. In their excitement, none of the other brothers appeared aware of it, so maybe I was wrong.

Cardinal Ugolino may have fallen under Francesco's sway, but he remained the astute observer and strategist he had always been. He watched and listened, as I did, and then he turned to me.

"Monna Giacoma, what think you of this? Is it wise?"

I hesitated. "Signore, if Francesco wills it, can it be other than wise?"

He shook his head. "I don't know. I wish I did."

Maybe I wasn't wrong.

I wished Elias were here to provide his clear-sighted observations and suggestions, but in the absence of pragmatism, enthusiasm prevailed. Eager brothers scrambled to join groups headed for faraway countries where they did not speak the language and did not understand the customs, to bring the word of God and their example of the gospel life to as many people as possible, whether those people wanted them or not. Men I knew, and more I didn't know, were impetuously committing themselves to unknown risks and hardships, out of love for Francesco.

So many brothers—hundreds of them, eager to carry their joy and faith to the world. Francesco moved among them, giving his blessing, speaking words of inspiration. Sixty men bound for Germany alone, and several other contingents were even larger. At least half of the brotherhood must have been committing to travel, including many men based at the Porziuncola.

I studied the forming clusters of new missionaries, looking for Ricco, then found him in the midst of the little knot of men bound for Spain. His face was radiant, and he was so achingly, painfully young. My heart lurched. Who would take care of the lad, so far away?

Egidio must have heard my thoughts, for he appeared at my side and rested his broad hand on my shoulder.

"You're not going too, are you, Egidio?"

"Not yet. My time will come—this is only the beginning."

"I fear for Ricco. He's still a child," I said, my eyes fixed on the men bound for Spain.

"God will care for him, Giacoma."

Then why did I feel so cold inside?

29

NOW that the chapter meeting was over and the initial whirlwind of activity as the missionary brothers set off in all directions, Francesco found time for me at last. We attended mass in San Rufino, and then I waited outside in the piazza, tapping my foot impatiently while he was mobbed by people who wanted his blessing, his advice, or just his attention for a moment.

Finally he tore himself away from his admirers to join me in Mengarda's palazzo. At last we were together, relaxing on a pair of window seats facing one another, a pleasant breeze ruffling the ends of my benda. Mengarda had finished fussing over us with plates of delicacies and cups of wine and water and had left us alone.

I wondered how much I should be saying to him. Should I express my misgivings? It was too late to try to persuade him that Ricco was too young for this mission. The group bound for Spain had left the previous day. I had watched them go, their bare feet stirring up dust from the road, carrying nothing with them for their journey as the Rule demanded. At least Brother Bernardo was among them. A good man, Bernardo—Francesco's first follower, and his childhood friend. Surely no ill would befall Ricco while in Bernardo's care.

Yet I still felt a chill inside.

"It must feel different at the Porziuncola, with so many brothers gone," I said.

"It's unusually quiet, except for the brothers who wanted to go but I ordered to stay behind. Some of them are still complaining." He smiled.

"I'm glad you're still here, at least. It would all fall apart without you at the center, with the others going so far away."

Francesco's brow furrowed. "I hope you're wrong about that, Giacomina, because I won't be here much longer. I'm taking Brother Pacifico and Brother Silvestro and we're leaving for France in two days."

I sat upright.

"France? Why?"

"To serve the brothers there, and others who would join us. And because the French have much to teach us about proper reverence for the Host." That was a favorite cause of Francesco's. He deplored the haphazard treatment of the sacred vessels in so many churches, the casual disregard, the dirty cloths covering the chalices, the Host itself tucked away in some inappropriate container.

"But who will look after the order here?"

"Brother Pietro Cattani. He knows what to do."

"Brother Pietro will do exactly what you've told him to do. It's what he always does. What if something happens and he has to think for himself?" My voice sounded sharper than I had intended.

"Then God will help him think for himself. Giacoma, I don't know why you're being so difficult about this. Or yes, perhaps I do. It's Ricco, isn't it? You're worried about him."

"Yes, I'm worried about him. I'm worried about all the brothers who are even now trudging off without so much as a roll of bread to eat, or a pair of sandals to protect their feet from sharp stones and snakes and other dangers. I'm worried that when they get to where they're going, they won't have the skill to talk to the people there and make themselves understood. And now I'm worried about you, most of all. Your health is not sound enough to permit you to do this, Francesco."

"So many worries. You sound like Elias. What has happened to your faith in God, Brother Giacoma?"

"My faith in God is as strong as ever, but my faith in mankind is another matter. At least let me talk to some of the Spanish churchmen in Rome. They can send messages back to their cities commanding the priests to treat our brothers with honor and permit them to preach. Without that, anything could happen to them."

To my astonishment, Francesco jumped to his feet, fury in his face. "No! You will do no such thing. I thought you, of all people, would understand. There will be no privileges, no exceptions, no special treatment. The *fratres minores* will make their way in the world as the smallest and weakest of men, their only strength being God himself. And what other strength is there? You will not speak to the Spanish churchmen, Brother Giacoma. I place you under obedience in this matter. If your faith is so small, at least do nothing to undermine your brothers." His voice shook.

I sat back, stunned. He had never spoken to me like that before. I couldn't speak, couldn't think. My embroidery slid from my lap onto the floor.

He composed himself and sat down. He must have seen my distress, because he went on more calmly, though I heard an unaccustomed coldness in his voice.

"I understand that you only wish to help. Perhaps it's a Roman thing, as the good cardinal is also determined to procure for us every possible privilege, completely counter to my wishes. But I must demand that you both cease this kind of meddling, for I know what is best for my order. It is God himself who has instructed me."

"I will obey, Francesco," I whispered, looking down at the embroidery in a heap at my feet. I felt the hot tears coming.

And then he was sitting next to me, the two of us squished together in the small window seat. His hand covered mine, and the familiar warmth was back in his voice.

"Giacomina, I'm so sorry. I know you meant well, and I had no right to be angry with you. I have no excuse, save that the chapter meeting has left me worn out, but you have never merited harshness from me, and I deeply regret the way I expressed myself. I promise you I will confess my fault and do penance." He picked up my embroidery and handed it back to me.

He regretted the way he had expressed himself. He did not regret what he had said.

"You couldn't have known that the cardinal and I have disagreed over this point many times."

I did know, actually, and I didn't think the cardinal's position was entirely without merit.

"I need my brothers, all of you, to understand." he said. "We do not seek any special treatment. We are the least of men, and we are subservient to all, for therein lies our power to do good. Smoothing our way, making it easy for us, undermines what we are trying to do."

He went on for some time, gently and patiently explaining his reasons for refusing any protection from the Church. As I gradually stopped trembling, I focused on the reassurance of his voice, now serene and kind, instead of on what he was saying.

I don't know whether he realized how distraught I felt, but he finally stopped his rambling explanation and fell silent. I kept my eyes on my embroidery, stitching steadily and precisely, willing my hands not to shake

"Giacoma, perhaps I don't tell you often enough how grateful I am for all you do for the brotherhood."

So it was wrong to try to smooth the traveling brothers' way, yet right to play the generous hostess, to introduce him to powerful churchmen, and to discreetly cover the brotherhood's costs and obligations? Where, exactly, was I supposed to draw the line?

I said nothing. Francesco waited for a little while, then let out a sigh and stood.

"I know I've upset you and I can see you don't understand why this matters so much. This obviously isn't a good time to discuss it further." Again he waited for my answer; again I was silent.

"Egidio will visit you tomorrow. You may speak freely to him about our conversation. He can assure you that you're not the first brother to feel my undeserved anger lately, but I think he can also help you see what it is I'm trying, so very clumsily, to do."

I still did not look up, not trusting either my face or my voice. He said nothing more to me, pausing only to say a few words to Mengarda on his way out.

I was shaken to my core. I retired early, pleading a headache, and while Mengarda looked at me sharply, she did not question me. I pulled a stool up to the window in my chamber so I could stand on it and look out at the cathedral, for whatever comfort that beloved sight might afford me, and my gaze fell on the three little men perched on their animals, forever holding up the great rose window.

They were so small, and the round and perfect thing they supported was so vast. How could I not see them all as Francesco, bearing the weight of this burgeoning movement he had somehow created? No wonder he sometimes felt overwhelmed.

And there was only one of him. Elias might have been able to hold up his share, but he was far away. Egidio's strength was Francesco's to call on, but it was not the right sort of strength for this task, and besides, he was increasingly drawn to a path of solitary retreat.

Only Francesco could do it.

I had been so full of my own hurt that I had failed to see how troubled Francesco was, but I vowed not to repeat that mistake. I would redouble my efforts to care for him, and I would show him my faith was not small.

*

When Egidio came, we talked of Francesco's words to me. He was sympathetic, as I knew he would be. He told me of several similar instances involving various brothers, including those who were closest to Francesco.

"Our spiritual father is preoccupied, inconsistent in enforcing the Rule, and quick to anger these days, Giacoma. I don't mean all the time—he's still often joyful, and prayer never fails to restore him. But he's trying to perform a difficult task, and it's one he fears he may be ill suited to."

"Is he right about that?" It had never occurred to me to doubt Francesco before.

"He may be. Francesco is a living saint, the best possible example for the brothers, but he has no gift for seeing to the practical day-to-day needs of his growing order."

"I hate it that I angered him so." I brushed a tear away. Despite my vow, I still felt devastated by Francesco's words, and by the coldness behind them.

"Giacoma, Francesco loves you still. What he fears is privilege granted by the Church, for he believes it will corrupt the brothers with pride as it has other monks."

"And would it really do that?"

"For some it would. For others, no. It wouldn't."

"Then isn't Francesco in his own way protecting the weaker brothers from temptation?"

"Do you think he has not thought of that, Giacoma? Our Francesco is a deeply troubled man. By himself, he followed in the steps of our Lord joyfully, but he is not by himself. Not with hundreds of brothers hanging on his every word and imitating his every action. None of us have his dedication and his purity of spirit, not even the best among us. From this point onward Francesco's path will become even more difficult, maybe impossible. Give him your love, your comfort, your understanding, but know that you will have to watch him suffer, and perhaps even fail."

"Can you tell me how I can help him?"

Egidio shook his head. "I wish I knew."

We lapsed into an easy silence, both of us dejected, yet warmed by each other's company. There was little left to say, so we prayed together. When we finished, I walked with him as far as the city gate.

"Will Francesco be safe on his journey to France?" I asked as we parted.

Egidio shrugged. "I hope so, but it will be as God wills. For myself, I'm going back to the hermitage. I need some time in solitude after being around so many brothers. They are dear to me, but they do make a lot of noise." He grinned. "God give you peace, Giacoma." And he was off down the path.

*

With so many brothers already traveling and with Francesco about to leave, I saw little reason to stay in Assisi. My talk with Francesco had left a bad taste, and I wished for a better resolution, but there was no opportunity, for he did take his leave within two days.

I began preparations for my return journey. It took me a few days to assemble a suitable escort, to pack, and to procure supplies, but I was becoming practiced at traversing this route, so I expected to make good time going home.

Home. To Rome and Marino, to my boys, to whatever chaos two toddlers and an overly-pampered sheep might have wrought by now. To Amata's cooking and Lucia's upcoming wedding and figuring out what to do about Lapo. To all the usual brash and colorful activity in the streets of Rome, to her white marble monuments and crumbling slums, to her beggars and church pageantry and the sludgy summer trickle of the filthy Tiber.

I could hardly wait.

30

LIGHT streamed through the parchment-covered window of my study, illuminating every detail of the massive account book propped on my reading stand. Parchment is better at admitting light than at keeping out the cold, so I had a small brazier at my feet, its embers glowing red.

I loved this little room. After Isotta died and Salvestra and Renzo married, we had extra space in the west wing, and I took over the small corner room once used for linen storage and extra bedding. All things to do with money were to be contained in this room where they would not pollute the rest of my palazzo.

Yet despite its dedication to Mammon rather than to God, the room itself was a delight, largely because of that light, but also because I was seldom interrupted here.

Now, though, I was waiting for a member of my household to report to me.

Footsteps approached, followed by a tap on the door.

"Come in, Lapo," I called, and he did. "Sit down."

He sat on the stool facing my writing table and waited, silent and respectful. He looked infinitely better than he had when he first came to us. Clean, nails trimmed, dressed in an old tunic of Graziano's, he was a different man than the unkempt creature who had appeared unexpectedly at our door, to his late mother's great joy. He had gradually become an accepted member of our household, and he had been grateful and eager to please us. To please me, especially. Massimo was teaching him to read and cipher, and he was becoming a useful employee to me.

I glanced at the cloak he carried over his arm. It looked like good cloth, and the rich red-brown color matched his russet hair. I hadn't seen the garment before, and it pleased me to see that even as he was diligently supplying our hospitals, he was tending to his own needs. He had come to my palazzo with nothing but the clothes he was wearing.

And then I remembered: he had no money. I had recently lent him a few coins to last him until payday, but they couldn't have been enough to pay for that garment.

"That's a handsome cloak, Lapo," I said, watching him. "Did you save enough from the hospital funds that you could afford it?"

He shook his head indignantly. "Giacoma, I spent every denaro of the money you gave me on supplies for the hospitals. I would never spend your money on myself." His voice dripped with wounded dignity.

"No, of course you wouldn't," I said slowly. With Lapo I never knew how much was sincere and how much was performance. "I was just wondering how you happened to have a new cloak. The last one I saw you wear was the one I gave you, Graziano's old blue one. What happened to that?"

"I still have it. I'm saving it for feast days. I needed a plainer one for errands."

"And you had enough money saved to buy one?"

"I... found it."

"You found it?"

"Yes. It was just hanging there, so I thought I might as well have it. No sense in having it go to waste."

"Where was it hanging, exactly?"

He looked down at his hands and mumbled something.

"Didn't hear you, Lapo. Where did you say it was hanging?"

"Clothesline."

"You took it off a clothesline?"

Another mumble.

I leaned both elbows on the table and rested my face in my hands. "Lapo..."

"I know, Giacoma. I promised. I don't know what comes over me—I guess I've been living this way for so long I just can't help myself."

"You've got to stop it, Lapo. I've told you, I'll make sure you want for nothing, just as I did for your mother, God rest her soul." We both crossed ourselves, and he closed his eyes and murmured a brief prayer.

"I was going to pay you along with everyone else, next week, but if you need it now, you may have it. If you want something, you can just buy it. But if you keep stealing, sooner or later you'll be caught, and it will mean no end of trouble for you and for the entire household. Even a bribe from me will go only so far." I glared at him. I couldn't understand his compulsion. Surely he realized that another conviction could cost him his right hand, or see him exiled, or both.

He scoffed. "I hardly think anything I do could cause you any real difficulty, Giacoma. Maybe a fine, or a bit of additional expense, but you wouldn't be in any danger. The only person I'm putting at risk is myself." His voice was shaking. Emotion, or theatre? "I know it, yet I can't stop."

"When you steal, you're sinning, Lapo. Do you confess it?"

"Of course. Always." Lapo was surprisingly devout, albeit somewhat selectively.

"I could send someone with you when you shop. Would that help you keep from stealing?"

"Maybe. It's worth a try. I do want to stop, Giacoma. You know I do."

I did know it, or at least I thought I did. And I could understand, just barely, how stealing could have become such a way of life for him that he found it hard to stop. But this could not go on.

"Have you prayed about it?"

"Every day."

My household, my responsibility.

"The cloak. Is there any chance you could unsteal it?"

"Un—what?"

"Take it back. Slip it back onto the clothesline in the dead of night, or something."

"Nobody leaves a clothesline out in the dead of night. Besides, you don't want me to take that chance. Not there."

"Why? Whose clothesline was it?"

"It was behind that big house over near San Nicola in Carcere."

The Pierleoni. Oh, God. They'd eat him alive, and they'd do it gleefully, knowing he worked for a Frangipane. "Don't pretend you don't know whose property we're talking about, Lapo. You're not stupid." *Though I might be, for taking a chance on you.*

It seemed Lapo had got himself a new cloak after all. Then I looked at it more closely.

"You can't wear this," I told him, aghast. "Look at that border. It's distinctive, and if the Pierleoni see you in it—or anybody who's currying favor with the Pierleoni sees you. . ." *Listen to me. Now I'm trying to help him cover up a theft.*

"I thought maybe I could just pull out the stitching and take the border off, leaving it plain," he said with a tinge of hope in his voice. "Plain is all I wanted, anyway. If there'd been a plain one, I'd have taken that instead."

"Let me see it, Lapo." I held out my arms and he draped the cloak across them. I stroked the supple cloth and felt the heft of it. Decent

218

quality, though nothing special. The trim was a simple woven band, dark green with decorative black stitching. It probably belonged to a servant, though a fairly high-ranking one. It was the sort of cloak Massimo might have worn, if my household still paid attention to that sort of thing.

That trim was going to have to go.

"Leave it with me, then. I'll remove the band." I couldn't believe I was doing this. What would Francesco say? Or Graziano, for that matter? They would both berate me, though for different reasons.

Lapo exhaled. "Giacoma, you are kind to me." He rummaged around in his pouch and pulled out a pastry, only a little worse for wear. He brushed it off and held it out to me. "May I at least offer you this, with my thanks?"

"Where did you get that?"

He gulped. "It was just..."

"I know. It was just lying there on the baker's table, waiting for a new home. No, I don't want your pastry, Lapo."

He looked aggrieved. "I didn't steal it. I swear I didn't."

"Yet you had no money."

"I won it fairly."

"You won it?"

"Just a little game of chance, out in the piazza."

"But what if you had lost? What would you have done?"

"I wasn't going to lose." He sounded quite certain of that.

"You mean you cheated?"

"Let's just say the outcome was under my control. But I didn't steal anything."

"If you cheated, how can you say you won them fairly?"

"That's how those games always work, Giacoma. It's only stupid and gullible people that get taken in."

I could see we were going to have to work on this. A small part of me tended to agree with him, though.

"Lapo, if you cheated someone in order to gain the pastry, then you stole it. Can we be clear about that?"

He hesitated, then nodded reluctantly. "I'll try harder, Giacoma. You've been good to me, and you saved my poor mother's life when I couldn't do anything to help her. I owe you everything, and I do want to please you. But stealing is all I've ever known, and I'm good at it. I don't know how to do anything else." Absentmindedly, he took a bite of the pastry.

"Yes, you do. You know how to drive a shrewd bargain when you purchase supplies for the hospital. You know how to find the little extras that mean so much to the patients, and you know what they need because you talk with them and listen to them with a saint's forbearance. They look forward to your visits as if you were bringing them the Holy Father's blessing. You're a kind man and a clever one. You work hard, you work efficiently, and you're able to make decisions for yourself when I'm not around. You're an asset to me, Lapo. I wouldn't want to have to do without you. You are my trusted worker and my friend, and you don't need to be a thief anymore."

"Am I really? An asset?" He looked stunned by my words. "Giacoma, I'll stop taking things. I swear it. This cloak will be my last stolen thing, I promise you. I swear it on my mother's soul."

Careful there, Lapo. Fortunately, I was fairly sure Isotta's soul would survive even Lapo's wavering intentions.

"The last thing except for the pastry," I couldn't resist saying.

"No, it really is the last. I got the pastry first and then the cloak."

"You're sure there's no safe way to get the cloak back to its owner?"

He shook his head. "Can't think of one."

I sighed. "So be it, then. You go on about your work, but take Gualtiero with you. Tell him I said you'd need someone to help carry things. Leave the cloak with me. What are you shopping for today?"

"Bedclothes for the women's hospital. New sheets, and you said to also get some secondhand nightshifts if there was enough money left. I'm ready to go now, and I won't need the cloak. I'll be warm enough."

"I'll give you the key to the money chest," I said, reaching for the casket on my writing table.

"I've got the money already. Don't need the key."

Did I want to know?

"No. Don't ask," he said, and his smile was somewhere between cocky and apologetic.

It was probably a good thing I had this one on my side.

"I'll take care of the cloak. But this is the last time. And Lapo..."

"Yes?"

"I need you to promise me you'll stay out of trouble."

"That I will. You have my word on it."

"Does that mean you won't do anything wrong, or that you won't get caught?"

He stroked his chin as he thought about my question. "I definitely won't get caught, at least," he finally said.

Good enough for now. "Go, then, and do your errand," I told him, and he left, whistling his favorite istampitta.

I knew I should give the cloak away as alms, but I feared someone would recognize it, and Lapo's light-fingered past was well known. Therefore, the richest woman in Rome was about to spend the next hour disguising a stolen garment.

As the door closed, I leaned back in my chair, hoping the sunlight on my face would cleanse the feeling of unease that followed Lapo around like an anxious puppy. He was immune to it himself, but Lapo's risks and equivocations alarmed everyone else in my household, even though we had become fond of him.

Perhaps it was *because* we were fond of him, I reflected. All of us had a better idea of what could lie in store for him than he appeared to.

A light, hesitant tap on the door took me by surprise. Amata opened the door cautiously, an apology in her dark eyes.

"Giacoma, I'm so sorry to bother you, but I must speak with you," she said.

31

I motioned Amata in and returned to my chair. She sat down, and the stool groaned in protest. Amata had always been plump, but since her daughter's stillbirth she had grown much heavier, to the point where she waddled when she walked, and going up stairs left her breathless. She hesitated, almost as if she was waiting for permission to speak.

"What is it, Amata?"

"I have to tell you something, Giacoma, but it isn't an easy thing to say."

"Is anyone hurt? Or ill?" First things first.

"No, it's not that."

Was it Lapo, perhaps? Had he done something else foolhardy? Warm-hearted Amata had been one of the first to trust him and welcome him.

"Tell me."

She appeared to be taking an intense interest in her apron, for her fingers busily explored the seams and smoothed the fabric over and over. She took a deep breath, but she would not meet my eyes. I waited.

"Your son is threatening Belfiore's virtue, and it's got to stop," she said suddenly, the words tumbling out.

My son? She had to mean Giovanni, robust and vigorous at fifteen, for fragile Uccellino was still very much a child. But that didn't sound like my Giovanni at all. Belfiore was our pretty new kitchen girl; I hardly knew her.

"How do you know this?"

"The girl told me. She's a good girl, Giacoma, and she has no wish to lose her virginity to the boy, even if he is the young master."

"He would never force her," I said, sure of my ground on that point at least. My Giovanni? And anyway, surely he was still much too young for such thoughts.

And then I remembered myself as a new bride at fifteen. Perhaps he was not too young.

Amata shook her head stubbornly. "She thinks he would. She's afraid—she told me so. She says he's being very insistent."

I didn't know what to say. That didn't sound like my son, and yet... He was a tall, powerful boy, and his voice had recently settled into its new, lower register. He reminded me more of his father every day.

"I love Giovanni too, you know," she said, finally looking at me. "He's a good boy, but he's at an age where he doesn't have much control over his desires, and even with all your training, he's still a wealthy young nobleman. It's no wonder he thinks he has the right, but he doesn't. We hired that girl because I needed the help in the kitchen, but it was also because she needed the work. She's undowered, and her family has nothing."

I knew this. Her people were among the families I had been helping for years.

"I don't want him taking advantage of her, and I know you don't either," she went on. "Will you talk to him, Giacoma? I feel like she's my responsibility, since I'm the one who suggested you hire her. She—"

A sharp rap at the door interrupted her, and without waiting for my invitation, Lucia stormed in.

"Giacoma, I don't know what she's been telling you, but it isn't true," she said, glaring at Amata. "Giovanni would never do something like that."

I rather suspected she did know, if she was ready to declare it wasn't true. I also knew that to Lucia, her former charges could do no wrong. I had run into this blind spot before, often. She refused to believe them capable of even innocent childish mischief, whereas I knew full well that they were not only capable of it, they were quite good at it.

Amata glowered back at Lucia, and I waited to see what they would do next.

"You do the boy no favors, Lucia, if you allow him to sin and do the girl harm," Amata said testily.

"He doesn't need any favors from me! He's a fine lad, and he always has been. You're imagining things."

"Are you going to raise that squalling brat of yours to be a sinner too?"

"My Lancelotto is the sweetest of children, and the only reason he cries is that your little monsters torment him incessantly." Lucia's left eye was twitching furiously.

Time to step in.

"That's enough. Lucia, either be silent or leave, and Amata, you be quiet too. I won't have this arguing."

I tried to sound stern but kindly, though I probably seemed exasperated instead. These two had been at each other's throats since Lancelotto started toddling. There was some truth to Lucia's accusation of torment, and Lancelotto did in fact whine a lot. Amata's boy Benino was a bully, plain and simple—a natural leader, his mother called him—and his twin Cilia was surprisingly sly for a tiny barely five-year-old girl. Both were also capable of great affection and could be delightful children, but they were going through a difficult age, and having them constantly besieged by an adoring but fractious two-year-old was a recipe for disaster. Nuta, our former wetnurse, had infinite patience with all the children, but now that she was wed to Gualtiero and suffering through the sickness of early pregnancy, I couldn't ask her to step in and help.

Lucia and Amata stared at me, each willing me to see her side of the argument, which clearly went far beyond their thoughts about my son. I had already been considering separating the two families by taking Amata, Massimo, and the twins with us to Marino for the summer and letting Lucia, Tommasso, and their boy stay in Rome, but if I did that, they'd probably both complain and want it to be the other way around.

Come to think of it, I wasn't sure I wanted the twins where I was going to be. Someday little Benino was going to have to find something to boss around. If not a city or a parish or a regiment, it would be his family, and I wouldn't wish that on anyone.

But for the moment, their sons were their problem. I had a problem with my own.

"You may both return to what you were doing," I told them. They hadn't asked my leave to come, but maybe I could at least get them to go. "Whichever of you finds Giovanni first, send him up to me. Do not tell him about this conversation."

Both continued to sit in stony silence.

"We're done here. Go, and send my son to me." I clapped my hands, and they finally got up. Lucia left swiftly, with one poisonous glance back at Amata. Amata looked as if she wanted to say something more, but my expression must have deterred her, because she finally lumbered out the door.

*

Giovanni stood before my table, flushed and defiant, his hands clasped behind his back.

"I won't deny I like the girl," he said. His newly deep voice startled me, as it did every time I heard him speak. Would I always think of my boys as children?

"She fears you, or so I'm told." That was the part I found hardest to believe.

"She has no need. I might have tried to persuade her, but I would never have done anything against her will." He spoke with conviction, and I relaxed a little.

224

"You will one day be a knight, my son. Your duty will be to protect the weak and the helpless. You are never to prey on them." Not every knight took this code seriously, but I knew Giovanni believed in it with all his idealistic heart.

"And I will not, Mother. But other men my age have a—a friend, or a leman. Why may I not?"

Hadn't he been a little boy just yesterday?

"The girl is a virgin. Would you lead her into sin?"

"Not if she doesn't wish to go there. But Pierino swives a servant girl—"

His bluntness startled me. "Your cousin is hardly a man I want you to emulate."

Giovanni gave an exaggerated sigh. "Mother, I don't see how you can understand. You're a widow, and you're sworn to chastity, but it's different for a man."

"Is Francesco a man?"

"Francesco is something more than a man, as you've told me yourself. You can't possibly know what it's like to want something so much. The girl is as fair as an angel."

I couldn't possibly know. What I couldn't possibly do was explain to my son how I still yearned for his father and resented the emptiness of his side of our bed. Sometimes even now, when I watched Amata with Massimo or Lucia with Tommasso, I thought I couldn't bear it any longer. Once a demon had almost convinced me to end my life and damn my soul rather than go on without Graziano. But I wasn't going to say any of that to Giovanni.

"Yes, she's fair." And she was—well shaped, graceful, with large eyes and full lips. "But if she doesn't want your attentions you are to leave her alone. Her virginity is all she has to offer on the marriage market."

"It needn't be. I could dower her."

"So can I, and I was planning to. But you will not be the cause of this angel's fall."

"Other men—"

"I mean it. You bed her, you wed her."

He looked at me in utter shock. "Mother, you can't mean that! I'm a Frangipane. I can't wed a kitchen servant!"

"Then don't seduce her, or you will have her for your lady for the rest of your life. You have my word on that."

"I've no intention of marrying her. I want to marry Saracena."

Saracena. This was the first I had heard of that particular ambition.

225

It wasn't a bad idea. She was the daughter of a noble line, a family prominent enough to keep our relatives from complaining, yet sufficiently lower than our own social standing for them to prize such a marriage. She was a bold and clever girl. I might talk to her people about a betrothal, though she was still far too young to marry.

"Someday that may happen. But it won't if you bed Belfiore. How could you persist in pursuing a girl who fears you?"

"Whatever you've heard, Mother, she doesn't act like she fears me. She's always putting herself where I can't help but see her, and she finds excuses to walk past me in the corridors. I swear she wants my attentions."

These things did happen in households like ours. Not that there were very many other households quite like ours.

"And how far have your attentions gone?"

He flushed a deeper red. "Not far enough to do her any harm."

"Not as far as you wanted, then."

"No."

"Good. I need not remind you of what Francesco would say if he knew of this."

For the first time since he had entered my study, Giovanni lowered his gaze. He said nothing.

"Avoid her, son. She won't be here much longer."

He looked up, startled. "You're sending her away?"

"I'm giving her a dowry and my recommendation to help her find another position. She can tell her new employers that our household was too odd for her to tolerate."

He balked for a moment, then bowed his head in defeat.

"As you will, Mother."

I almost felt sorry for him. Lust was natural in a boy his age, but I noticed he hadn't spoken of love, so there was a limit to my sympathy. He could turn his thoughts to Saracena instead.

*

Night was falling, but I sat quietly, not bothering to light the candles.

The girl would be on her way on the morrow, a generous dowry in hand. She could scarcely contain her glee when I told her, and it was clear to me that this was the outcome she had wanted. If I had turned a blind eye, would she have succumbed to Giovanni's efforts and then made her move? I thought it likely. And had she perhaps played this game before? Certainly possible.

226

Pity she didn't know she could have had it all—her dowry, my friendship, and a place in my household. But not my son. I was still too much a Roman noblewoman for that.

Lapo's cloak, now plain and anonymous, covered my lap to ward off the evening chill. I sat facing the window, watching the sky through the parchment as it went from dark blue to night black, and my thoughts turned to Francesco and the brothers in Assisi. On days like this I wished I could have joined Chiara and her sisters in their life of pious silence at San Damiano. For all its demands, it would at least have provided peace and quiet.

It was never to be. It would remain a dream, an imagination to soothe me when my responsibilities crowded in and threatened to overwhelm me. I treasured being Brother Giacoma, but I could no more join the brothers at the Porziuncola than I could become Sister Giacoma and live in prayer and peace under Chiara's benign rule. I was chained to Rome, and to my life here.

I fell to wondering how Francesco and the brothers were doing, and the missionaries—Ricco in Spain, Elias still so far away, and as of last summer, even Egidio, off to Tunis. Elias's letters came infrequently, and I'd not had a visit from any of the brothers in months, but now that the snows had melted and travel was possible again, I hoped to see some of them soon. Surely by now there would be news from the missionaries, and whoever visited would be able to tell me how Francesco's fragile health had held up during the winter. So much depended upon his strength and vitality. The order, its numbers increasing with alarming rapidity, was nowhere near ready to survive without him.

But I must wait here in Rome, surrounded by screaming children and contentious servants and a lustful son and an unrepentant thief and a resident sheep, until someone came to me.

32

"HOW long do you think it's going to take her to realize that hobbyhorse isn't going to move on its own?" I asked Prassede, but quietly, so Amata would not overhear and leap to the defense of her beloved daughter.

Amata, Lucia, and I were sitting on old sheets spread out on the ground, doing our needlework and watching the children. On three other sheets near us sat several women from the village, taking a day off from their labors to bring their children to play with Cilia, Benino, and Lancelotto at our lakeside villa. This was an annual tradition. I had issued my invitation at church last Sunday, and these were the women who had accepted it. All of us were glad for the breeze off the lake, as well as the shade from the trees behind us. It was unusually warm for May, and Rome would already be an inferno.

"Well, you never know. She just might figure out how to make it work," Prassede said, smiling at the sight of Cilia trying to sit on the stick with one end wedged against the ground.

"Cilia, just ride it the way the boys are riding theirs," I called to her.

"I can't. It's supposed to carry me, and anyway, if I have to make it go, my skirts might come up too high, and ladies have to be modest." The plaintive whine in her voice was enough to make Benino come running to her aid, dragging the oldest of the visiting village boys along with him. Benino may have been Cilia's twin, but he was a sturdy, swaggering child, larger by half than his tiny sister. He took over, gave orders to the other boy, and soon the two of them were carrying Cilia's hobbyhorse while she sat triumphantly. Unsteadily they moved forward, Benino in front shouting orders to the sweating boy in the rear, and Cilia held on to her brother's shoulders for support.

"See? She did figure it out. I thought she would." Prassede looked smug.

"She didn't make it go, Prassy. The boys did," I said, watching Amata as she chatted with Lucia, their longtime friendship gradually reviving in the relaxed atmosphere of our summer villa. I was glad I had decided to bring both families with us to the villa after all.

"She figured out how to use the boys."

"I think she's always known that," I said, amused. "It should serve her well in life."

Prassede leaned back against a tree. "This is wonderful, isn't it? Lapo is going to love it here." We were expecting Lapo to arrive at any time, bringing us some needed supplies from Rome, and this would be his first chance to see our villa.

Prassede was right—it was wonderful. The cool woods to our backs, the vineyard stretching off to the west, beds of flowers and herbs closer to the house, and in between them this expanse of lush green studded with tiny violets. It was a perfect play area for the children, who loved their change of scene so much that they were being uncharacteristically peaceful and pleasant.

Next to us, Lucia's son Lancelotto played happily with his toy horses, sitting in his nest of violets next to a little girl from the village who must have been about his age. The two of them pretended they were unaware of each other's presence, but occasionally one would sneak a glance at the other. Lancelotto steadfastly kept track of the whereabouts of his beloved Cilia, even as he murmured to himself and made the little horses gallop through the violets. Beyond where the older children romped, Lotario grazed contentedly, perhaps a bit closer to the herb garden than was wise, but so far he seemed satisfied with munching violets.

Cilia's mount had picked up speed, but unfortunately for the little lady, coordinating the two ends of her steed at that pace proved impossible, and she found herself unceremoniously dumped onto the lawn. Lancelotto jumped up, his mouth in a round O of alarm, and Amata heaved herself up and ran to her wailing daughter, while Benino pummeled the older boy with both fists. The poor child didn't dare fight back—to him, Benino was part of the ruling household—so he merely doubled over and tried to protect himself as best he could.

Amata, alarmingly out of breath from her sprint, ignored the boys and knelt beside Cilia, caressing and comforting her. Prassede and I looked at each other, shrugged, and got up to go rescue the village boy from Benino's ire.

A skinny young woman, the mother of the tiny girl playing next to Lancelotto, got there first. She grabbed Benino's wrist and held it firmly.

"You. You don't hit that boy. You're bigger'n he is, and anyhow he's done nothing to you." Her accent was pure street Roman. I didn't remember seeing her on any of our previous summer sojourns in Marino; perhaps she was new to the village. I had noticed her sitting alone, on the far edge of a sheet.

Benino struggled to free his arm, his pudgy hand still balled tightly into a fist. "Mamma!" he bellowed, and Amata reached over and yanked at the woman's shabby skirt. The fabric ripped, and the thin garment gaped, exposing a bony knee. Amata let go, and the woman clutched at her mangled gown with her left hand, trying to cover herself without releasing Benino, who was squalling louder and louder.

"Don't you touch my son!" Amata spat. "You let him go right now!"

As I stepped between the two women, the other boy's mother took advantage of the intervention to grab her son and pull him to safety.

"Amata, she's right. You can't let Benino attack the other children," I said, and she opened her mouth to answer me, pure fury on her round face.

Before Amata could speak words she would have regretted, Prassede took charge.

"Ladies, children, we will pray," she announced, her voice filled with authority. "We will kneel and ask God to restore us all to peace and friendship." She clasped Amata's hand in her right hand and extended her left to the thin woman, who reluctantly let Benino go so she could take it. Prassede sank to her knees, and both of the women followed her example. Benino and Cilia clung to Amata's skirts and wept, Benino angrily and Cilia with exaggerated pathos.

Prayer. Well, why not? I had no better ideas to offer. So I knelt too, and then so did all the other women, some of them tugging at their wide-eyed children to get them to do the same.

Prassede led all of us in prayer while we murmured appropriate responses. Amata was still furious, and she petted her two sniveling children with her free hand while she spoke the holy words mechanically. But to my surprise the other woman appeared lost in her devotion, her eyes tightly shut, her voice fervent.

The prayer would probably have droned on for a long time—this was Prassede, after all—but the children were growing restless, so when she paused for a breath, I inserted my firm "Amen." Prassede's eyes flew open and she looked at me in surprise, but when I gestured to the children, she caught on and promptly echoed the word.

My turn. I got up, and as the others scrambled to their feet I thanked them for coming and told them I had gift baskets for all of them to collect before they left. They waited obediently, their mood subdued. None of them would look at the thin woman, who had been the last to rise from her knees.

Amata was about to shepherd her children back into the house, but Prassede insisted that she first clasp hands with the woman whose dress and chemise she had torn. Impulsively, I added my hand to theirs.

"Make peace with each other, for Father Francesco's sake," Prassede instructed us. "Forgive one another, and be at peace."

"God give us all peace," I said, and after a brief hesitation both women repeated my words. The village woman was understandably wary, but I believed I saw Amata's anger recede, especially when I asked her forgiveness if my words had hurt her. My friendship with Amata was deep and longstanding, and however sensitive she was to any criticism of her darlings, it would take more than an awkward moment between us to destroy it. Or at least I hoped it would.

I was not so sure all was mended between Amata and the woman who had dared to halt Benino's tantrum, but both women were civil as they spoke words of forgiveness to each other. All the other women watched this procedure with interest. I was sure it would be the talk of the village, though I didn't sense much sympathy for the brave woman whose threadbare gown Amata had destroyed.

She held the tear in her skirt together as she contemplated her daughter, peacefully sleeping among the violets, and a look of concern crossed her face. I guessed she was trying to figure out how she was going to carry the child and her basket and her distaff back to the village without walking her skirt into tatters or exposing her bare leg.

I touched her shoulder gently. "Please wait a few minutes and let your child sleep. I'll mend that skirt for you before you leave us."

She swallowed hard but nodded.

It was time to distribute the gift baskets and let our guests return to their homes. Lucia and I had purchased the simple baskets in the Marino market and filled them with small treats: honeyed almonds, little cakes, and apricots from our orchard. Each one also contained a length of good white linen, enough to make a veil. The baskets waited in the shade of the biggest tree, and Lucia, Prassede, and I handed them out, with a pleasant word to each woman and her children. They thanked us shyly, eyes averted, and moved on, walking toward the path back to Marino.

None of them spoke to the thin woman as they passed her. I had thought surely at least the mother of the child she had defended would offer thanks, but instead she brushed past, talking in an exaggerated whisper to the woman next to her.

What I thought I heard her say was, "Whore."

Once all the other visiting women had filed past us, I turned back to our remaining guest. She stood calmly, watching me, and her golden-brown eyes met mine with no hint of evasiveness. She had a generous mouth, prominent cheekbones and a longish straight nose. Her hair didn't show under her veil, but her eyebrows suggested it would be a medium brown. She could have been pretty, had she been less careworn. I suspected she was younger than she appeared. I was curious about her, but I knew if I pressed her too hard she would flee, and I would never know her story. I admired her courage and decisiveness, particularly in the face of the other women's hostility.

She and Lucia and I sat on the sheet and I picked up my sewing things. I sent Prassede back into the house to find something the woman could wear. This battered gown must be the best she had, or she wouldn't have worn it to the villa. I could not send her away without giving her something in compensation for such a loss.

She squirmed a little as I approached her with threaded needle. "I could mend it myself, madonna, if you'd be so kind as to lend me the needle. I've only my spinning with me, or I'd use my own." Having the woman who owned all the feudal rights to her village about to sew up her dress while she wore it was apparently enough to make her uncomfortable. I could understand that, but still I wanted to do it, and I wanted to learn more about her if I could. This was one way to keep her with us a little longer.

"I'll do it, and it will only take a few minutes. But please tell me what name I may call you." I sat at her feet. She looked down at me, her expression one of mild alarm.

After an almost imperceptible hesitation she said, "I am Sabina."

"Sabina. Welcome to our villa, and I'm sorry you've met with this accident."

Lucia held the torn edges of fabric together while I did a quick basting stitch. "I thought more women would have brought spindles," I said, making conversation. "But most of them had embroidery with them."

"The other women, they brought embroidery like real ladies, but mostly at home they just spin or sew, like me."

Ah. All for my benefit, then. All that clumsy needleworking, just to impress me. I should have praised their efforts more effusively.

"You did well to stop Benino, Sabina. He has yet to learn to control

232

himself. I apologize, too, for his mother. She is one who cannot see the shortcomings in her children."

Sabina glanced at her own daughter, still sleeping in the shade. "Children will do such things, sometimes. But it doesn't help them to let them hit the other little ones. They grow into bullies and worse, and in time they become men who do evil things."

"Benino already bullies my Lancelotto," Lucia observed, watching me stitch the rent. Lancelotto was sleeping too, sprawled on his back with his chubby arms akimbo, not far from Sabina's daughter.

This would be only a temporary repair, for the cloth was so flimsy that my mending would not last long. "I was surprised that boy's mother didn't thank you," I said, hoping to elicit more information about her role in the village, but she said nothing.

"Your daughter is a sweet child," Lucia said. "I wish she could spend more time around my Lancelotto. He would so love to have company his own age, and not always be pushed around by the twins."

"She is a joy," Sabina said, smiling.

"What does her father do?" I asked.

She stiffened, so suddenly that I dropped my needle. I looked at her, perplexed. The smile had disappeared.

"She has no father."

Widowed? She didn't wear the benda. Abandoned? I remembered what the other woman had said.

"I'm sorry," I murmured, picking up the needle to finish the job. "When we're done here, I'd like you to let me give you a gown to replace this one."

"There's no need for that, madonna."

"Oh, but there is. I need to do it. I can't have people visiting me here and having their clothing ruined, can I?" I tied off my last stitch. It would do, for now, but a new gown was definitely in order.

"You are generous, madonna. But if you were to give me a dress they'd all know it, and they'd only hate me more'n they already do."

I pondered this. I wanted to replace her loss, yet I didn't want to do anything to make her life even harder. I also didn't want to risk humiliating her by asking why the other women didn't accept her, but how could I help her if she wouldn't explain her situation?

Lucia, in her gentle and artless way, came to my rescue.

"How is it you've come to live in Marino, Sabina? Your speech is Roman, and I'm sure we didn't see you here last summer. I know I would have remembered you." Her voice was warm and encouraging.

233

Sabina reached down and smoothed her skirt, examining my handiwork. She gave it an experimental tug, the mend held, and she nodded, satisfied. "Thank you, madonna," she said softly. But she did not answer the question.

Before I could try to approach the question another way, Prassede emerged from the house with a blue dress of Lucia's over one arm. She was already talking well before she reached us.

"Lucia, you don't mind if we give her this one, do you? I'll make you another. My clothes would be too short, and they're meant for a sister anyway, and all of Amata's are way too big, and we gave away everything extra that belongs to Giacoma ages ago. And this color will be lovely on our new friend, with her fair skin and pretty face. Oh, Giacoma, Amata wants to talk to you. Whenever you're ready to go inside, I'll help you gather up these sheets and the extra cakes and cups. Cilia's still fussing over her soiled dress, but she isn't hurt at all, and Benino's in the courtyard playing with his little soldiers, so he's fine. Would anybody like anything to eat, or to drink? I could bring something out for you."

With that she arrived at our sheet. Lucia assured them both that Sabina was welcome to the dress, but Sabina was reluctant to take it, or even touch it. At least I finally persuaded her to sit on the sheet with me.

Prassede settled herself next to me, and I whispered, "Prassy, remember the vow." The vow in question was a hypothetical and intermittently renewable vow of silence; it was our signal that something was going on and I needed her not to talk for a while. Life had gone much more smoothly since we put that in place. She held her finger to her lips to signal her assent.

"Sabina, you were about to tell us how you came to live in Marino," I said, knowing I was taking a chance.

33

SABINA folded her hands in her lap and looked down at them. "Had a bad situation in Rome. It's better here, even with... even though I don't fit in with the other women. Couldn't stay in Rome."

Lucia frowned. "But why don't they accept you? You tried to help one of their own when Benino got all cross and mean." Lucia's intentions were always benign and transparent; she could get away with asking questions that would have made their target retreat into silence, had anyone else voiced them.

Even so, Sabina didn't answer immediately, and when she did, she spoke reluctantly.

"It don't matter what I do here in the village. They don't want me here because of what I am. Or at least because of what I did, and what they think I am."

"Yet you tried to help the boy, knowing that his mother would turn against you," I observed. "That was brave, and it was also kind."

"Because it weren't fair, him having to suffer for something he hadn't done. I don't like things not being fair."

"What upset those women so much, Sabina?" Lucia asked sympathetically. "It's all right to tell us. We are all of us sinners, and God can forgive everything."

No answer.

Mentally I urged Lucia to keep talking. More and more I wanted to hear this story.

"Did these problems start after you moved here?" Lucia persisted.

Sabina shook her head. "Rome."

"Then how did they even know about whatever it was you did? Did you tell them?"

Sabina said nothing, but she glanced furtively over at her sleeping child before lowering her eyes.

"I think perhaps it was something done to you, rather than something you did," I said slowly, imagining some of the possibilities. A young wife abandoned, a maid betrayed, a widow left at the mercy of a callous family. Marino's conservative community would not easily accept such a woman, even if the fault was not her own.

"Madonna has the right of it," she said dully, "though I've done plenty as well. You think I haven't explained anything to you, but I have, if you'd understand it."

"But I don't understand, Sabina, and I want to," I said. "Perhaps I can help you in some way if I do understand."

She snorted at that, then caught herself. "Begging your pardon, madonna. You can't help me—it's too late for that. But if you really want to understand, I'll just tell you that my name wasn't always Sabina. That's the name I chose when I threw my old one away. And that's all I'm going to say."

Sabina. Sabina from Rome. The Sabine women. I shuddered as I realized what she was telling me.

"You were raped."

She nodded.

"By your daughter's father?" Lucia asked softly. Prassede shut her eyes tightly and prayed silently, her mouth forming the words.

"By him and five of his friends, not that I know which one of them was him." *Men who do evil things.*

"But the shame is not yours. It's the men who did this to you who should feel shame." The unfairness of it made me want to strike out at something.

She shrugged. "Tell that to the virtuous women of Marino. Or to my neighbors back in Rome."

"I wish you had come to me then. I could have helped you somehow. I help Roman people who are in need, sometimes."

"Madonna, everyone knows of your great charities. But I wasn't going to join those people who crowd around your door. I'm no beggar. I can spin, and I can do other work. I can take care of myself and my daughter."

"So you wanted to leave Rome and you came here. Do you support yourself with spinning, then?"

Her face flushed a vivid red. "It's harder to do that here than in Rome. Sometimes I have to. . . I have to do other things, or there wouldn't be any food for my girl. But when I earn our bread that way, it's all for her, and I don't eat any of it." She stared down at her thin hands.

Whore, they had called her, and not just because her child was fatherless. Likely it was those women's husbands paying Sabina for her services. Lucia caught my eye, and with her chin she made a tiny gesture toward the house and raised her eyebrows in inquiry.

Yes. My sweet Lucia was a step ahead of me.

"Sabina, will you join my household? You and your daughter can live here with us, and then come with us when we go back to Rome—"

At the word "Rome" she started, pulling her legs underneath her.

"No, it will be all right," I said hastily. "You'll see. You'd be in my

236

palazzo, and you'll never have to be out in the streets alone, and you and your daughter will have everything you need."

"No. My daughter isn't going to grow up in Rome. The same thing'll happen to her as happened to me. I can stay here in Marino. It don't matter what they say."

"And do you want your girl to grow up hearing what they say?" Lucia said, almost indignantly. "You can't believe they'd treat her any better than they treat you." Gentle as she was, sometimes Lucia could cut right to the quick of the matter.

And cut she had, for Sabina's tears started to come. Lucia held her tenderly while she sobbed in great hoarse gasps, and Prassede patted her hand and murmured soothing words, but the floodgates were open, and the storm did not abate for some time.

By the time it did, both children had awakened and toddled over to us. The little girl curled up on her mother's lap, and Lancelotto stood behind them, awkwardly patting Sabina's head as he often did Lucia's.

At last Sabina wiped her eyes with her sleeve. "Madonna, I am overwhelmed. You offer me a great gift, but I don't see how it can work. Your servant, that one that tore my dress, she won't want me here, and I don't know if I can go back to Rome."

"Amata will come around. She's a kind woman, and she will want to help."

Sabina looked unconvinced. "What d'you want me to do?"

"Oh, only what we all do—sew a little, help in the kitchen, care for the children, whatever needs to be done."

"How is it, madonna, that you know what I am and you'd still take me?" She sniffed loudly and wiped her eyes. "Are you sure I'd be welcome?"

"Yes," I said, and Prassede and Lucia both said it right along with me, which made us all laugh. Even Sabina finally smiled. She reached over timidly and touched the blue dress.

I got to my feet. "I need to talk to Amata," I told them. "Prassede, will you ready the chamber next to the twins' room, and Lucia, will you have a couple of the men take the donkey and go into town to fetch Sabina's things?"

"I don't have enough to need a donkey, madonna."

"No harm in having her along. Just give Lucia your key, and the men will take care of everything. You won't even have to go with them."

"Don't have enough to need to lock up, either."

"You leave your house unlocked?"

"'Tis a room, only. And the lock's broken. I'd fain lock it if I could. Sometimes the townspeople come in when I'm out and spread filth around, and wreck what little we have. But I've no money to get it fixed."

I shook my head, exasperated at the unkindness of my Marino folk. "I don't see why they are so ready to blame you for something you couldn't help. Though I suppose they do resent any doings you may have had with their men. May I have your word that you will not engage in such behaviors while you are under my roof? I must not encourage sin."

"Oh, you have it, madonna. They all think I do it for the pleasure, but I swear to you, there is no pleasure in it." She shuddered, then composed herself. "Or only the pleasure of seeing my daughter eat."

"Good. And your daughter will eat well from now on, I promise you. But there is one more thing, Sabina."

She looked at me suspiciously. "One more thing, madonna?"

"Yes. The people of my household are my friends and my companions, and I theirs. We call each other by our Christian names, and we do not use titles. So I must ask you to call me 'Giacoma,' and not 'madonna.'"

"I... I will try, madon... Giacoma."

"Excellent. We can talk about Rome later. If you really don't want to come back with us, perhaps you can stay here and help take care of the villa over the winter, under the protection of my steward and the few staff members who stay with him."

"Is Giulio still your steward?"

"In the winter, yes. Right now Massimo is here. He's my steward in Rome, too. Do you know Giulio?"

"Let's just say that for me to keep my promise to you, I'd best go back to Rome with you after all. Long as my girl and me don't have to go outside alone."

Ah. Tucking away that information for future reference, I left Prassede and Lucia to their tasks and went inside to find Amata.

She was sitting on her bed, her daughter on her lap. Cilia's tiny heart-shaped face was streaked with tears. Wordlessly she held out her grass-stained skirt for my inspection.

"I've told her she can have a new dress, Giacoma. That's all right, isn't it?" Amata said, stroking the child's abundant auburn hair. Cilia sniffed.

"Amata, she's a child. They get dirty. The dress can be washed, and most of that will probably come out. Besides, she has more dresses than I do already."

"But that's your choice," Amata said reasonably. "You could have as many dresses as you wanted, Giacoma. You could have a new one every day if you chose." At that, Cilia looked up at me, a spark of interest in her hazel eyes.

I tried not to show my irritation. Cilia was forming some fairly exalted notions about what was appropriate for ladies, and her mother did naught but encourage her. Amata was used to being part of my household; by now she probably assumed that her children's future was assured because of their connection with me. She wasn't far wrong in that, for I intended to provide a generous dowry for Cilia and comparable bequests for Benino and for little Lancelotto, and now I had a feeling I was going to make a similar commitment to Sabina's daughter, whose name I didn't even know yet. I did think, however, that Amata was unwise and certainly unkind to hold that her darlings were superior to the locals. But I had no energy left to argue.

"Fine. She may certainly have a new dress. See to it, will you?" Amata lifted Cilia off her substantial lap and started to struggle to her feet when I couldn't resist adding, "Amata, for her own safety, do teach the child that ladies ride in whatever way best gets them where they're going. Prassede and I rode all the way to Assisi and back, you know, and we didn't worry about our skirts."

She hesitated, then nodded. "You have to admit, though, that you and Prassede are not exactly typical of ladies." She grinned as she said it, and I smiled back, relieved to see her good humor returning, since I was going to have to tell her about Sabina soon.

"I have to go to the kitchen, Giacoma. I need to get started on supper. Would you like a frittata tonight? With cheese and spinach?"

"I'd love one. Come on, I'll walk with you. There's something I need to talk to you about."

34

IT was late afternoon. I had expected Lapo much earlier, but he still had not arrived. The children were quiet, Amata had grudgingly accepted the idea of Sabina entering the household, and Sabina and her daughter, whose name was Casta, were getting used to their new chamber. Both of them had reacted to it with wide-eyed wonder, seeing luxury where I saw only a simple, modest-sized room. Lucia and I had gone outside to make sure we hadn't missed any stray dishes or bits of food left behind by our guests.

I heard the crunch of footsteps on the path leading to the lawn and garden. Whoever was coming was still hidden from sight by the olive trees that lined the path.

As I expected, it was Lapo who emerged from the grove, but a panting, sweating Lapo doggedly trudging along next to his horse. Two hired pack mules followed behind him. The trip from Rome was not a long one, but it wasn't like Lapo to walk if he could ride.

"Welcome, Lapo. But why are you on foot?"

He gestured toward his horse, the roan gelding he usually chose for trips outside Rome. "Threw a shoe. I've been walking alongside him for miles and miles and miles."

He put one hand on my shoulder to brace himself and stood on one leg, removing the shoe from his raised foot with his other hand. "I've got blisters, and I think these shoes are ruined," he said ruefully.

Lucia joined us. "Couldn't you have ridden one of the mules?" she asked.

"Apparently not. Leastwise, they didn't seem to think so." He glared at the pack animals, and they stared impassively back at him. "Besides, we had to bring you all this stuff." He indicated the packs. "So instead I've walked for miles and miles and—"

"I know," I said. "And I appreciate your efforts. Come and rest, and tell me your news." My last visitors from Rome had been here only a week ago, so there shouldn't be much I hadn't already heard.

Lucia went to fetch someone to take care of the animals and unload the supplies, and Lapo sat down on the grass with a sigh of relief and tugged off his other shoe. Morosely he inspected his foot.

"My boys are well?"

"They are."

"Tell me, how is Nuta doing?" She was due to give birth in about a month. If I had enough warning, I hoped to come back to Rome in time to help her.

"She's fine. She's not as tired now as she was earlier, and Gualtiero says she eats more than he does."

That was hard to imagine. Nuta was reed-slender, or had been before her pregnancy, and her husband had the healthy appetite of a vigorous young man.

"Any other news?"

"Not really. Not from Rome, anyway. We did have a visitor from Assisi, though."

"Did you? Who was it?"

"That fellow called Brother Feo." Lapo grinned at the memory. "He's quite a lad, Giacoma. A fount of useful information. He's taught me a lot—for instance, do you know how to set up an ambush?"

I did, as a matter of fact, but I thought perhaps I wouldn't say so to my friend the erstwhile thief, lest it interfere with his ongoing efforts to reform.

"How interesting. And did you teach him anything in return?" I was confident that no follower of Francesco would be tempted by Lapo's wayward habits.

"Oh, yes. I taught him a few tricks for playing mosca, and also the game using shells or little boxes. He has quick hands, and he catches on fast."

So much for my confidence. Clearly the former urban thief and the former mountain bandit had plenty to say to each other.

I was about to ask him what news Feo had brought of Francesco and the brothers when Lapo looked up suddenly and blanched.

"Oh, God's hairy armpits, Giacoma, it's that damned sheep!"

Sure enough, Lotario was facing us, head down, snorting malevolently. His horns were aimed right at Lapo, who scooted behind me.

"I didn't know he'd be out here. Giacoma, can you make him go away?" Lapo put a shaking hand on my shoulder.

"Probably not." Lotario liked me well enough, but not as well as he liked terrorizing Lapo. The two of them had taken an immediate dislike to one another back in Rome, but there they usually made an effort to avoid each other. I didn't know what it was about Lapo that made Lotario forget he was a small, aging wether and start acting like a huge ram in his prime, but it happened every time. Even a little ball of wool like our pet could leave a nasty bruise, as Lapo had learned on more than one occasion.

"I don't know why that creature hates me so," Lapo muttered. Lotario eyed us balefully.

"Maybe because you insist on calling him 'Cutlets,'" I suggested, and from behind us, a woman laughed.

I turned to see Sabina, who had just emerged from the villa carrying a pitcher and a tray with cups and food. Still smiling, she assessed the situation, put her burden down on the ground, and walked toward Lotario.

I held my breath, hoping that Lapo's woolly nemesis would not threaten the newest member of my household.

"Hello there, signor Sheep," Sabina said, moving slowly and deliberately toward Lotario with her hand extended. Lotario turned his head to study this stranger and see if she posed a threat, or, like Lapo, an infuriating annoyance.

I needn't have worried. When Sabina got close enough, Lotario sniffed at her outstretched hand, then nuzzled it. She knelt beside him and scritched his woolly chin, and then the top of his head, and if sheep could purr, that's what Lotario would have been doing as he bared his yellow teeth in a kind of ecstatic smile.

"Aren't you the handsome one," Sabina murmured. "You like these violets, don't you?"

Lapo and I watched while she worked her magic on the animal, who settled down happily next to his new friend.

Lapo cautiously stepped out from behind me and sat on the grass, his eyes fixed on Lotario, who had apparently lost interest in him; certainly our pet had no intention of leaving Sabina's side just to indulge in the sport of ramming Lapo.

"Sabina, do you think you could persuade Lotario to let you take him back to the stables?" I asked. "It would be very helpful."

She nodded, and in short order had Lotario trotting along at her side. Soon they rounded the corner and were out of our sight.

I turned back to Lapo, ready to ask him more questions, but the expression on his face stopped me. His mouth was hanging open, his jaw slack; his eyes were wide and glazed as he stared after Sabina.

"Who is she, Giacoma?" he said breathlessly. "She's amazing."

Thunderstruck.

Before I could say more than "Her name is Sabina," Prassede came out the front door and hurried toward us, talking all the way.

"Oh, Lapo! It's such a relief to see you. We thought you'd get here much earlier! How is Nuta? How are all the others? Have you heard anything from the brothers? Do you know if our Ricco has come back from Spain yet? Is there any news? I see you found our villa. Did you get lost on the way? What do you think of it? Isn't it lovely here? Is it hot in Rome? I expect it's cooler here than there, but it's still been awfully hot. How long can you stay? Did Sabina bring you the food? She had some cheese and bread, and strawberries with a little almond milk and a few cakes we had left after the women went home." With that, she arrived.

"Prassy, Sabina had to take Lotario to the stables. The food is there, just outside the door. You walked right past it. Let's go get it." She and I went back and picked up the tray and the pitcher, but Lapo stood motionless, his eyes fixed on the corner of the villa where he had last seen Sabina. I would need to warn him away from her later, but best not do it in front of Prassede, who was not exactly the soul of discretion.

Egidio and I had once joked privately about how the appropriate greeting to Prassede should be "God give you peace—and quiet," and I thought of that now as she chattered, but Lapo seemed content to eat and drink and let her rattle on, so I did the same. I knew he would have shared anything important right away, even as distracted as he obviously was.

*

Amata, Massimo, Lucia, and Tommasso, as well as the children, all greeted Lapo happily. I introduced him to Sabina, but she reacted stiffly. Without a sheep between them, his presence made her uncomfortable— understandably so, because his eyes followed her whenever she was in the room.

After we had supped and the children were in bed, the others went their separate ways and Lapo and I sat down to talk in the hall. We left the front portal open for the breeze.

"Are the boys still at their lessons?" I asked him. Giovanni and Uccellino had elected to spend the summer in Rome, training in horsemanship and light weapons with a cousin of mine in Trastevere.

"They've been training hard, at least in the early mornings while it's still cool."

"May all their knightly battles take place early in the day, then," I said, and he grinned.

"Did Feo bring you any news of Francesco?" That was the main thing I had been waiting for.

"He's well. Or at least better than he was during the winter. And he sends you his affectionate greetings."

"And the other brothers? Are they well? Is Egidio?"

"Brother Egidio's off in the hermitage again, and the others are well. Leastwise the ones at home are, but he didn't tell me anything about the brothers who are traveling."

"So nothing about Ricco?"

He shook his head. "Still in Spain, as far as I know."

"I really wish we'd hear from those brothers. It's been a long time."

Lapo shrugged. "Could be worse—he could have been one of the brothers who went to Germany."

"Why? What happened in Germany?"

"Feo says none of the brothers there could talk the German language. They finally figured out that when somebody asked them a question, he might be asking if they wanted food, and they should say 'Ja.'"

"That doesn't sound so bad."

"It wasn't, until somebody asked them a different question. They figured out later that the man had been asking them if they were heretics."

Oh, dear. "And I'll bet they said 'Ja.'"

"Mm-hmm. And apparently it didn't go at all well after that. The locals beat them up and stole their tunics, and finally they had to give up and come back home." Lapo was trying not to smirk.

I understood the temptation. It was pure foolishness; still, someone could have been seriously hurt. And it could have been Ricco.

"Did Feo bring any messages for me?"

"Brother Francesco told him to make sure you got that letter he sent out to the Third Order people."

The Third Order was for lay people, both men and women, who wanted to follow Francesco yet still live in the world. They gave to charity and the church as generously as their circumstances would allow, and they agreed to refrain from taking oaths or carrying weapons. In exchange they would be subject only to canon law, and secular law could no longer touch them.

"I received it."

"Apparently Brother Francesco is telling people that you're the Principal of that Order, since you're the one gave him the idea for it. Did you know that's what you are?"

I shrugged. No, I didn't know, but if Francesco said I was, then I supposed it was so. I didn't feel like part of a Third Order, though, since Francesco had refused to let me give away my wealth and live in poverty. It left me feeling like no part of anything—not his First Order, though I was Brother Giacoma; not his Second Order, for I was no nun; and not a part of his Third Order either, since I was still rich. Always a duck, unsure whether to fly or swim or walk.

Lapo's expression grew serious. He cleared his throat. "There's one more thing you'll need to know, Giacoma, but I'm not so sure you'll like it."

Well, whatever it was, I'd rather hear it than not. "Tell me, then."

"Brother Feo says Brother Francesco is about to go to the Holy Land." He watched me anxiously. "He says tell you you're not to worry, that God will take care of him."

The same way he took care of the brothers in Germany? He was right. I didn't like it. Francesco had tried to do this before, and it took a shipwreck to stop him. The cardinal would have taken decisive action to prevent such a rash action, but the cardinal was in Florence.

"When?" I finally managed to say.

"Soon. Maybe already. Feo said it might be before he got back to Assisi, and he left four days ago."

"Who is he leaving in charge? Pietro Cattani?" I had my doubts about Pietro's leadership, but at least he had done the job before, for brief periods while Francesco traveled around Umbria to preach. But the brotherhood had never had to get along without Francesco for as long as a trip to the Holy Land would take.

"No, Brother Pietro's going with him. They'll find Brother Elias when they arrive."

"Who, then?"

Lapo shook his head. "I don't remember their names. One of 'em's the cardinal's nephew, though.

I did not find that reassuring. The Cardinal's nephew was young and vigorous, but I thought him overly ambitious and perhaps too inclined to run roughshod over gentler men. Yet Cardinal Ugolino doted on him, so there was no arguing with Francesco's decision. There never was, anyway.

"We will pray for them too, then, that they shepherd the brothers as Francesco would," I said, though that was hard to imagine.

Lapo nodded absently. "Giacoma, who was that woman in the blue dress? Does she live in Marino? Is she working for you? She's amazing."

"You said that before. Sabina works for me as of today. She's had a difficult time, but I think this will make things better for her, and for her little girl."

I watched him register the existence of a child, but it barely made him blink. "Is she married?"

"No. But, Lapo, don't get interested in courting her. I don't think she would want that."

Before he could ask me anything more, the night's stillness was broken by the forlorn cry of a child. I knew Lancelotto's whine, Benino's bellow, and Cilia's wail, but this cry was new. It had to be Casta, awakening in the night in an unfamiliar place and frightened.

Sabina, who had been in the kitchen cleaning up, hurried past the door of the hall on her way to her daughter, and Lapo stared after her, transfixed.

We heard the door of her chamber open, then close, and the child's cries subsided. Lapo turned back to me.

"Do you think she thought I was afraid of your sheep?" His brow furrowed.

"Lapo, you *were* afraid of my sheep."

"With good reason. But did you see how she handled him? She was amazing."

"Yes, you mentioned that. She does seem to be good with him."

"I thought she was wonderful with him, Giacoma. She wasn't frightened at all, and she was so gentle, and she moves so gracefully. . ."

"Be careful, my friend."

"I know, I know. But she was so remarkable. I was just. . . I don't know, I was. . ."

"Amazed?"

"Yes, that's it! Exactly!" He gazed longingly toward the doorway as if hoping she would come past again, returning to the kitchen, but all was quiet.

I sighed. Francesco heading into who knew what perils, the brotherhood under the control of people I didn't entirely trust, and now my friend the thief, utterly dumbfounded by a woman who, for good reason, wanted nothing to do with men.

At least it was a comfort to me that Elias would be waiting when Francesco arrived in the East.

If he arrived, this time.

Rome, September 1220

35

"I promise, Giacoma, Francesco hasn't died. It's only a rumor." Egidio patted my hand, but he spoke with a sort of brisk detachment that warned me he was tiring of my persistent questions. I had gone looking for him yet again, finding him outside the Roman palazzo where he had been lodging and working for the past week, and we were seated together on the stone bench his employer provided for tired passersby.

"Why do I keep hearing it, then?" I said irritably. "And if you haven't heard from him, how do you know it isn't true?" Or even if he had, considering how long it took for a letter to travel that distance.

"Because if he died I would know it, and so would you. Can you even imagine we wouldn't?"

I had to admit it: in my heart I did not believe Francesco could leave this life without my knowing the exact moment it happened, no matter how far away he was.

"Nobody has actually heard anything, Giacoma. It's just a story that moves quickly because it frightens people so much. You must have faith and know that God will protect him."

I took a deep breath. Given the order's dependence on Francesco, I supposed rumors were inevitable if he insisted on going into danger. No shipwrecks this time. He had reached the Holy Land and promptly thrust himself and his companions into the middle of the Crusader camp at Damietta. My most recent letter from Elias, written sometime after Christmas, had reported that Francesco was well, but so much can happen so quickly.

I made an effort to shake off my cloud of uncertainty and vague worry. Egidio had little free time lately, and I didn't want to spend it annoying him.

He periodically forced himself to leave his hermitage and come to the city to live and work among us for a while. Brothers were supposed

247

to work for the alms they accepted, he reminded me, but I was fairly sure there was also an element of penance about it for him. He knew he would have been a welcome guest in my home, but he was determined to earn his food and lodging, and apparently to do it by performing tasks as unpleasant as possible.

"Are you still sleeping in the kitchen?" I asked him.

He grinned. "Yes indeed. I've been very fortunate. It's the warmest spot in the house."

"Egidio, it's still so hot you could boil eggs in the Tiber." An exaggeration, but not by much.

"Ah, but someday it will be winter, and then I'll be the envy of all Rome."

I snorted. "Only for people who like lugging firewood, and carrying water, and whatever else you've been doing to earn your place on the kitchen bench."

"Those things here, and also helping at a building site and digging graves. And cleaning out latrines."

No wonder he was so sunburned. And I didn't want to know the nature of the black grime embedded under his fingernails. I would have been more sympathetic if I hadn't been so convinced that he was hiding something. He would never lie to me about Francesco's safety, but I was becoming increasingly certain he had other news I was not getting.

I had asked him specifically about Ricco. We had learned that his group left Spain for Morocco, and while I wasn't quite sure where that was, I knew the missionary brothers would do everything possible to stay in contact with the brothers at home. If Elias could write to me from the Holy Land, surely other brothers could write an occasional letter from wherever they were. But the more I asked, the more vague Egidio's answers became, each time I saw him. And today apparently wasn't going to be any different.

"Giacoma, I have to get back to work." He gave my hand one last pat and stood. "If you like, I'll meet you at your church for mass on Sunday."

"I'd like that, Egidio," I said, also standing. "I'll see you then. You'll stay for dinner?"

He nodded, then gave a quick farewell wave and went inside the palazzo.

My cloud expanded to include impatience and frustration. What wasn't he telling me? And *why* wasn't he telling me? I would just have to try again on Sunday. Or maybe Prassede could get something out of him. If nothing else, she could talk him into submission, and he'd give up whatever it was in self-defense.

*

My sunlit study was usually my favorite place in Rome, but I was weighed down with too much uncertainty to enjoy it. So when somebody tapped insistently on my door, for once I almost welcomed the distraction.

I should have known better. Prassede opened the door at my "Come in," and as usual she entered talking.

"Giacoma, there's a problem I have to speak with you about. Well, actually it's Lapo who wants to talk to you, but I told him I'd tell you he wanted to see you. I think it's about you-know-what." She gave me a knowing look and placed a finger to her lips, but she didn't stop talking. "He's having a very difficult time of it, and he needs your advice. Please be patient with him. He can't help what he feels, and he is trying really hard not to do anything dishonorable."

Prassede had only recently discovered the concept of secrecy. Lapo had been schooling her, and she was quite taken with it; she just wasn't very good at it.

I supposed, then, that "you-know-what" was going to be Lapo's desperate infatuation with Sabina. That was the open secret we all tried not to talk about, hoping it would somehow go away or resolve in a way that didn't hurt anyone. Everyone in my household—Lucia and Tommasso, Gualtiero and Nuta, my boys, Prassede and me, even Salvestra and Renzo—knew, probably including Sabina herself. None of us had spoken to her about it, yet surely she must have noticed the way Lapo paled whenever he saw her.

Amata and Massimo knew, and they didn't even live with us anymore. I had deeded them one of my town properties, for Amata firmly believed she had outgrown the status of a servant. Also, back in Rome her shaky truce with Lucia had fallen apart. It was worth it to me to cut down on the amount of childish squabbling I had to listen to, and only part of that had come from the children.

So it appeared everything was about to come out into the open. I would have been readier to cope with this conversation were I less worried about Francesco, but crises don't allow us to choose our timing. They happen when they happen.

Ah, well. Things had worked out well enough for Vanna, and she had been every bit as lovelorn and desperate as Lapo. "Ask him to come in, please, Prassede," I said, and she turned to the door and beckoned.

249

The Lapo that slunk into my study was a far different man than the one I had hired, or even the one who "found" his cloak on a Pierleone clothesline. His shoulders slumped, his face sagged, and his hair was lank and needed washing. His movements were hesitant, unsure. Nothing was left of the cocky ne'er-do-well I was so fond of. My heart went out to him, though I doubted I could do much to help. I waved Prassede away, and she slipped out and closed the door behind her.

He slouched into the chair facing mine, my writing desk between us. He looked at me from below knitted brows but said nothing. His hangdog expression was almost too much to believe, but I was sure he was not playacting.

"What is it, Lapo?" I asked him gently.

"You know what it is, Giacoma," he said, and he sighed heavily. "You probably think this is just lust, or infatuation, but I swear I love her. I want to wed her and take care of her forever. I want to give her a home of her own and have children with her. I want to be a father to Casta. I can't even think about anything else. She's been through so much, and I just want to show her that men can be kind, and she doesn't have to be afraid. But she won't even talk to me."

It was true. Sabina would not speak to a man unless her sense of duty required it, and even then she kept her speech to a minimum and her eyes averted. She scurried out of any room Lapo entered—or, for that matter, Gualtiero or Tommasso or Massimo, or even Giovanni. She was more tolerant of Uccellino, and she could put up with Renzo, though our bedridden tinker grew ever weaker, constantly watched and nursed by Salvestra, and he was no longer the casually outrageous amorous Renzo of old.

"Lapo, I don't know what to tell you. You know why she fears men, and I can't blame her for that." He knew only because Prassede was new to secrecy, but maybe it was well that he did. "She has nothing against you in particular. She just doesn't want anything to do with any man."

"Can't you talk to her, please?" he said, his tone somewhere between wheedling and begging. "Tell her I'll treat her well. I'll keep her safe. She doesn't even have to lie with me until she wants to, and if she never wants to, I'll accept that. But I can't do without her. I love her." He made a helpless little gesture with his hands and sank deeper into the chair.

My poor friend. "I will talk to her, Lapo. I'll tell her what you've said, but truly I don't think it will change anything. I wish I could help you, but don't get your hopes up."

He nodded. "I know, it isn't very likely, but please try anyway. I can't bear to think I haven't tried everything that might help." He got up and shambled out of my study, the picture of dejection.

*

Later that afternoon it was Sabina who sat, hands folded in her lap, in the chair opposite me, waiting for me to speak. This conversation was going to be harder. Sabina was unpredictable when anything reminded her of what she had been through. I aligned my account book with the edge of the desk and rearranged the quills in their holder, trying to think how I should begin.

"Sabina, do you ever think about what you'll do after I die?" That wasn't quite what I had meant to say, but I did want to know, so I didn't try to amend my question.

"If you go to your heavenly home while I am still living, I will enter a convent," she said promptly. "Casta and I will go to a house of women. I would like it best if it could be Sister Chiara's house. I've heard so many wonderful things about her, and it's far from Rome. But any house of women would be all right. My daughter and I will both pray for you every day. I would take vows if they allow me to, and otherwise I'll serve as a lay sister or as a servant."

"And I will certainly leave a dowry for you in my will, sufficient so any convent would be glad to take you both in. But have you considered any alternatives? You are still young, and fair."

"Alternatives such as marriage?" It was a challenge. She sat up straighter and looked me in the eye.

"Well—yes."

"Giacoma, I know who you're speaking for. You'll tell me he is a good man, and I cannot argue with that. I've seen nothing of him to make me think otherwise. But I will not marry, and I will not have anything to do with men directly, even the brothers. Not even for you."

"And I will never ask that of you, Sabina. But you're right, I will tell you that Lapo is a good man. He loves you well, and there is nothing he wouldn't do for you. Many women would envy you that."

She sniffed. "Maybe they would, but they wouldn't envy my life up until you took me in. It was men that did that to me, and I'll die, or even kill, before I'll let them do it to Casta too. That's my sacred duty as her mother. She will never know a man."

Casta, that bright-eyed child who was always singing, clearly would not have much say in the matter. That saddened me, for I knew, too well, how much joy can come from a happy marriage. I knew, too, how much pain can come from its abrupt ending. Yet I would never have chosen to give up the joy to avoid the years of pain.

"Women have not been kind to you either," I observed.

"That's true, some haven't, but other women, especially you, have been more kind to me than I could possibly deserve."

She was adamant. I would have pleaded Lapo's case further if I thought there was any chance for him, but I knew I could not change her mind. I could not even risk trying to persuade her, for to do so would be to forfeit her trust.

"Sabina, I have never known you to lie. Can you tell me with absolute honesty that you will never consider Lapo's suit, no matter what happens?"

"Yes." No hesitation.

I leaned back. "There's an end to it, then. I will tell him. And I thank you for being so forthright with me."

"Thank you, Giacoma, for your care for me and for Casta. And for Lapo, as well. He is lucky to have your friendship, as am I. If you wish, you may give him my thanks for his kindness, but tell him I cannot give him what he wants." She stood. "I must go check on Casta. She's playing with Lancelotto, and I want to take her back to our chamber before Tommasso comes for his boy." She ducked her head in what was now a familiar gesture, offering just as much of a curtsy as she thought I would let her get away with, and left me.

So now little Casta was not even to come into contact with Lancelotto's father. How long would it be before Lancelotto himself was forbidden her? This sort of thing was making life complicated, for my household had always had an easy mix of men and women, scandalizing some and confusing others. Years ago, it had had both effects on poor Vanna. Never had there been even a hint of impropriety, but my own friendship with Francesco had set the tone. And now this.

But my commitment to Sabina meant we were all just going to have to live with the consequences. I blamed the evil men who had done this to her—had done harm also to Casta, by cutting her off from possible futures, and to all of us, by introducing fear and divisiveness into our home.

I offered up a brief prayer for guidance, a longer heartfelt prayer for Francesco's safety, and then summoned Lapo to my study for yet another difficult conversation.

36

A loud pounding on the front portal made me drop my embroidery and hurry downstairs. No one else was free to answer the door. Tommasso and Lucia were busy teaching their class, Nuta was watching the children, Prassede was upstairs helping Salvestra bathe Renzo, Gualtiero and Lapo were running an errand, and my boys were practicing swordplay at my cousin's house.

I opened the door and gaped at Brother Giannuccio, wild-eyed and distraught, pouring sweat, openmouthed but saying nothing.

Oh, God. Francesco.

"What is it, Giannuccio? Come in, come in," I said, reaching for his sleeve and drawing him inside. Whatever he was going to tell me, I didn't want to hear it in public.

"Tell me. Is it Francesco?"

He nodded, and I felt my heart plummet.

"Is he..." I couldn't say it.

"He's back, and he's furious, and he wants me out of the brotherhood," Giannuccio gasped out. My hand was still on his sleeve, and he clutched it with both of his.

"He's back?" My head was spinning. "He's alive?"

Giannuccio stared at me as if I had suddenly gone mad. "Yes, of course he's alive," he said, and tilted his head to one side as if I might somehow make more sense that way.

Apparently I didn't, for he kept looking at me quizzically. He was still breathing laboriously, but my confusion focused his attention and he calmed a little.

I sank down onto the bottom stair, suddenly weak in the knees. Giannuccio was still holding my hand.

"Giacoma?" he said tentatively. He watched me with fear-filled eyes.

"I'm... not unwell."

Francesco was back. There must be something disturbing going on, but he was alive, and I felt my heartbeat beginning to return to normal. I exhaled slowly, only now beginning to realize how much I had feared another outcome.

Giannuccio released my other hand and sat next to me on the step.

"Giacoma, I'm so sorry," he said. "I was distraught, and I didn't realize you feared for Father Francesco's life. I, too, have heard the rumors, so I should have been more careful in what I said. Will you forgive me?"

"Oh, Giannuccio, there's nothing to forgive. You bring me welcome news. But there must be more, for you to be so troubled. Will you tell me?"

"I should not have come," he said, his voice catching. He started to get up, but I grabbed his tunic and pulled him back down.

"But you did come, and I want to know what ails you," I told him. "Brother, you are my dear friend, and what troubles you is also troubling to me. Is Francesco unwell, then?"

He shook his head. "No. Well, yes. He is ill, but it's the same sickness we have seen before, with maybe some eye trouble now too. A fever that keeps coming back, weakness, thirst. That is not what distresses me so, though if I were a better man I suppose it would be. Remember, I live and work among lepers, though God knows what will become of them now, so lesser sicknesses don't impress me much."

"What is it, then?"

He shook his head. "I meant it, Giacoma," he said. "I should not have come to you. Father Francesco will probably tell you not to allow me to come back, anyway. He has turned against me, and he hates me now as much as he once loved me. But I swear to you, I meant no harm. My sin springs from my lack of understanding, and not from any ill intent. I need you to know that."

"I do know it, brother. I have never known you to mean any harm to anyone."

Giannuccio's woebegone expression made me want to comfort him somehow, but I didn't understand. How could Francesco have turned on one of his earliest followers? Yet I vividly remembered the time he turned on me, and I shivered.

I wanted to prod Giannuccio for more information, but talking about whatever had happened was evidently painful for him, so I remained silent, waiting to see if he would say more.

He finally began to speak in a low monotone, staring straight ahead.

"I wanted to start a new order with my lepers and the brothers who nurse them. It would have included anybody who wanted to serve the lepers, men and women both. I thought it would help us all, and I thought Father Francesco would be happy about it. One of the brothers who knows how to write put it all together for me and wrote out a proposal to take to the Curia. And we were getting everything ready and thinking about the habits and the rules and what we would need, and it all seemed so right. I was sure it was what God wanted us to do."

He looked up at me, his eyes bloodshot. "And then Father Francesco found out. All the way out in the Holy Land, one of the brothers came to him and told him. And he wasn't happy at all. He was enraged. He started back right away, with Brother Elias and Brother Pietro Cattani and some others, and as soon as he disembarked, he sent a brother to me to tell me to stop all my activities immediately. The brother said he had never seen Father Francesco so angry."

I was confused. "Do you mean he came back from the Holy Land just because he heard about your plans?"

"No, not only that. There were things the vicars did that he didn't like, lots of them. But I was a big part of it. And the worst thing is, I still don't understand why. I know I've committed an awful sin, but I don't know what it is. Do you know, Giacoma?"

I shook my head helplessly, as bewildered as Giannuccio. Had Francesco thought it too much of a liberty? Did he want all the brothers to share nursing duties, instead of only a few? Was he thinking of the complaints that fear-filled people always raised whenever lepers were brought to their attention? Was it the idea of mixing men and women in an order? But that would have been easy to fix. I often found it hard to follow Francesco's thinking when it came to decisions involving the brotherhood. He was a visionary, yet he was, quite frankly, a terrible administrator. Not for the first time I wished Elias were here.

"I thought it would be a good surprise for him. I wasn't trying to do anything behind his back. And I can't bear to think about him learning about it all the way over there in Syria and starting to hate me, and I didn't even know." His craggy face contorted, and he lowered his head and sobbed like a child. I put my arm around his shoulder. For the first time, I noticed the gray in his unruly tufts of hair.

I knew from Elias's letters that Francesco had been exposed to many dangers while he was in Egypt, not the least of them his audacious encounter with the sultan himself, a tale so fantastic I was not sure whether to believe it or not. Had those experiences changed him?

"Where is Francesco now?" I asked, as Giannuccio's sobs grew shallower.

"In Orvieto. With the Holy Father. Probably telling him to excommunicate me." Giannuccio moaned at the thought.

So close. Then I would surely see him soon. "No, brother, he wouldn't do that. He might be telling the pope not to approve your new order, but I'm sure it's no worse than that."

I heard young men's voices out in the street, high-spirited and raucous. Giovanni's laugh rang out over the others, so it was no surprise when the portal opposite us burst open and my two exuberant sons barreled in, along with several of their friends. All of them still wore their practice swords, and their clothes were sodden with sweat.

"Hello, Mother," Giovanni began, then saw who was with me. His mobile face first lit up with pleasure as he recognized his old friend, then registered puzzlement, then fell as he saw the state our visiting brother was in.

"Uccel, take our friends to the courtyard. I'll be with you soon," Giovanni said, exchanging a glance with his brother. The other boys followed my younger son.

Giannuccio looked down, saying nothing.

"Francesco?" Giovanni whispered to me. I shook my head.

"Welcome, Brother Giannuccio," Giovanni said, a little hesitantly. Giannuccio mumbled something, but he did not raise his eyes.

"Come with me for a moment, son, and we'll bring refreshments for your friends," I said, and Giovanni followed me into the kitchen. I told him briefly what Giannuccio had told me, and he was as puzzled as I was.

"I don't want to leave him for long when he's this upset. Let's go back, and maybe he'll talk to you. That might help him," I said.

Giovanni nodded. "The refreshments can wait."

But the entry hall was empty. Giannuccio had gone, and the portal stood ajar.

"I'll go after him," Giovanni said, heading for the door.

"God be with you, son," I said, but he was already on his way, and my words hung in the air.

*

Rather than stew in my worries, I went upstairs to help Salvestra and Prassede. Salvestra seldom left Renzo's side; her wandering days were over, or at least suspended. I still wasn't used to knowing where she was all the time.

Renzo greeted me cheerily enough, but he looked even more gaunt than he had a couple of days ago. I would have to check on how much he was eating and see if we could devise a way to tempt his appetite, despite his shortage of teeth. Perhaps a pounded rice dish would do the trick.

"She's still a fine figure of a woman, isn't she, Giacoma?" he said, indicating Salvestra, who was standing in front of the window. Prassede pursed her lips, but she didn't say anything.

"Indeed she is, Renzo, as you're a fine figure of a man," I said, patting his shoulder. "How are you today?"

"Not as well as I'd like to be. Lucia says she'll make me a posset soon as she gets some time." He wheezed a little as he spoke.

"Lucia takes good care of you, doesn't she?"

"Oh, yes, she's a sweet thing. She loves to listen to my stories, and she tries to get me to eat, even rubs my legs when they cramp. I think the girl likes me." He winked. "She says I remind her of her grandfather, but I think she's attracted to me."

"Careful," I said in a loud, meant-to-be-heard whisper. "She's married, and besides, you'll make Salvestra jealous."

Salvestra continued to gaze out the window, but a faint smile brightened her wrinkled face.

Prassede scooped up the pile of soiled linen and I moved aside to let her take her burden out of the chamber.

Renzo's sharp cough made me quickly turn back to him. He had been coughing a lot lately, but there was something in today's cough I didn't like, some new quality I couldn't quite identify. Salvestra went to him and helped him sit up, but it didn't stop his harsh wheezing. She looked at me and I read a deep sadness in her eyes. Renzo didn't have much longer, and we all knew it.

Add that to my list of sorrows and worries.

When Renzo began to doze, exhausted by his coughing fit, I took my leave, squeezing Salvestra's hand as I passed her. Prassede had come back by then, so I felt comfortable leaving them.

No one was in the entry when I came downstairs, so I went to the courtyard to ask Uccellino if he knew whether Giovanni had found Giannuccio. Uccel's friends were still there, a lively group of aristocratic adolescents. They had found their own refreshments, and some of them sat dangling their bare feet in the pool. Uccel's exuberance had been replaced by something closer to lassitude. He kept up his end of the conversation, but he lounged beside the pool as if he had no intention of moving again, ever.

These knightly training sessions were hard on him, but what Giovanni did, he would do too, and there was no gainsaying him. It was yet another worry I added to my list.

I was in my chamber when Giovanni finally returned, but I had been listening for him, so I arrived downstairs before he had finished taking off his boots.

"Did you find him?" I knew the answer already, from the slump in his shoulders.

"No. I looked everywhere I could think of. I checked the Benedictine house, and the hospitals, and San Sebastiano and a couple of other churches. I did see Sister Bartola outside the women's hospital, and she said she'd watch for him."

"Thank you for trying. I don't understand this situation at all."

"Neither do I. But at least Francesco is alive."

I hadn't been aware that Giovanni too was tracking the rumors. I hadn't mentioned them in front of the boys, thinking to protect them from worry, but my firstborn was almost a man now at sixteen, and he was quite capable of worrying independently of me.

"Do you think I should get my horse and ride along the Tiber? Or look for him at Saint Peter's?"

"It's been long enough now that I doubt you'd find him."

Now that Giovanni was there to play host, Uccel went to his chamber to rest, and I went to the chapel.

First, I offered a prayer of gratitude for the knowledge that Francesco still lived. That was uppermost. But Giannuccio's troubles alarmed me, and Lapo's doomed love saddened me. I worried for Uccel's health, and with Renzo's condition deteriorating fast, I worried for Salvestra. As I did every day, I wished Graziano were still beside me, to help me sort through all these concerns and reach the best possible outcome. Or failing that, I wished Francesco would come and offer advice.

That, at least, might happen. If he was as close as Orvieto, surely he would come to Rome before he returned to Assisi. I wanted to hear from his own lips what was going on with Giannuccio, and whether he had news of Ricco. And if God was indeed good to me, perhaps Elias would be with him. I would so love to see them both, safe and close to home at last.

I should have known better than to equate "safe" with "home."

37

"WHAT do you suppose is taking Lapo so long?" I asked Prassede as we carried our burdens to the kitchen. I had sent him to my brother-in-law more than an hour ago, and he should have been back well before this. But I wasn't worried about him. Yet.

"I don't know, Giacoma." Prassede shrugged. "Maybe he got to talking with somebody, or maybe he decided to do an errand. Did you need him for something?"

"Not really. I'm just anxious to hear Cencio's reaction. I told Lapo to make sure he handed my letter directly to Cencio, and not to one of his hired thugs." To the thug in charge, in other words.

In my message I had refused to permit the sale of a jointly-owned family property, so Cencio was going to be as angry as the devil on a Sunday, and I didn't want him taking it out on Lapo. The building in question currently housed one of my hospitals, and I didn't see why we should oust my patients just so my in-laws could make a profit. True, I would have profited as well, but we were wealthy enough.

"I'm sure he'll be back soon," she said. We had reached the kitchen, and she put her bundle down on a corner of the bench and adjusted her garment, for we had both hiked our skirts up in order to safely carry our armloads down the stairs. Reminded, I did the same. "He'll probably be home before Father Francesco arrives this afternoon."

Francesco had come directly to Rome from Orvieto, but we hadn't seen him yet. New and disturbing rumors about him, hints of fragile health and erratic behavior, were making the rounds now that all knew he still lived, so I wanted to see him with my own eyes. He needed to get back to Assisi, so we wouldn't have him for long.

I put down my stack of neatly folded habits, a gift for the brothers from the women of my household. Prassede's stack was breeches, plain and simple but sturdily made, also meant for the brothers. They would await Francesco in the kitchen.

The two of us were sorting the coarse garments by size when we heard the front door open. Someone dashed in, and then the door and the bolt slammed shut in quick succession.

Lapo sprinted into the kitchen. "They're coming after me, Giacoma. I swear I didn't do it! Will you hide me?" He looked around wildly, saw the door to the garden standing open, and hurried to close and bolt it, too.

"Who's after you, Lapo? And what didn't you do?" His panic alarmed

259

me.

"Your brother-in-law and about ten of those musclebound peasants he employs," he said, panting and trembling. "And there's no time to explain—please, just trust me and help me! Don't let them take me!"

If it was Cencio versus Lapo, I was with Lapo. He was by far the better man, even if he had transgressed in some way. "Run up to my study. Bar the door, and I'll do what I can to keep them from looking for you there. Be as quiet as you can."

He took the stairs two at a time. I heard my study door open and then close. By then Sabina and Nuta had come in to see what the commotion was about, and I told them briefly.

"I think there's going to be trouble. Sabina, better go tell Lucia and Tommasso to dismiss their class early. We don't want the little girls in the middle of anything ugly. Have them leave through the garden. Nuta, please go upstairs and stay with the children, and look to Salvestra and Renzo." Both of them obeyed immediately.

Prassede's eyes were wide. "Will he force his way in, Giacoma?"

"He might try." Massimo and Gualtiero were fetching supplies from Marino, my boys were off somewhere with their friends, and Tommasso was a scholar and no fighter.

Five neighborhood girls between the ages of seven and ten, all clutching their wax tablets, filed through the kitchen, greeting us politely as they passed us. Lucia was at their head, Tommasso bringing up the rear. Lucia unbolted the door to the garden, and the girls went out. Lucia and Tommasso watched them until they were satisfied that the girls had returned safely to their homes, then they closed the door and joined us. All of us, by unspoken agreement, moved to the entry hall to await whatever was going to happen.

Loud, angry male voices out in the street, coming closer.

"If anyone would like to avoid this, you may leave through the garden," I said. No one moved.

Someone banged hard on the front door. I saw alarm on every face around me. Whoever was out there pounded again.

"Giacoma, you're harboring a criminal," Cencio bellowed, his voice only slightly muffled by the heavy wooden portal. "If you don't let us in, we'll break the door down." More banging.

I felt my stomach lurch. I didn't see that I had much of a choice. If he had ten of his men with him, he could splinter even that formidable door, and we couldn't stop him. I stepped forward and lifted the bolt.

My brother-in-law entered, glowering. His offspring Pierino was right behind him, and they were followed by a shabby servingman and eight of Cencio's notorious henchmen. Lapo's estimate had been close.

Let the show begin.

"Welcome to our home, Cencio. To what do we owe the honor of your visit today?"

"We want your man Lapo. He tried to cheat my man in a game of chance, and that's nothing more than base thievery. I will not tolerate such behavior from anyone, especially not someone from your undisciplined household."

Lapo cheating at dice? He certainly had a history, yet I had thought him well past that sort of thing. And he did tell me he didn't do it, whatever "it" was. Against all logic, I was inclined to believe him. Not that I would have turned him over to this blustering fool even if I hadn't.

Cencio grabbed the servingman's tunic and yanked him forward. "Tell the lady what happened, Fredo," he ordered.

Fredo shifted his weight back and forth. "Well, m'donna, he challenged me to a game o'dice, and I didn't see no harm in it. That's 'cause I didn't know he was a cheat." He looked up at Cencio, as if seeking reassurance.

Cencio nodded encouragingly. "Go on, Fredo."

Fredo turned back toward me, but he wouldn't meet my eyes. "He used cheating dice, m'donna. I ain't never seen such a thing before"—this delivered with exaggeratedly aggrieved innocence—"and I ain't never had a chance to win. T'weren't fair."

"Pierino, show Giacoma the dice," Cencio ordered.

Pierino reached into his purse and pulled out two unimpressive wooden dice. He held them out to me. I ignored him and continued to face Cencio. Pierino scowled and tossed the dice over his shoulder, where they clattered as they hit the stairs.

"Lapo is my servant, Cencio," I said. "If your man has a legitimate complaint against a servant of mine, I will offer fair compensation."

"This isn't your affair, Giacoma. It's about your cheating servant. Where is he?"

"It is my affair. And you're wasting your time—he's not here." I needed to know how far Cencio intended to pursue this. Hence, our first lie. *Sorry, Francesco.*

"I knew you would lie. Now let's see if all the members of your household will lie for you. Is this everyone who is at home? Are my nephews here?"

"Your nephews are out. The people here are the only ones at home, except for two children and their nurse and an elderly couple, all upstairs." I turned to indicate the people standing around me, and saw that only Lucia, Tommasso, and Prassede remained. Sabina must have slipped out before anyone noticed her. I didn't blame her. She was so frightened of men, and Cencio and his thugs could terrify anyone. That meant I had just spoken our second lie accidentally.

"You." Cencio loomed over Tommasso, who blinked rapidly. "Is this Lapo somewhere in the house?"

Tommasso swallowed hard, but he summoned his best teaching voice and said, "No, he is not, my lord. Had he come back, I would have heard him. I was teaching in a chamber off the courtyard." The third lie. *Thank you, Tommasso.*

Cencio turned to Lucia, who timidly met his gaze. "And you, woman? Is Lapo in this house?"

"Sir, he is not." Her voice was soft, but clear. The fourth lie. I knew I could count on her.

"Were you also teaching, as you call it, with this man?"

"That's enough," I said quickly, as Tommasso bristled. "If you have questions, you will ask them of me, and you will not speak inappropriately to members of my household."

"This is a legal matter, Sister-in-law. Your man stands accused. I will speak with each and every witness, and if you try to prevent me, it can only be because you are hiding something. Or someone. My men will testify to that. Now. Girl, I asked if you were teaching."

Lucia's telltale left eye twitched. "My husband and I were both in the classroom, yes, with the girls we teach."

Cencio sniffed and turned to Prassede. He looked her up and down. "And you, Sister. You're sworn to serve God, are you not?"

"I am, though that can mean different things depending on whether a person is a lay sister or someone who has taken the veil, and of course everyone should be a servant of God, even people who don't have any religious profession at all, but these days not everybody seems to understand that—"

"But you are sworn not to lie?"

She tilted her head to one side and looked at him.

Oh, Prassy. If only I had told Lapo to run instead of to hide, you would have talked Cencio into a stupor and given him plenty of time to get away. And please, just this once, lie. We can make it up with alms, later.

"I am sworn not to lie," she confirmed, and her voice shook a little.

"Then I ask you, before God, is this accursed Lapo somewhere in this

262

house? He was seen to enter here a short time ago."

Prassede drew herself up to her full height, which was not much, and placed her hand over her heart. "Before God, Lapo is not in this house," she said firmly. *Bless you, Prassede.* The fifth lie. I should never have doubted her.

Thank God Sabina had gone. She was the only one of us who I had never known to tell a lie, even a tiny harmless useful one. I wasn't at all sure she could have done it. She was more likely to refuse to answer, which would have set off a whole new set of problems.

Cencio had a snide little half smile on his fleshy face. "You've trained them well. So now we're going to search, and prove that you and your people are liars."

"No, you're not," I said, stepping forward until we stood toe to toe. I had forgotten what foul breath the man had. With that as a weapon, he hardly needed henchmen.

"How do you intend to stop me?"

It was a good question. If he followed through against my will, I could make all sorts of trouble for him later, but I didn't see any way to prevent him from doing it now—and seizing Lapo. Our immediate defenses were slim to nonexistent.

"I intend to remind you that I am your kinswoman," I said in a dangerously quiet voice, "and I control a substantial share of family resources. Are you really willing to sacrifice any cooperation between us in the future to enact your petty revenge scheme?"

"Cooperation such as you provided for the hospital sale?" Fury flushed Cencio's face.

Had I underestimated his anger or overestimated his good sense, or both? He was impulsive and stupid, and such men are dangerous.

"I think you know that I have friends in high places in the church, Cencio—"

"We'll have your pet pope off the throne and declared an antipope within the year and our own man in his place. And you forget, I have highly placed friends too."

"Comparing your church friends with mine is comparing a slingshot to a trebuchet."

Unexpectedly, Prassede spoke up. "But even a slingshot can kill, Giacoma. Like with David and Goliath. Except Goliath didn't have a trebuchet, but he was such a big man that he almost *was* a trebuchet—"

"Silence, woman!" Cencio towered over her, and she shrank from him. I stepped between them. My own anger was rising, but I forced myself to control it. The danger was here and now, and if Cencio was too enraged to care what happened afterwards, I had no leverage, and no way to protect Lapo. I had to think of something.

"We're going to find him. Now. You two," he pointed, "search down here. The others, upstairs with me." He motioned to his men to follow him and started toward the stairs.

"Wait," I said. It was a command, and instinctively the men took it as such, halting. "You will first allow Lucia to go up to the children and tell them you're coming. I will not have them frightened by your bullying."

Lucia shot me a grateful look and hurried up the stairs, keeping as far away from the men as she could.

To my surprise, Sabina had silently rejoined us. She stood impassively, her hands behind her back. Why was she here? Where had she been?

"Another one," Cencio muttered. "Very well, girl, I'll ask you the same question I asked everyone else. Is Lapo in this house?"

Oh, no. We were in enough trouble without this. I held my breath.

Sabina gazed at him calmly. No lowered eyes this time; she was taking his measure. She was in no hurry to reply, and I sensed his impatience growing even as my own tension mounted.

Finally she spoke, and her tone was matter-of-fact. "Lapo is not in this house."

I exhaled. Sabina had lied! The sixth lie, to be exact. I was so proud of her. She had gained us a precious few more minutes, so maybe I could stall him until I thought of something.

"You, man," I said imperiously to Fredo. "How much money do you claim you lost?"

He shifted his weight from left to right again. "I dunno. Some."

"How much?"

"Giacoma, this isn't important," Cencio growled. "Who cares?"

"This good fellow does, no doubt," I said smoothly. "I am offering to compensate him for his alleged losses, even though I don't believe his tale. You will then have no further reason to disrupt my household. Also, what is my brother-in-law paying you for your testimony, Fredo? I will double it."

Fredo stared at the floor.

"Well? Your losses?" I prodded.

"It were a few denari, m'donna," he mumbled. "Don't know, exactly."

"And what is Cencio paying you?"

"He offered—ouch!" Fredo reached down to grab his ankle where Pierino had kicked him. "He ain't paying me, m'donna. I'm just telling the truth, 'cause I don't never lie."

"Enough of this. Find him, men!" Cencio started up the stairs, the others close behind him. I followed them, with Prassede, Tommasso, and Sabina right behind me. Sabina was carrying a poker. That must be what she had been holding behind her back.

"Thank you, Sabina," I whispered. The men were blustering loudly, bragging about what they were going to do to Lapo; they wouldn't hear us. "I know you hate to lie."

"I didn't lie," she whispered. "He's not here."

Not here? But how...?

Cencio and his men were fanning out on the piano nobile, barging into each room. One of the men demanded an answer from Nuta to the oft-repeated question, since they hadn't seen her before; that didn't worry me, for I knew she would lie as the rest of us had. The seventh lie. And they didn't bother talking to Renzo or Salvestra. Just as well. If they thought doddering old people wouldn't know anything, they didn't know our doddering old people. I heard Renzo railing at the men who searched their room and warning them to keep away from his wife, probably wishing he had Sabina's poker.

At the head of the stairs I stopped short, gawking. My study door stood open. Two of Cencio's men were inside, exploring every corner. No one could hide in that room. It had nothing but a desk, a chair, and some shelves filled with books. Perplexed, I looked at Sabina, and she mouthed the word *stable*.

I should have thought of that. Lapo would have gone down the outside stairs, through the garden, and out to the stable. Risky, but not as dangerous as staying in the study. We almost never used the outside stairs. Everyone used the main staircase, as it was safer and more convenient. But thank God Cencio had been too stupid to post a man outside.

The thugs were thorough, but eventually they had to admit defeat. We followed as Cencio led his men downstairs and out the door, where they ignored the three humble friars waiting there, friars who were apparently on their way to see us, and who stepped courteously aside to let the men storm past. Was one of them Francesco? I couldn't tell; all three were wearing their hoods, which seemed a bit unusual on a bright spring day.

"We're not done here yet, men," Cencio bellowed. "Search the stable! If he's not there, we search the whole neighborhood."

My heart sank. Were we to lose Lapo now, after all we had been through? I turned to the friars, hoping that if one of them was Francesco or Elias or someone else we knew, they might find a way to help us.

I recognized Francesco first, then Elias. I would have been overjoyed to see them had I not felt such immediate fear for Lapo. I started to explain the situation to them, but Elias stopped me with a hand on my arm.

"Giacoma, I'd like you to meet our new brother," he said, his eyes twinkling, and only then did I look at the third man, whose habit was suspiciously clean and new.

Lapo managed a wan grin from within his hood.

My mouth gaped. I whirled around to see what Cencio was doing and whether they had noticed us.

He and his men were standing in a semicircle outside our stable, watching some sort of commotion inside. Some of the men were laughing. Then Pierino ran out, a panicked expression on his face, and Cencio and the men scattered to make way for him.

Pierino stopped a few paces beyond the men, turned back to the stable, and shook a fist at its open door. He said something to one of the men, who put his hand on his sword, as if to comply with an order.

But Lapo was with me. Wasn't he? I peered under the third friar's hood, to be sure. Definitely Lapo.

When I looked back, Cencio had his hand on his son's shoulder. The gesture was meant to calm, it seemed, and whatever Pierino wanted to assault in my stable—and I had a good idea what that might be—for now appeared to be safe. My kinsmen started for their home, which was within sight of ours.

Halfway there, Cencio all but collided with my sons, who were returning from wherever they had spent the day. They were disheveled and sweaty, probably from indulging in some of the rough physical games that young men love so much, the sort that energized Giovanni and exhausted Uccellino.

Cencio said something to Giovanni. He was too far away for me to hear, but his face made it clear this was no pleasant greeting. He stormed off, leaving my sons looking bewildered. With a quick apology to the three hooded brothers, I went to meet my boys.

"What did he say to you, Giovanni?"

"Something about Lapo and some dice, and you and our household."

"Was he threatening anybody?"

Giovanni shrugged. "He was pretty much threatening everybody, but I figured that was just Uncle."

A good way to look at it. I needed to think about extricating my finances from the rest of the family's. And possibly dropping a word or two in certain influential ears to make sure the Frangipani didn't create another antipope crisis.

We walked slowly back to the palazzo while I filled them in on the excitement they had missed. They absorbed the important parts: first, Francesco was back; second, that their uncle was a belligerent fool; and third, our friend Lapo was in hiding and pretending to be a monk.

Giovanni shook his head. "Mother, you never just live normally, praying and embroidering and doing charity work like other women, do you?" He sounded amused.

I thought about his question.

"I suppose not," I finally said. "Or rather, I do those things too, in between things like this. But why do you suppose Pierino burst out of the stable like that?"

Uccel grinned. "I'll wager it had something to do with Lotario," he said, and the three of us chuckled. My boys had long since outgrown their hero worship of Cencio's loutish son.

Uccel's forehead creased. "Does Uncle pose a danger to Lotario, Mother? We can't very well guard the stable all the time."

"True." If Cencio couldn't get at me by attacking Lapo, he would certainly be capable of committing ovicide. "Maybe we'd best send Lotario to Marino for a while. Will you see to it? And take his donkey friend too."

Uccel nodded, and we went back to the palazzo.

There we found Elias and Lapo, both still hooded, with the other people in my household gathered protectively around them. Elias told me Francesco had gone to the chapel to pray.

While my sons greeted Elias and sympathized with Lapo, I moved close to Sabina and spoke to her quietly.

"Sabina, thank you for getting Lapo a habit," I said. "It was very clever of you, and it saved the whole situation. But you can put the poker back next to the hearth now."

She blushed and went to the kitchen to return it.

I let everyone chat for a while, then suggested that Elias and Lapo join me in my study, asking the others to send Francesco up when he came back. I was going to find out, at last, whatever it was Francesco knew about Ricco.

38

As we started up the stairs, Lapo stopped, bent down, and scooped something from the edge of a step.

"It's dice, Giacoma. Did he try to tell you these were mine?" His tone was somewhere between anxious and indignant.

"Yes, but nobody believes Cencio about anything, Lapo. Don't worry."

We brought the stools and the dice into my study, leaving the door open for the breeze, now that the house was no longer full of Cencio's thugs. Lapo studied the dice, then clapped them triumphantly on my desk.

"See? These couldn't have been mine."

"Are they weighted?"

"They're shaved, but they're shaved so clumsily they wouldn't even work. See, look at this corner." He indicated a spot on the amateurishly-made die. "This wouldn't do it. If you want the die to fall on that side most of the time, you need to shave both of these corners equally. Mine were perfectly done—I mean, back when I still did things like that. So that proves these aren't mine." He sat back in triumph.

"Lapo..."

"I think what Giacoma is trying to say is that you're probably not making the most effective case for your innocence, Lapo," Elias said, a little smile playing about his mouth.

Lapo grinned sheepishly. "Well, yes. I see what you mean. But it's true, nevertheless."

"But you really didn't cheat?" I asked.

"I did not. You have my word."

"I believe you, then."

"Good. But Giacoma, he doesn't need an excuse, or a reason, or proof. If your brother-in-law has it in for me, it isn't safe for me to be in Rome. I don't see any way around that."

He had a point. I didn't see any way, either. It exasperated me that I could not protect my own servants in this lawless city, but such was Rome.

"You could come with us to Assisi," Elias suggested, "and come back someday when enough time has passed that you feel safe."

"That might work, Lapo," I said. "We know people there who would house you, in exchange for the same kind of work you do for me."

Lapo looked down at his hands.

"I know you don't want to leave, and I don't want you to, but I'm afraid you're right. It isn't you he wants to hurt, it's me, but he'll use you to do it. And there's a limit to what I can do to protect you."

Lapo nodded, but he didn't raise his head.

We sat in silence for a few minutes. Elias closed his eyes, in prayer or in thought—I never knew which, with him. I probably should have prayed, but I was still feeling too agitated. I doubted that God would welcome being approached by someone as full of anger and and worry and resentment as I was at that moment.

The silence continued until Francesco joined us. I jumped up, eager to finally greet him properly, but something in his face made me stop.

"Giacoma, my dear, I have to tell you some news." The gravity in his voice alarmed me. I was afraid I knew what was coming.

"Your Ricco has gone to God as a holy martyr. You must not grieve, Giacoma, but rejoice—he has earned a high place in heaven."

My legs gave way and I sat down abruptly. It was what I had feared.

Elias put a hand on my arm. "Giacoma?"

"This is what Egidio wasn't telling me, isn't it?" I said woodenly.

"I asked the brothers to let me tell you myself, Giacomina," Francesco said. "It was my duty."

And it was your whim that sent him to his death.

He went on. "It happened months ago, in Morocco. The local people turned on the brothers. News reached us first in the Holy Land. I communicated it to the brothers at the Porziuncola, but I insisted they wait for me to bring it to you. I put them under an obedience, so you mustn't blame them."

Ricco. My poor freckle-faced boy, always so cheerful and hopeful. I felt no shock, only a deep sadness glazed over with numbness. I wished I had given more thought to his education and started his lessons with Tommasso sooner. Maybe then he wouldn't have been so eager to join Francesco. He was so young when he came to us—he should have been like another son to me, but I had seen him as a servant, until it was too late to keep him.

"I need you to understand that this is an occasion for joy, though I know you will also feel sorrow. God has chosen Ricco to be one of his holy martyrs, and we must honor Ricco by praising God."

My tears began to flow, and the expression of helpless pity on Lapo's face made me cry even harder.

"God can choose his holy martyrs from somebody else's household next time," I said, sniffling.

Lapo blanched and Elias was stony-faced, but Francesco took it in his stride. He sat silent, watching me.

I had nothing more to say to him. I would mourn Ricco, I would pray for him, I would have masses said for his soul. But it need not have happened.

"I want you to understand—"

"—that God chose him to be a holy martyr. And you chose him to go over there and carry your precious message to evil men who would kill an innocent young boy."

Silence. I had probably gone too far, but I didn't care. I wept, noisily, and Francesco could do or say whatever he liked. If he took away the "Brother" in front of my name, or condemned me, or stormed out of my palazzo, maybe I and mine would be the safer for it.

Then came Francesco's voice, more subdued. "I share your sorrow, Giacomina. Both of us gave him something he needed and wanted, and we both wanted to see him take our gifts with him through a long life of serving God. But God had other plans for him."

So had some murderous scum in Morocco. But the catch in his voice made me look up.

Tears were streaming down Francesco's cheeks, and he looked at me with such anguish that I couldn't hold on to my anger. It drained away, a flash flood come and gone, and it only remained to assess the damage.

"Francesco, I'm sorry. That was unfair of me. Ricco volunteered to go to Spain. I know that—I was there. He wanted to go."

Elias released the breath he had been holding, and Francesco reached for my hand.

"If you had known how dangerous it was, would you have let him go?" Having no kerchief handy, I mopped at my dripping nose with my skirt.

"No. I should have, even then, for the glory of God, but I don't think I would have. Just as I should celebrate his martyrdom as I told you to do, instead of feeling this grief, for him, for the others, for you... I am such a sinner, Giacomina."

We clasped hands, and by some miracle our deep connection was back. Even a capricious god has to be kind sometimes, or he would not be capricious.

"Francesco, I can't think about it any more now. I'll think about it after we solve Lapo's problem." I wiped my eyes on my sleeve.

"Very well. Tell me what you need."

With an effort I set my grief aside. I told Francesco everything that

270

had happened before his arrival, and I said we feared for Lapo if he stayed in Rome. Could he go to Assisi with Francesco and Elias? I could arrange for his lodging. Lapo watched us both intently.

Francesco hesitated, exchanged a troubled glance with Elias, and then, almost reluctantly, nodded. "Yes. He can come with us, and he can stay at the Porziuncola, if necessary, until something else is available. I can't guarantee his safety on the way if your brother-in-law decides to pursue him, though. Giacoma, may I use your chapel? I need to pray on this, in solitude."

"Of course, Francesco."

He left us.

Ricco and Lapo. So much loss threatened to overwhelm me, but I couldn't give in to that. Not yet. Not while my brother-in-law was a vicious fool bent on vengeance.

"It's a shame your noble relatives don't have anything better to do than to harass your servant to get back at you," Elias observed, leaning back against the wall.

I snorted. Suddenly it was all just too much for me. "That 'noble relative' is a bullying, evil, small-minded, avaricious blot on the landscape, and the world would be better off without him," I said fervently.

Elias stroked his chin in a contemplative way, gazing off into the distance as if thinking about what I had said. Finally he turned to me and remarked, "That's quite true."

His calmness somehow struck me as funny, and I giggled, in spite of everything. Lapo looked up at that, puzzled.

"Lapo, before I forget, tell me what happened after you went upstairs to my study. I know Sabina must have given you the habit, and I suppose you went down the outside stairs, but you weren't in the stable. What did you do once you got out of the palazzo?"

Lapo colored. "I did go to the stable, but that damned sheep of yours was loose, so I ducked into a stall. He was snorting and snuffling and crashing around trying to get at me. The brothers heard all the noise, and they came in and saved me. I was already wearing the habit, so I asked if I could stay with them. They said they wouldn't lie for me, but they wouldn't keep me from standing next to them, either. So they saved me, but Sabina saved me too. She was the one brought me the habit to wear."

"She did a brave thing. But Lapo, don't read too much into it. She isn't going to change her mind."

"I know. But she did save me. I'll always have that."

That was one question answered. But I had many more, and this was my opportunity to get some answers.

"Elias, can you tell me what is going on with Francesco? We hear all manner of rumors."

"What do you observe?"

"I don't see much difference. He's thin, but he's the same Francesco he's always been."

"Yes, for the most part I think he is. Yet his experiences in the Holy Land have not left either his body or his soul untouched."

"What do you mean?"

"I hope I'm wrong, but he seems distraught much of the time, and I don't know whether his illnesses are the cause, or something else. And the circumstances of our coming home were not the best. But I must not speak of these things in front of someone who isn't a brother." He looked pointedly at Lapo.

"Lapo, would you please go to your chamber? You may want to pack your things. You can't take them with you if you're going to travel in the habit, but I can have them sent later. You are welcome to rejoin us as soon as you hear Francesco return from the chapel."

Lapo got up and left without a word, his posture dejected.

"Now. What exactly happened before you returned?"

"A young brother—not someone you would know—left the Porziuncola without permission and made his way across the sea to where we were, in Syria. As you can imagine, it took an extraordinary situation to drive him to it."

It was an almost unheard-of act. It spoke of desperation, and of courage.

"Why?"

"He came to tell us of something that distressed Francesco beyond anything I've ever seen from him before, and I've known him a very long time. Longer than I've been a brother."

"And that was?" Surely Francesco's anger at Giannuccio couldn't have been this extreme.

"The brother came to us to complain about some of the overreaching actions of the two vicars Francesco had left in place. For one thing, they took it upon themselves to make our order more like other monastic orders, adding extra fasting days and other stringent requirements."

"I thought Francesco had always said we should follow the rule of the gospel and eat what is put before us, as long as we respected the Friday fast."

"Exactly. The vicars feared what men would say of them if they were less strict than other orders, and that was precisely what Francesco hated—that cowardice, that bending to the opinions of man rather than the laws of God. When the young brother arrived, a few of us were about to eat our dinner. If we had adopted the new rules he told us about, we couldn't have eaten the meal set before us. Francesco said to Pietro Cattani, 'Signore Pietro,' as he called him in jest, 'what should we do?' And Pietro replied, 'Signore Francesco, do what you will. You have the power here.' So Francesco told us to eat what was put before us, just as the gospel says."

Pietro had spoken wisely, but also predictably. I knew there were brothers who wanted to outdo monks in other orders in their austerity; others opposed them, wanting more privileges, more concessions to ownership of books, more exceptions to the simplicity of Francesco's early rules. It sounded like the rift had become more serious since my last visit to Assisi.

"That wasn't all, though. Before we took ship, we got two other pieces of news that upset Francesco as much as his vicars' insubordination."

"What were the others?"

"One was Brother Filippo Longo. He obtained a privilege from the Holy Father for Chiara's sisters, something involving sanctions against anyone who disturbed them, and you know how Francesco feels about privileges of any sort, for the brothers or the sisters. And Chiara hates the idea even more than Francesco does."

"Yes, I can see how that would distress them both. Was anyone disturbing the sisters?"

"Not that I know of. But there's more to it—Brother Filippo wanted to be personally granted the authority to excommunicate anyone he thought was interfering with the sisters."

I whistled softly at that, a habit I had picked up from Lapo. The Friars Minor, we Lesser Brothers, were to consider ourselves beneath all others, worthy or not. Never in positions of authority. Even Francesco accepted authority over the order only reluctantly. Yet I could imagine that Filippo's error sprang from zeal and could be corrected without any permanent harm done.

"And the other?"

"Brother Giannuccio. He's formed his own community, based around his lepers, and Francesco was having none of it. You'll ask me why, Giacoma, and I honestly can't tell you. I don't understand his anger over this, when it's so obviously well intentioned, and he won't explain. He just says it has to be stopped. That's the main reason we went to Orvieto, though the fasting days and Brother Filippo were part of it."

"It can't be because so many people are frightened of lepers. He could hardly fear what people think in one situation and rail at his vicars for fearing it in another."

"I know. I can't make sense of it either, but I trust Francesco and his wisdom. Don't you, Giacoma?"

Never before would I have hesitated to answer that question, but this time my recent memory of poor Giannuccio gave me pause.

"He was here, Elias."

"Brother Giannuccio?" His brows raised in surprise.

"Yes. He doesn't understand it either, and it's tearing him apart."

Elias closed his eyes, a pained expression on his handsome face.

"I'm sorry to hear it."

"Will Francesco really cast him out of the order?"

"Giannuccio has cast himself out. And Francesco has persuaded the pope to put a stop to this new so-called order."

"Do you suppose he fears that if Giannuccio's people care for the lepers, the other brothers can avoid that duty?"

He shook his head doubtfully. "Maybe. But I don't understand where his deep anger comes from. It would be easy enough to reprimand Brother Giannuccio, put a stop to the new order, and just go on as before. Giannuccio could do penance, and all would be well."

"Giannuccio followed Francesco even before you did."

"Yes. I wish I could explain it to you, Giacoma. I can only accept Francesco's judgment, even though I don't like it."

I wasn't sure I could even do that much, but I would pray about it. We lapsed into a dejected silence, which lasted until Francesco entered, Lapo right behind him.

They both sat. Francesco looked serious.

"Giacoma, Elias, Lapo, I have prayed about this situation, and I know now what I'm going to do. I've said that Lapo may accompany us, and I will keep my word. We will not lie on his behalf, but we will do nothing to add to his problems. He has been unjustly accused, and we will not help an injustice along.

"At the same time, I remain concerned that we are taking part in a kind of implied lie. This makes me uncomfortable, but I take the full responsibility upon myself, and when we are back in Assisi I will do severe penance for the dishonesty in what we are about to do. I don't like seeing a layman wearing a brother's habit. Yet I see no other way to get him safely out of Rome, if Cencio's people are watching." He turned to Lapo. "No blame accrues to you, Lapo. The sin is mine. I take it from you."

Elias and I met each other's eyes. Francesco was in no shape to take on anything that even he would describe as "severe penance." I was trying to figure out some other way to accomplish what needed to be done, but Lapo's hoarse voice jolted me out of my ruminating.

"Father Francesco, maybe there's a way to fix things so you won't be participating in a lie," he said, almost too softly to hear. "I don't want to ask you to do that."

Francesco looked at him, waiting.

"Brother Feo is my friend, and he told me I ought to join the order. He tried hard to talk me into it, but I didn't think much about it then. Now I'm thinking maybe that's the best thing to do, after all. Then I'd be wearing the habit fairly, and you wouldn't be lying, and I'd have somewhere to go, somewhere that would accept me."

Lapo a brother? I could barely imagine that. Yet he had been so miserable here, ever since he fell in love with Sabina—maybe it could work.

"Lapo, you know our way of life. It's very different from yours. Could you be content to shed your old ways and follow ours?"

"I think so. I wasn't ready to think about it yet when Brother Feo tried to persuade me. He's happy, though, and he and I aren't so very different. I think I could do it." He turned to me. "Giacoma, please understand—I can't keep going like this. It's too hard. I need a fresh start, somewhere far away. You've saved me so many times, but you can't keep me safe from your brother-in-law, or from my own heart. May I go?" His eyes pleaded with me.

"Lapo, of course you may. I will miss you, more than I can begin to tell you, but I will rejoice in your new life and in knowing that you're safe. Go, with my blessings." It hurt to let him go, but not as much as it would hurt to see him stay and be miserable, or, worse, to become Cencio's victim, sacrificed to my brother-in-law's desire to get back at me.

Francesco studied him for a long time. Lapo met his eyes and did not flinch or evade his scrutiny. Elias and I waited, both of us sitting completely still.

"Will you give me your oath as a brother, Lapo? You have said you know what's involved."

"I do, and I will."

"You realize this is a commitment for a lifetime?"

"I know."

"You leave behind your family—even your adopted family, here in Giacoma's household—and you come away with nothing. You will never again have anything that is your own. You will be chaste and celibate, you will humbly follow the gospel way, you will glory in your poverty and take joy in your unencumbered closeness to God. You will be one of the *fratres minores*, the smallest and least of men, and every other man will be your master. Can you do this?"

"I can."

"Will you?"

"I will."

Francesco stood, and a glorious smile, like the sun coming out from behind a dark cloud, spread across his face. "Then welcome, Brother Lapo, newest of the Little Brothers!"

39

MY exhausted household slept, but before I went to bed I wanted to peek into Lapo's room. I supposed I would give his meager possessions to the poor, but first I wanted to see the room as he had left it, so I took a candle and entered.

His belongings were scattered about in a cheerfully disheveled state. The bedcover was carelessly spread over his narrow pallet, and his clothes were hanging haphazardly over the wooden rail on the far wall. The cloak he pinched from a Pierleone clothesline so long ago was draped over a stool. He had a small table; on it were the current book of hospital expense records, some knucklebones, his purse, a wax tablet and a stylus, and a half-eaten almond cake. I picked up the thick book and saw behind it his keys on a sturdy ring.

It was that last item that made the tears spring to my eyes. Lapo had carried duplicates of the few keys I restricted—the money chest, my study, and the door to the tower, which I had kept locked for years. Only he and I could open those locks. It had meant so much to him to have my trust, and he did have it, for he had earned it.

Tucked underneath the table I saw his shoes, sturdy leather meant for getting around on city streets. That made me smile, remembering him leaving, ready to set off on the long walk to Assisi with Elias and Francesco.

"Barefoot?" Lapo had asked faintly.

"Barefoot," Elias had confirmed, grinning.

Lapo gave a self-deprecating shrug, and then they were gone.

I left everything as it was for the moment, except the account book, which I took back to my study. I would take care of everything else later. I pulled his door closed as I left.

I was slow to find sleep. The tumult of the day, followed by the pain of having to share the news about Ricco with my household, had left me drained and empty, and I could not find rest. I longed for Graziano, for the chance to talk everything over with him and let his calm competence soothe me and reassure me.

In all my years of widowhood I had never found a friend who shared the secrets of my heart the way Graziano did. Francesco was so far beyond me in his closeness to God that he serenely ignored my faults, my imperfections, my contradictions. Graziano saw them all, but he loved me anyway. I would have given much to loose my grasp on earthly life and join my husband, but I knew now that taking that decision into my own hands would cut me off from him forever. Had it not been for that, how could I have continued to live in this world, so full of greed and viciousness? Greed had cost us Lapo, viciousness Ricco.

The body will eventually assert itself and take what it needs, and so it was that in the small hours of the day I finally drifted into sleep. Fragmentary images of the day's events flitted through my mind, breaking up before they could achieve coherence. They eventually subsided, and I slept deeply at last.

*

An unearthly wailing shattered my dream. I jolted awake and sat straight up in bed, disoriented. The wailing was coming closer.

"Giacoma! Giacoma! Oh, come!" It was Salvestra. She was now outside my door, pounding on it. I scrambled out of bed and ran over to open it for her.

"What is it, Salvestra?"

"Renzo. It's Renzo, Giacoma—he's. . . he's. . ." She was panting.

"He's what, Salvestra? Tell me." I grasped her fragile shoulders and tried to steady her.

"He's not breathing. Please, please come!" She pulled away from my grip and started back to her chamber, looking over her shoulder to make sure I was following.

Other doors were opening as my household awakened to the noise. Tommasso and Lucia stood in their doorway, wrapped in their blanket and blinking in confusion. My boys emerged from their chamber, and Sabina from hers. Prassede, who slept in the tiny room next to mine, was already dressed and standing in the doorway of Renzo and Salvestra's chamber. She stared into the room and crossed herself.

Salvestra pushed Prassede aside, rushing to Renzo's bed. I was right behind her. Renzo lay on his back on his usual side of the bed, eyes and mouth open, one hand raised slightly as if he had been about to lift the coverlet.

Salvestra threw herself across his body. "Renzo, Renzo, wake up!" she cried. My heart broke for her, but it was clearly too late. We had lost Renzo too. Lucia wept, and Tommasso put his arm around her shoulders. All of us by now were crowded into the chamber.

Prassede tried to draw Salvestra away, but without success. She looked at me.

"You'll have to do it, Giacoma. You're the only one she'll listen to."

I finally managed to pull Salvestra into my embrace. She sobbed in my arms while Prassede reached over and closed Renzo's eyes.

"Giovanni, bring the chair from my study for Salvestra," I said, and he nodded and left. "Tommasso, could you fetch a priest? Or should we wait until full morning? What do you think, Prassede?" It was too late for unction, not that Renzo had been in any position to sin much for a long time.

Prassede sighed. "I think we might as well wait. Nothing can be done right now, and with the way things have been going the past little while, I don't really like to think of any of us out on the streets before it's light."

Giovanni set the chair down next to the bed. It had a sloping back and a wide seat, much better than the three-legged stools and the linen chest that provided seating in this chamber. He and I gently eased Salvestra into it and she sat there sobbing, never taking her eyes off Renzo. She was shivering, and Prassede draped a shawl around her thin shoulders.

I don't think anyone returned to bed. Lucia's eyes were red and her face blotchy, and Salvestra refused to budge from her chair. Somehow we got through it, all of us looking after each other as best we could. When the sun was up we made all the necessary arrangements. Two priests arrived for a vigil, though it would have to be an abbreviated one, as we wanted to inter Renzo's body that same day. They placed him on the bier they had brought with them and supported it on two stools. They chanted and prayed, and I had good wax candles brought, and we lit them around him. Through it all, Salvestra never moved.

Prassede got her to take a little water, but she would not eat. I was worried about her, both her state of mind and her frail body, but she ignored us all, seeing only Renzo.

When two more churchmen arrived and it was time to take Renzo to the church for his funeral, I distracted Salvestra by kneeling in front of her and taking both of her hands in mine.

"Salvestra, we will bury Renzo in my family tomb. And I will have a stone carved with his name and the year of his death. Do you by chance know what year he was born, or the names of his parents? I would like to give him his true name, if I can, but I never knew it." Behind me the churchmen were hefting the bier to take it away.

She shook her head. Her eyes followed the bier, but she made no attempt to get up. I thought she might have been too exhausted.

"He never told me his parents' names. He said he was eighty years old, though, so you can figure out his birth year. Except that sometimes he said he was eighty-five, and once just last year he said he was seventy-five."

She actually smiled a little at that.

"Eighty sounds like a good average, then. And since we don't have a full name, I'll have the stone carved with 'Lorenzo dei Settesoli.' Will that be acceptable?"

A bigger smile this time, though a little shaky. "He'll be a part of your family, then, Giacoma."

"He always has been."

"When I die, can I be buried next to him? And can I be Salvestra dei Settesoli? I'd rather have that than my birth name. Then Renzo and I will be together in heaven, too."

"Salvestra, I will be honored, as I am honored to share my name with Renzo."

She squeezed my hands, and a tear rolled down her cheek.

"Do you mind if I tell you it won't be long?" she asked.

I started to say that she must live out her life for Renzo's sake, and all that sort of nonsense that people say, and then I thought about it. A flood of memories overwhelmed me; she waited patiently.

"If it isn't long, I'll understand."

She nodded, satisfied.

*

I felt as if I was severing my ties to Rome. I had always been Roman, I couldn't imagine living anywhere else, but the boisterous, raucous city no longer felt like home to me. Everywhere I looked, I saw corruption, avarice, ugliness. It was as if Cencio's foul nature had become reflected in the city itself, though in truth nothing had changed, at least nothing outside of my own soul. I blamed my mood on grief and tried not to think about it.

We worried about our sorrowing midwife. She mourned and she prayed, and she ate almost nothing. She spent endless hours wandering through every part of the palazzo, as she had before Renzo became bedridden. She visited Renzo's tomb, though for her safety we made sure at least two people went with her each time she walked to the church. In spite of all her wandering, she was no longer steady on her feet.

We all missed Renzo. Though we grieved for Ricco too, it had been years since he had been a part of our daily lives. Not so with Renzo, whose diverting company had meant more to all of us than we realized while he was still with us.

Nearly a week after Renzo's death, I was walking along the corridor outside the bedchambers, looking down to see how the potted herbs fared in the courtyard below, when I felt something amiss. I don't know what it was I perceived, maybe a sound, or a draft where there shouldn't have been one, but I trust that instinct, so I went looking for whatever had triggered it. All seemed in order at first, nothing out of place or unusual, until I ventured down the north corridor, which was still mostly unused.

My unease was growing stronger. It was late afternoon on a cloudy day, and the corridor was gloomy and dark, so I had to go all the way to the end to check every door, every room. And there I saw the door to the tower standing open.

At first I was puzzled. I touched the keys on my girdle, though that formidable bundle of keys was heavy enough that I couldn't possibly have lost them without knowing it. Then how...?

Lapo's keys. The duplicate keys on the table in his chamber, where I still had not returned to pack up his things. And I had left those keys where anyone could walk in and find them, just as I had found them.

Intruders? No. People didn't come and go unnoticed in this house. Someone in the household, then. But who would have had business in the tower? And if anyone did, wouldn't they have come to me for the key?

Salvestra.

My stomach knotted. I had been in this story before. "Is anyone up there?" I called, already starting up the stairs. No one answered. I didn't know if anyone in the house had heard me. Lucia was at the mercer's shop trying to match some thread, the men were who knows where, Prassede was probably in the kitchen.

As I climbed, as fast as I could, Sabina appeared at the bottom of the stairs.

"Giacoma? Did you call? Do you need me?"

"Yes! Come with me!" I hiked my skirt up and sprinted across the landing and up the next, steeper flight of steps, listening as I went.

Sabina's footsteps, coming up rapidly behind me. Above me, nothing but a whistle of wind through a window slot.

At last I emerged, panting, in the room at the top of the tower. "Salvestra?" I gasped the name out, but no one was there. Only one of our kitchen stools, toppled, directly under the window, and Lapo's key ring on the stone floor next to it. Nothing else but the wind gusting through.

The wind, then agitated voices in the street, and then Lucia screaming.

*

"It was an accident," Sabina insisted. "She would never have imperiled her soul in that way. She was a good woman." Her voice shook. It was evening, and she and Prassede and I were huddled in my chamber, still agitated after a nightmarish few hours.

"But the stool—"

I interrupted Prassede as smoothly as I could. "I think what Sister Prassede is trying to say is that while we know Salvestra would never have harmed herself intentionally, the stool suggests that some madness caused by her grief may have made her do this." Sabina was rattled, not thinking clearly, and I wanted to soothe her.

I sympathized, but with that telltale stool, nobody was going to believe it had been an accident. Better to blame madness, or demons. That—and a generous donation—was how I had persuaded the clerics to let us bury Salvestra in consecrated ground. They wanted to know why we had not called in churchmen to confront her demons, but I told them the madness had come on her suddenly, and we had no warning. They were not going to contradict me, but Sabina had been there with me, and she must have seen the suspicion in their eyes.

Egidio and some of the other brothers stationed in Rome had spoken eloquently on her behalf, which had probably been enough to tip the balance.

The worst of it was over. No one from our household saw her fall; Lucia arrived as passersby gathered around Salvestra's broken body, crumpled far beneath the window like a shattered pot, yet with a tiny secret smile on her ancient lined face.

Salvestra's body rested in our courtyard now, with young priests at her head and feet, chanting as the day's light dimmed. Lucia was so distraught that she had taken to her bed, and Tommasso didn't want to leave her alone. Egidio had joined us as soon as he heard. Amata and Massimo had come with their twins, and I had charged Uccellino with entertaining Benino in the garden so Lancelotto could enjoy a little time with his adored Cilia, though she ostentatiously ignored him. All the children were asleep now.

Sabina and Prassede were the ones who truly feared for Salvestra's soul. Everyone else had been quick to seek comfort in my theory about demons and the madness they had caused. And a person cannot be blamed for madness, or so I kept insisting.

I was trying to convince myself, as well as the others. Had I given my permission to her? Or to her demon? Was it my fault? Should I have known what she intended? *Did* I know, and let her do it anyway? I couldn't even confess my doubts without throwing into question Salvestra's right to burial in holy ground. I needed to talk to Francesco, but he was back in Assisi.

Sabina desperately wanted it to have been an accident. The idea of demons terrified her, but we couldn't help her with that. Demons were indeed terrifying, as I well knew. That was more or less the point of them—God's enforcers, Francesco called them. And grief was a powerful demon in its own right.

Prassede found it easier to believe it had been demons, but she was so traditional, so conscientious about all matters dictated by the church, that she kept going over and over the event, trying to convince herself beyond any doubt. Being Prassede, she naturally did this out loud. And every time she did, Sabina became more agitated.

We needed to break this loop.

"Sabina, please come with me to the kitchen. I'd like to bring up a little wine, and maybe some fruit." We had not given a thought to supper, its hour now long past.

Obediently she started to get up, but Prassede jumped to her feet. "I'll do it, Giacoma," she said.

I shook my head and indicated with a gesture that she should sit down. Puzzled, she complied.

In the kitchen, Sabina and I went through the motions of filling pitchers, gathering cups, and putting out cheese, dried fruit, bread, salt, and oil. Once we had everything assembled, I asked her to sit next to me.

"Sabina, there's something I want to tell you. But I must ask you not to tell anyone else. It isn't something I have discussed with anyone here." Egidio was in the house, so that wasn't quite true, but almost.

Her forehead creased. "Can I be silent without sinning?"

"You can."

"Then I will keep your confidence."

In as few words as possible I sketched for her the circumstances of my own bout with demons, all those years ago. I told her of my overwhelming grief, and of the madness that overtook me, leaving me cut off from God and from any clear understanding of what I was doing. Her expressive face showed first horror, then profound sympathy, and finally, when I described what Francesco had done to save me, awe.

"If Francesco hadn't been here, I would have ended as Salvestra did," I told her, and her face crumpled as she started to weep at the thought. I patted her hand. "Salvestra had no one who could save her. Yet I believe God will accept her soul. She was very old, at the end of a long and virtuous life, and she had just lost the person she loved best in the world. Maybe that's why God didn't send us to her in time to stop her. He will take pity on her. He is good, and he knows human hearts. He would not turn his back on our Salvestra, even if her grief left her open to demons. You know he wouldn't, Sabina. And she may have cast off her demons at the last moment and repented, but she was frail and unsteady on her feet, so maybe she couldn't catch herself. If so, then it was a kind of accident after all."

Sabina wiped the tears from her cheeks with a kitchen towel. "God is good," she agreed. "In spite of everything that has happened to me, everything I see around me every day, I still believe that. And I am so glad Francesco was here for you when you most needed him. That must have been God's work. So yes, I think I can accept that Salvestra was taken over by demons, and that it was the demons rather than her who did this thing."

Demons it was, then. We were all agreed. Not that it was up to us, really, but the safest answer was demons. Though recalling Salvestra's incongruous little smile, a heretical thought flitted through my mind: *angels?* I crossed myself and immediately discarded the idea. Angels would have engineered a less messy end.

Sabina drew a deep breath and went on. "And I can believe her soul rests with God. And with Renzo."

"Good. I don't doubt it either. Do you feel more at peace now?"

She hesitated. "Yes, I think so. Yet I can't help wondering whether the demon actually did her a kindness. Is that even possible?" The thought clearly troubled her, but I was glad she had voiced it. It made me feel less alone with my own heretical thought.

"I don't think a demon can intend a kindness," I said slowly, thinking carefully about my words. "But maybe it's possible for a demon to intend to do evil, yet instead God causes him to do something that brings a good result." Or perhaps human beings were not the only ones who were capable of staggering levels of incompetence; maybe demons could achieve them too. Theologically I was on shaky ground here, as was she, but there were no churchmen present. Still I thought it best to leave it, lest we stray into errors of thought. Sabina made no answer, but she appeared to be weighing what I had said.

Time to exert a bit of authority. We had decided; now we had to let it go. "We'd better take the wine and food in, or the others will wonder what happened to us," I said briskly, and she smiled and picked up a tray. I took the other one, and we returned to the hall.

It was getting late, so we found bedding for Amata, Massimo, Egidio, and the children, and got everyone settled in for the night. On the morrow we would lay to rest Salvestra dei Settesoli, wife of Lorenzo, in the family tomb. And if Cencio didn't like it, he could go eat rocks, for all I cared.

So many losses in such a short time. I couldn't help feeling that the ties binding me to Rome were fraying like an old bowstring. How much longer could they last? And if they snapped, where would they fling me?

40

RAIN behaves differently in Assisi than in Rome. It never washes Rome's streets clean, but only turns dust into mud and makes people irritable as they slog through the drizzle, or the shower, or the downpour, going about all that business they are so sure cannot possibly wait.

In Assisi rain has a different aspect. It does wash everything clean, and it mutes the city's already subtle pinks and peaches and pale bluish grays into something even softer.

It was my fifth day in my temporary home, and already I loved it here. I pulled my stool over in front of the open door to enjoy the distant rumbles of thunder and occasional diffuse flashes of lightning beyond the mountain while I shelled what would probably be the last beans of the season.

This simple two-story wooden house had stood vacant for some months until I rented it, knowing this visit would be longer than I could impose on Mengarda. Sabina, Prassede, and I had spent hours cleaning, but now all was tidy and pleasant, with ample light from the windows and the door even on this gray day. And the garden was still producing, which was why I had a wooden bowl full of beans on my lap, and why there was another bowl piled with early apples on the bench next to the hearth.

Sabina peered out the door. She was thrilled to finally have a chance to meet Chiara, whom she revered. She fretted that the weather would cause us to postpone our visit to another day, but already the rain was beginning to slow and the sky was growing brighter.

She turned to me. "Are you sure it will be all right to bring Casta?" Her dearest wish was to see her daughter safely brought into Chiara's sisterhood, though the child was too young, at seven, to make that commitment.

"Certainly she may come. The sisters will love her, and she'll get a glimpse of what their life is like."

Casta was a sweet-natured child, contented and obedient, always singing, her voice surprisingly adult and pure. I wondered what she would make of the silence at San Damiano, but then, they had their musical moments as well, and perhaps that would be enough. Or she could dedicate herself to nursing the sick in Chiara's hospital, where her songs would be welcome.

In the meantime, it was good to have her here in Assisi. When the child turned seven, Sabina had laid down the law: no more playing with Lancelotto. It had been nearly impossible to keep the two heartbroken children apart while they were living in the same house. Finally, to achieve some peace, I had presented Lucia and Tommasso with a small house of their own, formerly one of my rent-producing city properties. And life had been easier with no risk of the children seeking each other out, or bumping into each other accidentally. I allowed Tommasso to continue teaching his classes in my palazzo, but Lucia seldom accompanied him, as someone had to stay with Lancelotto. I missed her, and her little one. It was one more small loss, one more change, relentlessly driving me away from Rome.

The rain had stopped. Sabina and I bundled up the apples in a cloth to take to the sisters and got Casta dressed in a simple blue gown that very nearly matched her eyes. We put on our outdoor shoes for the muddy walk down to San Damiano and set off, Casta and her mother singing a lauda in sweet harmony. Sabina's soft alto supported her daughter's clear soprano, but in no way competed with it. The result was charming and lovely, and it made the walk seem even shorter than I had remembered it.

*

Chiara was ill and confined to her bed. "Bed" was not the best word for it; Sister Berta escorted me to Chiara's spot in the dormitory, where she was lying prone on a thin straw pallet, a smooth stone supporting her head. A coarse sheet covered her, but I could still see tufts of straw sticking out here and there underneath her. Her still-beautiful face was drawn, and she was thinner than the last time I had seen her, but she smiled at me and extended her hand, which I took and held gently between my own.

I had left Sabina downstairs in Vanna's care, my former servant shepherding my present servant, and Casta in the midst of a circle of delighted sisters, who had quickly discovered her extraordinary gift and persuaded her to sing for them. As always, the rule of silence was relaxed for visitors. I hoped Casta would not get the wrong idea about what life in the sisterhood would be like.

"Welcome, Sister Giacoma," Chiara said.

Part of me wished I was a sister in truth, but I wouldn't have lasted a month at San Damiano, and I knew it. Yet something I valued remained out of my reach, and there was no better reminder of that dissonance than Chiara herself.

"I thank you, Sister Chiara, and I am sorry to see you unwell. Do you lack anything?"

She shook her head. "God is with me, so I have everything I need. How long will you be in Assisi?"

"At least a few months. I won't travel back to Rome until spring at the earliest, and I might stay longer, depending on how things work out. My son is getting married in less than a year, and I will have to return for that." Saracena was eager to join our household, though I suspected it would hold some surprises for her.

"Yes. May his marriage be blessed and bring you and him great joy."

"Thank you. I have a woman with me who wants very much to meet you, and to have you bless her little daughter. Will that be possible, or are you too ill?"

"When you and I have finished talking, send them up to me, and I will be happy to greet them."

I told her a little of Sabina's history, and of her hopes for her daughter and herself, and she nodded her approval.

"She sounds like a good woman, and you did well to rescue her from her sin and give her a safe home. Unless God advises me otherwise, it will be my pleasure to welcome them to San Damiano when they are ready. It does her great credit that however much she wants to come here, she is not willing to leave you while you have need of her. And her care for her daughter is also laudable."

"I am grateful to her. She has become a real friend."

Chiara adjusted her position, grimacing a little as she moved. She managed to sit up, lean back against the wall, and reach for her spindle.

"With the sickness upon me, I can do little of my work here in the convent, but I need not be completely idle." She began to spin a fine, even thread.

As I watched her, I considered asking her about Francesco, but I wasn't sure I should. He was still on his mountaintop retreat, so I hadn't met with him since my arrival in Assisi. I knew Chiara didn't see him often, for he was very careful about mixing the brothers and the sisters in any way, but somehow they kept in touch with each other.

"You are afraid for Father Francesco's health," she observed, her eyes still on her spinning.

She always did that. "Yes. I hear rumors."

"Many are true. His old sickness had worsened by the time he returned from the Holy Land, and now he suffers from eye disease, as well. Light pains him, his fevers come and go, and he is often weak, so weak that he rides a donkey rather than walking. He rode to his retreat on La Verna, which he's never had to do before. He hates to pamper himself, but if he is to continue to do God's work, he has to make some concessions to his body."

"Was it wise, then, for him to climb a mountain and spend forty days depriving himself of food and comfort?"

"All that Father Francesco does is wise. Whether his body will suffer because of it, I could not say."

I decided to leave that alone. "How fares the brotherhood?" I asked.

"There is dissension. Not long ago, several of the brothers were ordained as priests."

"There have always been priests in the order—Brother Leone, Brother Silvestro..."

"Yes, but they were already priests when they entered the brotherhood. These new ones want clerics to have special privileges, and you know well how Father Francesco feels about that. Others cleave to the earlier ways. And also, there are brothers who want the order to be more like the Benedictines, and those who are content to be radically different."

"Is that four factions, or two?"

She laughed. "Sometimes four, sometimes two. Probably sometimes three, or six, or twenty. There are so many brothers now, we can't expect them all to be like the first ones. But it is hard on Father Francesco when they squabble among themselves and demand contradictory things of him."

Francesco had officially given up leadership of the order soon after he returned from the Holy Land, but he was still, and always would be, The Brother. Even after he handed the reins to Pietro Cattani, and then, after Pietro's sudden death, to Elias, Francesco led by example. According to Egidio, Francesco longed to become a hermit, yet he couldn't let go of his position as decision maker for the brotherhood. Torn in two directions, like my own dilemma, but with much more at stake. And he had taken on the responsibility of composing a Rule, a protracted effort that had misfired before. He finally had to face the reality that no single version was going to please everyone.

"Can you tell me anything about Giannuccio?" I asked cautiously. I had gone back and forth on whether to bring him up or not, but if there was news, I wanted to know it.

She shook her head. "It's as if he has simply disappeared. You were the last of us to see him."

I fell silent, thinking of my friend and his distress. Chiara clearly didn't want to discuss it, so I changed the subject.

"What about Greccio? What was it that happened there?" I was curious about the extraordinary thing Francesco had done there, last Christmas. Greccio was the site of a hermitage Francesco loved to retreat to, perched on a rugged cliff looking out across a wild valley.

"You know that he decided to celebrate Christmas by setting up a stable and a manger in the church there?"

"I had heard that. It has never been done before, has it?"

"No. God gave Father Francesco the idea, and he obeyed. One of his followers carved a wooden image of the holy child to place in the manger on Christmas Eve. They had an ox and an ass, too, real ones, there in the church."

So I had heard. I wondered how that had worked out. I had a sheep I could have lent them, but I could just imagine Lotario eating the hay around the Christ child, or ramming the manger if he was in a bad mood. Maybe not the best idea.

"The townspeople gathered, and all the churchmen, and they sang hymns, and Father Francesco served as deacon for the mass. And then he lifted up the image of the Child and placed it in the manger, and witnesses swore they saw the wooden image come alive. It was a beautiful miracle."

Egidio had told me the local people collected hay from the manger afterwards and fed it to ailing animals, and it healed them. It even was said to have helped pregnant women deliver their children easily, though I don't think the women had to eat it. Francesco's reputation as a miracle-maker and a living saint grew each time the story was repeated. I suspected he was not comfortable with that.

Chiara apparently had nothing more to say about it. She set her spindle down carefully, then eased her body back into a prone position.

"Sister Giacoma," she said, "it would be best if I met your servant and her child soon, before my little strength runs out. But first, there is something I must confess to you, and for which I must ask your forgiveness." A small furrow appeared in her otherwise smooth forehead.

Chiara? Asking my forgiveness? I couldn't imagine what she meant. Not the egg, surely, after all this time. If anyone should be asking forgiveness, it was me, for coveting her special position in Francesco's heart. It still hurt that he would never call me Sister Giacoma. I felt it made me less to him than I might otherwise have been. Less than she was.

Gazing on her lying there, suffering, a wave of remorse swept over me. What right had I to be jealous of this extraordinary woman, as much a saint as Francesco himself? Impulsively I started to apologize to her, but she was already speaking, and our words tumbled out over each other's.

"I have envied you your closeness with Father Francesco—"

"Sister Chiara, I have wished I could be more like you, and be a sister in truth—"

"—and I have resented you for taking the place I wanted."

"—and I was hurt that I could not be what you are to him."

We both stopped speaking and looked at each other.

A long silence followed. Finally, wanting to finish it, I said, "He calls you Sister."

Her gray eyes opened wide. She let out a long breath and murmured, "He calls you Brother."

Again we studied each other. Did she want what I had, even while I yearned for what she had? It was absurd, yet that seemed to be what faced us.

Finally the corner of her mouth quirked as she came to the same realization, and she chuckled. I couldn't help joining her, and soon we were both laughing aloud. I reached for her hand. At last the barriers between us had crumbled, and we sat together as friends. Not sisters, exactly, but friends. It was no small thing, this acceptance at long last between the two women Francesco loved best.

I felt as if a burden had been lifted. I floated downstairs to find Sabina and Casta and bring them to Chiara, and I couldn't stop smiling as Vanna and some of the other sisters showed me around the garden and the hospital. Sabina and Casta rejoined us in the courtyard, both of them awed and nearly speechless, and I asked them to wait for me while I went up to tell Chiara goodbye.

Her eyes were closed. Disappointed, I halted at the top of the stairs, watching her gentle breathing. I had no wish to wake her, knowing how weak she was.

As I started back down the steps, her voice came from behind me, light, a little amused: "Farewell, Brother Giacoma."

41

AUTUMN gradually shifted from warm and wet to chill and wet. Francesco had been atop the mountain La Verna for nearly two months, and no news had reached us in Assisi. I had received several messages from Rome, so I knew all was well there. Or at least all was well in my little portion of the city. Rome's political turbulence never ceased; it only ebbed and flowed, like the Tiber, which could never rest inside its banks for long without becoming restless and threatening devastation.

One of the pleasures of being back in Assisi was seeing Lapo occasionally. My quintessentially Roman friend had settled into the brotherhood remarkably well. His friendship with Feo had helped, but what may have helped even more was that Elias thought highly of him. Lapo was finding a number of outlets for his unique talents there at the Porziuncola. His hospital experience made him a natural choice for caring for patients, but he had ample opportunities to do other service too.

On this particular day at the beginning of October, I waited for him outside Santo Stefano, because it was the first bright day in a week and I wanted to enjoy the sun on my face while I could. I had prayed inside, and now I sat idly on a stone with my mantle pulled about me. Despite the sun, there was a chill in the air. I was beginning to wonder if Lapo had been detained by some task that would not keep, and perhaps I would have to meet him another day. But then I saw him running toward me, his bare feet pounding the ground.

"Giacoma! He's on his way back!" Lapo was panting. "But he's not at the Porziuncola yet, because he's really sick, and they had to stop at the hermitage in San Sepolcro to let him rest, and Brother Elias is planning to go to him, and the brother who brought us the news said they thought he might die when he first got there, and they don't know when he'll be able to come home, and something happened to him while he was on the mountain, but nobody's talking about it 'cause he told them not to—"

"Slow down, Lapo! I assume you're talking about Francesco, but you sound like Prassede. Tell me one thing at a time. Now, start over, please."

Lapo plopped down next to me on the stone and took a deep breath. "All right. A brother came to us from the hermitage in San Sepolcro and told us Father Francesco was much sicker than he was when he left here, and he wasn't doing very well then, I can tell you. Anyway, now he can hardly see, and even fire hurts his eyes so he doesn't want to be near the hearth, yet he gets cold so easily, and the brothers try to make him wear warmer clothes, but he says they're a luxury, so he won't do it. Am I going slow enough?"

I nodded. "He didn't walk all the way to San Sepolcro, did he?"

"No, he couldn't. They borrowed a donkey for him, and Brother Leone walked alongside him. He's thin and weak, which you'd expect because of all the fasting, and in a lot of pain."

"Is Elias on his way to San Sepolcro, then?

Lapo shook his head. "He was going to go there, but before he had finished assigning brothers to take care of everything while he was gone, another brother came and told us that Father Francesco and Brother Leone were moving on to the hermitage at Monte Casale. So now Brother Elias is going there."

"He must be better if he's able to travel."

"I hope so," Lapo said, but I heard the doubt in his voice. "They have a better infirmary there, though, so maybe Brother Leone thought they could help him more."

"Will you tell me as soon as you hear anything more?"

"Absolutely, Giacoma. I promise."

By tacit agreement, we entered the church and knelt to pray for Francesco.

*

I woke every morning thinking about Francesco and waiting anxiously for news. It was tempting to arrange a journey to wherever he was, but I couldn't keep up with his movements, not with news taking days to reach the Porziuncola, and once it arrived there, Lapo having to arrange to meet with me to pass it along.

Elias traveled back and forth between the Porziuncola and wherever Francesco was, giving himself the dispensation of riding because of his many responsibilities. Some of the brothers grumbled at that, but I thought it was reasonable—he needed to check on Francesco, but he also had an order to run, and without that savings in travel time, it would have been impossible to do both.

Elias did his best to make time for me whenever he was in Assisi. He was always honest with me, and while I hated to hear how ill Francesco was, at least I knew I was getting an accurate picture. But he would not tell me what had happened to Francesco on the mountain. He would only say that God had honored our brother, and he must not say more. His silence fueled my unease. The last time brothers kept information from me, it had been bad news.

One day, early in February, Elias was sitting with me in front of our fire, filling me in on the latest developments.

"I think he will be back in Assisi soon, Giacoma. He needs nursing care, and protection from light and cold, and he needs nourishing food. Chiara has agreed to house him at San Damiano, and the brothers assigned there are making a hut for him."

The brothers who served as questors at San Damiano were tasked with doing any construction or repair jobs that needed to be done, and with begging alms for the sisters, who could not leave their cloister to beg for themselves. Lay sisters went back and forth between Chiara and the questors, communicating the sisters' needs and collecting the alms.

Knowing the extreme poverty of the Poor Ladies, I was skeptical that Francesco could get adequate care, but nobody was asking my opinion. Still, since this was Elias, I gave it anyway. He listened patiently.

"You may well be right, but it's been almost impossible to get him to agree to even these poor provisions. I've had to exercise my authority as minister and actually order him to submit to this, and I can tell you, it is not easy to give orders to Francesco, even for his own good."

These days Elias was looking like someone who gave orders. He had taken to wearing a pair of slippers he brought back from the Holy Land, claiming a foot problem. Even if that were true, it was hard to understand why he had also affected an oriental cap, which he now wore every day. Both the slippers and the cap were finely made and exotically embroidered in the eastern style, and the brothers grumbled about that, too. Elias, unlike poor Pietro Cattani, led in more than just name. But even though Francesco professed to be the smallest and meekest of men, he was led only by God, and he was never slow to tell other brothers how they should behave.

"Let me know how I can help."

"I will. He might accept help and care from you that he wouldn't from anyone else."

"I wish I had Lotario's wool here, but it's back in Rome. I'd make him a warm garment. Maybe he'd wear it to make me happy."

"Really? You've been saving Lotario's wool?"

"Oh, yes. When the boys were young, they used to love to pull it out by handfuls. I saved it all. There's quite a pile of it now, already washed, and it's just waiting to be spun and woven into cloth. It's not the best quality wool, but it will serve." I had always intended to have it made into a tunic for Francesco.

Elias stood. "I must get back. I had no idea being minister of the order would take so much time, but I try to do all that Francesco would want me to do, as well as anything I see that needs doing." He hesitated for a moment. "I'm pushing Francesco to let a physician treat his eyes before they get even worse and he loses his sight altogether. This isn't the season for eye treatment, but as soon as it's spring, I'm going to want him to travel to Rieti and get it done. I may need you to help convince him."

I shivered at the thought. The painful treatment involved cauterization of the delicate skin at the temples and around the eye with a red-hot poker.

"Couldn't we spare him that?"

"I dread it too. But we have to try. The order needs him. I can't let him just fade away because he won't accept care."

"But are you sure? Is he really that sick?"

Elias looked at me gravely. "He's that sick. There's a thing I haven't told you yet, Giacoma." Something in his voice chilled me.

"What is it? Was it what happened to him on the mountain?"

"No. That I am still not free to tell you. This was a dream that came to me when Francesco and I were in Foligno, before he went to La Verna. He was resting for a few days because he had exhausted himself preaching, and I was waiting for him to be ready to travel."

My heart was beating fast, though I didn't know why.

"I dreamed of an elderly priest dressed all in white, who came to me and spoke a prophecy. He reminded me that it had been eighteen years since Francesco renounced the world, and then he said it would be only two more years before our beloved brother would go to his eternal glory. He told me to tell Francesco."

Two years. Blessed Lady, let Elias be wrong for once. Let it be only an idle dream. Francesco couldn't have seen many more than forty years, and the world—and I—needed him so.

"Did you tell him?"

"Yes. He believes it."

"Is he afraid?"

"No, not at all. In fact, he was remarkably cheerful after I told him."

We stood together in dejected silence for a few moments. We should have prayed, but I couldn't, and I don't think Elias did either.

"Giacoma, I must go," he finally said.

"You'll send Lapo or someone to me as soon as he gets to San Damiano?" I said as we walked to the door.

"Yes, though he may need a day or two to settle in before he receives guests."

Guests?

"Elias, I am no guest. The podestà is a guest. The bishop is a guest. I am Brother Giacoma, and I have as much right as any other brother to attend to him." I glared, and Elias put up both hands as if to ward off my anger.

"Yes, you are Brother Giacoma. There has never been any doubt of that. And since Francesco will be in a house of women, or at least right outside it, there's no reason at all why you cannot be with him every moment he allows you to be."

Unlike the Porziuncola, the heart of the order, where the rules said I could not go. And where Elias was now returning, to take up his duties.

*

Some weeks later, I sat on the hard ground next to Francesco's pallet as a brother, not a guest, brushing the mice away from him with a leafy branch. He was sleeping restlessly, constantly shifting position, making small sounds of distress, and this aggressive army of mice was not helping. While I stood guard, he had at least a chance of gaining a little rest, and he needed it.

We were in a hut made of reed mats, hastily thrown together in the courtyard at San Damiano to make a sickroom for Francesco. Chiara would have abandoned all caution and convention and taken him inside, but he would have none of it. I supposed he was right; his enemies would have seized on that and made a scandal out of it, and the church would have reacted badly. But the hut was drafty and flimsy, and it gave him little protection from the cold.

The worst of it was the mice. There were so many of them, and they tormented him. They skittered across him as he lay on his pallet, they attacked his food if he set it down for even a moment, and they fouled everything with their droppings. Francesco in his weakness was convinced they were demons, and I was beginning to agree with him. I had always had an intense dislike of the creatures, and sitting on this filthy floor in their midst was not making me any fonder of them.

Francesco was terribly ill, worse than I had ever seen him before. His eyes troubled him most. Even though he never left the hut, if the day was bright he wore his hood with its scrap of cloth stitched across the opening to shade his eyes, which were red and swollen and watered constantly. He could not walk. His feet and hands were swathed in bandages, rags that should have been changed and washed more often, but he wouldn't permit it. He wouldn't let me touch them at all, though I brought fresh cloths each time I came. I had to leave them behind, and mostly they piled up and became nests for the mice, though Rufino or Elias could sometimes persuade him to allow a change of bandages.

He needed warm clothing and blankets, but he wouldn't accept them either. He insisted they were luxuries, and he did not want them. He was a difficult patient, alternately demanding care and rejecting it. The brothers who nursed him had a trying job, yet they did it with infinite love and gentleness. For years Francesco had tended to lepers and ailing brothers, never losing his patience with them, but he found it much harder to receive care than to give it.

I wanted to take him to my house and make him comfortable, but he wouldn't have it. So I brought food, though he ate little. Sometimes while he slept I pulled my cloak over him for a time, though the mice inevitably got in underneath it and made his life a misery.

I had one success. The pillow I made for him so long ago finally supported that beloved head, though my embroidered cover was not on it. Elias had warned me that Francesco would never accept the decorated version, so I offered the naked pillow, and to my amazement he allowed it. Not particularly graciously, but he allowed it.

Elias had been surprised, too. He told me about a time not long ago: Francesco had briefly been the guest of a nobleman and had become convinced that the soft pillow on his bed was possessed by demons, eager to torture him. In his agitation he had flung the offending pillow at his traveling companion, and then suffered agonies of guilt over having done so. It was clear that Francesco's illness had taken its toll on his mind, though at least his experience hadn't completely soured him on all pillows.

I was brushing at a particularly persistent pair of rodents when I heard Lapo's voice outside. He was on an errand for me, so I scrambled to my feet to go meet him. As quietly as I could, I stepped outside the hut, and Rufino slipped in to take my place. I handed him the branch as he went by me.

"Where's the cat, Lapo?" I asked. He held up an empty wooden cage, his expression woebegone. His hands were badly scratched.

"Couldn't get it. The creatures don't want to be picked up. I tried, really I did, but they just weren't going to let me grab them. Not even the little ones."

"But we need one desperately. These mice are horrible, and he gets so upset with them—"

"All be well, Brother Giacoma," Feo's ever-cheerful voice said from behind me. I turned, and there he stood, a big black cat nestled in his arms. The creature was nuzzling Feo's beard and purring loudly.

"Feo, you are wonderful," I said, and he grinned. "Now, Lapo, see how easy it is? Just go make friends with it."

Reluctantly Lapo took a step toward the cat, which hissed at him, though it clearly had no intention of giving up its berth in Feo's arms. Lapo hastily backed away.

"It doesn't matter, Lapo. We've got one now, thanks to Feo. I'll go to the kitchen and get a dish of water for it," I said.

"It wants some milk, I think, Brother Giacoma." Feo stroked the animal affectionately.

"We need it hungry. You should see the number of mice in there. I guarantee it won't stay hungry for long. Just pop it into the hut, will you, Feo?"

He complied. As I headed toward the convent's kitchen, I heard a commotion inside the hut, then a delighted cry from Francesco, and Rufino's voice, saying "Oh, excellent! What a fine cat you are!"

I smiled to myself. We were off to a good start.

*

It helped. It helped a lot, and we got about a week and a half of a reduced mouse population. Francesco couldn't bear to watch the cat kill the mice, which it did with great vigor and enjoyment, but then he couldn't see much of anything anyway, so he managed to ignore the mayhem and enjoy the benefits. In Francesco's view, it wasn't a cruel thing if the mice were in truth demons. The brothers cleaned up all the various partially-eaten mice, and everyone reported the situation much improved.

And I liked it that the cat, named Mousebane by the brothers, curled up next to Francesco once its stomach was full, providing him with at least a bit of warmth.

What ruined it all was a visit from the cardinal. Cardinal Ugolino had a number of difficult personality traits, but the brothers were witness to one I hadn't suspected.

He was frantic with worry about Francesco, as were we all, and he needed to see for himself how our spiritual father was doing, so he slipped away from his many responsibilities and paid a visit. I wasn't at San Damiano that morning, but I heard about it from Lapo later that day.

299

"The cardinal went into the hut to see Father Francesco, and Rufino said his face lit up when Father Francesco sat up and greeted him. He tried to get Francesco to agree to go somewhere else, but Francesco said God had told him he was in the right place, so that outranked even a cardinal. He went over and sat down on the pallet next to Father Francesco and they were talking when Mousebane strutted in through the door, cocky as can be, and meowed.

"Father Francesco was glad, but the cardinal jumped up and screeched something about demons and Satan's servants, and he picked up the stool and he threw it as hard as he could at Mousebane."

"Did it hit him?"

"No, but it came close. Mousebane yowled, a loud, horrible sound, and he arched his back, and that scruffy black fur stood straight up, and then he hissed at the cardinal."

I had known people who reacted badly to cats, but I had no idea Ugolino harbored such views. I rather liked the creatures, myself. Apart from cats' obvious usefulness, I found them lovely, graceful, and affectionate. Apparently that was not the way Cardinal Ugolino saw them. Indeed, I could not imagine the cardinal putting up with the indignity of being hissed at.

As for Mousebane's reaction to the cardinal, I knew a few Romans who shared it, but that was neither here nor there.

"The cardinal actually pulled out his dagger—did you know he carried a dagger?"

I did, in fact. "Go on," I said.

"He started toward Mousebane, angry and menacing-like, and Francesco was trying to get him to stop, and Mousebane kept hissing, and I don't know what would have happened if Feo hadn't come by just then. He's not one of the brothers who usually takes care of Father Francesco, but somehow he knew to go into the hut at that very moment. The interruption distracted his lordship, and Feo scooped up Mousebane and scuttled around the cardinal to get to the door, all the while stroking the cat and saying things like 'I'll get the animal out of here, your lordship,' and 'He's going now, all gone, don't worry.' He took Mousebane out, and he took him to the shelter where the brothers sleep and kept him in there. They had enough mice of their own to keep Mousebane busy."

I sighed with relief. "Good for Feo."

Lapo frowned. "The rest of it wasn't so good, though. The cardinal ranted on and on about how cats were the devil's creatures and he didn't want one near Father Francesco, and finally Father Francesco had to agree not to allow Mousebane to come back."

"Can we get another one, after the cardinal goes away?"

"That was the first thing I thought of, too, but I guess we can't, because he made Father Francesco agree not to have any more cats around him. And you know Father Francesco keeps his promises."

I knew it. It was a nuisance sometimes, but it was part of who he was.

Mousebane's story wasn't quite finished. He kept trying to get back in to Francesco, and Feo kept going in and taking him back out, until finally one day Francesco beckoned to Feo to set Mousebane down on his pallet. He stroked the cat and murmured to it, explaining the situation, and thanking the animal for its service to him. Then he asked it to kindly respect the church's wishes as conveyed by the cardinal and go live somewhere else. Mousebane stood up on the pallet, nuzzled Francesco's hand, hopped down, and strutted out the door, never to be seen again.

The mice, however, came back in droves. It took a few days, during which time they crept in a few at a time, but soon the situation was worse than ever.

And the winter days grew colder.

42

FRANCESCO had a way of driving all of us to distraction with his recalcitrance and his irritability. Then, just as we despaired of ever having another peaceful hour, he would do something so breathtakingly wonderful that we fell in love with him anew. It might be a flash of compassionate insight about a troubled brother, or a prayer that lifted him and all around him into a state of exaltation, or an unexpected expression of gratitude to the brothers who cared for him, thanking them with a passion, warmth, and intensity that left them dazed. With me he was always gentle, but it never fell to me to minister to his failing body in all the unavoidable ways that caused him so much distress. And even with me he was sometimes distant, locked into his body's pain and whatever spiritual pain it was that tormented him.

Those manifestations of grace served to remind us of who he was, underneath the sickness and pain and doubts. Those of us closest to him sensed, maybe only dimly, how his physical blindness mirrored his dread of spiritual blindness. He spent a lot of time with Elias, and Elias had told me privately that Francesco expressed grave fears for the order—fears I shared. How would the troubled brotherhood fare if Francesco continued ill? Or if—when—he died?

I was present for one of Francesco's magical moments on a chilly day late in March. Bernardo was gatekeeper, and I asked his permission to enter the hut. While we were whispering about Francesco's health, I heard that beloved voice from inside the hut, singing.

We both listened. The melody was simple but joyful. I had not heard it before, but I would never forget it. And the words were so extraordinary, so uniquely Francesco's, that I knew I was listening to his own composition.

He sang of God, as he always did, but he also sang of God's creation—Brother Sun, Sister Moon and the stars, Brother Wind, Sister Water, and

Brother Fire, and our sister Mother Earth herself. Each of these creations was a vehicle for praising God, as well as a reason to exalt him. His song held such ecstasy, such gratitude that it brought tears to my eyes.

When he finished singing I heard the song start up again, but this time in the more hesitant voices of three of the brothers. I recognized Elias's resonant voice, and Rufino's, low pitched and soft, and guessed that the third, powerful and moving, belonged to Brother Pacifico, who had been a minstrel before he joined the order. They faltered occasionally, and Francesco prompted them with the words, but soon they had it, and they sang it through perfectly.

Before the last note had faded, Francesco called out, "Come in, Giacoma. Don't just stand outside. I have a song to teach you."

I didn't even pause to wonder how he did that. I pushed the threadbare curtain aside and went in. The inside of the hut reeked. The stench of mice was overpowering, and I noticed a fainter stink of human waste and sour sweat. But Francesco's music made me forget all of that, or at least push it into the background.

Francesco taught me the song. Propped into a sitting position, his eyes covered with a cloth band, he patiently sang me one line at a time until I had it. The other brothers in the hut sang along with me. I had the tune in my head already, so it didn't take long. Soon I was adding my higher voice to those of the brothers.

When I sang with Chiara and the sisters, my voice was usually the lowest. While their voices soared and arched, mine trudged along in support. But when I sang with the brothers it was my voice's turn to float above the others. I had spent most of the previous decade being something of a brother and something of a sister in everything I did. Why should singing be any different?

"What's your favorite part, Giacoma?" he asked, like an eager child. I had to stop and think about his question.

"I love it all, Francesco, but I think the part I like best is Brother Fire: 'Through him you light the night, and he is beautiful, and merry, and robust, and strong.'"

Francesco smiled in satisfaction. "I knew it. There is much of fire in you, Giacoma. You, too, are beautiful and merry and robust and strong, and you have brightened many a night for me and for the other brothers."

I blushed, but his words pleased me greatly. "Do you have a favorite part, Francesco?"

"All of them are important. But now that I can no longer gaze upon either Brother Fire or Brother Sun, I think singing of Brother Sun gives me the most pleasure."

"'And he is beautiful and radiant with great splendor,'" I quoted.

"'And he bears your likeness, Most High,'" Elias said, finishing the line.

Francesco sank back down on his pallet. "I tire, brothers. I will sleep awhile," he said, and we filed out, Elias holding the curtain door for the rest of us.

*

I never wearied of hearing Francesco's song, or singing it. It was a good thing I didn't, for he wanted to hear it often. Whenever he called for it, any brothers nearby would gather and sing it—with him, if he was strong enough; to him, if he was not.

The brothers assigned to San Damiano taught it to the lay sisters, who went back and taught it to all the other sisters. They sang it at the hospital, while they worked in the garden, and as they crossed the courtyard. That last was a joy for Francesco, for he could hear them there and he said they sounded like angels. Silence still prevailed inside, but Francesco's song was given the status of a prayer, and it was sung often, in chapel and outside.

The sisters had a special focus for their prayers. Assisi was in the midst of troubling times, and the rift between Bishop Guido and the city's new podestà, messere Oportulo di Bernardo, grew colder and more bitter along with the winter days. The two men had never liked each other, though they maintained a certain grudging mutual respect. But everything had deteriorated precipitously since July, when Oportulo got himself—and his city—involved in Perugia's civil war.

Perugia and Assisi had a long adversarial history. As a young soldier almost a quarter of a century ago, Francesco had spent many bleak months in a Perugian dungeon. His father finally managed to ransom him, and from all reports he had returned a changed man. But this time Perugia's conflict was with itself.

Messere Oportulo had sound political reasons for siding with one of Perugia's factions, but he also must have known that the Holy Father had already dissolved one such alliance, hoping to defuse the situation.

Not surprisingly, Bishop Guido excommunicated Oportulo. He probably felt he had no choice, but I could imagine he took a certain satisfaction in the act.

Oportulo was enraged, but he had his own cudgel to wield. He declared it a crime for any citizen of Assisi to have legal dealings with the bishop.

Check, but not checkmate. This posturing on the part of both men was disruptive to both business and religion, and business and religion were the two poles that defined Assisi. Something had to be done before the hotheads among the citizens took sides and performed actions they would regret, or we would have our own civil war to contend with.

Both of these eminent men admired Francesco, but that commonality was not enough to bring them together, for each wanted to rule the other.

Oportulo was a stern ruler, but to the citizens of Assisi he was one of their own, and many of them sided with him against the bishop.

Bishop Guido had long been a true friend to Francesco, but he had a temper that rivaled the cardinal's, and no holy finger bone to smooth it over. He had made a number of enemies.

Francesco grieved for the strife growing all around him. Confined to his miserable hut, he kept going over the situation, trying to think of something he could do to help. His influence in Assisi was enormous, but he was too ill to go to the bishop and the podestà and negotiate peace. Unsurprisingly, it was in prayer that Francesco found his answer.

I was there that day, trying to persuade him to put on a new tunic while I washed his old one. My private plan was to come back and tell him that the old one was so fragile it had disintegrated in the washtub, and he'd have to wear the new one. I might have needed to launder it with considerable vigor to make that be the truth, but I was prepared to do whatever was necessary to get him out of that filthy rag. No luck. He wasn't about to give up his tattered tunic for one that was clean and whole.

Clearly preoccupied, he asked me to step outside the hut while he prayed, and I did. I was standing nearby talking with Rufino when I heard Francesco's exultant voice cry, "I have it! To me, brothers!"

Rufino and I hurried in, with Elias and Bernardo not far behind us. Francesco lifted his hood with its improvised blindfold and squinted at us, his dark eyes red and swollen and watering. It hurt just to look at them.

Finally making out who was present, he said decisively, "Summon Brother Pacifico." Then he pulled the covering back over his eyes and sank back down on his pallet, his sweaty head resting on the pillow I had brought for him. Bernardo hurried away.

"What is it, Francesco?" asked Elias solicitously.

Francesco shook his head. "Wait," was all he said.

Once Bernardo and Pacifico had entered the hut, Francesco told us his plan.

"Elias, I want you to gather as many brothers as you can find. Choose one of them to go to the podestà and one to the bishop, with this message: 'I, Brother Francesco, the smallest and least of the Little Brothers, humbly ask the most honorable messere Oportulo to come to the piazza in front of the bishop's palazzo with as many men as he wishes to bring with him, at the hour of Sext. And I ask the wise and holy Bishop Guido to meet him there with as many men as he wishes in attendance.' Do you have that?"

"Yes," said Elias, and he turned to go.

"No, wait, brother," Francesco said. "I want you to hear this plan before you leave. You're part of it." Obediently Elias returned to Frances-co's side.

"I have made a new verse for my song, and God tells me that this verse, along with the rest of our praises, will move these two men to seek peace. It will make them humble and forgiving and patient with one another."

I looked around me to see if anyone expressed any doubt. No one did. Even Elias, so practical and clear-eyed, would never question Francesco's prayerful insight.

Did I doubt? Of course I doubted. Francesco was a holy man, but even he was sometimes wrong. I have seen too many proud nobles and high churchmen in my life to believe there can ever be an easy answer when they quarrel. Asking them to invite as many men as they liked could be setting the stage for a melee.

And yet... this wasn't just anyone talking, this was Francesco. So while I doubted, I also believed. And I hoped.

"I am going to teach you the new verse, and you four are going to teach it to the others on your way to the bishop's palazzo. Giacoma, I want you to go along and observe, and then come back and tell me what you see. Understood?"

"Yes, Francesco."

"Good. At first I want only two brothers to sing. Brother Pacifico, you are to be one of them, and I leave it to you to choose the other. If all of you sang from the beginning, the audience would join in with you, and this one time, I don't want that. Now, after you sing the verse about Mother Earth, I want you to end by singing these words." Laboriously, Francesco sat upright. He took a long slow breath, lifted his head, and sang.

"Be praised, my Lord, for those who give pardon for your love, and who bear sickness and trials. Blessed are those who endure in peace, for by you, Most High, they will be crowned."

Give pardon for your love. Endure in peace. Francesco had found his way of saying to both powerful men "God give you peace." Or perhaps it was more like, "God has given you peace, if you will only take it."

Everyone in Assisi had heard Francesco's song by now, and this new verse, made for the occasion, would surely move his listeners. But would it move them enough?

"Once the two of you have sung it, I want everyone to sing the new verse again, all together. Understand? Good. Go now. Gather the others. Giacoma, you won't be singing this time, because a woman's voice might distract the listeners, so you'll be in the best position to observe and report to me. Brother Pacifico, choose well. God be with you all." He sank back down onto his pallet, exhausted but smiling.

My voice might distract the listeners. True, and it might also make the townspeople more aware of the woman in the brothers' midst, and talk might ensue, since the brothers made it a point to avoid the company of women. The only reason I could come to Francesco's bedside at all is that he was at San Damiano, not the Porziuncola. Still, I had no wish to sing in public.

It didn't take long to muster a group of perhaps a dozen brothers. Others from the Porziuncola might hear of the meeting in time to join us, but they wouldn't know the new verse, so this dozen was what we had. They drew lots to see who had to stay behind to meet the sisters' needs, and the others prepared to go. Pacifico had chosen Rufino to join him in giving Francesco's new verse its first performance, and Rufino, painfully shy, accepted his choice as if he had been given a penance.

I walked with them. Along the way they rehearsed, Pacifico and Elias coaching the others until all had a firm grasp of the new words. As we approached the city gate, Elias turned to the rest of us, his finger to his lips.

"No more now, until it's time. We don't want to give away Francesco's gift too early."

The piazza was already full of townspeople, but the bishop and the podestà were not yet there. The people peered at our approaching group, probably hoping to see Francesco himself, though everyone knew of his illness. So many people were praying for a miracle that one could scarcely blame them for hoping one had occurred. I woke every morning with the same hope in my heart.

Which of the two men would appear first? I suspected it would be the podestà, for I thought it likely Bishop Guido would wait until he saw his adversary before he emerged from his palazzo.

From up the hill, the cathedral bells began to ring for Sext. Almost intolerably loud in Mengarda's palazzo, here their voices were more melodious, less overpowering. They were soon joined by a brief cacophony of overlapping peals from churches closer to us.

As the last note died away, messere Oportulo rode into view. Three other men rode a few paces behind him, followed by a substantial entourage of wealthy and influential men on foot. All were dressed in a glittering array of rich colors and fabrics with a substantial amount of metal decoration.

At least I hoped all that metal was only decoration. The podestà had not gone so far as to come armed into the bishop's presence, but he did wear the padded garment that was the first layer of his armor, and his mail and his sword were conspicuously present, borne by two of the mounted men with him. The third man carried a bundle of weapons, probably those of the other knights in the podestà's retinue, wrapped in cloth but flagrantly poking out at one end of the bundle. The townspeople registered all this and murmured among themselves.

Would Oportulo dismount? He reined in his horse but made no further move. I wondered if Bishop Guido would come to meet him if he stayed in the saddle. All these little details, so fraught with meaning, so full of symbolism, and yet Francesco wanted only to bring together two men he respected and have them simply talk to one another.

Please let the bishop come forth. Both men had to be there for Francesco's plan to have any chance of working.

The door of the bishop's palazzo opened, and all eyes turned in that direction. Several churchmen stepped out and stood to either side of the door. A pause, then Bishop Guido emerged, dressed in full regalia. He took three measured steps, stopped, and looked straight at Oportulo.

Please let the podestà dismount. Oportulo stared back at him, his face expressionless, for a long moment, then, with deliberate slowness, he dismounted, never taking his eyes off Guido. His mounted companions followed his example.

He did not step forward. He made no obeisance, nor did he approach to kiss the bishop's ring. He was, after all, excommunicate.

Guido took three more paces into the piazza, then halted. Elias came forward.

"May God give you peace," he said, and the crowd murmured the same words. "Good my lords, we give you thanks for accepting our invitation. Father Francesco sends both of you his blessings and his gratitude. He has asked us to sing for you his song of praise. Will it please you to listen?"

Oportulo and Guido still held each other's eyes. Oportulo gave a single decisive nod, and at the same time Guido said, "We will listen."

Elias stepped back, and Pacifico and Rufino came forward. Pacifico caught Rufino's eye and mouthed the word "Ready?" Rufino looked terrified, but he mouthed "Yes," and took a deep breath. His hands were shaking.

"Most High, all powerful, good Lord, yours are all praise, all glory, all honor, and every blessing. To you alone, Most High, they belong. No man is worthy to speak your name." Pacifico's voice was strong and filled with its customary magic. Rufino wavered a little, but slowly he gained confidence, until the two voices blended to create something of intense beauty. At first, some people in the crowd had started to sing along with the familiar melody, but in the face of what Pacifico and Rufino were weaving, they soon dropped out.

"Be praised, my Lord, with all of your creations, especially my lord Brother Sun, who brings the day, and through whom you give us light, and he is beautiful and radiant with great splendor, and he bears your likeness, Most High."

Guido touched the cross he wore.

"Be praised, my Lord, for Sister Moon and the stars: in heaven you have formed them, bright and precious and fair."

Oportulo closed his eyes. Was he thinking of his beloved daughter, one of Chiara's sisters at San Damiano?

The brothers sang of Brother Wind, Sister Water, and Brother Fire, and both men swayed with the music, transported.

And finally Pacifico and Rufino finished singing "our sister, Mother Earth, who sustains us and governs us, and produces myriad fruits and colorful flowers and herbs."

It was time for Francesco's new verse.

Pacifico, with the instincts of a true showman, paused. It wasn't a halt, or a hesitation. He simply paused, and the pause was part of the song. The crowd didn't know that something new was coming, yet it held its breath.

Then they sang it:

"Be praised, my Lord, for those who give pardon for your love, and who bear sickness and trials. Blessed are those who endure in peace, for by you, Most High, they will be crowned."

Silence. No one spoke, no one moved. I knew Pacifico planned another dramatic pause before all the brothers joined in to sing the new verse a second time, so I watched him, waiting for his signal.

It never came. Instead, Oportulo flung himself forward and dropped to his knees in front of the bishop.

"I should have acknowledged you as my lord, messere Bishop. I was wrong. I am ready to do whatever I must to satisfy you—you have only to tell me what that is. I say this for the love of our Lord Jesus Christ and also the love we both bear for Father Francesco." Tears were running down his cheeks.

All eyes were now on Bishop Guido. I knew him for a proud and forceful man, but the same could be said of the man who knelt before him. We had one miracle. Would we get two?

Guido spoke, slowly. "To serve Mother Church I should be a humble man. Yet all know that I fail in that, too often. I am hotheaded and impatient by nature." He reached for Oportulo's hands and helped him stand. "I humbly ask your forgiveness, messere Oportulo."

The two men embraced and then exchanged the kiss of peace. The crowd's excited murmuring turned to full-throated exultation, and Pacifico seized the moment to signal all the brothers to sing Francesco's new verse. This time the bishop and the podestà listened arm in arm, smiling.

I watched the crowd break up, everyone chattering happily. Bishop Guido led a beaming Oportulo into his palazzo, calling to his servants for refreshments for his honored guest. The brothers gathered to walk back to San Damiano and I joined them, thrilled to be able to give such a good report to Francesco.

We walked briskly, delighted with the success of our mission. Elias had already figured out what this shift might mean politically, and he tried to explain it to us, but we were so exhilarated that we were in no mood to listen.

As Rufino reminded us, though, the accomplishment was really Francesco's.

Francesco hadn't even been there, but somehow he had done it. I should never have doubted. My giddy relief surprised me. Had Assisi become more of a home to me than I had realized? Was it possible this was where I belonged, now that I didn't feel like a Roman any longer?

It was something to think about, but not something to act on immediately. It was almost time to return to Rome to see my older son wed to his Saracena, so Rome was on my mind and in my immediate future as I prepared to make my report to Francesco. Yet for all our joy in the moment and my mind full of travel plans, I couldn't forget Elias's dream. Exactly how much time did Francesco have left?

September 1226, Rome

43

"But Mother Giacoma, we've already given the beggars plenty of food, and extra clothing, too. Surely they don't also need our coins. What would they buy with them? We've given them everything they require." Saracena had a tendency to speak to me as if I were a rather stupid child, and I was losing patience with it.

"They must pay their rent. They need firewood, and medicines, and furnishings, and bedding, and many other things, just as you and I do. We have so much—can we not think on these things, and show a little compassion for those who have so little?"

Saracena lowered her dark lashes. "I'm sorry, Mother Giacoma. I only wanted to protect my husband's goods. As his wife, I feel it's my duty to be thrifty and frugal, for his sake." The silky sweetness of her voice grated on me, and I couldn't help noticing that the gown she was wearing was a long way from frugal.

"It's not his money yet. This is still my home, and it's still my money." Most of it was, at least. At twenty-two, Giovanni had come into some of his inheritance, but the palazzo was mine, as was a substantial portion of Graziano's estate, and all of what we gave the beggars. "There will be plenty left for you and Giovanni. We've been giving alms for years, and we haven't run out of money yet."

"As you say, Mother Giacoma." Slowly she held out the purse full of coins. "They have already gone, though they'll doubtless be back tomorrow, and empty-handed, regardless of what they took away today." When I said nothing, she continued.

"Perhaps my judgment is clouded because the child takes all of my attention." She smugly patted her belly with her other hand. She wasn't showing yet, but all the other signs were there. Sometime next spring, I would be a grandmother.

I repossessed the purse. "I applaud your good sense, daughter, and by all means be frugal and thrifty if it seems good to you, but there are other places to economize that don't harm our beggars. For example, you might want to reconsider your plans to have the hall frescoed. I know it's the fashion, but it isn't necessary, and it will be quite expensive."

Her sullen expression told me what I had suspected: she hadn't intended to talk to me about that plan until it was too far along for me to stop it.

I almost felt sorry for the girl; she underestimated me so consistently. Almost.

"Also," I went on, "you might think about whether you really need two maids who do nothing but dress you and sit and sew." *And giggle with you, and poke fun at Nuta and Sabina, and probably at Prassede and me too, though I haven't actually overheard that part yet.*

She flushed. "I need Lena and Becchina. They help me run this house so you can pray and embroider and do all the things you want to do, and your women can chase after those children of theirs."

Sabina's daughter, Casta, was nine now, a sweet-natured child who sang as easily as most people breathed. And Nuta and Gualtiero's little Ginevra was a shy seven-year-old who worshiped Casta, so the two of them were usually together, and they required very little chasing after.

As for "praying and embroidering," I also managed a business empire and a number of charitable activities. But I wouldn't expect Saracena to notice any of that. And as for running the house, that house included a kitchen, and without Prassede and the help she received from Nuta and Sabina, none of us would eat. I wouldn't want to have to count on Lena and Becchina for a decent dinner.

"Fine. You have your maids, and if you must go ahead with the frescoes, then of course you may, though it will be your husband's funds you're spending and not mine. But when I entrust you with money to hand to the beggars, you give it to them. Is that clear?"

A pause, then "Yes, Mother Giacoma."

I didn't want to leave things this unpleasant, so I changed the subject. "How are you feeling now? Are you past the nausea yet?"

Maybe it was pregnancy that was making her so difficult. She could be personable, and my son was smitten with her. Although that might have had something to do with her impressive bosom, which she dressed to show off. It would probably become even more formidable as she progressed through her pregnancy.

"I was only thinking of my husband, you know," she said instead of answering me. "Sometimes it almost looks like you're giving away his rightful inheritance. I don't think his father would have wanted that, do you?"

"I'll decide about that," I told her curtly. *No, my girl, you do not talk to me about Graziano.* "Giving alms is for the good of Giovanni's soul and yours, as well as mine. The church requires no less of us." Even as I said it, it sounded inadequate to my ears. I had never thought of feeding beggars as an investment in getting us into heaven. I fed them because they hungered.

"As you say, Mother Giacoma," she murmured. "And you kindly asked about the nausea. It still troubles me, and when I do have a craving for a certain food and I think I might be able to eat it, your women often don't have it for me. Sister Prassede has been here all day, and she knows I want some sugared almonds, but she hasn't made any yet. Could you talk to her, please?"

"Sister Prassede was nursing the sick yesterday at the women's hospital. She lost a patient she thought she might save, and it hit her hard. You are not to trouble her today. If you require sugared almonds, send your women out to buy you some."

She curtsied and left. I thought I heard her mutter "Prassede's are better" as she went.

All in all, I didn't think the role of mother-in-law was a good fit for me. I had tried to give Saracena as much responsibility for the household as she wanted, but the results were unsatisfactory. Still, I needed to find a way to get along with her. If all that took was money, perhaps I could be more generous.

I resolved, not for the first time, to stay out of her way as much as possible. The palazzo was big enough for our lives to remain separate for the most part, and I was sure she wanted it that way as much as I did. Perhaps when Uccel married he would choose a woman who was a better fit with our family.

I went upstairs and tapped on the door to Prassede's chamber.

"It's Giacoma, Prassede," I called. "May I come in?"

The door opened, and Prassede blinked at me, her eyes red and teary. I followed her into the small chamber and sat with her on the long chest at the foot of her bed. I took her hand and squeezed it.

"You did everything for Tosa that anyone could have done."

The mention of her patient's name made Prassede tear up again, and she sniffed into a handkerchief. "I know, but it's so difficult when someone is that young," she said, her voice muffled by the cloth. "All she wanted was to live long enough to have her baby."

"You kept her comfortable, and you prayed with her, and you brought her a priest in plenty of time, and you made sure her husband and her little boy got the help they needed."

"You did that last one, Giacoma," she pointed out, wadding up the cloth and setting it aside.

"Only because you let me know about their situation. We'll have masses said for Tosa's soul, and we'll do whatever we can for her widower and her child. It's all we can do now, except for praying for her ourselves."

"Yes. But it still makes me sad."

We sat in silence for a little while, then I judged it was time to broach the subject I had come to talk about.

"Prassy, Cardinal Ugolino will be visiting this afternoon, and he'll have news of Francesco and the brothers." She looked up with interest. "Would you like to join us?"

She brightened. "Oh, yes! Thank you, Giacoma. I've been eager to know how Father Francesco is doing. It's been so hard to get news of him."

That was true. At times I felt I could not wait another minute to know how he fared, and I wanted to jump on my mare and go flying to him on my own. Hardly a practical thought, but the temptation was there.

"The cardinal has seen him recently. Whatever he tells us will at least be reasonably current."

"Do we even know where Father Francesco is, these days?"

I shrugged. He was too sick to walk, too sick even to ride most of the time, yet I couldn't keep up with where he was. It was exasperating.

He had been here, there, hither and yon—in Rieti for the dreaded medical treatment, at a hermitage, in Bishop Guido's palazzo in Assisi, in half a dozen nearby villages. What little news we did get was confusing. He was cantankerous, refusing food and medicine, yet he eagerly gave away each tunic the brothers provided for him to the next poor person he saw, and they had to scramble to beg another, or he would have gone naked. He was anguished about the state of his order, yet people everywhere were crediting him with miracles, especially healings.

If only he could somehow heal himself. But his condition had deteriorated to the point where no one still expected him to get well. Elias's dream had said two years, and we were getting alarmingly close to that. I could barely imagine what it would be like to lose him, but I pushed that thought away for now.

Prassede and I went down to the kitchen to find some refreshments to serve the cardinal, who should be joining us within the hour. Maybe while we were there we could sugar some almonds for my daughter-in-law.

*

"But where is he now?" I asked Ugolino, interrupting. He had started to summarize Francesco's astonishing travels for me, but I didn't need to hear it.

"He's back in Assisi, though that wasn't the brothers' idea. The citizens of Assisi were afraid he would die somewhere else and his relics would wind up there instead of here. Somewhere like Perugia. So they sent a delegation of knights to escort Francesco back home."

I nearly wept, first at the thought of Francesco's imminent death, then at the pain and exhaustion so much travel must have caused him, then at the idea of his body seized by the hostile Perugians. It would have been a coup for them. After his death, even before he was officially made a saint, his relics would draw crowds of pilgrims and their coins to whatever city held them. My beloved friend had become a commodity.

"How did he bear that awful treatment with the hot poker?" Prassede asked. Her voice trembled, even though the ordeal had been months earlier.

"Gallantly. Bravely. I wasn't there when it happened, but Brothers Leone and Rufino and Bernardo and several others were, and in the end they fled the room before the doctor began. They couldn't watch."

"I cannot believe Elias would flee," I said.

"He wasn't there. He was busy elsewhere with his duties as vicar, and they decided to go ahead without him. Perhaps Elias would have found the courage to stay, but the brothers who were there couldn't stand to see it. Yet the doctor told me later that Francesco simply made his petition, asking Brother Fire to be courtly to him so he might bear it, and told the doctor to proceed. He did not cry out, and he never complained, even as the doctor seared his temples and both sides of his face."

How like Francesco. If only the treatment had worked, perhaps it would have been worth the fear and the pain and all the suffering afterwards. Unable to eat, he was losing strength daily. He constantly complained of cold, even in the ferocious heat of midsummer. No wonder the brothers wearied of him constantly giving away his clothes.

"He has refused all further treatments." Ugolino's face was haggard. "If we had anything available that might help, Elias and I would argue with him, and as vicar, Elias could even put him under an obedience. But no doctor has been able to suggest anything."

316

"Where is Elias now?" I offered the cardinal the almonds and he took one.

"With Francesco. Word reached him that Francesco had been vomiting blood, so he left the order's business unfinished and rode to him immediately. He has been helping Francesco to compose his final testament."

Prassede made a strangled little sound.

"Are they at the Porziuncola?"

"No, they're back in Bishop Guido's palazzo. The bishop is traveling, but he sent word that they were welcome to stay as long as they wanted. He also gave orders for an armed guard to be posted outside the door at all times."

Assisi was protecting its property.

"How much time does he have left, your lordship?" I had to ask.

"Do you know about Elias's dream?"

"Yes."

He sighed. "I think it's a true one. Not much longer, I suspect."

It hurt to hear that, though I knew it was true. Twenty years had passed since I first saw Francesco, dressed like a peacock and enthusiastically flinging coins at San Pietro's tomb. It was hard to think of a world without him.

"He will go to glory and dwell with the other saints in heaven," Prassede said. She had that ecstatic expression on her face again. I tried not to let it annoy me. Acceptance always came so much more easily to Prassede than it did to me.

The cardinal's eyes met mine. We were just two people who would much rather have our beloved friend here on earth with us than dwelling with the other saints. But nobody was asking us to decide.

"He has written another verse to his Canticle," the cardinal said.

"Has he? Would you sing it for us, my lord?"

"I don't think you're going to like it, my lady. I didn't, at least not at first."

"Then perhaps I need to hear it, if you would be so kind."

Ugolino cleared his throat and after a false start or two, he sang the verse for us. He could barely carry a tune, but I knew what it should sound like.

These were the words he sang:

"Be praised, my Lord, for Sister Death,

from whom no living man can escape:

317

woe to those who die in mortal sin;
blessed those who she finds in your most holy will,
for the second death will not harm them.
Praise and bless my Lord and give him thanks,
and serve him with great humility."

He was right. I didn't like them.

44

MECHANICALLY I prepared to travel. Everything was nearly ready. I had laid in a stock of good wax candles, fine and white and delicately scented of honey. Incense, too, in a sufficient quantity to honor my friend, for it would be hard to obtain enough in Assisi. I would bring the cover I had made so long ago for his pillow, and some embroidered cloths, a few towels, and a small casket with all the ingredients for almond cakes. I had already pulverized the almonds, and I added some good honey, small cloth bags of spices, a lidded pot, and a jar of oil from our Marino estate. All I would need when I got there was a fire. Amata had taught me not to prepare the cakes too far ahead of time lest they go stale, and I wanted these to be perfect.

Thinking of Amata, I crossed myself and said a silent prayer. We had lost her to what Prassede called the "sugar sickness" almost a year ago, and it was still hard to believe she was gone. Massimo was desolate.

Gualtiero and several of his men were on alert that I would need them as an escort soon. Messages had been sent to towns on the way to arrange accommodations, though I planned to make the trip as efficiently as possible and not linger. Giovanni was going with me, over Saracena's protestations. However much she insisted she needed him with her during her pregnancy, Giovanni was not going to lose an opportunity to see Francesco. Besides, the baby would not come for months yet. Uccel unfortunately was ill again. We would have to leave him behind, though he too wanted to see Francesco.

Prassede wanted to come too, but she wouldn't be able to keep up with us on a fast-paced ride. I was traveling light and lean this time. Lucia was coming, since I did need at least one other woman on the trip for propriety. Not that I cared much for that, but she had persuaded me.

The other important thing we were bringing was the cloth for Francesco's burial tunic. Lotario had died in Marino over the summer, but we had many years' accumulation of his wool. We sent it out to be combed, spun, and woven, and it came back to us as a length of coarse ash-gray cloth, sturdy but not particularly pretty, like Lotario himself, but cleaner and better smelling. I kept half a braccia of it to remember my woolly pet by, not that I was ever likely to forget him.

All was ready. My intention was to leave in a week, or sooner if I received word from Elias that the time was close. Yet I worried—what if things shifted suddenly, and there was no time to get the news to me?

Should we go ahead now, and wait close at hand rather than so far away? Giovanni wanted to take the rest of the week to make the rounds of our properties outside Rome before the cold weather set in, and I had agreed, but I was unsure.

So I prayed. I knelt on the cold stone floor in our chapel and prayed to Our Lady and her son, and said my paternosters, and contemplated the wooden crucifix that hung above the altar. Should I wait, or should I go? I needed an answer.

As usual, what I got was silence. I offered a few more prayers, and then, on impulse, I sang Francesco's Canticle. Even the new verse, which I still hated.

I was about to get up and leave, and the last note of the song was still echoing in the chapel in my not-high and not-low voice, when I heard another voice echo all around me.

"Giacoma, it is time. You must go."

I had heard that voice before. Was it the voice of God, or the voice of Francesco, or the voice of God sounding like Francesco to make sure I would listen? Whoever it was, I would obey. I would, in fact, give thanks and serve him with all the humility I could muster, as Francesco's Canticle counseled. Whichever one of them it was.

I waited a few seconds to see if more would follow, but it did not. I murmured my prayer of thanks and scrambled to my feet. It was late afternoon, so tomorrow was the earliest we could leave, but we were going to be on our way at dawn. I hurried to spread the word.

*

The resulting preparations lasted well into the evening. Giovanni canceled his estate visits without complaint, though Saracena's protests about his upcoming absence were becoming more and more frantic. She worried about bandits, wolves, and other dangers of the road, and while all of those were completely legitimate fears, I began to think it was her pregnancy that was making her so hysterical. The girl had a voice like a trumpet when she was upset, so I overheard her complaints as I passed by their closed chamber door on my way to fetch the cushion cover.

"Vanni, what if something happens to you? What will I do? What will happen to our child?"

Giovanni murmured something inaudible, probably trying to reassure her.

"Your mother hates me! She would let us stay, yes, because it would look terrible if she didn't, but she doesn't want me in this house. You're the heir here—this house should be yours, not hers."

A sharp retort from Giovanni, her noisy sobbing, and another soothing murmur from my son.

I walked on past, shaken. I had never meant for my impatience with Saracena to become so obvious, or for her to feel unwelcome. She was my son's wife, soon to be the mother of my grandchild, and I didn't want to put Giovanni in the position of having to choose between us.

And maybe she was right. I didn't need this palazzo. I didn't even really want it any more. I owned plenty of more modest properties in Rome, and any one of them would be enough for my needs. Maybe it was time to give over the palazzo to Saracena and let her decorate with frescoes and fripperies to her heart's content. I had neglected the place in recent years; she could put her considerable energy into restoring it. I could leave it all to the next generation and go somewhere simple, somewhere quiet. Maybe nearby, maybe in another part of the city.

Maybe in Assisi.

That thought roiled around in my head as I rummaged through the trunk looking for the cushion cover. It was almost enough to distract me from thinking about the somber purpose of our trip—almost.

I had just put my hand on the embroidered fabric I sought when Giovanni poked his head in.

"There you are. Everything's packed, Mother. We can leave first thing in the morning."

"Good. I'm eager for us to be on our way."

"So am I." He shook his head. "As a matter of fact, if we could leave tonight, I'd do it. That woman is going to drive me mad."

I almost told him he was about to become the owner of the palazzo, but there would be plenty of time for that as we rode. For now, I would do what I could to smooth things between my son and his anxious wife, since apparently I was the cause of her anxiety, or at least some of it. Her husband was about to travel, and no woman approaches childbirth completely free of fear.

"Son, you'll be a father soon," I reminded him, as gently as I could. "Saracena has been a loving wife, and she naturally fears for you. Be kind to her."

His face brightened at my mention of the child. "Do you think the baby will be a boy? Becchina says it will, because when Saracena walks, she always starts with her right foot. Was it so with you before I was born, and Uccel?"

I hid my smile. "I would say that in my considered opinion, there is a good chance Saracena's child is a boy." About a fifty percent chance, in fact. I didn't have much faith in women's predictions of such things. It was all too easy to celebrate accurate results and ignore those that turned out to be wrong.

"But did you start walking on your right foot?" he persisted.

"I don't know. Probably. But whatever the child is, it's a Frangipane, it's yours, and there will doubtless be many more of both sexes." Instinctively I fingered the keys on my belt, touching iron to make sure my words did not tempt fate.

He beamed. "Yes, Saracena is well made for childbearing."

"We shall see. Danger is always present when a woman brings a child to the light, but Saracena is strong and young, and we will support her with our prayers."

"And find her a midwife who's not as mean and bitter as Sister Donata," he added, grinning.

"That shouldn't be hard. But now, we have a trip to think about. Will you check the horses and make sure all is ready, before you go to bed?"

"Yes, Mother," he said, and we went our separate ways. I was glad he would be with me. He would be a comfort on this difficult journey.

That night, later when all was finally done, I knelt again in the chapel and asked God to kindly keep any pesky brigands out of our way, for I wanted to blaze on through to Assisi with as few stops as possible, and I had no patience for any unnecessary encounters. Fair travel weather would also be welcome. I would provide the fast horses and capable bodyguards.

I intended to reach Francesco while he still lived.

October 1226, Assisi

45

My party was almost within sight of the gate. We rode along a winding path through the trees, which were showing the beginnings of autumn color but had not yet shed many of their leaves. We had made the journey with practiced efficiency, but this time it seemed to take forever.

I had never been to the Porziuncola before. Near it, yes, but never beyond the gate. Or even past the rope stretched across the path, tied to trees on either side, which had been the extent of the brothers' security in the early days. Then, when I stood on the path, I had looked beyond the barrier to the almost random scattering of crude huts surrounding the tiny chapel. Behind them was the infirmary, a structure only slightly larger and sturdier than the flimsy huts, and behind that was a trench latrine, not visible from the path but making its presence known nonetheless.

No woman could set foot inside the complex, and no brother was ever turned away. This raised the question of what they would do about Brother Giacoma. But for me there was only one possible answer: Francesco was in that infirmary, and that's where I was going.

Giovanni rode close at my side, Lucia and the rest of our escort following us in single file. I didn't know who would greet us at the gate, but I was prepared to argue, cajole, yell for Elias, or claim God's own safe-conduct—whatever it took to get in. A friendly face, someone who knew me, would help. Explaining myself to one of the newer brothers would waste time I could ill afford.

I prayed as I rode: *Please let this part be easy.*

We passed a landmark, a huge dead tree split by lightning. The Porziuncola, Francesco's beloved "little portion," was just around the next bend.

And there it was, with two brothers guarding the gate. A few more paces, and if they were men I knew, I would recognize them.

To my relief, I did know them. Even better, they were Lapo and Feo, and they both stared at me in openmouthed amazement as I approached. I hoped that wasn't a bad sign, but it made my stomach clench with fear. Were they amazed that I was here at all, or dreading to tell me I had come too late?

I pulled up and dismounted, and they came to meet me.

"Does he still live?" I asked, my voice shaky.

Lapo nodded.

"Giacoma, how are you come already?" Feo sounded perplexed. "The messenger hasn't even left yet."

"What messenger? What are you talking about?"

Lapo put a hand on my arm. "Father Francesco just dictated a letter to you. We all heard him. He told you to come quickly, if you wanted to find him alive, and to bring certain things with you. Brother Bernardo and one other were to take it to you straightaway, and they even had permission to ride, so they could reach you sooner."

Ah. Then the voice had probably been Francesco. "Well, I'm here now, and I want to see him."

Lapo and Feo looked at each other.

"He invited her," Lapo said. "You heard him dictate the letter."

"I know, but..."

"He wouldn't have said that part about finding him alive if he didn't want her to come in. He can't go out to her, after all."

"Yes, but shouldn't we check with Brother Elias? What about the rules?"

I could feel my impatience rapidly growing unmanageable. I was Brother Giacoma. I took that role as seriously as any man who dwelt at the Porziuncola. I had the right to see Francesco, and I would not be kept away from him by my sex, which forced me to work so much harder at being a brother than the men did.

I turned to Lapo. "Well?" If I sounded a bit imperious, he was just going to have to forgive me.

"Wait, Giacoma." Lapo turned to Feo. "Brother Elias said to bring her in, Feo. Go and get Bernardo and the letter, if you're not sure."

Feo turned and walked rapidly toward the infirmary.

"He worries about doing things right," Lapo said with an apologetic shrug. "It won't take long. And I'm afraid only you will be able to come in. It's just brothers now, until it's over, so the others can't come in with you. I'm sorry."

"It's all right, Lapo. I didn't expect everyone to be admitted." *Just as well I didn't have Prassede with me. It would have crushed her to be turned away.* I turned to Giovanni, now in charge of the party with Gualtiero as his reliable deputy. "Go, son, to my house in Assisi and see if there's room there for Lucia." I had purchased the little house near Santo Stefano, but two indigent families were currently living there while I was based in Rome. No point in leaving it vacant while people needed shelter.

"Mengarda should have received my message sometime last week," I went on. "She knows to expect us at any time, and she will have worked out lodging arrangements for the rest of you. I will send you word as soon as I know anything. But before you go, let's unload the candles and cloth and incense, and the casket with the almonds and the other ingredients. Lapo, could you help?"

But Lapo was again staring wordlessly. What had I done now? What had I just said?

I began to have a suspicion. "What are the things Francesco wanted me to bring?"

"Gray cloth," Lapo said slowly. "And candles. And almond cakes. But he didn't mention the incense." Lapo was always a stickler for detail.

Well, good. At least I had thought of one thing Francesco hadn't already considered. Or maybe he thought incense for his funeral would be too much of a luxury.

Gualtiero, Lapo, and Giovanni unloaded the two packhorses and Lapo went to get some brothers to help carry our gifts inside. I said my farewells to my son and the others. The party awkwardly reversed itself on the narrow path and started toward Assisi, the last bodyguard in line leading my mare and the two unburdened packhorses.

As I watched them go, Lapo returned, with Feo and Bernardo. Wordlessly, Bernardo handed me Francesco's letter. My hands trembled as I unfolded it and began to read.

To monna Giacoma, God's servant, Brother Francesco, Christ's beggar, sends his greetings and fellowship with the Holy Spirit of Our Lord Jesus Christ. Know, well beloved, that Christ has, of his grace, revealed to me that my life's end is at hand. Therefore, if you would find me alive. . .

I turned to Bernardo. "Would you take me to him now?"

*

Later that afternoon I watched Francesco as he slept. He had greeted me joyfully, but even those few moments of animation had been enough to drain what little strength remained to him. He lay on his side on the grubby pallet, under a thin blanket. The skin on his face was stretched

325

taut over the bones of his skull, and the contorted position of his legs looked painful. He stirred restlessly, as if he could not find a comfortable position. One bandaged hand was thrust out from under the covering, and his feet, enclosed in cloth slippers, stuck out at the end of the pallet. But his dear head rested on the pillow I had brought him at San Damiano.

Elias sat on a stool next to Francesco, and Rufino and Bernardo moved quietly around the infirmary, their bare feet soundless on the dirt floor. Francesco was the only patient. A single window covered with cloth admitted a little dim light, but most of the room was in shadow. Elias was sorting a pile of rags, pulling some out to launder. Bernardo crushed herbs in a mortar, occasionally adding a drop or two of oil from a small bottle. Rufino took Francesco's urine flask out to empty it, and Leone arrived with a bucket of spring water and set it down just inside the door.

The brothers had hailed my visit as a miracle. Elias told me Francesco had given instructions for me to be admitted as soon as I arrived. "The cloister rules do not apply to Brother Giacoma," he had said, but that very specific message had not reached poor Feo, who had just returned from an errand in town.

Though he expected me, Francesco had appeared mildly surprised to see me at the infirmary door before the seal had hardened on his letter. When I explained about the voice I had heard while I prayed, he laughed. "You see, Giacoma, you did get my message, only not quite the way we expected."

Now he rested. Elias, his sorting finished, stood and shooed me out temporarily so he could replace Francesco's bandages, and I took the opportunity to go explore the Porziuncola.

There wasn't much to see, though I greeted several brothers I knew well. Their huts were even tinier and shabbier than they appeared from a distance. The cookfire was in front of a lean-to, so I directed Lapo to put my almonds and other foodstuffs under the meager shelter. I needed to make my almond cakes soon, before the mice and rats made off with my supplies. The chapel was spotless, dark, and peaceful, though bare of any ornamentation whatsoever.

I even made use of the latrine, with Feo standing by to guard my privacy, and then I briefly considered fasting and abstaining from water, to minimize the need to repeat that experience. But if the other brothers could put up with it, so could I.

I felt humbled. For many years I had thought of myself as living simply, because I had stopped wearing elaborate clothing and adding fashionable touches to my palazzo. But apparently I had not understood what living simply really meant. Even my sturdy little house in Assisi was luxurious compared to this, with its well-equipped kitchen and the closestool in my chamber and two comfortable beds with thick, soft mattresses supported by rope netting and outfitted with sheets and pillows. I so wished I could nurse Francesco in my home and give him ease. But he was determined to die at the Porziuncola and be buried there.

When I returned to the infirmary and tapped lightly on the door, Elias opened it. He motioned me in and quickly closed the door behind me, shutting out the light that so pained Francesco's eyes. Care, grief, and exhaustion etched Elias's still-handsome face. The only brother who was not barefoot except for Francesco himself, he wore his Oriental slippers and his cap. Lapo had told me Elias seldom left Francesco's side. I wished I knew of some way to help him bear his burdens, though I struggled with my own responsibilities and my own dread of losing Francesco.

Francesco had awakened. He was in a cheerful mood, though very weak. Even with his eyes covered, he knew it was me.

"Are there almond cakes, then, Giacoma?" he asked.

"Not yet. I'll make them soon, but I wanted to see you first." I sat on the dirt floor next to him, though I knew he wasn't strong enough to talk much. Being with him at last was a balm.

"My brother," Elias said, "I have letters I must write, now that Giacoma is here to stay with you for a while. May I go and discharge this duty, so I can return to your side soon?"

"Go, brother. I thank you for your care for me, and for your diligence on behalf of the brotherhood. I will be fine," Francesco assured him, and Elias left.

I was alone with Francesco, except for Rufino, who sat on the floor in the far corner, nodding drowsily. None of the brothers closest to Francesco had enjoyed an uninterrupted night's sleep for many days.

Francesco lay on his back and asked me about my household: my boys, Prassede, Lucia, and all the others. It pleased him to learn that Giovanni and Lucia had come with me, and he offered his apologies for not welcoming at least Giovanni to the Porziuncola.

"Elias has decreed that only brothers may enter now, and I think he is right. This is a time to share among ourselves, and I am no longer strong enough to give outsiders what they want from me, even if they are dear friends." Even that much speaking exhausted him, and he grew quiet, his breathing ragged.

Everyone, brothers included, always wanted so much from him, I reflected. Had we drained him of his strength? Were we the reason he lay dying? Yet men die of many causes. No one escapes death, even a saint. And if his Canticle truly expressed his thoughts, this saint of ours had no desire to escape.

I remembered Elias's prophetic dream, and the prediction of one of Francesco's doctors, Bongiovanni of Arezzo, whom Francesco playfully insisted on calling simply Giovanni, since "no one is good save God."

Bongiovanni had bowed to Francesco's demands to know the truth about his illness. "Your disease cannot be cured," he had said, "and I believe you will die between the end of September and the fourth day before the Nones of October."

The fourth day before the Nones of October. Tomorrow.

We sat in silence in the gathering darkness. I thought Francesco slept, and Rufino snored gently in his corner. A mouse emerged from a pool of darkness and skittered to the middle of the room, where I could barely see it twitching its nose. I made a face and flapped my hands at it, to warn it away from Francesco.

A sudden movement from the pallet startled me. Francesco pulled himself almost to a sitting position and yanked the cloth from his swollen eyes, which were fixed on the door of the room. I followed his gaze but saw nothing. What did he perceive there? More mice? I turned back to him, about to ask him, but he spoke first.

"Giacoma, do you see her?" He raised his arm and pointed with his bandaged hand at the door.

My vision blurred momentarily, and for a fleeting instant I thought I saw a woman standing in the open doorway, gaunt and pale and clothed in dark shreds of rotting fabric. I smelled earth, and darkness, and worms.

I gasped and turned to Francesco, whose rapt attention was fixed on the door. I looked back almost immediately, but she was gone, and the door was closed. There had been no sound of it closing.

Francesco sank down on his pallet, resting his sweating head on the pillow. He was beaming.

"Was she not beautiful, Giacoma? The next time she comes, I think she will take me with her."

No. She is not beautiful. She is hideous, and evil, and avaricious. She wants my Francesco, and I don't know how to protect him from her.

When I didn't answer him, Francesco placed his hand on mine. His bandage was rough and scratchy.

"One day she will come for you, too, Giacoma. When she does, she will take you to your Graziano, and then you will find her beautiful."

To Graziano. I sat back, stunned. Yes, if that was her mission, I would find her lovely indeed, and I would welcome the earth and the darkness. I began to understand, a little. Francesco was ready.

He couldn't contain his exhilaration. "Rufino! Wake up!" he called, and Rufino, who had been sleeping deeply, jerked awake. "Bring me more brothers! I want to hear our Canticle." Francesco pulled the cloth shield back over his eyes, and Rufino stood up groggily. He stumbled to the door and flung it open.

"Brothers, let us sing for Father Francesco," he called, and soon we were joined by Bernardo, Leone, Elias, and several others. They began to sing, and it was clearly something they did often, for Elias made only a tiny hand signal, yet they all began together, on the same note.

I remained silent at first, but Elias motioned for me to join them, so I did. I lent my voice to the verses about Brother Sun, Sister Moon and the stars, Brother Wind, Sister Water, Brother Fire, Mother Earth, and those who pardoned for God's love, my mind roiling all the while with what I had seen, but when we came to the new verse, the one about Sister Death, I fell silent. I could not give my voice to Sister Death. Not yet. Francesco may have been ready, but I was not.

The brothers finished the song. Francesco gave a sigh of contentment, thanked us, and announced that he would sleep for a little while. Bernardo offered to stay with him, and the rest of us filed out. As I stepped over the threshold I thought I caught a faint whiff of damp earth.

46

ELIAS joined me in the lean-to as I crouched next to the fire, prodding my lidded pot into the embers so the almond cakes could bake evenly. He sat down heavily on a rock.

"It won't be long now, Giacoma."

"No."

"Will you stay?"

"Of course. That's why I'm here. But what will happen when... what will happen next?"

"The entire city is waiting for Francesco to be born into sainthood. The people will come, and they will walk with us to take his body into Assisi. The podestà will provide an honor guard, well armed, and the city's standard bearers, and we'll supply the populace with olive branches. When we reach the city, all the bells will sound in Francesco's honor. We will carry him to San Giorgio, where I have a stone sarcophagus waiting for him."

"San Giorgio? I thought he wanted to be buried here at the Porziuncola."

Elias shook his head. "Not safe. If the Perugians decide to come after his relics, they will send soldiers. We brothers could not stop them. He'll be safer in town, in San Giorgio. The city has promised to provide armed guards for his tomb."

Francesco had once said to Bishop Guido, in defense of his beloved poverty, "If we have possessions, we will need arms to protect them." Now he himself was Assisi's possession.

I must have looked dubious, because Elias tried to reassure me.

"His burial in San Giorgio is only temporary, Giacoma."

"Oh, you mean he'll be reinterred here later? When it's safe?"

"No." Elias's face had a peculiar expression, one I had never seen before. It was almost like Prassede's religious ecstasy face, but with a kind of steely determination behind it.

"Where, then?"

"There will be a new church. In Assisi. I've talked to the cardinal about this many times, and we are in agreement. We will build it, he and I. It will be the greatest church in Christendom, with two levels and a vast worship space where all can stand together, with no divisions between high and low. Pilgrims will come from everywhere to revere Francesco's relics. And all of it will celebrate our brother. It will be a wonder, Giacoma. We will begin it immediately, and once the Holy Father canonizes Francesco officially, his relics can be translated to the new church. The cardinal says canonization won't take long—one year, two, three at the most. Already Francesco works miracles while he still lives."

"Does he know?" I doubted that Francesco would find this picture appealing.

"He's too sick. I don't want to upset him now. He will have his wish to die at the Porziuncola, but we must keep his relics safe. That's our responsibility. And when we have a wonderful new church dedicated to Francesco, that is where his relics must lie. He would certainly agree with that. Will you help us build it, Giacoma?"

"I don't want to talk about that now." Francesco wasn't relics yet—he was a living, breathing man, whom I loved.

Elias drew back. "Very well. Not now, then. We'll speak of it later."

Such an undertaking would require an enormous amount of money, and if both Elias and the cardinal were determined to go ahead with it, I knew I could not avoid making my contribution. But for now, I wanted to concentrate on the living Francesco and his imminent passage to heaven, so I murmured something noncommittal and poked at my pot with a stick, scattering the embers on top and dislodging the lid so I could see and smell the baking almond cakes.

*

Francesco did eat part of one. He nibbled at it with evident pleasure and then gave the rest to Bernardo, who had always been fond of those cakes. Reverently Bernardo took a small bite, and then he slipped the rest into his sleeve.

It grew late. I was sure Francesco needed to rest, but when the others got up to leave him to his sleep, he asked me to stay behind. The rest of the brothers filed out, murmuring "God give you peace," except for Leone, whose turn it was to stay with Francesco through the night.

After the others left, Francesco spoke to Leone. "My brother, I must speak with Giacoma alone. Please leave us for a little while, and I will send Giacoma to fetch you soon."

Leone looked surprised, but he got up to leave. "You'll find me in the chapel," he told me as he left.

I sat close to Francesco's pallet. Tears stung my eyes. His sunken cheeks told me this would be the last time we two would speak alone, and that certainty nearly overwhelmed me.

He lay on his back, and his breathing sounded labored.

All the myriad things and people I had wanted to talk to him about—Saracena, Lapo, Ricco, Salvestra and Renzo, the Frangipani's alliances with the emperor, Sabina's loathing of all men, my perennial fears for Uccel's health, my concerns for my future grandchild—all these thoughts fled from my mind and I waited, empty, to learn why he had wanted this time with me.

Finally he spoke. "Will you do something for me, Giacoma?"

Anything, Francesco. Whatever you want, now and always. Only please don't die. "Yes."

"I need you to help Elias."

That was not what I had expected to hear. Elias had never seemed to need any help from anyone. "Help him in what way?"

Francesco's voice had an undercurrent of sadness. "He has challenging times ahead. God has permitted me to see some of what will come, and I fear Elias's path will soon become very difficult."

"I don't understand. What will happen to him?"

"Most of what will happen to him will be his own doing. And yet I love him well, and the order needs him, even though many of our brothers will decide they don't."

"He loves you too, Francesco, and he would never knowingly do anything against your wishes." *Except bury you in the wrong place and build you an elaborate church that you don't want.*

Francesco shook his head, weakly. "Giacoma, I don't have enough strength left to tell you more. I need him to do exactly what he's doing, what he does best. Yet I fear the demands of the order will cost him dearly. I can only pray they do not cost him his soul."

I was speechless. I had never heard Francesco speak of a beloved brother in this way before.

"I have asked much of him, perhaps too much. Giacomina, I have made so many mistakes. If the brothers understood them all, they would never forgive me." His expression was downcast. "It is only because God can forgive anything that I have any hope at all."

I had to ask. "Was Giannuccio one of your mistakes, Francesco?" No word had ever come to us of our vanished brother.

He nodded, and a look of such pain crossed his face that I hastily changed the subject back to Elias.

"Do you mean the brothers will not support Elias?"

"Many of them will not. They won't understand his decisions or his actions, and they will try to make him into a Judas. Elias may not fully understand it all himself. So what I want you to do is what *you* do best—

help him. Support him. Don't turn your back on him, no matter what happens or what he does. Don't give up on him. Love him, Giacoma. He will need you." He reached out his bandaged hand and I took it gently.

"Francesco, I will never turn my back on Elias. No matter what happens. You have my word." *What had Francesco seen?*

He nodded, satisfied. "Go now and get Leone. Have him show you where you will sleep, and then he can come back to stay with me. God give you peace."

I wasn't ready to leave him yet.

"Francesco, how can I help Elias?" I had no idea how to even start.

"Just love him, Giacoma. That's all you can do. Do it for me," he said. "Go now."

*

That night I slept in a hut. No one would tell me who had vacated his cell so I could have a place to sleep, and since the brothers had nothing of their own, I couldn't guess from the hut's furnishings—a thin pallet, a threadbare blanket, a gray hood hanging on a nail. I lay awake for hours. When I finally dozed, I dreamed of Elias, but I gained no clarity from it.

I woke stiff and cold from sleeping almost on the ground, and I knew right away that this day would change my life. I had slept in my clothing, for the blanket was thin, almost transparent. I prepared myself to brave the latrine, but then I noticed that some kind brother had left me a chamberpot from the infirmary, so I was quickly ready to seek out Francesco.

He was worse. Pain pinched his features as Elias and Leone gently rubbed his arms and legs with a salve that smelled sharply of nettles. Rufino stood watching, idle for once, anguish vying with exhaustion on his thin face.

Francesco murmured something to Elias, and Elias turned to Rufino.

"Summon the brothers," was all he said, and Rufino left without a word.

The rest of that nightmarish, blessed, hideous, beautiful day blurs together in my memory. Francesco suffering, singing, weakening, praying, whimpering, laughing. Dying. The brothers kneeling around him as he touched each one's head and blessed him. Tears flowing unchecked, unnoticed, as if all of us wanted to keep company with Francesco's streaming eyes.

Francesco insisting that the brothers wrap him in sackcloth and lay him on the ground, then sprinkle him with ashes and leave him there at least long enough for Bernardo to read the story of the Passion from Saint John's gospel, for he wanted to die in poverty, owning nothing, not even his tunic. Elias and Leone, the only two brothers allowed the intimate care of Francesco's body, stepped forward to obey him, shielding him from our view with their bodies as best they could. But in that moment of nakedness, stripped of his tunic and not yet covered in the rough, punishing cloth, Francesco raised his arms to assist them, and I glimpsed what appeared to be an open wound in his side.

What was that? I had not heard of any injury happening to Francesco. It didn't look like a bedsore, nor was it in a place where it was likely to be one. His pale skin stretched tautly across his ribs. He seemed almost bloodless, yet the bright drops were there. I was not imagining it.

Quickly Elias covered him. He and Leone secured the sackcloth around Francesco with a rope belt and together they lowered him carefully to the cold ground. Rufino came forward with a handful of ashes scooped from the seldom-used brazier and wept as he scattered them over the length of Francesco's shrunken body.

Bernardo began to read the gospel aloud, his voice flat and expressionless. As he read, Elias looked around at the brothers. *He wants to know if anyone saw the wound.* His eyes met mine and held them; he knew.

Apparently no one else had noticed, or perhaps everyone but me already knew of it. What could have caused such a wound?

As I listened to the words of the gospel, a strange thought pushed its way to the surface. *Impossible. It cannot be.*

Francesco's hands and feet were still bandaged. *Why? Why are they bandaged? No one ever told me.* The errant thought persisted, grew stronger.

Bernardo finished his reading, and Elias and Leone hurried to help Francesco up from that chill floor and back onto his pallet. Again shielding his body, they pulled off the sackcloth and started to dress him, though Elias had to command him under obedience to accept the clothing. This time it was a new garment, sewn overnight by some devoted brother out of the cloth made from Lotario's wool. I hadn't seen it before, folded on a stool, but I recognized the rough cloth. It couldn't have been much easier on his fragile skin than the sackcloth, but at least it was clean.

This time, in spite of Elias's and Leone's attempts at subtlety, I was sure that when Francesco raised his stick-thin arms for Elias to guide them into the sleeves, I saw the wound. I watched Elias closely, and he carefully avoided touching the area.

This time I was the one who surreptitiously looked around me to see who else had noticed. Perhaps two dozen brothers were packed into the small room. Elias and Leone, supporting Francesco's body, must have been aware of the drops of blood. Several brothers had their eyes closed as they prayed; others watched the scene through their tears, and Rufino had turned away, as if he could look no longer. But Bernardo was watching Francesco with something between awe and terror. I was not the only one who had seen.

"Brothers, let us sing the Canticle for Father Francesco," Elias said to the others. Obediently, if raggedly, they began it, and Elias, under cover of the music, took Bernardo by the arm and steered him over to where I was standing, in the back of the room.

"So now you two have seen it," he said quietly, while the brothers sang. "Soon all will know, but Francesco has asked us not to speak of it while he lives. Giacoma, now you know what happened on La Verna that I couldn't tell you about."

"Why are his hands and feet bandaged, Elias?" Bernardo's voice shook. "Is this... what I think it may be?"

Elias nodded gravely. "It is. It is his greatest miracle, and the world doesn't know it yet. God has marked him with the stigmata of Our Lord— hard black bumps like nail heads in his hands and feet, and the wound in his side that never closes."

The Canticle was nearing its end.

"Who knows?" I asked him quickly, while I still had the chance.

"Leone. Rufino. Egidio. Me. I think Masseo may have seen it, but if he did, Francesco swore him to secrecy, as he did us. And now you two. Keep his confidence for a little longer, and soon all will know. This is the most powerful sign of favor God could have given him."

The music ended, and Elias left us to return to Francesco's side. Bernardo and I exchanged a few whispered words, but there wasn't much to say. All the moving about and changing clothes had exhausted Francesco, so most of us left the infirmary to give him a chance to rest. Elias and Leone stayed with him.

The stigmata. A few eccentrics had laid claim to that extraordinary honor before, but all had been exposed as frauds. The real thing, the thing that had happened to Francesco, was unprecedented.

I kept thinking of the words in Francesco's Canticle: ... *and he is beautiful and radiant with great splendor, and he bears your likeness.*

*

Later that afternoon, as the slanting light began to fade, Elias summoned us back to the infirmary. Not only Francesco's closest disciples were there, but all the brothers currently in residence at the Porziuncola, including Lapo and Feo, though many had to stand outside. They made way for Elias and me, and we squeezed into the chamber. It felt strange not to have Egidio among us, but he seldom left the hermitage these days. I could only assume he had found his own way of saying goodbye.

"Our brother Father Leone has done his priestly duty and administered extreme unction," Elias told us. I heard the strain in his voice. "Now we will keep company with our Brother Francesco as long as we may, and then, when we must, we will bid him farewell and send our prayers with him as he ascends into his heavenly home."

We wept; we prayed and we sang as Elias directed, while he orchestrated this final act of Francesco's life. Francesco sank ever deeper into himself, until he gave no sign of awareness. Did he know we were all with him? Or were we with him in truth, or only with his body? Already he had gone somewhere we could not follow. Yet he still breathed.

I had seen my share of deaths. This death was not so different from the others—unconsciousness, skin taking on a grayish cast, one rattling breath after another, each shallower than the last, until finally there were no more. Only silence, and sorrow, and relief, and exhaustion for those who watched and waited. Joy at the birth of a saint would follow, but our first reactions were those of bereaved human beings, nothing more. If Sister Death had come for him, I had not seen her.

Later it would be said that Santo Stefano's bells rang spontaneously at the moment of his death. Lambs bleated piteously, images of the Virgin shed tears, clouds dimmed the moon and stars and miraculously lifted as Francesco entered heaven.

I don't know about any of those things. But I did hear the larks.

Larks are birds of the day, not the late evening. Francesco had especially loved them because they had such simple, plain plumage, suggesting a friar's hood, and they sang God's praises constantly. It was not yet full dark when Francesco breathed his last breath, but it was far past the time for larks. Yet they were there. A huge flock of them, just overhead, circling the infirmary and singing with all their hearts. We heard them above us, and all of us looked up, as if we could somehow see them through the roof.

"They will sing him into Paradise," Rufino murmured.

After a period of prayer, Elias set about making ready for the vigil. Brothers would sit with Francesco's body all night, reciting prayers for the dead. Some of the candles I had brought would be lit and placed around him. Messengers were sent to Assisi, to inform the city officials and the churchmen. They would begin to arrive soon, to venerate Francesco and eventually to help convey his body to San Giorgio in the morning. We would travel via San Damiano, so Chiara and her sisters could see their spiritual father one last time, as he had once promised her. Many, many citizens of Assisi would come too, bearing olive branches and candles, singing and chanting.

But for this brief time, he was still ours.

I couldn't help wondering what would happen when the citizens came. Would they see the marks on Francesco's body? Should they?

Before Elias gave the brothers leave to go and do their assigned tasks, he gathered us all together.

"Brothers, some of you know what I am about to show you. Tomorrow everyone will know. But tonight, before the townspeople arrive, I want all of you to see what until now only a few of us have seen. Brother Leone?"

Leone stepped up to Francesco's body and untied the rope belt, then gently, slowly, he opened the tunic to show the wound. A low murmur passed through the assembled brethren, followed by cries of amazement as Leone removed the bandages from Francesco's hands and feet.

The black marks were unmistakable. We crowded around to see them, and Elias was right—they were like black nail heads protruding from Francesco's flesh. Despite what Elias had said, for some reason I had expected to see wounds such as nails would leave, but instead we saw the nails themselves. The wound in his side no longer dripped blood, but it was open and raw.

One man, braver than the others, asked Elias why the brothers hadn't been told of such a miracle before, and Elias told him of Francesco's wish for secrecy. "But soon all the world will know," he added triumphantly.

"But, Brother Elias," the man said, "is it right for us to make this known to the townspeople if Father Francesco wanted to keep it secret?"

Elias's eyes flashed, but he quickly brought himself under control. "My brother, I appreciate your concern, but this is a sign from God, and when people see it at last, they will know of Father Francesco's saintliness. It must be shown. There must be witnesses, and not only brothers. For the world to believe, the world will have to witness. If we tell them but do not show them, they will say we are blinded by love, or that we seek power. But if these respected men who are not part of us bear witness, all will believe."

He was right. I had asked one of the messengers to go find my son and tell him to come, for I knew a prominent Roman nobleman would be an influential witness. Many people would join us as the night wore on, but they were few in comparison with the multitudes who would hear of this miracle and be amazed. Witnessing it was a privilege and a blessing, one I wanted Giovanni to have.

*

Rufino fetched candles, and he and Elias placed them all around Francesco's body. Bernardo left and came back with a burning brand, and he lit the candles, one by one, as Elias prayed aloud.

The flames blazed and danced, and my first foolish thought was distress that the light would hurt Francesco's eyes.

Then Elias beckoned to me. I came closer, and he stepped forward, swept Francesco's body up in his arms, and thrust it toward me, almost knocking over a candle.

"Sit, Giacoma. Hold him. You loved him in life, and you should hold him now."

Numbly I sat, and Elias placed Francesco's body on the floor in front of me, his head in my lap. I ran a finger along his cheekbone, traced the contours of his face, caressed his hair. I saw the nail heads on his hands up close, though the wound in his side remained covered. I murmured words of love and farewell, and then I dissolved into tears. Despite larks and saints and processions and miracles, this was my Francesco. I would never laugh with him again, never sing or pray with him, never take my problems to him, trusting completely in him to help me.

Elias let me weep, Francesco's head in my lap. When I finally became calmer, he and Leone lifted the body up and put it back on the pallet. Francesco's limbs were supple and relaxed. The painful contortion was gone, and he looked like a young man—the young man who had saved my life and my soul so many years ago.

I got up and thanked Elias for the privilege he had given me.

"It was a privilege you are entitled to, Giacoma. We brothers have only this brief time to say our farewells, those of us who were closest to him. But now he belongs to the world. Even now the crowds are gathering, just outside our gate. We've asked them to wait until morning, to give us this time, but they grow restless. I know these men. They will insist, and when we admit them they will jockey for position and push their way in, eager to partake of Francesco's holiness. For most citizens, following behind his body in procession will be all they can hope for, but for those with power and influence, they will want to witness his wounds, once they learn of them. And we must let them, however much it feels like a violation."

"Yes. We must. But I dread it, Elias."

"I do too. But at least you were here when he needed you. When *we* needed you. Soon you will be on your way home to Rome to resume your life, and we will handle all that will come next."

I shook my head. "I'm not going back. I am a brother, Elias." My sons, my household, my city, my grandchild to come—all slipped gently away from me. I mourned them, but I let them go. "My place is here, in Assisi. I will tell my party to go back without me, and I will never leave Francesco again."

Elias looked at me with a depth of tenderness that rattled me to my core, and he nodded. "It is well, my brother. I will be glad to have you here. But now, we must do the things that are necessary." He indicated the door, where already people were knocking, demanding entrance.

He was right. The intrusion was inevitable, and it was necessary. Elias waited while I composed myself; then he called the brothers in the room together and gave us our final chance to say our farewells. But the knocking was becoming louder and more insistent, and we could hear agitated voices outside, many of them. They were inside the gates, and they would soon glut the tiny infirmary.

It was time. We brothers moved back, hugging the walls, to make space for the newcomers. Elias turned to Francesco's serene body and said softly, "God give you peace." His voice broke as he spoke the words.

And then he moved decisively to the door and flung it open to let the world in.

Thank you for reading *Lady of the Seven Suns!* If you enjoyed it and would like to help others find it, please consider writing a review, either on a retail site, a review site, or wherever you are in the habit of looking for books. It needn't be lengthy - even a line or two with your honest reaction to the book would be enormously helpful in improving this tale's visibility and findability in a world where many new books are published every day.

About the Author. Tinney Sue Heath has a journalism degree, but somewhere along the line she realized that for her, the classic journalistic questions of Who? What? When? Where? and Why? were getting shunted aside by "What if. . . ?" And thus a fiction writer was born. She lives in Madison, Wisconsin with her husband. The two of them enjoy playing medieval and early Renaissance music on a variety of period instruments. They travel to Italy as often as possible; while research may be the excuse, they also take pleasure in that country's natural beauty, art, music, food, wine, language, and history, as well as the wonderful people they meet there.

For more about her work and about the history of medieval Italy, consider signing up for her monthly **newsletter** on her **website:** http://www.tinneyheath.com. New subscribers will be able to download her *Cantilena for Seven Voices: Dante's Women Speak*, a novella-length collection that channels the voices of seven women we know from Dante's life and works. These reminiscences, character sketches, and vignettes will give you a picture of life in Florence around the turn of the 14th century, and it is not available elsewhere. She is also on **Facebook**. Search for "Tinney Sue Heath" or go to https://www.facebook.com/tinneyheathauthor/.

Author Notes

Who is historical and who is fictional? One of the first things readers of historical fiction often want to know is which of the characters really lived and which are invented for story purposes. *Lady of the Seven Suns* contains a mixture. Most readers will know that Francesco and Chiara (St. Francis of Assisi and St. Clare) are historical personages; fewer may realize that Giacoma is as well. Readers wishing to learn more about Giacoma but preferring to use English language sources may wish to look up Jacoba of Settesoli, as her name is anglicized.

Information given about the Frangipane family, about Francesco's family, and about Chiara's family follows the historical record for the most part.

Giacoma's immediate family members (husband, sons, daughter-in-law) are historical, but her brother-in-law Cencio is not. The name "Cencio" recurs frequently in the Frangipane family, and some men of that name figure in the historical record, but this character is fictional.

All of the named high churchmen (popes, antipopes, cardinals) are historical. There was a recluse named Prassede who followed Francesco, though my character takes little from her besides her name.

Most named Franciscan brothers are historical. A reader who wishes to know more about Brothers Egidio, Leone, and Giannuccio from English language sources will want to look up Brother Giles, Brother Leo, and Brother John of Capella, respectively. Bishop Guido (both the first and second of that name) and messer Oportulo (podestà, or mayor, of Assisi) are historical.

Giacoma's employees and associates (Vanna, Lucia, Amata, Massimo, Ricco, Donata, Bartola, Lapo, Renzo, Salvestra, Nuta, Sabina, Gualtiero, Feo, Belfiore, Mengarda, Arnolfo, and other more minor characters, as well as all the children associated with them) are fictional. Some early brothers did meet the fate described here for Ricco; the one biographer who lists their names does not include a Ricco, but since nothing else is known about those men, I chose to make my character part of that group.

Giacoma's claim of a childhood friendship with Lotario Conti is fictional. She married into a family that certainly felt no friendship toward the Conti; still, her birth family (the Normanni) was not always politically aligned with the Frangipani, so I concluded it was possible, and adopted it for story purposes.

Lotario (the sheep, not the future pope) is, believe it or not, historical, though unnamed. Mousebane is fictional.

How much information exists about Giacoma? Francesco's first official biographer was Frate Tomasso da Celano, a Franciscan friar who was Francesco's contemporary and almost certainly knew him personally. He wrote three works based on the saint's life; Giacoma is not mentioned in the first two, but the third covers her role in Francesco's last days. St. Bonaventura (born Giovanni di Fidanza) was a Franciscan of the next generation who also wrote about Francesco and contributed to our meager knowledge base about Giacoma. Writings by Frate Leone and some of the other early followers, collected in volumes like the Assisi Compilation, give us a few more details and amplify what Tomasso and Bonaventura have written.

Some Franciscan scholars believe that Giacoma's role in the early Franciscan community was suppressed or minimized, both by church authorities and by later generations of Franciscans. Tomasso of Celano's first two biographies of Francesco, for example, where Giacoma is not mentioned, were commissioned by ecclesiastical authorities. This may have been out of fear that Giacoma's relationship with Francesco might be misunderstood, considered scandalous, or might encourage overly warm friendships between friars and devout women, to the detriment of Francesco's, Giacoma's, or the order's reputation.

Because Giacoma married into a prominent Roman family, extant documents pertaining to her property, as well as that of her husband and her sons, fill in the picture a little more. Even with that, the surviving information about Giacoma is sketchy.

Names. In almost all cases I have elected to retain the Italian form of names, which these men and women would have used to address one another. The main exception to this rule was Brother Elias, whose Italian name—Elia—might have sounded like a female name to a reader unfamiliar with Italian nomenclature.

The Frangipane family name has an interesting history. This noble Roman clan proudly traced its origins back to Aeneas himself, and the surname is said to have come into being in the 700s, when an ancestor named Flavius Anicius Pierleone took it upon himself to relieve the Roman people's suffering from a flood-induced famine by delivering bread to them, thus earning the name *Frangens panem,* or distributor of bread. And yes, this does show how far back the connections between the Pierleoni and the Frangipani go. They intermarried frequently, and their relationship was not always as contentious as it was in Giacoma's time. NB: Frangipane is singular (the Frangipane family), and Frangipani is plural (the Frangipani).

Giacoma's embroidery. Giacoma was a skillful embroiderer. Visitors to

Assisi and Cortona can see examples of her needlework in the reliquary collections of two churches: the Basilica di San Francesco in Assisi, and the Chiesa di San Francesco in Cortona. Assisi holds an embroidered silk veil said to have been used to wipe the sweat from Francesco's face in his final illness. Cortona is home to the cushion with an embroidered cover described in this book. The cover is red silk, embroidered in gold thread as well as green and yellow silk thread in a motif of heraldic lions and eagles, with additional figures of flowers and geometric designs. A local legend says that Giacoma gave the cushion, with its cover, to Francesco on his deathbed; an alternate tradition says that while she did give him the cushion at that time, the embroidered cover was added posthumously, when his body was transferred from its burial place in the Chiesa di San Giorgio to the newly readied Basilica.

Mengarda's palazzo. On a trip to Assisi some years ago, my husband and I rented a vacation apartment in precisely the spot I have given Mengarda's palazzo. Thus, the view from the window, looking down to the left toward San Rufino, and the prized location just a few doors away from the house where Chiara grew up, are very precise in my mind. It was a privilege to be there, even if the wifi did decide to quit halfway through our stay. And I felt about the façade of San Rufino much the way Giacoma does in the book.

Miracle Boy. While the incident with the child and the oxcart is recorded, there is no mention of the child beyond that point, so the character of Miracle Boy is fictional.

Almond cakes. We know from the works of Tomasso da Celano that when Francesco dictated his letter to Giacoma from his deathbed, he asked her to bring a certain food that she had often made for him before. We learn from Brother Leone (in the Assisi Compilation) what that food was: a sweet made from almonds and honey. Some historians have interpreted this dish as *mostaccioli*, a sort of Roman almond cookie. Others have associated it with the almond pastry cream used as a filling for tarts, cakes, and pastries, and called, appropriately, "frangipani." Still others have concluded that it was marzipan, a rich sweet almond paste.

It is the custom in some Franciscan communities to mark Saint Francis's feast day by sharing a modern interpretation of these sweets. Thus, there are numerous recipes available online. I have tried several of them— those that didn't include blatantly modern ingredients—and I'd have to say my results were not entirely successful. But then, I didn't have the advantage of Amata's expert tutelage.

Fourth Lateran Council. My description of Pope Innocente III's Fourth

Lateran Council is taken from historical records, which include some fascinating eyewitness accounts.

Lamb. San Bonaventura (*Leggenda Maggiore*) tells us that Francesco presented Giacoma with a lamb, which lived with her, followed her around, and even woke her in the morning to make sure she would not be late for church. This creature's name and personality are my invention. Author and sheep rancher Prue Batten advised me on ovine behavior, but any errors are my own.

Ugolino's relic. Cardinal Ugolino, who was to become Pope Gregorio IX, did indeed wear the finger of a Belgian holy woman in a portable reliquary. I have treated the cardinal's concern with blasphemy rather lightly, but historically it appears he went through a period when he experienced a crisis of faith, and that is when Jacques de Vitry presented him with this holy object. Jan Vandeburie, from the University of Kent, has written a paper entitled "When in Doubt, Give Him the Finger: Ugolino di Conti's Loss of Faith and Jacques de Vitry's Intervention," presented at the 52rd Summer Conference of the Ecclesiastical History Society at the University of Sheffield, July 2014.

Bandits. Feo and his fellow bandits are fictional. The idea, however, came from one of the stories often told about Francesco, in which he and his brothers "turned the other cheek" when they were harassed by a gang of thieves, bringing their tormentors food, fuel, and clothing. This so disarmed the miscreants that some of them abandoned their thieving ways and joined the brotherhood.

Marino. Marino is a community in the Alban Hills, located about 13 miles southeast of Rome. In Giacoma's day it was a Frangipani fief, and her family would certainly have had a residence there—Marino was, after all, a summer resort community for wealthy Romans all the way back to the Roman Republic.

An interesting document exists, dated 1237, in which Giacoma and her son Giovanni made a contract with her vassals in Marino, confirming their "*consuetudini vigenti*" (existing customs [habits, practices, traditions, conventions, possibly rights]). This document tells us that in 1237 Giacoma was still very much the lady of Marino.

Mice. The mice that plagued Francesco in his hut at San Damiano are based on the historical record, as is his belief that they were a torment sent to him from the devil.

Ugolino and cats. Did Ugolino really hate cats? Here I've probably been unfair to the cardinal. The idea for his antipathy to Mousebane comes from his authorship (later, when he was Pope Gregorio IX) of the papal bull *Vox in Rama,* issued in the early 1230s. The bull condemned a German heresy that included a ritual involving kissing a black cat on the buttocks, among other strange practices.

Some have extrapolated from this that people began harassing and terrorizing cats as a result of Pope Gregorio's words. It has even been claimed that a pogrom against cats allowed the rat population to surge and was thus the indirect cause of the plague that hit Europe in 1348. This appears not to be true. During this period, monks and nuns often openly kept pet cats—unlikely if the church had taken a stance against the creatures. Cats were valued for vermin control in many a medieval home and farm. Certainly there were times and places in the middle ages when cats were persecuted, whether for entertainment or out of superstition, but blaming it on Gregorio is a stretch. Still, that was the germ of the idea, and I turned the poor man into an ailurophobe. Apologies to Pope Gregorio for the liberty.

Peacemaking and the Canticle of the Creatures. The sequence of Francesco's composition of the Canticle (the initial part, the verse composed to make peace between messer Oportulo and Bishop Guido, and the later and final verse) is as it happened. The Canticle's role in making peace between the two warring dignitaries is also historical.

The translation of the Canticle here is my own, though informed by the work of many scholars.

Saracena. Saracena (birth family unknown) did marry Giovanni and was the mother of his two children, Pietro and Filippa, both of whom died very young. Widowed, Saracena remarried, acquiring two stepchildren. Records exist of sales transactions involving properties that had once been Giacoma's and were being sold by Saracena. A historian describes her as "a woman of great vivacity of spirit and great ability." Certainly she seems to have been a shrewd handler of money. Saracena's relationship with Giacoma and her personality as depicted in this book are fictional.

Francesco's death. I have told the story of Francesco's last days and hours as accurately as I could, based on surviving information. Historical (or hagiographical) points include the letter to Giacoma; her appearance before the letter was sent; her explanation of why she arrived when she did; the revelation of the stigmata; the townspeople's response; Elias's gesture offering Giacoma the chance to hold Francesco's body; and the flight of the larks.

Giacoma in Assisi. Giacoma did move to Assisi and end her days there following Francesco's death, but this probably didn't happen immediately, as I have written it. Some believe that she relocated to Assisi only shortly before her death, which probably occurred in 1239; others think she relocated soon after Francesco's death in 1226. For story purposes I have had her make a more immediate decision.

Additional reading. Little is available in English about Giacoma (or Jacoba), with one significant exception: Darleen Pryds has done some very interesting work on Giacoma's history. I recommend her chapter, entitled *Lady Jacopa and Francesco: Mysticism and the Management of Francis of Assisi's Deathbed Story*, in the book *Death, Dying and Mysticism: The Ecstasy of the End*, edited by Thomas Cattoi and Christopher Moreman. See also *Francis of Assisi and the Feminine*, by Jacques Dalarun.

In Italian, the Angela Seracchioli translation of Édouart D'Alençon's book *Frate Jacopa: La nobildonna romana amica di san Francesco* is very helpful. It is also available in the original French.

For more information on Francesco, the reader will find a wealth of information. There are quite literally thousands of books about *il Poverello*. To select a few favorites: the modern biography I found most helpful was *Francis of Assisi: A New Biography* by Augustine Thompson, O.P. Other useful biographies include *Francis of Assisi: The Life and Afterlife of a Medieval Saint* by André Vauchez, translated by Michael F. Cusato, and *Francis of Assisi* by Arnaldo Fortini, translated by Helen Moak. Fortini, a former mayor of Assisi, has a wealth of material about medieval Assisi and its residents, as well as about the Franciscans.

Readers wishing to learn more about the early days of the Franciscan order may want to seek out works by Rosalind Brooke, including *The Image of St. Francis: Responses to Sainthood in the Thirteenth Century; Popular Religion in the Middle Ages: Western Europe, 1000-1300;* and especially *Early Franciscan Government: Elias to Bonaventure*.

Additional information about Giacoma's Rome can be found in these books, among others: *Rome Before Avignon: A Social History of Thirteenth Century Rome* by Robert Brentano; *Rome: Profile of a City, 312-1308* by Richard Krautheimer; and *Medieval Rome: A Portrait of the City and its Life* by Paul Hetherington.

Also possibly of interest: *Innocent III: Leader of Europe 1198-1216* by Jane Sayers.

Acknowledgements

I would like to thank the people who helped this book come into being. I couldn't have done it all on my own, and while many people provided me with ideas and insights (some of them not even realizing they did so), the following were the most intimately involved in the writing and editing process:

My beta readers, all of whom had valuable suggestions and who were generous with their time and thoughts, provided me with timely and useful assistance: Elizabeth Caulfield Felt, Susan Keogh, Lucy Pick, Kim Rendfeld, Judith Starkston, and Eileen Stephenson. Judith Starkston in particular saved me (and you!) from having this manuscript cover another thirteen years, which it didn't really need to do. It's all still on the cutting room floor, if you ever get curious about What Happened Next. Writing can be a lonely occupation, but all of these talented authors underscored for me that we are part of a mutually supportive community, and I thank them. I also recommend their work to my readers. Seek them out—you won't be disappointed!

Prue Batten provided expert advice about ovine behavior (another author whose work I recommend, she is also a sheep rancher in Tasmania). Like my character Lapo, I'm an urban sort, and I need a lot of help with this sort of thing. Any remaining aberrations in Lotario's behavior are neither her fault nor his, but mine. Lucy Pick, a medievalist and another fine writer, shared a number of useful insights on religious life, terminology, and thought in this period.

Kim Rendfeld and Susan Keogh are the other two-thirds of a critique group that I feel extraordinarily lucky to be part of. They have seen me through every phase of this book from the very beginning, and I would be lost without their insights, delivered with tact, humor, and a willingness to brainstorm until it's right.

My cover designer, Jennifer Quinlan of Historical Fiction Book Covers, has been a pleasure to work with. Her professionalism, expertise, and talent have been invaluable.

Last but not least, I thank my husband Tim, for patiently troubleshooting every technical dilemma I manage to create for myself, for listening to me talk about my books at great length, for providing ideas, and for coming with me to Italy to do research—and for navigating once we get there, so that I could actually find all the places on my list. I couldn't do any of it without Tim.

Made in the USA
Monee, IL
21 April 2020